CLOAKED IN DARKNESS

Hannah Hanvey

Copyright © 2022 Hannah Hanvey

All rights reserved

The characters and events portrayed in this book are fictitious. Any similarity to real persons, living or dead, is coincidental and not intended by the author.

No part of this book may be reproduced, or stored in a retrieval system, or transmitted in any form or by any means, electronic, mechanical, photocopying, recording, or otherwise, without express written permission of the publisher.

ISBN-13: 9798357150097

Cover design by: Art Painter
Library of Congress Control Number: 2018675309
Printed in the United States of America

*To the people who find comfort in darkness and warm their
souls with the fire in their veins.*

*To my grandfather, who pushed me in every
possible way and I wish could hold my book.*

CONTENTS

Title Page
Copyright
Dedication

Chapter One	1
Chapter Two	11
Chapter Three	22
Chapter Four	33
Chapter Five	48
Chapter Six	53
Chapter Seven	62
Chapter Eight	78
Chapter Nine	87
Chapter Ten	92
Chapter Eleven	105
Chapter Twelve	112
Chapter Thirteen	119
Chapter Fourteen	127
Chapter Fifteen	136
Chapter Sixteen	151
Chapter Seventeen	163

Chapter Eighteen	175
Chapter Nineteen	182
Chapter Twenty	197
Chapter Twenty-One	202
Chapter Twenty-Two	209
Chapter Twenty-Three	215
Chapter Twenty-Four	225
Chapter Twenty-Five	240
Chapter Twenty-Six	253
Chapter Twenty-Seven	266
Chapter Twenty-Eight	272
Chapter Twenty-Nine	282
Chapter Thirty	295
Chapter Thirty-One	304
Chapter Thirty-Two	314
About The Author	321

CHAPTER ONE

Silence enveloped the market's bustling atmosphere, reducing to whispers. Vendor stalls layered with customers halted to stare towards the middle of the dirt path. A figure concealed under a midnight cloak stalked through the crowd. Men draped an arm over their wives, mothers huddled their brood closer to their skirts, and street orphans peeked over stocky objects they cowered behind. Every person stared at the being with fearful curiosity.

The figure prowled through the parting crowd to a building with crossed swords posted above its iron doors. Unable to distinguish whether the person was a woman or a man, the crowd observed the individual enter the guard's station without a backward glance at the motionless crowd.

Kivera Galveterre never understood why guard stations were designed in bland taste. Not a single decoration marked the drab walls nor was there any furniture occupying the chipped wood floors that weren't meant for function. Underneath the cowl, she scanned every personnel ambling around the enormous room and her gaze snagged on an oversized oak table in the room's center.

Stacks of parchment and pinned maps overloaded the plain surface despite the massive size to fit twenty people. Desks and chairs separated Kivera from the vital information of the case and she wended between the furniture to the table. With gloved hands, she breezed through gruesome details of bloodied bodies and notes on the body locations before she landed on the face behind the horrific reason she was there.

A man's rough sketch inked a well-worn parchment. His small mouth askew in a smirk but was void of any emotion. Sunken cheekbones highlighted his black, depthless eyes with dark, unkempt hair flopping over his brow. His taunting gaze whispered a cunning mind and the caption under the photo scribbled "Petyr Rocne" in the common tongue.

"Who are you? What are you going through in this case?" A gruff voice rumbled behind Kivera and she turned. The owner towered over Kivera with an unshaven face and brown eyes squinting down at her. By the uniform and the various medals, she assumed the man to be the town's Chief of the guard, Danel Gousen. He searched her hood's shadows for her face, with nothing to offer him beneath the heavy darkness.

"My name is Kivera Galveterre and the Alcerian Council dispatched me. I'm briefing myself further with your evidence. They didn't send me much and wanted me here as soon as possible."

The Chief studied her closer before he peered at the papers she was holding. "He committed brutal acts, didn't he?"

"Intricately so," Kivera drawled.

His face scrunched up in premature disgust and crossed his arms across his worn cobalt uniform. "That man is a perverted killer. A monster. Nothing about him is 'intricate'."

She was used to defensive authorities and didn't blame their reactions. They invested their lives in hunting killers and don't want to see the crimes from a detached viewpoint.

"He is a monster of the darkest breed without a doubt, but his crimes depict a man with high intelligence and cautious discipline. He executed the perfect murder many times and followed a killing routine he planned to an extraordinary degree. It's a miracle you even caught him."

He didn't seem inclined to agree, but thought it better than arguing with her. "The message from the royal guard ordered you to interrogate Rocne," Chief Gousen searched Kivera's ensemble for a royal seal that wasn't there and narrowed his eyes in scrutiny. "*Are* you with the guard? You sound young for this sort of work."

"I have certain capabilities that have made me useful to the Council for severe cases such as the one you're facing. Mainly as the last resort. They made too many mistakes in the past to afford to convict innocent people, so I am dispatched for a death sentence's accuracy." She tried to keep the bitterness off her tongue and hoped he didn't notice her fists at her sides.

Chief Gousen stared at her in puzzlement, but exhaled through his nose before rubbing the back of his neck. "We've been interrogating him for hours now. I'm not sure how much longer my men can hold out before they snap the bastard's neck. He's been playing with us since we brought him in. The worst part is he knows damn well we don't have enough evidence to arrest him." Worry and exhaustion laced his voice in heavy chords.

Kivera's heart twanged unexpectedly and she almost reached out to comfort the man. Almost.

"Ten minutes is more than enough time for me. He'll be singing soon so let me begin." The question is never *if* Kivera will get a confession, but *when*. A guarantee for Kivera's substantial fee.

Chief Danel escorted her down a dim hallway lined with iron doors. The musty air suffocated Kivera's nose, and she averted her eyes from the cobwebs plastered to the gray stone walls. She stifled a rising shiver at spiders crawling on the ceiling.

The pair turned into the third doorway on the right and passed through into a viewing room. There was enough space in the room to fit a long table in the center and a wide desk on the left wall. Fingertip sized holes carved into the wall to allow sounds to float through the adjacent room. In modern guard stations, they install a false wall or darkened glass to avoid suspicion from the suspect for any listening ears.

Limp candles in their holders cast elongated shadows on

those standing in the room. Staring at the holes, a huddle of pale officers observed two men sitting on opposite sides of a table. Most glared, crossed their arms, or muttered something nasty under their breath, but no one glanced at the newcomers hovering in the doorway.

Chief Gousen leaned towards a stoic officer next to him. "Has he confessed to anything?"

"No, sir." But he blanched when he noticed Kivera in the Chief's shadow. His mouth and eyes widened at the silent wraith.

A deep rumbling echoed through Kivera and she shushed the source dwelling in the pits of her soul. An iron chain constricted her core, and she forced herself not to pay the grumblings any heed to avoid spreading her curse. Once a beautiful magic long ago, now rooted in destruction. That part of her desired to delve into his mind.

But she engaged her energy at the true evil in the building and directed the darkness to the suspect, ignoring the normal twinge of guilt she felt. Within a split second, she slinked through Rocne's weak mental guards and filed through the slimy, evil memories. Once she found the information she needed, confirming the truth, she turned towards Chief Gousen and nodded at him.

The Chief escorted her to the interrogation room and spoke into the haggard deputy's ear. He stormed out of the room with unchecked rage burning in his eyes.

Kivera swallowed the rising bile before Gosen followed behind him and the door slammed shut with a death-swing ring. Knowing full well of the audience behind the wall, she eased the cowl off. She sensed the men in the room behind her inhale a sharp breath and mutter words she could barely hear despite her extraordinary hearing. Shoulder-length obsidian hair framed pointed cheekbones with predator ocher eyes illuminating her olive skin. Her full lips set in a straight line. She moved on silent feet before sitting across from the murderer. She cocked her head and stared at him, waiting for him to begin.

Seconds passed before his impatience tasted the air, bubbling to the surface of his skin and he practically vibrated in his chair, but discipline rooted him. His features remained cool and disinterested, though his scarred hands fumbled with the tin cup he received for water. Before long, he finally spoke and tilted their game to Kivera's favor.

"And who are you?" he drawled in a gravelly voice. The corner of his mouth pulled up in a smirk, but Kivera watched his calculating mind spin at the sight of her.

Kivera sensed the guards in the room behind her bristle at his predatory voice, but she did not react and didn't blink. "Kivera."

"Who do you belong to, Kivera?" Rocne's smirk deepened.

Kivera's evaluation of Rocne's mind was complete. "Myself." She scribbled a note on parchment leftover from the departed investigator and jumped to her feet. Petyr snapped his head and began asking what Kivera was doing before she hurried out the door to Chief Gousen.

A question formed on his lips as a gloved hand extended from the depths of her cloak's dark folds to pass the note. She met his gaze and prayed that the human trusted the note.

Kivera turned on her heel and strolled back into the room.

Petyre eyed her movements with a dark, hungry gleam until Kivera eased herself onto the wooden chair again. She leaned back and continued her cool assessment of his memories. Nausea wracked through her at the vile images contained within, but the frozen mask remained. Someone had to see these women's last moments, to bear witness to their tragedies that weren't this monster who delighted in them.

He picked at his nails and examined his hands. "So, what are you? Assassin, mercenary, King's Champion?" Petyre's thoughts frenzied with the beautiful creature across from him, envisioning the lustrous trophy she would be and bile coated her throat.

The power within Kivera growled at his arrogance, but she didn't worry about his assumption of living in freedom again. Petyre Rocne would leave the room in shackles, she reassured herself. Most likely won't even make it to the gallows alive by the look of the starved wolves in the observation room. "I assist the royal council by investigating severe strings of cases involving violent crimes, such as the one we're both here for today." She tipped her chair back on two legs.

He processed the curt words and planned mental theories, all ranging from madwoman to executioner to a mercenary. The latter two were close. "What does that kind of position entail?"

"It means I have the pleasure of hunting down vicious sadists with the royal family's protection."

"Must pay pretty good if you come walking in like that." He waved his hand at Kivera's apparel. Kivera guessed her black velvet cloak with a matching tunic underneath, and loose pants were worth a couple of decades of his wage. He would balk at the cost of her closet in her home. Longing lashed through her for the cottage on the beach below the palace, but she flicked those emotions away.

"I'll get by." She checked her watch from the cloak's inside pocket and noticed a quarter of an hour already passed. Longer than she said, but she needed to stall for Gousen's men. "Why didn't you seek counsel for today's questioning?"

His dark eyes twinkled with rage and annoyance but in a blink, he resumed his bored expression and shrugged. "I'm not guilty. Why would I need a solicitor if I was innocent?"

"By the gods, I don't believe that crock of shit and neither does anyone else." She raised a brow and deepened her head tilt to the side with a brash grin on her mouth.

"I didn't kill those damn women." Clenching his fists across his chest, his eyes brightened with anger. Gone was the easygoing persona.

Another move in Kivera's favor.

"No? You didn't assault these victims a profuse amount of times? Didn't torture them for hours, mutilating their bodies beyond recognition? I know that's a lie." He opened his mouth in denial, but Kivera grew tired of his poisonous lies. The long trip to the rural, small town placed Kivera in a nasty mood and she longed to go home to Tymern. "You committed inhuman, heinous acts against innocent people, women for gods sake, drawing sadistic excitement and pleasure from the deepest pits of your evil soul. You dream and think constantly of each session with each woman, wanting to commit the acts again and again."

The man stilled, mentally calculating an escape plan, but struggled to focus with the onslaught of images from the gruesome murders he committed Kivera was channeling into his mind.

In Kivera's experience, men like Petyre couldn't stop and wouldn't desire to stop unless they were chained to cage bars or dead. She leaned towards him and shed the glamoured facade Kivera wore for too long.

The torches flickered as magic whisked by and she loosened a glamoured sheen shrouding her ocher eyes and they brightened to a predator gleam. Her grin widened as she leaned toward him. Her face sharpened and faded into shadows as darkness slithered up the wall between Kivera and the guards, shielding her from sight.

Blood drained from Petyre's face.

"There's nothing like the first time you kill. No one describes the rush of *life* flooding your body. You aren't told of the excitement you feel as you watch their life drain from their eyes." His saucer-sized eyes locked onto the beautiful face borne of wicked Night and his mouth opened slightly. "Power courses through your veins and you lust for more, the desire wracks through your body, every heartbeat pounds for more. More blood, more screams, more death. Until one day, you just," Kivera lifted her fingers and snapped her fingers. "Crack."

Petyr Rocne watched from the tangles of the hypnotic trap she weaved and she allowed the magic to pulse through the room and drag him deeper into her web.

"Would you like to know a secret?" Kivera's voice was a death purr as she readied her final blow. He nodded slowly, his chest barely moving. She stared at him through lowered lids and the corner of her mouth curved. "The authorities are on their way to your mother's house and they're looking for your recent victim as we speak."

Petyre's face drained to the color of bone. Fear wrapped around him and drenched the room in its scent. Kivera breathed in, energizing herself, knowing full well his latest victim hung spread eagle in chains, awaiting his delusional fantasy that won't arrive. Rocne would have the turn to suffer.

Kivera cocked her head and tapped a finger on her chin. "She's chained in the barn, right?"

"It's not-" He began, but his eyes swiveled side to side as his impending demise was approaching.

"Say it." She challenged him. A predator challenging the murderer.

"I don't-"

"Just say it," Kivera repeated in a slower, huskier prowl of the tongue. Her stare bore into his own, coaxing his mouth to speak his cruel confession.

Dozens of emotions flashed across his face, but after a moment, defeat dimmed his eyes. "I killed them."

Kivera's enhanced hearing listened to the commotion from the room behind. Relief reverberated through Kivera, elated at the humans' reaction. She withdrew the power and shifted into the familiar human-like mask. The inductile, fragile skin she masked over herself signaled for the dark magic to be shoved down into the dark abyss, where chains beckoned. A danger for any human to witness a fraction of the destruction it's capable of.

Kivera stood to leave, her black cloak swooshed around her legs, but turned her head to glance at Petyre Rocne and she slipped on her hood as she spoke.

"In the years I've been in this sector, Petyre Rocne, the consequences of peace will always outweigh those of evil." With that, she strode out of the squat room as the earlier interrogating officer entered the room to record Petyre's confession. Her glamoured mask was back in place before she moved to the door.

Kivera moved down the hallway toward the hub of desks and guards, desperate for a cup of water to cool the wildfire raging beneath her skin when a voice came from behind her.

"What the hell was that?" The voice belonged to Chief Gousen.

Kivera whirled to his blotchy face and a paper clenched in his fist at his side.

The scribbled note regarding the victim's location she handed him earlier.

"A confession. What you wanted, right?" Venom burned her tongue, but the small use of magic against Rocne soured her mood further. Magic coiled tight in her soul craved a release, one to rattle the world and introduce herself to the ignorant, mortal population. The need for release increased each day, so Kivera took precautions to release small amounts to ease the fire consuming her.

"Brief me on what happened in there. On all the ot-other stuff that happened in those clouds." The chief spluttered.

She frowned. "A man confessed to raping, mutilating, and murdering innumerable women. Otherwise, nothing *else* happened."

"Those black cloud things-" He struggled to find the right words as he scratched his temple. "Those clouds *swirled* around the room. I just-I don't know what to-to say or think."

"Not the right question you want to ask, Chief." She softened her words after feeling a bout of sympathy for the poor human. His beliefs shattered before him and he grasped for an explanation for the inhuman person standing in front of him.

A truth Kivera could not reveal.

"It's my right-" he began.

But Kivera raised a hand, cutting him off. "Not regarding this, I'm afraid."

He paused. "But you did something incredible."

Shock squeezed her stomach tight and Kivera's mind went blank, not knowing what to say. No one has spoken words like these to her in years. She's used to the harsh threats from the Royal Council from a young age.

"Thank you," she swallowed before continuing, "Enjoy your celebrations."

He let her reach the doorway to the lobby before speaking once more. "How'd you know she was at his mother's barn?"

Kivera didn't turn around. "It was all he could think about," and she strode out the exit.

As Kivera walked out of the dingy building, a dark wind swept through the station, and memories from every person who saw her identity and witnessed the interrogation. She replaced them with new ones. All that remained was a bland woman, without the horrifying curse, working away at the confession that eventually came after a miracle. Kivera and the Crown didn't want there to be common knowledge of the mysterious woman with dark gifts.

Not yet.

CHAPTER TWO

Smoke filled every clean air pocket in the pub's cavernous room and Kivera almost gagged on the stench suffocating her nose. She never understood the appeal of substance packed into pipes, but everyone lives with their demons. When she walked past after leaving the guard station, scenting the sharp smell of liquor, and aching to forget who she was, the floors were already sticky with long-forgotten beer and the air tasted of sweat, muck, and whiffs of urine.

Tavern patrons chattered around rickety furniture, cackling at the nonsensical conversations and throwing back drinks to celebrate the town's recent victory. Without fail, the entire town flocked to the bar's simple doors.

Packed with laughing bodies and flailing drinks to maneuver through, Kivera yearned for home. Yearned for Masga's silent company, a friend she discovered when the old woman was cast out from the castle for her age, and drinking expensive liquor as she read a novel. Instead, she choked down a piss-poor drink and sat on a sticky barstool. For a moment, her thoughts drifted to the older woman and how she may handle this longer trip away alone in their home. She made a mental note to send a message to order more supplies for her friend.

Kivera exhaled loudly through her nose and gulped the brown liquid sloshing the glass. Calculating how long the trip back home to the glittering city would be if she were to leave at this moment before a voice interrupted her.

"You seem lonely, sugar." A voice slurred next to her.

A shiver slithered down Kivera's spine and immediately probed his mind to find vile images of what this cretin sought after. "Not lonely enough for your company," she raised the glass to her lips and bristled when she felt him step closer into her personal space. Magic nestled deep and prowled the length of its cage, waiting for the chance to be unleashed on him. Discipline was an effort for the cursed power in times of boredom or adrenaline coursing through her veins.

She's learned how much darkness loves to play.

He ignored her and played with Fate as he remained a hair-width distance away from her arm. "What's a woman as beautiful as you doing in a place like this all alone?" the fool asked with his best smile, increasing his unattractiveness with rotten teeth and canine features. Taller than her by a few short inches, but she could overpower him with ease.

Kivera continued to stare straight ahead, sipping her drink as her patience began fraying.

"Did you have a long day, princess? Tired?" Unfazed at her lack of response, he continued with his devilish suggestions. "I could always give you a good, long zap of energy."

As Kivera was preparing a smart response to suppress her body's instinct to rip him apart, a voice came from behind them.

"Trib, what do you think you're doing to this young woman?" a musical soprano voice asked. Kivera turned to see a curly-haired woman with hands on her hips. A scar savagely raked down her left eye, milky from vision loss during the scar's initial trauma, interrupting the piercing blue glare aimed towards the man called Trib.

Trib jolted upright and faced the newcomer. Kivera scanned his frantic thoughts spinning in his tiny brain and she smiled into her drink. "Uh, she-, I-" he tried and ran his hands through his hair before bolting.

A scent caught Kivera's attention and she inhaled deeper. Familiar to her, yet foreign to these human lands. Unease tightened around her bones.

The intriguing female perched herself on the empty barstool next to Kivera, her mess of dark curls brushing against Kivera's forearm. Her pretty features tugged into a smile and stared at Kivera kindly.

Kivera crept into the newcomer's mind with half a thought. The beauty within immersed Kivera immediately. Her sparkling eyes watched the world in vivid colors but in the back of her mind lived a field of thorns protecting a palm-sized, locked box at its center.

A box containing a soul-crushing secret. From the woman's scent, Kivera had a good guess, but wondered if there was anything else within.

After a moment, confusion swept across the stranger's mind about Kivera, but her ingrained manners managed her tongue.

"Hi, there!" Her face brightened and she crossed a leg over the other.

"Hello," Kivera replied with as much enthusiasm as she could muster. She signaled to the bartender for another drink before facing the stranger. She needed another for this surprise.

"My name is Mavis and I'm sorry about that blithering idiot. He doesn't take rejection well, but he's mostly harmless." Mavis paused for a hiccupping breath and flipped her hair to place the entire mass on one shoulder and raked her fingers through the ends. "Although, there was a bonfire a couple of years ago that ended in disaster. The town guards were summoned and they threw him into a holding cell for a couple of days for trying to be with a girl that was too young. She shouldn't have been at the party at all, but nothing horrible happened. Trib was beaten nearly to death by the girl's father, a member of the guard." Mavis's words blended without a single breath impressively.

"My name is Kivera Galveterre. It's a pleasure to meet some interesting company," Kivera lifted the corner of her lips and threw back another long swig. Mavis's secret nagged at her more than her scent.

"What are you doing in town?".

"Visiting for a case." Kivera shrugged her slight shoulders.

"Do you mean the Petyre Rocne case?"

Cold surprise coated Kivera's spine at Mavis's correct guess and all she could manage was a stiff nod, trying to keep her expression neutral.

Mavis shook her head and Kivera watched the curls dance to their beat from the movement. "I've never liked the boy. He once killed my favorite cat to 'test out an experiment', whatever that means." Her eyes rolled but the scar on her left eye prevented an actual eye roll. Kivera snorted into her drink from the effect all the same. "He only spent time with his mother. She was troubled, too, with her drinking and beating him all the time. It's no wonder, honestly, what he did, I mean. Those poor women. Everyone in this town grew up with them, ya know?"

Mavis loved to talk, easy for Kivera to sit in content silence. Not as lonely or as gloomy. Most humans, on instinct, stay far away from Kivera, afraid of death staring at them.

"I'm glad the guards caught him and that confession!" Mavis finished, blood flooding her cheeks in a pretty flush.

"Getting his confession was easy." Kivera blurted. Whether it was the alcohol or Mavis's welcoming demeanor, she *wanted* to talk to her. Talk about Petyr Rocne or anything of the smallest importance. Tonight, Kivera craved company to air out her day to anyone, even a stranger. An unprecedented move for Kivera.

"You *talked* to him?!" Mavis spun towards Kivera with an awestruck smile plastered on. "That's fascinating. Mother always said Petyr was trouble and funny enough, she was right."

"Funny enough," Kivera mumbled into the rest of her drink before slamming the remaining liquid. Kivera slid her eyes to Mavis, opening her mouth to say more, but the latter was focused on the door, searching for something Kivera couldn't see.

At a glance, a few people disappeared out the front door but nothing of remote interest to Kivera.

Mavis, ignoring Kivera entirely now, tapped her forefinger on the tip of her nose before mumbling an excuse then walked out the door.

"All right," Disappointment soured her tongue and she craved the comfort of a bed. Kivera paid the bartender, leaving a more than generous tip for his watered-down booze, and stomped to the door.

Weaving through the drunken bodies dancing to the mediocre three-man band on the raised platform, proved harder than expected for Kivera. With a few well-executed elbows, she finally drank in the fresh night air. Turning east towards the inn a couple of blocks down, Kivera walked a few steps down the road when a noise behind her pricked her ears. She swiveled and crept along the bar's prickly wood exterior towards the sound. She was turning towards the entrance to the pub's alley when the noise emitted again from within the shadows on the opposite end but was cut off.

Nocturnal lids slid into place over Kivera's golden irises and revealed two burly figures standing around another smaller figure cowering against the dead end.

But what shook her the most was Mavis standing in the middle of the alley, pleading with the men. "Boys, let her go." Her voice shook and she clenched her fists to her sides but she stood tall.

"Get out of here unless you want to join us!" one man yelled back and something glinted in his hand as he waved Mavis away.

A dagger the size of Kivera's forearm.

Before Kivera could step forward, Mavis's hand flashed up and pointed a blade at the men.

Kivera raised her eyebrows.

They shrieked with laughter.

But they missed a fleeting, crucial moment when the puddle at her feet *shuddered* from Mavis's arm motion. Kivera wouldn't have believed the event had she not witnessed the abnormality herself and inhaled the familiar scent of burnt sugar.

The secret in Mavis's locked box clicked together for Kivera. Holy shit, there was another magic wielder in the mortal realm?

Mavis's knife rattled, a fact the men and Kivera noticed. Holy gods, where did she get a knife, and does she know how to wield it?

Holding up their weapons, the men turned away from the cowering girl against the brick wall, chuckling as they stalked towards the brave, stupid girl clutching a knife.

Kivera waited at the entrance for Mavis's reaction, wondering if she'll defend herself if she *could*. After an extra two seconds and Mavis didn't move from her rigid position, Kivera stepped into the alley as a shadow-dipped wraith.

"Now, boys, the lady said to let *go*." She prowled into the small space and within a fraction of a second, her face shifted into a goddess of death.

Mavis spun towards her, saucer-eyed and fear oozing from her still form as she noticed the approaching nightmare.

Shock warped the men's arrogant expressions as the moon-faced pair saw Kivera with hands in her pockets.

Kivera lifted her hands and darkness from the edges of the alley lengthened into an extension of her limbs, molding to her will, eager for blood to spill. Clouds of darkness burst from her palms and speared the men as she stepped closer to herd them away from their victim. She didn't dare split her attention to the girl, but focused on the magic she cast overeager to do her bidding. The darkness slithered up the length of the attackers' bodies before reaching their necks. Without warning, she closed their throats with shadows, and a maroon ribbon formed around their necks, and she savored the fear tainting their scent. She choked their airways with mist and night sky to prevent any screams from escaping into the quiet night.

As the dark magic worked, Kivera pierced their minds, already in a tortured haze, and forced them to feel engulfing pain. Their faces opened in a petrified expression with mouths hanging askew in a silent scream to the forgotten gods lounging in the heavens. Kivera stepped around Mavis, who watched the scene with her mouth gaping.

The attacked girl cowered against the wall, eyes switching from the cloaked savior to her two assailants frozen in silent pain.

As Kivera neared the trio, she retracted the magic into the cage within her core, but the tendrils put up strong resistance. The pushback wore on her energy, but she shook off the fatigue as the men collapsed in a vomiting heap to the soiled ground. She reached for the girl, but she flinched away with a whimper.

Can't blame her. Don't know what to think of this either, Kivera thought and ignored the sting in her heart. Kivera approached slower and held out her gloved palms to appear as non-threatening as possible. "It's okay. You're safe now," Kivera murmured as if speaking to a fawn.

Reluctantly, the petrified girl accepted her outstretched hand. Kivera shrugged out of her cloak and placed the heavy garment on her exposed skin. The pair turned to walk towards Mavis when one man spoke.

"You'll regret this, witch," he snarled between large gulps of air.

Kivera stopped in her tracks and she inhaled to clear away the red mist in the corners of her vision.

She straightened her spine and handed the young woman to Mavis and murmured the inn's name to her and gestured to leave.

Mavis obeyed, either out of fear or respect, and hurried from the alley. Once she disappeared, Kivera turned in a rigid circle to face the two men.

"A witch?" A dark chuckle accompanied her advancing steps. "Better a soulless witch than a coward preying on innocent women." One creeping step in front of the other to drink in their fear until she stood over their shaking bodies. She crouched down and yanked the sharp-tongued one by his chin, forcing him to look at her.

He vibrated with anger but nearly pissed himself when he saw the living demon, equipped to slaughter and ravage the streets with blood, staring him down with luminous eyes.

"She was fine before *you* got here," the ensnared man growled, but Kivera didn't miss the sweat drenching his shaking limbs.

"Just fine?" Kivera huffed another chuckle and cocked her head to the shorter male who struggled against his invisible restraints to escape. His effort amounted to rising long enough to stumble a couple of steps.

A huntress's smile curved Kivera's mouth as she threw icy darkness at them, taking hold of their bodies and slamming the pair against the dirty wall.

"Let us-!" the tall one started.

"Enough," she clamped their vocal cords shut. She rose from her crouch in slow motion, and their terrified eyes followed every movement. Fear of the inevitable, fear of the oncoming torture, fear of her.

The mortals should be frightened.

"If either of you dares to attack a woman from this time forward," Kivera snarled from a deep place inside her, a part of her locked up from this world, and stared them down. "Wherever you're hiding, I will find you and bring you a glorious death, unworthy of your sea-scum living years. I swear this to you." Her word was the only currency of value in Kivera's life.

Kivera neared their vile breath and a dull ache began in her fingertips as dark amber talons lengthened from her knuckles. She gave them a split second to observe before slicing the shorter of the two men down the arm. Cold shadows covered his mouth to stifle his screams as she sniffed the dripping blood before flicking her tongue out to taste the richness. Human blood isn't necessary for Kivera's diet but regardless tasted delicious as spices exploded onto her tongue and her phantom limbs tightened until the males turned blue in the face. Their bodies sagged on the vomit-covered ground before she released the magical hold. She hoped they didn't hear the unpreventable soft moan before darkness took them.

Kivera strode away from their collapsed forms and wove heinous nightmares into their unconscious minds. Disgust gripped Kivera's stomach as she walked out of the alley, but a seed of blooming gratification planted itself within her. Never would Kivera regret saving a life or mourn the loss of the wolves walking in sheep's clothing. But how could she be so foolish to expose magic in front of humans or taste their life's nectar?

As she ripped the memory of herself from the men, a figure departed from the bar she drank at only minutes ago, fuming and muttering under their breath.

With their head down, they strode toward Kivera.

Alarm bells blared in Kivera's head and her instincts braced for an attack but told herself the drunken person would leave her be. Cold shivers passed through her limbs as the dark magic readied.

As the distance closed, the figure snapped its head up and a man's chiseled face with summer leaf eyes stared at her.

For a split second, Kivera craved to trace the outline of his strong jaw up to the high cheekbones below his piercing eyes and stroke his close-cropped curls.

What the hell is wrong with me? Kivera would have rolled her eyes had she not been focused on his movements.

Relief flashed across the stranger's face and he hurried to Kivera. Her defenses immediately raised and without a thought invaded his mind.

She didn't spare any chances. Those were for the weak or

dead.

In seconds, she assessed the stranger and passed through his mental shields, mere cobwebs to protect his memories, knowledge, and person. Hunting through his mind for anything of threatening intentions but the flash of the man in a decorated uniform presented to Kivera's mind and she blinked.

Why does this guard recognize her?

"Are you Kivera Galveterre?" His rough voice disguised a concealed hope, but Kivera didn't care about what he hoped for. Only cared why and how this man knows her name and bothered her at such a weary hour in a town she's never traveled to before.

"Depends on the day and who's asking," she squinted up at the taller man. His mouth twisted into a scowl before molding back into a polite smile. She didn't care about his annoyance. Her fraying curiosity left him unharmed, though diminishing with every passing second. *Who could know me in this backwater town?* Kivera wondered.

"My name is Captain Jexton Tidefal." With a deep umber hand, he gestured to a pristine brooch with the roaring lion's seal of the Guard clipped to the dark cape on his shoulder. A Captain of the Royal Guard.

"What do you want?" She lifted her chin and sized him up as he did the same.

"I'm here on behalf of my commanding unit for an assignment we're investigating and need your help. Do you have a moment to talk about the case inside?" He gestured to the bar entrance with a raised arm.

Kivera debated for a moment, part of her needing to go to the inn for reasons receding from her with a handsome man in front of her, and the bigger part of her, the winning side, wanted to follow this uniform into the bar.

Impossible to deny such a striking face, Kivera thought to herself with a secretive smirk, but nodded and sauntered through the doors. Quite a turn of events for tonight, she thought as she approached the doors.

CHAPTER THREE

"So, what does the Guard want now?" Kivera examined her nails and leaned into the booth. The Captain found seating in the darkest alcove in the grimy pub. Her mind drifted to her serene cottage by the sea more with each passing minute as the desperation for the bliss rather than the cesspits she traveled to.

The man's harsh face didn't waver and he held out his hands. "It's about a case.".

Kivera rolled her eyes and folded her arms across her chest. "You've said that, Captain. It's always about a case. The council knows to contact me as a last resort."

A youthful and frazzled barmaid reached their table in a dirty gown covered by an even dirtier apron. She glanced at Kivera and fidgeted with a loose strand of hair.

Kivera kept her order simple with a glass of ale and their popular appetizer for the already overwhelmed waitress. The captain passed on ordering and stared at Kivera, waiting for the barmaid to leave. Color flooded the waitress' cheeks with each fluttery glance at him, but left in a resigned huff.

"My team and I are currently investigating in Oakheart to investigate several related unsolved murders. There have been ten murders connected to one or more suspects," he said when the waitress left and pulled out a file from the inside of his uniform and slid the parchment from within across the table.

Kivera thumbed through the pages and her stomach rolled at the horrific details about the victims' violent deaths.

"They took each woman for nine days, tortured, and each body drained of blood then disposed of in the woods. All dark-haired and in their twenties, but that's the only connection," he stopped as the barmaid dropped off Kivera's order and sashayed away, glancing over her shoulder at the unobserving Jexton. Her lower lip bulged in disappointment.

The corner of Kivera's lip tugged upwards. "When was the first victim killed?" She asked while sipping her drink and twirling a potato sliver in the air.

"Half a year ago. The victims are taken a month apart but escalated to a fortnight from each other. We've checked records of anyone traveling to Oakheart during those times, but no success." He frowned and his eyebrows pulled together before continuing his thoughts. "My unit has been there too long and your name was mentioned about a week and a half ago when the latest victim was discovered."

Jexton slid his eyes to the carefree patrons, laughing at feeble stories with glazed eyes. Different emotions flashed across his face, but composed himself quickly until he finally met Kivera's stare.

"Do you know why I was named as a resource?" Her voice was soft as velvet.

"I only know bits, Ms. Galveterre." His brown eyes didn't falter, but his scent changed.

She blinked at his lie but decided not to press the issue for now and let her reputation precede her.

"You must have some lead, Captain." She didn't want to travel across the country for nothing, even for a string of murders. Not enough to warrant Kivera's help.

He frowned at the waitress's sudden appearance. "We have nothing."

"Do y'all need anything else?" she purred at Jexton and fluttered her lashes. She planted a hand on her hip in a way that accentuated her large chest.

Kivera waved the flushed waitress away, and she bolted with a nasty side-eye aimed for Kivera.

Kivera leaned back in the booth and twirled her mug as her mind processed the information. How does a clumsy, forgetful human not leave a trace behind? After so many victims known to the public eye and the increasing pressure from authorities, a human would leave something behind. Why was every drop of blood drained before they dumped the body in the woods? She looked across at Jexton, head bent and engulfed in his thoughts. Using this bubble of silence, she peered into his mind again.

Images of various details in the case flit around. Broken bodies, crime scene evidence found, and a random memory of his team gathered around a table. Hazy memories sped past of the team chatting together, usually at a nondescript round table, sometimes regarding serious points of the case. Other memories of his team laughing were cocooned in a warm brilliance, and she took care not to damage those thoughts. His mind kept steering to a woman discarded in the woods with cuts and bruises marking her gray body. From what she could gather from his mind, this woman was the seventh victim, Val Sybia. The youngest victim was barely eighteen years old, and a young maid without family in town.

But something caught her attention with horrifying clarity. Small enough to barely notice, but a mark marred the naked body's outer thigh.

Ice soaked Kivera's core as she focused on the mark. One she hadn't seen in years and especially not in Alceria, but the impossibility of the two being the same rattled Kivera.

"Kivera?" a rough voice asked in faraway echoes through her mental fog.

When she was immersed in others' minds, Kivera lost her surroundings on an undisciplined occasion. Kivera yanked her mind with care from Jexton's mental depths and found him staring at her with unveiled curiosity.

She blinked in the grimy surroundings and stole time to calm her racing heartbeat. "When's the soonest we can leave?"

Jexton Tidefal cracked a grin and his gleaming smile

brilliant against his deep umber skin. Kivera's mouth dried at the sight, but her thoughts ran bleak with the mark at the forefront of her thoughts.

He won't be this happy if Kivera's impossible suspicions prove true.

Instead, she raised a brow and pursed her lips before tossing back the rest of the honey-colored liquor and placing coins on the table, and rose from the unforgiving seat.

Captain Tidedal followed and they stood like pillars at the end of the booth a couple of feet apart. Kivera tilted her head to look up at him but thought she would have to reach on her tiptoes to clear past his shoulders. Impressive considering she was a head over most people. He returned a commander's gleam as if he discovered the latest weapon for his arsenal. He plowed towards the door through the drunken crowd, and Kivera trailed behind. "We leave at dawn?"

She nodded and checked her pocket watch. The dials pointed to one in the morning as they stepped into the night's air. The shocking lateness brought all the night's events rushing back and Kivera swore. Cursing herself for forgetting about Mavis and the girl attacked in the alley, she swiveled back to Jexton. Without another thought, Kivera sent out the magic in search of their whereabouts, praying they located her inn and waited there. "Are we all done here?"

Jexton raised his brows and his victorious expressions melted off. "Well, sure. I require a room, so I'll go to your inn to inquire about any vacancies if that's suitable for you?"

Kivera nodded. "I'm going there now but have someone to meet so we need to hurry." She spun on her heel and led the way for the quick trip down the street. They walked side by side in silence for a few paces when his voice interrupted the peaceful night.

"Did that man confess? Rocne?" Kivera felt the invisible touch of the captain's stare as he peered at her sideways and chuckled at Kivera's surprised expression. "My superior found out you were here for the Rocne case and sent me some details to debrief. I read the file before traveling here, and the case was legendary among the locals. There haven't been murders like this in generations."

Kivera's lips thinned and she stared straight ahead. "Didn't want to waste your time coming this far?" She sucked a tooth, not letting his words sting. Jexton choked and struggled to find his words, but Kivera waved him off. "No need to explain. Chief Gousen's officers arrested the right man based on suspicions from one officer but had hardly any evidence to hold him, nothing of worth to deem him a prime suspect. Just the officer's gut instinct. Witnesses said they spotted Rocne in the same area as the women when they disappeared, but he found an alibi. His mother, of course. Weak, but an alibi all the same." Kivera shook her head. "I questioned him and used my... abilities to discover his truth. Afterward, officers found a woman he kept in his mother's barn for the past few days being tortured."

Jexton whistled and shoved his hands in his overcoat pockets. "Damn. Makes you wonder how many more innocent people you save from catching one man."

Kivera blinked and exhaled. "How long has your team been there?" They were a couple of blocks away from the inn's entrance. She peered into an empty bookstore they passed and glanced at the bland book covers and trinkets sprinkled around. She ached to roam the store and devour more tales to occupy her days. *Maybe in the next town*, she thought glumly.

"A couple of months." He angled his head up as they reached the dim lights of the inn.

A dark awning drooped over thick wood doors etched with bear designs. The windows were clean enough to show the vacant lobby, save for the lone attendant at the front desk. Kivera prayed there was a sole cook awake to soothe her grumbling stomach. The energy exertion ravaged her appetite and frayed her patience.

Jexton opened the door and the musky odor of oak and cigars welcomed the pair to the inn. Kivera pointed Jexton in the direction of the guest attendant and walked away to search for Mavis. Next to the front desk, a stone staircase, once white rock now dirtied to brown, led to her room on the second floor but Kivera passed through the main lobby towards a hallway adjacent to the staircase. The room expanded into a vacant seating area. On the opposite wall of the entrance, a roaring fire encased in faded brick and scorching heat slammed into Kivera's face when she removed her hood. As the only source of light, Kivera didn't mind her bare face being exposed and she relied on humans' poor eyesight. Wide bookcases stocked with dust-coated books overlooked the room on either side of the stocky fireplace. Lounge chairs and couches were dispersed around the fire with one being occupied.

Two familiar forms huddled on the shabby couch closest to the fireplace. One with a handkerchief grasped in her fists. The other one, Mavis, rubbed the sobbing woman's back while cooing comforting murmurs.

Kivera strode to the sitting chair next to their couch and perched on the armrest. She waited as the woman attempted to compose herself when she noticed Kivera next to her. Tears stained her pretty face but enhanced the bruises on her cheeks. Kivera searched for additional injuries in case she needed to dispatch a healer. The victim's long brown hair escaped from her ponytail and her ripped clothes exposed lengths of skin. Cuts and faint bruises lined her lower arms and hands from defending herself. Otherwise appeared unharmed, but Kivera swallowed the urge to find those men and rip out their cowardly throats for putting hands on a woman.

Shadows in the room clawed up the corners of the room and Kivera forced herself to focus on her breathing. She didn't want to frighten the shaking woman further, but Kivera entered her mind for a moment to verify the entire ordeal and what she saw Mavis do.

The two men had followed the girl out of the bar and shoved her into the alley. They haggled and pawed at her clothes until they pushed her against the bricked dead end.

Kivera's mental self could smell their sour breaths when Mavis arrived at the alley, hollering for their attention and begging for her release. Kivera could feel the girl's relief through the memory.

Kivera stared at the image of Mavis in the middle of the alley, her curly hair illuminated under a kiss of the moonlight and her blue eye and scarred, white eye braced for trouble. An unmistakable warrior glinted in her eyes. The sight twisted a thorn in her stone heart and Kivera fled the girl's mind. Before she departed, Kivera brushed the frightened mind with the magic of the night sky and the woman immediately relaxed her shoulders and her breathing eased.

After a few calm breaths, the other girl lifted her brown eyes to meet gold ones.

"Hello, my name is Kivera. How are you feeling?" Kivera hoped her voice sounded as gentle as she intended. She couldn't look at Mavis now, with her blue eye volleying between them and picking at the leather seat she sat on. Kivera needed to process the new information and how to proceed.

"H-hi." She stuttered, her round face frozen in a mix of awestruck and fright. She hiccuped and tried again. "My name is J-Janesa."

Kivera smiled. "It's a pleasure, Janesa. Now, is there anywhere safe I can take you?"

Janesa's eyes widened, and she picked at the ends of her hair. "No, th-thank you. I can go home from here." She sniffed and looked down at her clasped hands. "What happened to them?"

A pause choked the room, and the crackling fire was the only sound. No one noticed the shadows inching up the walls.

Kivera chose her next words with care. "They're nothing to be afraid of anymore. They're taken care of."

Out of the corner of Kivera's eye, Mavis leaned to stare at her, questions clasped at the floodgates, but Kivera shook her head once when Janessa wasn't watching.

Thankfully, Janesa nodded as if the vague reply

answered everything and stared at her hands.

"Hello," a pleasant, deep voice interrupted the women's bubble and Kivera snapped her eyes to the source and she scowled. Jexton's green eyes met her narrowed eyes first and held them for a second longer before looking at the other girls. He walked to the women with his back to the fire and his attention on Janesa. "Is everything okay?"

Silence emitted from Janesa and Kivera didn't blame her for not wanting this man clothed in black to know what happened. She didn't know where Jexton's Royal brooch disappeared.

"Janesa and Mavis, this is Captain Jexton Tidefal, a new colleague of mine." Everyone nodded their greetings and Kivera's insides shriveled at the awkwardness. "Captain, I met these ladies at the tavern down the street and I'm ensuring they arrive home safely.".

Jexton's eyes flicked to hers, and he raised an eyebrow. *Yeah, right*, his eyes contested, but he said nothing.

"I'm tired and need to go home." Janesa stood from the couch. "Thank you for what you did."

Kivera nodded her goodbyes with a smile pasted on her face, but didn't move from her spot, not wanting to startle Janesa further.

Mavis led the rattled girl out, a hand rubbing Janesa's shoulder. They stopped before disappearing from view and Janesa turned her head to smile at Kivera. She returned a soft smile and watched them exit the lobby.

Once they were out of sight, a shadow loomed over Kivera and she looked up to Jexton's frown.

"What happened, Ms. Galveterre?" He growled.

She stood up to have equal standing in the conversation and counted to five to keep her temper in check. The chained-down magic poked up, but Kivera swallowed down nausea from pushing the beast back down. She stacked each spinal disc on top of each other until she became as tall as her spine would allow and peered at him down the bridge of her nose.

"She was attacked." Each word coated with ice.

He stepped back. "You should have reported the incident to me." He snapped when he composed himself and leaned down.

"I've dealt with much scarier monsters than those canal rats. I said I took care of it." Kivera's upper lip curled at the sheer dominance of the human man and released a cord of darkness. The shadows in the room pulsed with power and she settled herself into the armchair, crossing an ankle over her knee.

He paused, and Kivera could see his mind working behind his hooded eyes. Eventually, he scrubbed his face and the back of his neck. "When did this happen?".

Kivera picked at her nails. "A little before I ran into you."

The captain threw up his hands. "Seriously? You couldn't have told me during the time we were talking?"

Kivera's eyes narrowed to slits. "Before I go assist your failed attempt to solve a case, first things first, I don't answer to you. I outrank you." Jexton attempted to interrupt, but she held up a hand. "I'm a special investigator and only answer to the pigs who hand me gold. Not you. Third, I didn't know a cloaked stranger in the dead of night would be a guard member, so why would I tell you I helped a woman getting assaulted? I said I took care of the incident, so trust my words."

Rage radiated from his body but ebbed into annoyance. His clenched hands loosened and he sighed through his nose. "Is she okay, at least?" He finally met Kivera's glare.

His genuine worry pricked warmth in Kivera but didn't soften her features.

"She'll be better soon once she sorts out the trauma," Kivera glanced at the fire, shying away from his too-attentive gaze, but she couldn't bring herself to meet his eyes.

Footsteps in the hallway tickled Kivera's ears, and she flicked her eyes to the entryway. Mavis strolled through and Kivera let out a whoosh of breath. It surprised her how excited she was to see the female again.

"Janesa's gone but I think she'll be okay." Mavis's curls were in disarray but her eyes were bright.

"Do you want to stay here?" Kivera rose from her seat.

"I don't live far from here so I'll be alright. But, I would like to talk to you." Mavis gave Kivera a pointed look.

Kivera nodded and slid next to her. "Myself, as well. I'd like to talk about future employment. With me." The words held in surprised silence and Kivera gazed at Jexton, who already planted his curious eyes on Kivera but stayed silent.

Mavis's pretty face contorted in confusion. "What do you mean?"

"How about you join me here for tea before dawn to talk?" She shoved her hands into her pockets. Kivera could imagine all the questions swirling around Mavis's head without peering in.

Mavis nodded and turned on her heel. "Tea in the morning would be nice." She moved to the exit and waved over her shoulder before disappearing.

A quirky smile lay on Kivera's lips at Mavis's departure. She followed out of the sitting room and strode for the stairway ascending to her room. She sensed Jexton following her to go to his room.

Once they arrived at the massive staircase, Jexton finally spoke. "You want to hire her? Do you even know her?" He was at Kivera's side now, close enough for her cloak to brush his shins. They marched up the staircase, and for a man so large, he moved like a cat.

"I find she has peculiar qualities I find intriguing. I don't know her, but after this evening, I'm curious about her."

"Hmm." was all he said.

Kivera peeked past her curtain of black hair to watch him scratch his clean jaw, but noticeably not carrying a bag. Strange to not pack belongings for a few days' trip, she thought as they landed on the top step.

"No bag? Did you flirt with her for your room?" Kivera's mouth curved up.

Jexton shook his head. "The attendant is keeping my brooch for a night's stay. Didn't care for payment. I think she wanted to touch something shiny and important."

"Or sell off for more than what the room's worth." A grin flashed across her face before wiping away. "It'll be an early morning, Jexton. I suggest you get some sleep." She turned towards him with the full force of her eyes and dipped her head in a shallow nod before turning on her heel to make the short distance to her room and didn't spare a glance back at the Captain.

CHAPTER FOUR

A tapping sound filled the seating area from Kivera's finger on the armchair. She despised waiting. I despised sitting in an armchair in the inn's lobby watching the sunrise and passing into the early morning. Despised the empty second cup of tea she choked down. Most of all, she despised the thought of staring at the door for a second longer. With a sigh through her nose, she dropped coins on the table for the measly porridge and pushed from her seat. She prowled to the guest attendant and left instructions for Jexton, paying for his night's stay so he could have his brooch returned, before walking out of the inn. Kivera flicked up her hood against the blaring sunshine and strolled down the main street.

The road remained empty save for a few scuttling souls, but Kivera ignored them and dark waves of magic radiated from her body and onyx tendrils burst from her skin to find Mavis. In a small town, it was a matter of time before latching onto her scent.

Kivera pondered if this was too invasive or a waste of effort, but after witnessing Mavis last night, she would try one more time for the chance to learn her secret. With Jexton planning to leave a while ago, Kivera needed to be swift.

A tingle reverberated in Kivera's spine as magic detected Mavis and nudged her to the southern portions of the town, so she set off at a brisk pace. Gods, if she was oversleeping, Kivera would throttle her.

The morning's gentle sun woke the sleepy town and painted the homes and buildings with a loving rosy brush.

Voices rustled from homes as families and workers began their morning routines with the singing birds.

Tickles of memory in the back of Kivera's mind from long ago replayed. A small hand frets over her with feather-light touches and a childlike voice cooing at her to calm. A breeze whistled across her chubby face in the early morning light and female shouts rang in her ears. Kivera shook off the recollection and shoved her clammy hands in her pockets as she increased her pace.

Magic pulsed intensely in the base of her spine as she neared Mavis until one final throb in front of a shabby cottage and the magic's warmth disappeared.

Dirt crusted the once white stone, and the cramped front yard was a wilderness of weeds. The front door rested on the mercy of a single hinge and revealed the shadow of someone roaming the house.

Kivera lifted her knuckles for three light knocks.

After a couple of moments, shuffling feet opened the door and thick odors of rotten fruit and musty furniture slammed into Kivera and pricked her eyes.

Open-mouthed and flustered, Mavis stood in the open doorway.

"What are-?" She stepped out of the doorway and closed the wood slab behind her.

Kivera tilted her head. "Why didn't you show up this morning?"

Mavis lowered her eyes. "I couldn't make it."

"Why is that?" Kivera itched to bite off her curly-haired head for causing a delay in her departure.

Mavis opened her mouth to rattle off her reasons when a voice vibrated the house.

"Mavis!"

The first mistake was not scanning the entire house, and now she's unprepared. A foolish mistake, she chided herself.

Mavis grimaced before setting off into the house, not glancing back to see if Kivera followed. Which she did.

The stench throughout the tiny hovel threatened to choke Kivera's windpipe as she walked further into the home. Debris scattered throughout the small space, mud blanketed items left around, and patches of wet spots dotted the packed dirt floor. A messy table hid away within a pocket of shadows in the farthest corner, covered with newspapers in different shades of yellow on the chairs and open spots on the table. Stacked on the floor were books in varying tattered states and a puny fire cackled at the hearth next to the table.

Two closed doors across from the fire marked the bedrooms of the home and Kivera wondered which was Mavis's. If she had her own.

In the middle of the living room was a broad, chipped bench and an overgrown rocking chair, and both were occupied. Sitting on the bench was a plump woman with graying frizzy hair and a nasty sneer twisting her face. Bloodshot eyes slid to the visitor and her slippery gaze injected oil down Kivera's spine. A gigantic, balding man sat in the rocking chair. A smirk thinned his lips, and he raised eyebrows at Kivera.

Instincts roared at Kivera as she eyed the man wearily and she raised shields to protect Mavis and herself.

"Who's this?" the old woman's raspy voice slurred.

"Noone, Mother. She was just leaving," Mavis replied, realizing Kivera followed behind her and her hands wrung in front of her dirty apron. The apron barely covered the loose pants and sleeveless, stained white shirt she wore. No less than an hour after dawn, Mavis already had sweat on her brow from chores.

"No one?" the grizzly woman cackled and clapped her hands together once. "She's a somebody. Now tell me who, girl."

Kivera bristled at the demanding tone with Mavis and with the flash of fear across Mavis's pretty face.

"Mother," Mavis pleaded, "she was just going." She emphasized the last word for Kivera's benefit and she cast desperate eyes at Kivera, but she didn't budge.

Kivera studied the humans across from her, letting her magic roam the frail mental shields of their minds. With a fragment of a thought, she entered their minds.

Memories burst at the entrance. Countless moments of cruelty against Mavis, wretched incidents of abuse at both the man and woman's hands.

A ringing sound in Kivera's ears, it became louder as she flipped through the brutal life of Mavis. The cruel life Mavis lived at the hands of her *mother* and *brother*. Rage boiled through her and stirred the beast caged at the bottom of her stomach.

The man's mind, Mavis's half-brother, wasn't any better as Kivera watched the chronicle of his years of hurting his younger sister.

Kivera snapped out of their minds, glaring at them before turning towards Mavis, and a plan formed in her mind.

"You don't know me or trust me, but I can take you away from here. Far away to people who don't know who you are or the cause of that scar," Kivera murmured to a flushed Mavis. Voices from the furniture attempted to interject, but Kivera pointedly ignored them and kept her eyes locked on Mavis. "Grip your freedom and I can show you the world away from this shit-hole. Give you the chance you deserve to *live*."

Mavis's face crumpled and Kivera didn't dare peek inside her mind, never violating that line again. They locked gazes, unspoken words thick between their eyes until a nasty voice interrupted.

"I'm talking to you, bitch." Mavis's mother snarled. "You answer me when I speak to you, girl."

Kivera waited for a heartbeat to breathe and revel in a daydream of the old hag's blood splattering the floor. Envisioning her talons swiping across the older woman's rotten mouth. Instead, Kivera faced the woman to cock her head and her mouth slashed into a wicked grin.

"I am none of your concern, wench. My business here is

none of your concern. If you speak once more, I will rip that privilege from you." Kivera flashed her teeth in promise but didn't swivel at Mavis.

The fools stared at her with open mouths.

The man jumped to his feet, redness shiny on his beefy face and clenched fists shook at his sides. He spits filthy names and nearly sends Kivera into a fit of giggles if Mavis wasn't cowering behind her. She tried to disappear into her tiny frame and inched towards the door. Her lower lip quivered as her blue eye volleyed between her brother and Kivera.

This brave woman who willingly faced off against armed assailants the night before was now *cowering* from her kin.

"How dare you speak to me like that?!" the woman on the bench screeched.

Kivera could only stare at Mavis's shaking hands.

Kivera dragged her eyes away from Mavis and gave the humans the full force of her stare. "How dare you put your daughter through so much misery?" She spoke with a fatal softness.

"You don't know a damn thing about us, don't know a thing about what I've been through." Spit flew from the human mother's mouth.

Her son gravitated closer to his mother's side and readied to be unleashed at her command.

"I don't give a damn. It's inexcusable." Kivera narrowed her steely gold eyes and waited for the next words to come out of that shriveled mouth.

The wench barely opened her mouth, inhaling to scream more, and a gust of air swept through the room. Her mouth opened and closed, but no sound came out.

Kivera smirked.

The woman lifted her wrinkled hands to clutch her throat and attempted to speak before her arms flailed around. Her son's bear-sized hands patted her back, but the attempt was futile against the dark magic's hold.

Kivera glanced at Mavis. The female stared open-mouthed at her frantic family. "Never again would you have to hear their voices again and that's a good enough reason to leave," Kivera leaned closer. "You would never have to see either of them again. You'll be safe."

Their eyes met for what felt like an eternity and emotions swirled in Mavis's eyes before she dipped her head in agreement.

Kivera smiled a genuine smile for the first time since coming to this town.

Out of the corner of her eye, Mavis's brother charged at them with enraged shouts.

But Kivera moved faster.

She lunged towards him and slid low to land a blow on the side of his knee. A satisfying crunch impacted her knuckles, and he dropped to his other knee. She jumped up at dizzying speeds before his knee touched the ground and landed a blow to his jaw. Red spit and white chips flew from his mouth as his head snapped to the side. He buckled to the ground in a moaning heap and a generous mark was blooming on his left cheek.

"You bitch," He choked out.

Kivera leaned down until she was a breath away from his face and in a venomously sweet voice, she said, "Now you'll remember me every time you raise a hand to a female. I will not forget you and the moment Mavis allows me to, I will come back for you and bring true horror upon you."

Before he could blink, Kivera brought her foot down on his hand clutching the ground and a loud crack echoed through the room. His screams echoed throughout the shack and she stepped over the writhing man and strode towards Mavis's mother in a couple of strides.

She sat as an unmoving statue and watched Kivera, but the scent of her fear was unmistakable.

Kivera flicked her fiery gaze to the old woman, lowering her eyelids as she spoke quietly enough Mavis couldn't hear. "I know what you've done and how she has lived. The treatment of your *daughter* is deplorable. Here on out, your lives hang on Mavis's mercy. The moment she wishes for your death, I will swiftly oblige."

The woman fixed Kivera with crackling hatred and her wrinkled mouth thinned to a distasteful line but unable to utter a word.

Kivera strode to Mavis and leaned down. "Let's retrieve your belongings and we'll leave, okay?"

Without another word, Mavis stepped to the doors behind them and Kivera followed close after. Cracking the door behind her, Kivera scanned the room and maintained a blank expression.

No more the size of a closet, Mavis's "room" fit a padded roll on the floor and a feeble stack of books on a chipped dresser. No windows or enough room to extend her arms.

Mavis glanced at Kivera with a sheepish smile. "It's not much, but it's home." Her short legs zipped around the room, pulled out her few belongings, and piled them in a thin pack.

Kivera shrugged. "Don't feel embarrassment on my account. I've lived on less. Do your mother and brother share a room?"

Mavis snorted. "No, Mother sleeps close to the fire for her joint pain. A few years ago, she let me use Mart's old room and he nabbed hers."

Kivera nodded and leaned against the doorframe, one ear towards the living room as she watched Mavis.

Within a few minutes, Mavis's belongings were bundled in her pack and she blew out the stout candle on the floor next to her mat after one last look around.

She reached a hand forward to open the door when Kivera touched Mavis's arm. "Are you sure about this? About leaving your home to go with a stranger?"

Emotions flit across Mavis's face, faster than Kivera could follow but Mavis nodded and straightened her spine then opened the door.

She entered the living room to find Mart struggling to rise from the dirt floor. Her mother, silent and fuming, nursed a glass of amber liquid left on the table at her side. Beady onyx eyes followed their movements.

Kivera pulled the magic from her vocal cords to see if she'll talk.

Mavis faced her mother, silently beseeching for kind words of departure in her eyes. "We're leaving now." Mavis choked on the announcement as her family glared at her with frozen contempt. Her bottom lip quivered, and shadows throughout the shack grumbled at the sight, but Mavis turned away, reaching the door before a hoarse voice spoke behind them.

"Don't die, girl."

Mavis didn't look back at the hovel she once called home. Instead, she faced the rising sun and set a swift pace on the main road.

Kivera remained steadfast at her side, allowing her to work through her thoughts.

After a few minutes on the same path she walked earlier, Kivera couldn't breathe in the suffocation of the quiet morning. "Are you okay?"

"Not how I expected my morning to go." Mavis shook her head. "Didn't think I'd see you ever again."

Kivera raised her brows. "Were you going to have tea with me this morning? Or were you going to blow me off?"

A blush crept up Mavis's neck. "I woke up believing last night to be a dream until you showed up on Mother's porch." Her eyes widened as last night's events clicked. "You saved us from those men with those dark clouds, right? Was that how you found me?"

Kivera turned her head away. "The magic in me sniffed you out. I wanted to find out about you before I left."

"You're leaving?" Mavis's head snapped to Kivera in surprise.

A small smile brushed Kivera's full lips. "We're leaving.

Not sure where to yet, but do you remember the captain you met last night? His name is Jexton Tidefal and will lead us there." She briefed Mavis on the conversation between her and the Captain, save for the symbol branded on the victim.

Mavis pursed her lips and her scar shined under the sun. "What exactly do you do? Talk to murderers?"

"Interrogate them, yes, and then some. I work for the Royal Council and they send me to the bloodier cases around the country."

"Wow," Mavis stared at her in awe. "Have you met-"

Kivera shook her head. "I've met the royal family once, and they stood in the same room with me for a few minutes before they fled."

"Did you show them a shadow trick? Perhaps those scared them," but her eyes twinkled with mischief.

Kivera laughed. "No, but I should have. Maybe they'd let me leave for vacation more often."

"Do you live in the palace? Do you attend royal balls? Is the prince as dreamy as the rumors say?" Mavis's words blurred together, but it was clear to Kivera that she was trying to distract herself from leaving her only family so Kivera would indulge her.

Kivera lifted her hands and chuckled. "I live on the beach below the palace's cliff. They want me close, but not too close." She looked away to the surrounding houses and blinked away the prickling sensation in her eyes. "I've attended a few royal balls, but find them quite boring after the same snobby folks attend the events. As for your last question, I'm sorry to disappoint you, but the prince looks like a bull rammed him in the face. Not very dreamy."

Mavis's face slumped in disappointment.

Stables appeared from the road, where Kivera instructed Jexton to meet her at, and was thankfully a short distance from Mavis's family house. Yawning families and workers milled about the streets, bracing for the day. Businesses opened shops and filled the morning with bells ringing.

"How do you do what you do? For the Council, I mean," Mavis asked as they passed the bar they met at the night before and neither peered into the pub's alleyway as they passed.

Thousands of answers pressed against Kivera's lips, many were deceits but the truth was more insistent. "I came here by accident and wasn't careful when I arrived. The Crown hunted me down until they cornered me in a small town. I don't remember the name too much time has passed. My magical abilities depleted from starvation and lack of sleep. When I was captured, I was offered a choice: work for them or be executed."

Mavis's jaw dropped. "They would have killed you?! How old were you? Seventeen?"

"Twelve."

A pause. "Twelve," Mavis breathed.

They passed by the inn Kivera stayed at and walked around the brick walls to the wooden stables against the forest line.

With his back to the road, Jexton spoke to a youthful stable hand. His russet curls glinted in the dawn and his splatter of freckles brightened with each smile. Absent-mindedly, Jexton extended an apple to a cream horse between them.

The sight rolled Kivera's stomach and she let out a sharp cough. The captain's eyes snapped to their arrival, and all softness hardened into the stoic commander.

Captain Tidefal crossed his arms. "You're late."

Kivera shrugged. "Had last minute business to take care of."

Jexton's eyes slid to Mavis, pensive as she faced the man. His upper lip curled but refrained from remarking on her puffy face or the limp pack on her shoulder.

"You're here now. Let's get going," He sighed through his nose and turned to pay the stable hand.

Mavis gawked at the horses. "They're pretty babies."

Kivera smiled. "Beautiful creatures, aren't they? Have

you ever ridden before?"

"Years ago, my friend owned one and she let me ride in the foothills." Mavis's eyes darkened. "Mother found out about us and stopped it."

There was something Mavis wasn't willing to say and Kivera frowned but didn't know what to say, so she squeezed Mavis's shoulder.

After a few minutes of gathering their horses, the trio began their journey north. Hooves beat the earth and the brisk wind whistled through Kivera's ears. Jexton led the group at a swift pace through the woods and in no time at all, the town became a speck on the horizon before vanishing altogether.

Mavis didn't look back once.

Kivera covered Mavis with a magical shield to keep her out of the cold. Cloaked in darkness and clutching her horse, Mavis smiled at her warmly through tendrils of darkness.

The sun rose into mid-morning and pressed down through the robust trees on both sides of the narrow path. The forest blurred into whorls of rich green, joyful yellow, and playful oranges melted together in a grand display.

The trio traveled in silence, but that didn't seem to bother any of them. Thoughts of the victim's mark consumed Kivera. The shock of the sight had worn off and replaced by endless questions. Who knows what it means? What does it do exactly? Who else knows about magic in the human world?

A feeling nagged at Kivera for miles until she demanded to stop.

Jexton growled with impatience but slowed their speed to a stop and a warning to make the stop quick. After finding a stream for the animals, Kivera slid off the horse's bare back and helped Mavis off the saddle.

"We're not stopping long, so hurry with whatever you need to do," Jexton shouted from the stream as he filled his waterskin.

Kivera rolled her eyes and hooked Mavis's arm through her own. The action was foreign to her now, but there was comfort in touching another person. "Let me show you something." Kivera's accent curved the words of her request and she led Mavis through the shrubbery, weaving between trees and thick shrubbery before sitting on a patch of grass. Kivera pulled off her worn leather riding boots, eager to feel soft blades of wild grass with her feet.

Mavis watched Kivera's toes wiggling in the grass.

"When I was a child, my father would tell me legends of travelers who didn't thank the gods. Gruesome stories of vengeful gods punishing ungrateful people. Seduction led men to their death, females succumbing to cannibalistic mania, and shreds of children mixed with pine needles." Kivera swallowed, remembering the vivid nightmares that followed his rare bedtime stories. On nights he couldn't scam money to spend at the pub drinking himself into oblivion, he told bedtime stories. He told them more stories of distressed damsels, heroic knights, and happily ever afters, but the brutal, unforgiving tales piqued her interest the most. No matter how bad the nightmares plagued her afterward. "Forgotten gods or not, I make an offering regardless and I breathe easier. It's a trick of the mind, but I haven't encountered a creature worse than a bear or mountain cat."

"Do you have to kill a goat or something?" Mavis's nose crinkled in disgust.

Kivera chuckled and shook her head. "Nothing like that. The gods were brutal but required the sacrifice of blood for more major celebrations or requests. I'd like to think these days they like to be remembered at all." Kivera gathered twigs and began weaving the woodland material into a rough circle. Mavis observed the motions.

"Aren't there some people in the land that worship them?"

"Generations ago, there were priestesses who worshiped the gods. The priestesses conducted ceremonies with masses watching them. Nowadays, money and survival have become gods consuming the world." She paused in her work to shrug off her cloak and tilt her face towards the sky to bask in glimmering sunshine. Kivera could spend hours basking in sunlight, lounging around like a cat in the afternoon.

"Do you honor other gods?"

Kivera opened her eyes to Mavis. "A few. Honoring too many gods would bring mischievous luck rather than good fortune." She wrinkled her nose. She remembered a time as a child she left a small gift for a river goddess, a few yellow flowers bound with her favorite silver bracelet. When she turned to leave, a slippery filament yanked on her arm and threw her into the same river, swallowing the murky waters. She crawled out and cursed the waters with foul words she overheard her father say. Kivera hasn't honored a water goddess since.

"It's sad really," Mavis commented with her head down and her teeth gnawed on her bottom lip as her curls swayed to the music of the wind. Leaves rustled and joined the melody, twirling to the rhythm. "To be forgotten so easily. Maybe it's easier to not be known."

The thought of being left alone, not a single breath whispering your name, sent tingles down Kivera's spine. *How blissful a quiet life would be*, she mused a[1]nd finished the band of twigs weaved into a circle. She fashioned it to create a miniature replica of a crown. Delicate twigs weaved together with long blades of grass and plump berries Kivera plucked on the way in.

They both were deep in their thoughts and their eyes trailing the trickling creek when Mavis broke the silence, her voice husky. "I don't think anyone will think of me fro-from there." Kivera snapped her eyes to her and narrowed her eyes. She wanted to demolish that shithole of a town. Mavis was barely into womanhood and she wondered for the hundredth time about the other scars Mavis kept veiled. "It's difficult to leave the place I've lived all my life, but I don't think one person will ask Mother where I've gone."

Neither of them dared to discuss what her family would

do.

"You do not know what anyone will do. But do not waste thoughts on things you cannot change." Kivera moved closer. "Time helps, Mavis."

A choked noise came from Mavis, and Kivera glanced over to find tears streaming down her pretty face.

Kivera couldn't remember the last time she needed to comfort another person. She hasn't needed to extend compassionate warmth or share comforting words in a very long time. But she shoved down her doubts of inexperience and gripped Mavis's icy hand.

Gods, even the way Mavis cried was delicate. How could anyone be cruel to a person with a heart as pure as hers? Broken her heart enough to sob with a near stranger. Unsure of what to do or say, Kivera held her hand for a few minutes and listened to the sound of sniffles filling the air.

Even without her enhanced ears, Kivera would have heard the crashing footsteps coming toward them miles away. Her whole body tensed and she sent magic to the source, then relaxed slightly at who caused the racket.

"The captain is coming through the woods. He probably thinks it's time to go, but take your time," Kivera murmured to Mavis and they rose to their feet.

Jexton burst through the low-hanging branches in a flurry of foul curses.

Kivera snapped her head to glare at the man as Mavis swiped her eyes quickly and scrubbed her face behind Kivera's shielding body. Kivera's upper lip curled to reveal perfect white teeth, but enough poison in her expression slowed his steps and he understood her silent message. *Be nice or I will rip you apart.*

His gaze immediately went to Mavis sobbing and his eyes softened before he met Kivera's withering look again.

Captain Tidefal cleared his throat and shoved his hands in his pockets. "The horses are ready to go when you're... when you're ready."

Kivera nodded once and he bolted the way he came. Kivera turned back to Mavis. Color stained her cheeks and her teary eyes remained downward. Kivera put her forefinger under Mavis's chin to demand eye contact. "I promise you I will remain by your side until you wish otherwise. You will never be alone in this world or the next. We will conquer each sadness as they come. Together." Her golden eyes blazed with an unflinching will.

Mavis's lower lip quivered again, tears pooling and spilling onto her cheeks, but she nodded slowly. She brushed away the flowing tears and lifted her lips in a small smile.

"I'm in," she said hoarsely, "if you are."

Never have five words struck Kivera's core so deeply. A promise to walk each day one at a time together. She cherished these words creeping towards a friendship. Those five words opened a gate for a warm future and she felt the warmth budding in her chest where her husk of a heart thrummed.

Kivera smiled at the words, embracing the feeling of Fate's threads settling around them, twining the females' lives together.

For only gods know what.

CHAPTER FIVE

Kivera landed off the horse with a soft thud, exhaustion wrapped tight around her bones after the rough day's ride. Even though they arrived in Oakheart a little after dusk with Jextons's breakneck pace, beating the estimated arrival time, she glared daggers at him.

To pass the time, Kivera took some liberty to view a map of Oakheart inside Jexton's mind. Not allowing the magic to peek at anything but the map, the guilt of invading his privacy didn't lessen.

With Kivera's position taking her around the continent, Oakheart would be an easier territory to navigate. Woods surrounded miles of land between the northern mountain range and the town. Twin rivers flowed down the mountain on either side of the town and trickled east to the sea. Anyone familiar with the land, even the mountains, could hide anything, or anyone, without ever being found.

That'll be where she begins her hunt.

For the most strategic position, Kivera wanted an inn closest to the forest. During another brief stop, she told Jexton so. He thought of one established between the forest border and the guard post where his team was based. Under the cover of the night and only the moon to guide them, they thundered on the outskirts of town, toeing between trees and people.

Flashes of nocturnal eyes tugged at Kivera's enhanced vision and she reinforced the surrounding shield. She let out a low growl, and they vanished.

Jexton looked over his shoulder at her but said nothing,

and Kivera didn't offer an explanation. Let him think about what he wants. She doesn't care.

They arrived at the inn as the moon peeked in the sparkling night sky. The dingy inn was nothing but a sturdy wood frame and lamps around the building lit the way to the door. The ominous forest blanketed the northern side and the mountain peaks winked above the treetops.

Kivera helped Mavis down as she fell asleep miles back and she magically tethered the woman to the saddle. Bleary blue and pale silver eyes met Kivera's as she helped Mavis down, supporting her while her body swayed. They walked towards the inn's front doors with dark magic protecting their backs from the shrouded forest behind them.

Upon their arrival, a stable hand with a lantern in tow dashed toward them and collected their reins. His eyes swiveled to the forest as if watching for a monster to jump out and enhance Kivera's nerves. Nothing about this town settled with her, but she couldn't place what it could be. The stable hand directed them to the front and Jexton handed him a few coins, then the boy hurried away with the horses.

Jexton led them through a side door and into a stuffy dining room. Kivera blinked to adjust to the firelight. Some men sat at the bar on the far wall while others meandered around. A few men watched their arrival with a carnal appreciation and Kivera stepped closer to Mavis, snarling under her breath at anyone looking too long.

Mavis didn't look up from her lowered gaze to notice the pigs staring at them.

Jexton left Kivera to arrange a room with the innkeeper. He stood near Mavis and shot her glances from time to time.

The pinched-face innkeeper informed Kivera there's one room left but with a two-person. Kivera groaned internally, but she peeked over her shoulder at Mavis. Her eyes were puffy and she swayed on her feet, so Kivera slid a gold coin to the keeper.

The wrinkled woman's eyes widened, and she transformed into a blubbering host, offering an upgraded room with two beds and private bathing quarters.

The corner of Kivera's mouth quivered, but she held back the rising smirk. How easily situations can brighten with the shine of gold. Once the arrangements for the room finished, the keeper left to bring hot meals to their room and Kivera turned back to her companions. Mavis's eyelids drooped over halfway and Jexton glowered at patrons of the inn. Kivera wondered if it was for the same reason she entered snarling, but she brushed the thought away. "We're sharing a room, if that's suitable for you, Mavis," Kivera murmured and Mavis nodded. The former looked up at the captain. "I assume we're meeting at a ridiculously early hour to go over the case with your team."

Jexton nodded. "We're staying at the guard post, so find us when you're ready."

Kivera nodded once after he provided details of how to find the station, then grabbed Mavis's stiff arm and strode to the stairs leading to their room. Jexton's footsteps sounded behind them.

"I'd like to go to the crime scenes tomorrow to view them with your fresh eyes," Jexton raked his fingers through brown hair. Kivera didn't mention her heightened senses and how she could see what the human eyes missed; hair, footprints, anything the killer could leave behind. That's none of his business, anyway. "My team will lead you through each crime at the scenes. Out of anyone, you could be the one to find damning evidence."

A sharpness in his tone caused Kivera to turn, and he watched her with eyebrows knit together and frowned.

She raised her chin. "It does not matter who finds those responsible as long as we do and as fast as possible. We have victims to protect and seek justice for. We cannot let our pride interfere, Captain." Kivera felt Mavis's eyes on her, but she couldn't tear herself away from Jexton's gaze.

"But we've been trying." Color stained his cheeks and his fingers curled into a soft fist.

They arrived at Kivera's door and Mavis watched them, her sleepy eyes volleying lethargically back and forth.

"You have been searching for him for so long. It was not a weakness to ask for help." Kivera unlocked their door and guided Mavis in. "We will find the bastard. But in the meantime, sleep. Dammit, I will."

And slammed the door in his twisting face.

"He's angry," Mavis stated from the small-framed bed closest to the window. She deposited her measly pack on the wood floor and sat down on the bed.

Kivera surveyed the comfortable living space in a slow circle. Two beds were next to each other with enough room for someone to walk between. An enormous dresser stood facing the beds and an oversized armchair in the room's corner next to the window. A door to the bathing room was next to the front door.

"Yes, he is," Kivera held out her palm and an onyx seed appeared before unfurling into waves of darkness and expanding to the walls. After a few moments, the shadows filled the room, and she hardened them to an impenetrable shield. No one could enter without her or Mavis allowing them in. A skill she learned a long time ago and told Mavis such.

"You can-can do that?" The whites of Mavis's blue eye shone in the room's candlelight.

Kivera moved to the bathing room and spoke through the bathroom door after she shut it while she changed out of her dirty riding clothes. "Shields are the first ability magic-wielders master."

"There's more of you? With your magic?" Mavis asked, quiet enough Kivera thanked her enhanced hearing.

"Yes and no. I haven't encountered one with the magic I possess but I know there are others out there with magic for different elements," Kivera left the bathing room in her simple silver nightgown, a relief for Kivera with the heat under her skin, despite the cool autumn air. Magic roiled beneath her muscles and boiled her skin if she didn't release any. She walked out to Mavis staring out the window overlooking the dense forest below.

"I've never heard of magic being here," Mavis commented absentmindedly.

Kivera was tempted to watch the gears spinning underneath her head of curls, but didn't dare cross the line. "There should not be magic on this continent." Veils framed each word.

Mavis looked up and curiosity replaced her exhaustion. "Not meant for here? How are you here?"

Kivera sucked on a tooth while her thoughts were frantic. "Magic is not meant for humans. Though lifetimes ago, mortal lineages contained drops of magic. Families bore elemental benders, healers, or farmers. Not enough drops of magic to rein over powerful gifts but able to aid their villages."

Mavis chewed over Kivera's answer and lifted her eyes to stare at Kivera. "And, you? How are you here, then?"

Kivera flicked her shuttered gaze out to the horizon at the glittering stars, before turning towards her bed. "A story for another time," Kivera waved her hand and hoped Mavis didn't notice them shaking. "For now, we should sleep. We have an early rise."

A pause. "What am I to do?" She didn't mean for the day.

Kivera stopped, pulling the bedcovers to turn to the girl. "You're under my employment. You can join me or ask around town about the victims. Or none of those things and eat tarts and nap all day if it pleases you. Do as you wish, Mavis." Then slid into bed, careful not to think about who else had laid there, and sighed when her head laid on the pillow.

Mavis followed suit in her bed, quiet as the mice scurried through the alley beneath the window. She stared at the ceiling before speaking. "I'd like to join you and earn my wages."

Kivera extinguished the candles with a flick of her wrist and let her vision adjust to the swollen darkness. "It will be nice to have nice company to spend the day with." She drifted off to sleep on the last word with a smile on her lips.

CHAPTER SIX

Blood streamed into my eyes and darkened my vision to crimson. Screams and the sharp ringing of unsheathing swords echoed throughout the red-misted air. Not able to see the source, but I knew what would be right behind me. Knew of the beheaded body, broken on the cell's floor.

A dark chuckle came behind me.

A choked sob escaped my constricted throat.

My hand gripped a fallen dagger, discarded from a soldier with a ragged slit cording from ear to ear.

I can't look at him I can't look at him I can't look at him I can't look at him.

The dagger shook in my weak hand.

My body froze to useless prey in the predator's thralls.

I deserve to die I deserve to-

Liquid pooled at my feet.

I couldn't look down, knowing everything would change. My traitorous body betrayed every instinct, though my mind screamed to not *look down. Blood soaked into the pads of my bare feet and stained the hem of my ripped nightgown.*

The screaming began anew and fire clawed up my throat, my hands clawed my throat.

Kivera sat up in bed and panted heavily. Sweat claimed her skin, and she raked a hand through her shoulder-length hair. She closed her eyes and focused on calming her ragged breathing.

The magic imprisoned in Kivera's body grumbled at the rude awakening and stroked her spine with whorls of darkness. Cords of the night sky cooled off her heated skin and thickened to wrap around her until darkness cocooned her. Tears streaked her cheeks in quiet sobs, careful not to wake the sleeping body in the bed next to her. Her head filled with blood and death and screaming. She trembled as the nightmare tumbled around her mind, unable to stop the long-ago memory.

For hours, Kivera remained in her shadowy cocoon, unblinking at the ceiling until dawn light crested the wooden beams. She threw off the drenched sheets, mentally noting to request extras with the innkeeper, and quickly changed into plain, loose clothes. She snuck out of the room, listened through the wood door for Mavis's change of breathing, and hurtled down the stairs when she didn't hear a difference. The nightmare's coppery scent engulfed her nostrils, the image of blood filling her mind and she tied back the top of her short hair as she swept through the lobby. She paced around the side of the building before bolting into the forest at a brisk pace.

The steady beat of her shoes pounding the rocky ground filled her ears. She inhaled in careful controlled breaths and lithe arms pumped her curled hands. Blood in her ears pulsed in her head in harmony with echoes of sinister chuckles.

Under the forest canopy, Kivera weaved in between trees and shrubs with nocturnal lids in place. Swift miles passed in whorls of colors as she hurtled over fallen trees and through dewy meadows while ignoring her ankles barking in complaints. Sweat drenched her spine and beads stung her eyes.

Liquid soaked her toes, and for a moment, she traveled back to the blood-soaked cell from her nightmare.

Bile rose in Kivera's throat and after half a heartbeat, the contents of her stomach emptied. Shameful tears pricked her eyes, but she scrubbed them away in between retches. Once finished, she wiped her mouth and jogged in search of a creek.

Creature heads poked out of their nests, beady eyes peeked around tree limbs, and furry tails leaped out of view.

Kivera heard the gurgles of a creek to her right and crumpled to her knees at the bank. Her aquatic reflection stared back at her with dead, gold eyes. Blank features rippled in the waters before twisting in disgust. Kivera immersed her head beneath the serene water and forced herself to stay under until her lungs burned. She lurched away and gasped for crisp air as she fell back on the soft grass.

Her breathing regulated minutes after laying down when a snapping stick broke the serenity.

Stupid, stupid, stupid, Kivera thought to herself as she raised feeble shields and flipped onto her feet, and slid into a defensive crouch.

She released a breath when Jexton walked into view between trees across the creek.

Jexton stopped at the creek to assess Kivera, and he smiled.

Kivera straightened her spine as instincts ebbed away and loosened her fists.

"What are you?" he breathed, but didn't move from his spot on the grass across the creek.

She narrowed her eyes and didn't deign an explanation for the coward across the water. She spun on a heel and stormed away from a few paces before stopping. The flush on her face was unmistakable when she turned to him.

Jexton opened his mouth. An apology or explanation for sitting away from her, Kivera didn't find out or care.

Kivera sprinted towards the creek, bound over the creek, and landed on the grass in front of him with a soft thud, all a blur to Jexton's human eyes.

"What are you doing here?" she hissed.

"I run when I can't sleep," he shrugged, but the laid-back gesture didn't meet his eyes. "Why are you here?"

Kivera straightened. "Same as you." She glanced at the golden rays streaming into the wooded area. Pinks and golds and oranges danced on the creek water and sang with the birds. Kivera and Jexton remained like that for a few minutes, watching the world wake up and intermingle with the divine light.

"We should get back. I want you to meet the team as soon as possible." Jexton murmured.

Kivera nodded. "I need to get back to Mavis." She jogged away before he could say anything and began the journey back to the inn. Her ears caught Jexton's subtle huff before his running footsteps followed behind her at a silent and steady pace.

"Where did you go?" Mavis asked before Kivera could shut the door with a soft click. Mavis stood in the entryway, hands on her waist and her mouth pressed in a thin line, and eyes bright.

"I went for a run" Kivera held out her hands and allowed Mavis to survey her sweaty and disheveled appearance.

Mavis lowered her eyes. "Sorry. I thought you left."

Oh.

"Mavis, I'm never going to leave you. I thought we established that yesterday." Kivera stepped further into the room.

Mavis' body deflated into a slump. "I'm used to people not caring. It'll take time for me to adjust."

Kivera offered a small smile. "Take all the time in the world. I am not leaving you, Mavis."

"Thank you."

Kivera squeezed Mavis' arm once before turning to the bathing room. She filled the tub with water, adding magic to the coals beneath the basin to heat them quicker, and added lavender oil she brought from her sea cottage. Once the stone room swirled with enough lilac steam, Kivera left the bathing room to gain her simple uniform but found Mavis on the edge of her bed holding a book in her lap. The book was falling apart at the seams and the colors faded.

"I drew you a bath whenever you're ready."

Mavis didn't look up. "This was my first book. Mother said it was the only possession my father left us. Well, except for a dagger, but nothing else." Mavis commented absentmindedly and Kivera perched on the armchair beside her. Kivera has been aching to see the dagger up close since the alley last night but didn't want to rush her new friend. "Not money, nothing of value, not even himself. But he left me a book. *Me*. A children's book."

"That has to mean something, Mavis," Kivera offered, unsure of what to say.

Mavis huffed a humorless laugh. "Mother would agree with you. She would shriek if the book was even in view. She always thought it was worth something, but all the trading posts and libraries she traveled to don't think a book they couldn't read was worth anything. When she came back from that trip, she threw the book at me but never wanted it back."

"Books carry more power than you realize. They carry knowledge, relief for the mind, and easy companionship." But Mavis' words nagged at Kivera. Why couldn't they read the words? "Why couldn't they read the child's book?"

"But a child's book full of bedtime stories?" Mavis shrugged. "The booksellers said the language wasn't workable to translate. No one knew what the language could be."

"Maybe those are stories he wished he could share with you if he raised you." Kivera gently touched Mavis' chilly hand with a foreign softness and tucked away that piece of knowledge.

"Possibly."

Kivera squeezed her hand once more before pushing her to her feet and extending a hand to Mavis.

"C'mon, a bath and a full stomach to help your morning, then we'll face grouchy guards."

Mavis placed her hand on Kivera's with a small smile as she rose to her feet.

A light knock rang at the door and Kivera ushered Mavis towards the bathroom before she strode to the door.

A petite barmaid with dingy brown curls escaping her beige headscarf clutched a platter of breakfast Kivera ordered when she arrived from her morning run. The shabby wood platter quaked as the waitress saw Kivera and her hazelnut eyes inhaled her onyx hair cut short to a razor point surrounding burnished gold eyes and a full mouth pulled up in a little smile. Kivera's smile widened, and she released a fraction of magic and let go of her crafted glamours she created to dim her otherworldly appearance to allow a subtle glow to kiss her skin.

"Aren't you pretty," Kivera purred and leaned on the doorframe with her arms crossed.

The pale woman shuddered like a leaf in the wind. "Ma'am."

Kivera leaned forward, capturing the barmaid's wide gaze, and lifted a hand and brushed a curl off her cheek.

Quivers erupted anew at Kivera's touch and she licked her lips.

Kivera licked her own. "Your name, love?"

The barmaid's eyelashes fluttered, and a deep blush washed over her smooth skin. "Mareena, ma'am."

"Mareena is a beautiful name." Kivera reached for the platter, grazing Mareena's hands. Satisfaction at the pretty human's trembling pooled deep in her stomach. Months have passed since she's been romantic with a woman and hunger for Mareena's company pricked her.

Mareena dipped her head. "Thank you, miss."

Kivera opened her mouth to say something when Mavis shouted a question from the bathroom.

"Another time then, Mareena," Kivera winked as she handed over a silver coin and watched the blushing woman leave with the scent of arousal with each step.

The early morning sunlight blinded Kivera and Mavis as they exited the inn's doors. A bitterly breeze lifted strands of Kivera's hair and sliced her cheeks. Grateful for the thick sweaters and loose fleece-lined pants Kivera brought for the pair of them, she thrust her gloved hands into her pockets and flared magic in search of Jexton.

Minutes passed before she realized the bastard wasn't at the guard station and, after checking with the innkeeper, he didn't leave a note regarding his location. She couldn't sense him anywhere in town as she hopped on each foot in front of the inn.

"Was that-was that you?" Mavis' cheeks were rosy but complemented the pale gray sweater she wore.

Kivera tilted her head and nodded. "How did you know?" She lowered her eyes to hide the spinning thoughts, but occasionally glanced at Mavis while she surveyed the town.

Run-down buildings lined the dirt road, and people milled around the hushed street. The residents were quiet in grief's suffocation and fear of who lurked in the shadows.

Finally, her magic snagged Jexton's energy north towards the teeming mountain range circling the town. Tree canopies in vibrant hues of citrine, topaz, and garnet concealed the foot of the mountains.

"The magic felt like a summer breeze calling me and wrapping around my body." Mavis' blush deepened. She held her hands under her armpits and followed Kivera as she led the trek to Jexton's team.

Kivera studied Mavis out of the corner of her eye. "Calling you?"

They veered off the main road of town to enter the slumbering forest without a marked path to follow. Mavis slowed her steps at the start of the woodlands, but Kivera tugged her arm. She always found peace among the wild timber and couldn't bring herself to be frightened of the beasts harbored in the thicket's darkness. Not with her darkness beneath her skin tugging to be released. Without looking back, she sauntered in with wide-eyed Mavis in tow.

"Sounds funny, doesn't it?" Mavis said with a half-joking laugh and her breath was visible in the frigid air.

"Not at all. Makes sense."

"Why didn't Captain Jexton tell us where he went?" Mavis changed the subject and her eyes darted at every sound echoing through the forest. Nocturnal eyes blinked behind branches, birds trilled throughout leaves, and shrubs rustled. Every sound sent Mavis' eyes frantically searching for the source of the noise.

Kivera strolled through as though the forest would unveil each thorny secret to *her* will. Magic shielded their presence from detection and the exertion released a knot of tension building at the base of her spine from idle magic. Releasing small spurts of power managed the strain and kept the power in check.

"I don't know, but I'm about to find out," Kivera promised, and they weren't more than half a mile from Jexton's energy pulse. They continued another few minutes in comfortable silence as Kivera viewed the scenic trail and thoughts buried Mavis.

"How old are you?" Mavis blurted.

Kivera frowned. "Twenty."

"You seem so much *older* than twenty," Mavis squinted at Kivera and she felt those milky white and blue eyes stripping her soul.

Kivera chuckled despite the shiver creeping on her spine and shrugged. Voices and footsteps cracked the silence up ahead with Jexton's pulse leading the way to the sounds.

"Where are you from?" Mavis questioned.

Kivera struggled to think around the thick emotion choking her as she thought of the place before these mortal lands. Maybe someday she would share the grief, the memories, and the agonizing pain coiled around her scarred heart from her homelands.

But today was not that day.

"That's a story for another time. Perhaps after a few ales. At the moment, we've arrived." Indeed, they arrived at the location of Jexton's team. Quietly, they watched from the tree shadows, and the team hadn't noticed them. Guards in royal uniforms, cobalt blue and glistening silver and sturdy knee-high boots, roamed around a creek and the surrounding trees. Jexton's familiar shape passed in between trees opposite the creek and glimmers of his brown hair peeked through.

Kivera stormed from the tree line towards his brown hair. Not one guard noticed her until she approached the creek. Within a heartbeat, she leaped over the creek and landed on her feet right in front of him and she snarled inches from his face.

A sharp outcry and slew of curses spit from Captain Tidefal's mouth.

Satisfaction heated Kivera's blood as she exposed her teeth and the scent of his fear deepened. "You kept me waiting, Captain."

CHAPTER SEVEN

"Not a patient person, I see." Captain Tidefal raised his hands and attempted a smile.

Kivera's eyes flashed in warning, but straightened and backed away. She gestured for Mavis to come forward from the shadows.

Mavis searched for a safe passage across the creek and the guards nearest to her unsheathed their swords and pointed them at her.

A breeze swept through the woods and pulsed with a warning. Kivera stepped once towards the men. "Make a move towards her and it'll be your last."

Jexton sighed and ran his fingers through his hair as he ordered his men to continue investigating. They relaxed as he commanded without their complaints.

"I didn't realize the time. It slipped my mind to leave you a message." Jexton looked away to scope the woods. He slipped his hands into his pocket while Kivera assisted Mavis across the water by placing solid blocks of darkness in a bridge formation.

Mavis tentatively stepped on the bridge and hurried across the short distance.

"You're fortunate that I'm in a good mood, otherwise I wouldn't have come all this way for gods know what," Jexton muttered something about what her good moods must be like which she ignored with a curl of her lips,

"I would have given you my report at our meeting," He started, but Kivera held up her hand.

"It's no matter now. You asked for my help and if you want it, it's yours. Continue to be uncooperative, then I'll move on with the number of other cases requesting my attention." Kivera released her magic. Shadows in the forest darkened and rumbled as dark power filled the air.

Jexton's head swiveled at the rustling leaves and the raw power kissing his skin. His mouth gaped as he looked at her with awestruck eyes.

Kivera's eyes burnished, the only sign of the well of power hidden deep within her core. This was a reminder to not forget *what* she was.

The guards froze and observed the unusual turn of events. A couple pulled out daggers to face the rumbling depths of the forest. Not realizing the dark-haired beauty with strange eyes controlled the changes.

"What are you?" he breathed and his wide eyes flicked to Mavis when she cowered at Kivera's side.

His worry jolted Kivera out of the power-hungry reverie and focused on her breathing to recoil from the power. The release soothed a cramp in her spine but wasn't worth the relief if Mavis was afraid, so she peeked at Mavis, who was observing the confrontation with curious eyes. There wasn't an ounce of fear as she stared at Kivera and even smiled at the powerful female next to her.

Kivera raised her eyebrows and smirked. "What I am is cranky for being left behind without a clue of where to find the captain who desperately hunted *me* down. So, please, share with us what you're doing out here before I pack our bags." Kivera avoided his question and picked her nails instead.

Captain Jexton lifted a hand to have them follow away from the stream and deeper into the forest.

Mavis reached for Kivera's hand and squeezed once before releasing it.

Kivera returned a warm smile before focusing on Jexton's back. They didn't travel only a hundred yards to the largest tree in the immediate area. A thick base and gnarled branches and, at its feet, a couple of guards clustered over something on the forest floor.

The stench reached Kivera before her companions, biting her senses with decay and a coppery tang.

Blood.

Kivera halted, pulling Mavis to a stop. Jexton kept going. She could slit his throat for not warning them.

"This might be overwhelming to see, Mavis. If you'd like, wait over here and-" Kivera started but stopped when Mavis's lips tightened.

"Is it-he or-s-she dead?" Mavis' brows furrowed together and Kivera nodded. "I'll come, but thank you. I need to learn to handle this stuff." With a determined gleam in her eye, she trailed after Jexton, and Kivera followed her.

The guards parted for the newcomers with a nod from Jexton.

Kivera didn't glance at the men and focused wholly on the pale mound on the ground. A simple white cloth stained with crimson covered the body, but pulled back to reveal the upper torso, and the image would forever haunt her dreams.

The corpse was a woman only a few years older than Kivera. They beat her delicate features to an unrecognizable mess of flesh and broken bones. Brown liquid covered nearly every inch of the exposed body and soaked the stringy hair. Mutilated limbs skewed at odd angles and burned away to the charred bone in some parts. Carved into her thigh was the mark, similar to the victim Jexton showed her in the file. Blood drained from Kivera's face. The mark had three triangles, two going the same direction and the last facing the opposite way, and three lines dragged down each apex.

Kivera couldn't believe her eyes and crouched for closer inspection of the body and noted every wound. She muttered a stream of prayers through bloodless lips.

Gods, she thought, *who could stomach doing this?*

Jexton and the others froze, watching Kivera.

Mavis locked an unwavering gaze on the body with

nostrils flared at Death's scent.

"Mavis?" Kivera scanned her friend's face, waiting for a reaction.

"I'm okay." Mavis raised her chin.

Kivera nodded and lifted a tendril of brown hair, packed with dirt, and inhaled the scents. Underneath the usual smells of a rotting corpse, a faint scent of unnatural dark magic pricked her nose. She jolted back with teeth bared and glared at the source of the abhorrent scent.

The guards jumped back a few steps as if witnessing a wild beast and their weapons leveled toward her. Someone even exclaimed to stay back from Kivera.

Mavis stepped closer to her with concern etched into her features. "Kivera, what's wrong?"

Kivera's breathing was ragged as she contemplated *what* the scent was. The magic chained inside her soul roared and thrashed against the iron restraints. Smoke curled in her throat and ash coated her tongue as the magic was seeking release. She focused on expanding her chest and filling her lungs with precious air to dampen the raging magic building up inside.

Like calls to like.

Kivera couldn't answer Mavis's question with bile threatening to choke her. She hurled her magic outwards, tunneling deep into her well of power, hunting for a whiff of the scent, and remained silent in her frantic search.

Birds squawked their annoyance at the magical wind canvassing their terrestrial home but remained in the blanket's comfort of leaves warming their feathers.

"What is it?" Jexton asked with sharper impatience than the sword his fingers rested upon. But the seed of fear in his eyes was unmistakable, and she didn't need the ability to read his mind to know that Jexton pondered what could frighten someone like her.

Kivera swallowed once before she could breathe through her constricted throat.

"This is not something I have ever encountered before. I need to investigate more to be certain of what touched this poor woman." Chaotic thoughts erupted with the scent and the symbol cut into the victim's skin. Within the catacombs of her mind, Kivera couldn't depict what either meant or where they could have come from. But a truth she was certain of, Kivera was not the only magically gifted soul in the human lands.

Chills skittered down her spine.

"What do you mean? What is it?" But to Jexton's frustration, Kivera shook her head and her hair brushed against her chin.

"I am not sure, but I'm going to find out. Mavis and I will check out the surrounding woods. Search for any mistakes the suspect made and I'll signal if there's anything."

"Be careful." Jexton's lip thinned, but nodded.

Kivera grabbed Mavis's hand and ventured deeper into the forest with Jexton's stare burning into their backs.

Kivera didn't signal all morning while they searched and eventually returned to the team when Mavis's stomach grumbled at midday. They crossed the treeline where Jexton's team converged and settled down for a meal on logs. Any conversation halted as the pair emerged from the shadows of the dense forest.

Jexton rose to his feet to meet them halfway. "Find anything?" Jexton's usually tidy brown hair flopped into his eyes and he brushed the strands away with scar-flecked hands.

"No, we couldn't find any physical signs of whoever killed the victim," Kivera fumed. Humans were reliable in making mistakes, but that scent coating the body wasn't mortal. Kivera trudged deep into her mind as they hunted for clues in the forest, trying to recover anything from her past teachings but without success.

Jexton shook his head. "You did as well as us. They found

nothing in the area or on the body. The methods are like the previous crime scenes."

"How many victims so far?" Mavis spoke for the first time since approaching.

Jexton's lips twisted. "After this morning, six women." He led them to the circle of logs his team perched on as they ate.

Kivera sat across from Jexton at the northernmost point with Mavis to her right, chewing on her lip as she gauged the crew around them and pressed herself into Kivera. The ring of guards only glanced at them before looking away except for an older man sitting a couple of seats to the right of Jexton, who stared at Kivera. She maintained his stare with an unflinching gaze waiting for him to speak.

"This is her?" He asked without blinking away from Kivera.

"How could it not be? Did you not see her jumping and the spooky silence in the woods?" Their youngest member exclaimed to the old man's right.

Unable to help herself, a shadow of a smile touched Kivera's lips, but she nodded.

"See, beautiful and young, like me yet pissing terrifying," The auburn-haired young man leaned back and flashed Kivera a playful grin on his face. The old man chortled and slapped his knee before staring at Kivera again.

"Bout time you arrived. These damned bugs have been eating me alive. I'm ready to get the hell outta here," the old man smirked.

A corner of Kivera's quirked up and hid her hand behind the log she sat on, careful not to show the human the onyx sphere in the center of her palm. With a flick of the wrist and the ball sped in an arc and her eyes tracked, the orb circled the team. Human eyes couldn't detect the slight glimmering shift in the air, so Kivera wiped her face blank to not frighten them. The ball surrounded the entire group before melting into the earth behind Kivera.

A heartbeat later, the buzzing died away, before leaving entirely.

Some members of the team looked around in silence.

You're welcome, the magic chained to her core growled but Kivera shoved the grumblings down.

"Good trick," the older gentleman's eyes danced and Kivera immediately liked the older man.

"Safe to assume that's why Jexton brought me along." Kivera leaned back and extended her legs, crossing them at the ankle.

There were six, including one woman Kivera mistook to be a man from the hood masking her face. The woman appeared only a few years older than Kivera with a round brown face bespeckled with freckles and curly, chestnut hair that tumbled to her backside. She was content to silently eat while gazing around with stunning green-blue eyes.

Jexton cleared his throat. "Kivera and Mavis, that's Rex, our team's physician, and next to him is his grandson, Maserion." They both nodded at Kivera and she returned a bow of her head. Jexton held a gesturing hand to the gargantuan man next to him. "This is my second-in-command, Tillirius, and Syt, over there next to him." Neither acknowledged Kivera but stared at her and she stilled under the heat of their eyes.

"Forgetting the best one, eh, Jexton?" A towering man next to Mavis with scars ravaging his face chuckled and crossed his massive arms.

Jexton sighed, but a ghost of a smile rested on his lips. "Kivera, this is Arcian. He's our extraordinary weapons expert."

"Hello." Mavis spoke and looked at Kivera, but loosened her shoulders when she beheld the man. His eyes crinkled, smiling down at her.

"Well, miss Kivera, I'm here as a pretty face to adore for these runts, so I'd say you have me beat," Rex smiled before he resumed eating and conversed quietly with Maserion. The interaction seemed to thaw the tension emanating from the group. As a whole, the party loosened a breath and murmured to one another.

Kivera pulled out her pack and rummaged for breakfast leftovers. She leaned close to Mavis, who eyed the loaf of bread Kivera brought with a hungry glint.

"How are you doing, Mavis?" Kivera handed her a generous half of the loaf and the water canteen.

"It's all very new. I'm still trying to process yesterday." Mavis shrugged and drank a heavy gulp.

"Give yourself time. Healing requires lots of time and patience with yourself," Kivera smiled but felt eyes on her. She looked over to Jexton, gazing at them with an unreadable expression. Kivera raised a brow, and he scowled back.

Jexton cleared his throat, and his unit immediately quieted.

"Since we're all together, let's go over the case's details so we're all on the same page. Take it away, Tilly." Jexton nodded at the bald man to his right, who watched at Kivera and Mavis with distaste.

"We have a string of murders in this town that have been going on for months. The sadistic bastard takes each of them for a few weeks and they turn up in the forest naked with injuries related to torture."

"Any similarities with the victims?" Kivera's brows furrowed while she tore into some bread.

"All women living in the city. Otherwise, they're different in age, appearance, and live in different parts of the city." Tillirius's almond eyes hardened.

"Any special markings on the bodies?" Kivera questioned, but she knew the answer.

But this time the man next to Mavis turned to Kivera. He was the largest man out of the group and with a thick scar carved from ear to ear on his wide neck. Various malicious weapons gleamed in the noon sun strapped to his body. Despite the polished uniform, Kivera wrapped a shield around Mavis in case of Arcian and prepared to rip out any throats that threatened her.

"Each woman had a marking on her thigh. I suspect from a dagger or a short-blade that can easily wield craft the symbols with care," Arcian passed over a crude drawing of the mark. He was a breathing mountain with broad shoulders and thick muscles corded around his body.

"How do you know how to recognize the blade type, Arcian?" Kivera studied the various symbols. Her blood froze at the sight of the arched letters and scrunched formations, but she wiped the recognition away.

"I've seen marks similar used by a short blade and are easier to carve into flesh than a long blade."

"Have you determined what the symbols mean?" Kivera didn't breathe, making sure no one could glean hints from her body language.

"There is nothing in the city library. I've sent messages to larger libraries neighboring the city, but nothing has come of it yet." A soft voice spoke and Kivera glimpsed over to the woman, Syt, and she set a calm gaze on Kivera.

"What do you do?" Mavis asked and leaned forward to the woman across from her, which she mirrored.

A fresh scent entered the air and Kivera sniffed towards its source and discovered Mavis's cheeks deepening into a lovely rose. Kivera hid her smile behind the parchment Arcian handed her.

"I like books and research anything related to the cases." Syt didn't break contact with Mavis, and Kivera could detect a similar arousal scent from her as well.

This will be interesting, Kivera thought to herself, and her smile deepened.

Mavis hummed deep in her throat. "A woman with brains. Quite a deadly combination."

"Don't let her fool you," Jexton interjected and covered Kivera's muffled snort into the paper. "Syt's lethal with knives and her knuckle. But her mind is her greatest weapon."

Syt's high cheekbones bloomed with color, and she

nodded in appreciation to her commander.

"Anything of significance from the other crime scenes?" Kivera lowered the parchment, her smile gone, and peered at the body across the creek, now fully covered with a white sheet. She shivered at the mysterious scent clinging to her nose.

"Not much changed between killings. All the victims were tortured, brutalized, and left naked in the woods. How any *man* could ever dare to do this to a woman is disgusting," Tilly sneered and crossed brawny arms across his chest.

"We'll put the animal in a cage and he'll face his crimes, Till," Arcian swore and knit thick brows together.

"Or her." Syt chimed in, but everyone, save for Mavis, ignored her. Mavis pursed her lips and touched Kivera's shoulder with her own.

"We have a witch now. Why can't we use her?" Tillirius asked Jexton with a curl to his lip.

Jexton opened his mouth to answer, but Kivera straightened her spine to the fullest height sitting on the log. "I'll make myself stunningly clear. I am not a witch bred for savage cruelty," Kivera said calmly, but her insides were churning with white-hot rage. They didn't know who, or *what*, she was, at no fault of their own. But the thought of being a weapon at anyone's disposal boiled her bones. Being *used* as they pleased. Kivera focused on her breathing and to calm her rapid heartbeat as the surrounding air pulsed with dark magic. "I am not some plaything for you to use anytime you please."

Tillirius leaned forward with a wolf's grin stretching across his face. "Care to share with the rest of the group what you are then, lady?" Tillirius threw out the proper name like a dagger, edged and poisoned sweetly.

Rather than bare her teeth and wrap her hands around his tanned skin like Kivera ravenously desired, she inhaled one more deep breath and stared at the man. Mavis stared at the Second with thinly veiled contempt and her small hands clenched in her lap.

"What concerns you and this team is the series of murders that your commander went through headaches of trouble to request me to investigate. To investigate *with* you. Do not make this even more troublesome for the rest of us." Kivera lifted her chin, not lowering her gold eyes from his hostile almond ones.

"We should know who we're working with. Threat or no."

"Kivera a threat? Is that a joke?" Mavis rose to her feet and her cheeks blossomed with roses, her clenched hands at her side.

"Do you not question her, girl? A human, like you, with someone dangerous like her?" he squinted at Mavis as he remained sitting with his arms crossed over his chest. Kivera wondered if he knew the consequences if he stepped once towards Mavis. The rest of the group stayed quiet, but their eyes followed the volleying words.

"I do not have to question someone who saved my life," Mavis lifted her chin. "Kivera is allowed her privacy and to share about her life as she pleases. It does not need to be pried apart by an arrogant man who wishes her to be caged like an animal."

"I don't need to take this from you, girl," Tillirius sneered and Kivera had to clench the seams of her black pants before she launched herself at him. Mavis appeared unaffected and didn't buckle under the weight of his narrowed eyes. "We can all hope she restrains herself from burning the forest down anytime she has a tantrum."

Mavis smirked. "Someone will undoubtedly test her restraint while working with such a pig-headed man."

Rather than replying, Tillirius shot to his feet, and after a warning growl from Kivera, he stalked off past the dead girl. Maserion followed behind, his whispered words unheard from Kivera's vantage. Jexton sighed loudly through his nose before wandering to his horse to fumble around in his saddlebags. Rex remained eating and wiggled his gray eyebrows when

Kivera met his eyes. Kivera couldn't help but give the old man a small smile.

"Don't worry about him. Tilly has been hot-headed since I've known him." Arcian leaned over to Mavis, who had returned to sitting. Her face was still flush from the outburst.

"Temperamental, ain't he?" Mavis jokes.

Kivera nudged her shoulder and handed over an apple.

"Thank you, Mavis. You have an incredibly kind heart." Kivera whispered and bowed her head. Mavis blushed further and bit into the blood-red fruit.

"Is your scar because of your home?" Arcian asked, not unkindly. From one scarred man to a scarred girl.

"It happened when I was a child a long time ago." Mavis lifted her shoulders, but her attempted indifference was futile. Kivera could only imagine taunts from vile mouths and stares and whispers behind raised hands Mavis endured. Who could do such a thing to a child? With a jolt, Kivera realized she met the monsters. She met the two individuals capable of harming a child of their blood and the thought almost convinced Kivera to pay a visit to the heartless mother and brother just to repay their mercy on Mavis.

"I was sliced when I was a young man, fresh into the army." Arcian's umber eyes glazed over but didn't continue as he was lost in long ago memories haze.

Mavis waited a moment or two, waiting for him to speak before curiosity bested her. "If it isn't too intrusive, what happened?" Mavis threw the apple core into the trees as Kivera remained silent, checking the magical shields for any holes.

"No one has ever asked." Arcian's jaw clenched as his mind spun with the mental battle to share but sighed in defeat. "When I was out of training camp, only twenty, they sent me to a legion stationed in Basilt."

The name rang a bell in Kivera's mind from a case she worked on when she first was employed by the Royal Council. A few children were discovered ritualistically murdered by a sadistic schoolteacher. Kivera vowed never to visit the swampy backcountry unless a case was severe enough. Basilt rested on the banks of the Caomado River and most of the town were fishermen. Women and men teemed the fruitful river sporting nets and poles until the sun drew to a close. As soon as the moon peeked her sleepy eye open, they exchanged their muck for ale in the few pubs.

"I kept my head down and trained harder than anyone at the post and moved up to captain within a year." Arcian continued. Rex pretended he wasn't listening as he picked at the red-haired boy's food, but Kivera knew his ears perked at the story. "In the Spring, we received word a commander from another legion would arrive to inspect how my legion's training was faring. While he visited, he invited a group of us into town for drinks to blow off a day's stress."

"After the blubbering cronies drank their weight in ale, they ordered me to follow them to camp. On the way back, they grabbed a lady walking down the street minding her own business," Arcian's throat bobbed. "They snatched her into an alley and by then I knew what they were going to do and I had to stop it."

Kivera couldn't stop herself from leaning forward and gazing at him while he stared at the cloudless sky. Mavis clenched her shaking hands and rested them in the warmth of her armpits.

"I hit the commander with a single blow and he didn't get back up. The girl escaped and the other officers hanging around pinned me down to give me this scar." Arcian tugged the edge of his collar down further to give them a clear view. Rex craned his neck for a clearer sight. "They told me my military career was over and were going to make sure I wouldn't talk."

"How did you make it out?" Mavis whispered.

"The girl came back with her father and they carried me to her grandmother. The women cared for me while I healed. Her brother scared anyone away with a cane that bothered us." Arcian smiled faintly, as if the twisted memory was pleasant.

"Did the commander stay true to his word?" Mavis' lip curled.

"When I returned, I dishonorably discharged and never saw those bastards again," Arcian nodded. "I didn't return home and found odd jobs wandering the continent. I found Jexton five years ago, and I thank the gods for meeting him."

"You killed the commander?" Mavis asked, even softer than before.

Arcian glanced at her, then at Kivera, gauging how to say his words next. "I did," Arcian replied cautiously, his mouth tightened making his brutal necklace shine in the autumn sun.

"Good." Mavis' answering grin was nothing short of feral.

Kivera rose to her feet, desperate for some movement and to walk away from haunted memories. Mavis looked up, a question to follow in her eyes, but Kivera only shook her head.

"I'm going to scout around again to see if I can find anything useful." Mavis didn't seem inclined to leave her new friend and waved at Kivera. "I won't be gone long."

Kivera shrouded Mavis in another layer of protection as she rose to her feet and her knees crackled from sitting too long. Rex glanced at her and waved at her when she strode past him. She patted him on the shoulder before sauntering into the forest.

Without a visible path, Kivera weaved through the pine trees, doing her best not to trip. During each snapping branch, her heart raced, and she quickened her pace. Though she was a weapon herself, the mysterious scent introduced a new player to this case and one not from this continent.

Deep into the woods, Kivera hopped over a fallen log only to stumble down a sudden steep decline. Rocks slid under her boots and branches clawed at her sweaty skin. She swung her arms out to maintain balance but slammed her shoulder into the base of a pine tree before skidding to a halt. Her shoulder exploded in agony and colorful swears poured out of her lips, frightening away the furry tails and feathered wings nestling in the trees.

The decline leveled out and led to a band of trees circling a magnificent oak tree overflowing with branches. Kivera couldn't help but marvel at the sleeping giant, gently colored with the dying season. In another life, she wouldn't hesitate to climb to the top with determination coursing through her limbs. She stepped forward with a hand extending toward the cracked bark.

Something caught her attention before her fingertips connected with the rough bark.

The forest was deathly silent. Gone were the cheerful chirping and busy rustling and snapping branches that filled the air.

Kivera swiveled around, keeping her back pressed against the massive oak, and her aching fingers curved into claws. She blanketed herself in the cool embrace of shadows, avoiding the detection of whatever roamed the forest. Worry for Mavis spiked throughout her body, but thank the gods the creature was closest to her and not her friend, surrounded by fragile mortals. The animal was most likely a lion or bear, but not whatever carried that mysterious scent on the dead girl. Kivera dispatched magic to find the nuisance and didn't have to search far.

Out of the corner of her eye, a dark form slunk through the tree shadows.

Slowly, Kivera turned to the shape to not make a single noise. She kept her shallow breathing quiet, but feared the creature could hear her thundering heartbeat. The dark body stayed hidden in the security of shrubs, only a stone's throw away, and only its head was visible in the brief spokes of sunlight.

It was nothing Kivera had ever seen before. A bizarre cross between bear and wolf, the enormous head was triangular with a curled snout revealing sharp teeth the size of Kivera's thumb. But the eyes were the most fearsome quality. Frozen orbs of ice eyed Kivera, despite being hidden within her shadows, as if he could see past the darkness. A low growl reverberated from the beast and pulled back its lips further.

Corded muscles tensed and before the night-black creature could lean back into its haunches to pounce, Kivera threw a shadow orb at the beast's eyes and bolted for the steep incline. Not bothering to check behind her at the ear-splitting howl of rage, Kivera pumped her arms harder as she sprinted for her life. Pounding earth and enraged roarings followed behind, too quick for her liking.

Kivera cast a single message to the one person who wouldn't question her as she careened through the forest. Despite the repercussions and the disdain that may come for the secret gift she wielded, she would unveil it. For Mavis' safety, she would.

Get Mavis out. Run.

CHAPTER EIGHT

Oh, gods. Ohgodsohgodsohgodsohgods.
Kivera hurtled through the trees but was miles away from the team and even further from the safety of the town. The chances of outrunning the beast were slim despite her daily runs. By some miracle, she was ahead of the monster, but the earth vibrated beneath her boots.

She flicked wall after wall of darkness to halt the beast but only stunned it momentarily before provoked it further as it shook off the shadowy blindness. She plunged deep into the well of power, molting down a few of the chains and reining in the monster prowling beneath Kivera's skin.

Amber flesh-shredding talons slid from Kivera's fingers, wispy shadows entangled around their sheen. Kivera reveled in unleashing a small portion of the cursed night-cursed magic enslaved in iron chains in her core. An absence she felt like a phantom limb and the burst of emotion added to her courage and a plan formed. Before judgment soured her bravery, Kivera struck.

She spun when a hot breath burned her neck and slashed across the creature's face, leaving its pointed ears to a scarred snout in ribbons. Its enormous head reared up in surprise and Kivera swiped for its jugular and tore through ragged fur. Its massive, agile body rose on its back paws and roared again. Not having the favor returned, Kivera bolted down the path. Blood roared in her ears and her heart pounded against her ribcage a couple of beats before the creature pursued again.

Kivera twisted through the trees and cut in tight turns.

The beast crashed through tree bases and bushes as if they were stalks of wheat, though a challenge to navigate for its large body. Still, she shot wall after wall of shadows behind her with shaking arms.

Leaping from a rocky ledge onto a patch of wild grass, Kivera landed with a soft thud and glanced behind her for a split second, catching the creature's human-like brown eyes centered on her. Kivera flicked her fingers to send a surprise blast of darkness as it leaped from the same rocky bank before she whirled around and dash ahead once more. The earth trembled when the burly body smacked against the ground and roared an ear-splitting howl that made Kivera's ears ring before it hunted her again.

Keep going. Keep running, A faint voice, both old and young, whispered in Kivera's head.

Without a second urging, Kivera pushed her legs harder with the aid of her magic intertwining her limbs. A slow, aching burn began in her lungs, and a piercing cramp in her side.

She was halfway to the hopefully vacated crime scene, yet the distance to safety yawned wider. Even if Kivera arrived safely in town, a snarling beast would be a threat to the town's residents. She either had to lose the animal in the thicket of the woods far away or slaughter it. Neither felt easy, with the creature's hot breath inching closer to the exposed skin on her neck.

Panic ransacked Kivera's stomach, threatening to disrupt the strategies trying to form. Rot and decay from the creature pricked her nose, and she almost gagged on the stench. Her breaths turned ragged as fear coiled around her heart, wondering if those might be her last.

Kivera didn't notice the branch partially hidden in the path and she tumbled to the ground. Time slowed and Kivera's heartbeats ticked loud in her ears. The creature's putrid breath seared the back of her neck as she fell. Monstrous jaws neared her neck in uncomfortable proximity and would easily rip

Kivera's body apart the moment she landed. A molten ball of darkness palmed in her right hand and floated to open air as she reached out for it, as if grasping for safety. The motion of Kivera's falling body released the growing magic, leaving her back exposed when the creature closed in on her.

The beast's flesh-shredding claws pierced through Kivera's jacket to the soft skin as her slow-moving body collapsed into the shadowy magic. She screamed at the fire-hot pain lancing through her blood. Darkness swirled around her body, tugging her soul and the movement churned her stomach. Night sky cocooned her body in a foreign chill and a faint whispering hummed through the darkness. Water leaked from her squeezed eyes and hair whipped her cheeks while she hurtled through the black.

Gods, what's happening to me? Someone help me. Please save me.

The rocky ground appeared after a heartbeat and time returned to a blood-churning pace. Kivera landed ungracefully on all fours and her knees barked in protest. Her torn shoulder, the monster ravaged, burned and failed to support her. She rose to a low crouch and hissed as she cradled her injured arm. She surveyed the tranquil woods around her where the beast was nowhere to be seen.

The shadows deposited her in a new area. Safe from bloodthirsty teeth and sharp claws as if the magic answered her pleas.

Questions buzzed in Kivera's head. How did she get here? Where was *here*? Is her power still growing? Magic grappled at the iron chains containing its shadowy tethers while chuckling at her shock, as if to say, *How could you forget me? About what I can do.*

Kivera choked on the rising panic and swept her dirt-encrusted hair out of her eyes.

A deafening roar clapped against the mountains and scattered birds into the skies. The beast's thunderous cry was far enough away but angry enough for Kivera to scale to the top of the nearest tree. Climbing proved difficult with her injured shoulder and she hissed at every movement until she finally grasped the highest branch.

Puffs of air burst from Kivera's mouth from heaving and panting as she clung to the tree's rough bark with one arm and cradled the other painfully close to her trembling body. Enraged howls exploded in the distance and rattled the tree she had clasped to. Exhaustion wrung out her body and she slid to sit with her legs dangling below the branch.

"What a godsdamned day," Kivera shook her head and raised a shield to inspect her wound so predators wouldn't sniff her out. Claw marks marred her shoulder blades, deep enough for rivulets of blood to stream down her chest and back. She would need to clean out the dirt before the skin knit back together.

Eventually, the roars disappeared miles south, and the forest returned to the serene normalcy as before. Kivera groaned as she stood to plot her route to the ground. Climbing would be painful as adrenaline seeped from her bloodstream and her shoulder was in blazing pain. An idea popped into her mind and before she could reason with herself, she leaped into the open air.

Shadows danced in her vision, and this time she reached for them. The air pulled from her lungs and her core yanked her before slamming face first into the base of a close by tree but on a lower branch than before. She scraped her hands on the unforgiving bark for a secure hold. Kivera's mind buzzed at the revelation and a grin tugged at her lips. Kivera focused on the next landing spot at the tree next to the one she was on and shakily hopped through shadows, nearly falling off the edge. Her arms windmilled frantically, and she caught her balance. Kivera whooped and her grin spread as continued shadow leaping until she reached the safety of the earth.

Kivera could have kissed the dirt and glanced at the horrendous heights of the trees. She near giggled at the past few hours but felt like a lifetime. A dead body, bloodthirsty beast, and new powers surfacing. She wondered what the next few hours could bring as she hopped short distances back to town.

The dirt road yawned open as Kivera walked through the grimy town. Darkness crept in from the east as the sun dropped below the staggering mountains in a vibrant finale. Kivera ached to sail among the fiery clouds, staining the last breaths of daylight and to graze her fingers against the colorful wisps.

Kivera desperately needed a steaming bath to cleanse off dirt and blood caking her skin. Her stomach grumbled after leaving the food with Mavis before she left for the woods hours ago. The thought of a warm bath, piles of food, and sleep ached her bones, and she jumped through shadows quicker out of the woods.

As Kivera journeyed back, the distances she jumped lengthened gradually, but drained her energy. The magic purred at the new revelation and rallied to discover what else Kivera could do despite the physical cost. She despised the cursed power more as new layers were unfolding. But Kivera couldn't deceive herself as her blood race and admitted to reveling in the discovery. But how could she contain the advancing power? How does she chain the growth to her will before the magic rips her apart?

Kivera decided those were questions to answer tomorrow after a deep cup of tea. She dispatched magic in search of Mavis and Jexton, who she hoped were together and safe. At the cursed magic, nausea roiled through her, though a tiny part was thrilled at the power. She had used only a small amount of magic today.

Thank the gods, the pair were at the inn and the rest of the team was absent.

The inn's front door, a decrepit slab of wood older than the town, creaked as Kivera stepped over the threshold. Musky air slammed into her senses and amplified her headache.

The innkeeper didn't glance up even when Kivera approached the front desk. "I need the largest platter of food and pot of tea you have available."

The attendant didn't glance up from her novel and waved her wrinkled hand at the request. Kivera received the message clearly. It'll get done when it suits the wizened woman.

Kivera exhaled through her nose and walked towards the dining room where two familiar people were waiting. Double doors led into a rectangular room with a blissfully roaring fire across from the entrance. All the mismatched, chipped tables were unoccupied except for the one closest to the ornate fireplace.

The smaller figure shot up from the chair and raced towards Kivera with twin red braids trailing behind her. Mavis.

She halted a foot away from Kivera. Her body trembled and wide eyes inspected Kivera's every inch. Not knowing how to embrace Kivera yet, Mavis grasped her frozen hands.

"Are you okay?" Mavis's inspective eyes landed on Kivera's injured shoulder despite the black sweater covering her wound. She had summoned clothes during a long stretch of walking, which did wonders for her mood. "You're hurt. What happened?"

Kivera smirked. "Met a new friend in the woods today. But I'll tell you the story with Jexton." Kivera raked her eyes over Mavis's body but found no bodily harm. "Are you okay?"

"Yes, but I'll let you know it's terrifying when a humongous man rushes you onto a horse because you supposedly told him to do so with your mind." Mavis searched for denial or confirmation and she squeezed Kivera's hands.

The other figure at the table, Jexton, coughed at Mavis' remark and slid out of the chair closest to the fire. Kivera nodded at him with gratitude for more than the chair.

"I did. It's a little curse of mine." Kivera shrugged and pulled Mavis with their clasped hands towards the warm table.

Kivera would discuss her magic with Mavis in private and noted to do so later.

"Tell us what happened." Jexton crossed his arms as Kivera plopped on the chair's hard surface and rested her arms on the backing. She complied with Jexton's request and described in terrific detail the interaction with the beast of nightmares, but left out the growing magic.

The fire warmed her frozen bones and heated the tender muscles of her torn-up shoulder. Graced with healing magic, the shredded flesh began knitting fibers together and clotted the flow of blood. After being able to rest and not use her magic on tasks like jumping, her body could prioritize energy for healing. She only hoped to clean the wound out before anything healed underneath the skin.

Kivera's slim hands gestured in lazy motions during the debrief and Mavis' sea and silver eyes remained on Kivera's face but flicked to her shoulder once in a while.

Captain Tidefal concentrated on her features to check for signs of deception, occasionally rubbing his sharp jaw. As Kivera finished her last word, Jexton wasted no time asking questions.

"What was it? Did it have that scent you talked about on the victim?"

Kivera shook her head and rumpled dark hair tickled the sensitive skin on her neck. "It was an abomination of nightmares."

As you are, a voice in her head sneered.

Jexton clenched his jaw, and the curling tendrils of his hair glinted in the firelight. "The question is, why was the thing so close to the body?"

"And where the beast came from." Kivera included.

"Is it not a coincidence?" Mavis piped in, her voice low, as if the creature prowled close in the shadows.

"It could or not, but interesting enough to find out." he angled his head to stare past Kivera into the depths of the flames behind her. "You can speak with your mind and I assume powerful enough to read them as well."

The abrupt change of topic question stilled Kivera's breathing and Mavis didn't say a word. The only noise was the crackling fire in the otherwise empty dining hall. Kivera surged deep into the strength of her willpower to not snap at the glaring captain. Her mind drifted to the comforts of plush blankets and steaming tea surrounded by mounds of food. She did not have an ounce of energy to be pestered with questions.

"Yes, I can. A gift I use with caution and only in situations with consent or emergencies," Kivera raised her pointed chin and her burning gold eyes challenged him.

"Is that how you're successful in interrogations?" Kivera nodded and didn't waver from his stare. "Do they get consent?"

"They are suspects of heinous crimes. That, I do not regret or second guess. The royal council is aware of my tactics and approves."

His fist clenched on the cracked table, and the room froze from his tone. "Do you invade my mind whenever you feel like it? Even Mavis? You've only recently met us."

"Initially, yes I did, to both of you." Kivera slid an apologetic look to Mavis and returned to Jexton's glare. "But I did so to find out why a cloaked man hiding in the shadows knows my name in a town I've never visited."

"It's our privacy I'm concerned about," Veins swelled in his forehead as he leaned further into the light.

The magic in Kivera grumbled at the move, and she stifled the instinct.

"Kivera's used magic to save our lives and allowed us enough time to get away." Mavis reasoned.

Gratitude crashed over Kivera like a wave and she nearly choked on the benefit of the doubt Mavis gifted her. "I've been on my own for a long time, Jexton. I need my precautions otherwise I'll be crucified."

"What if you're wrong about the suspect?" Jexton raised his eyebrows.

Kivera's eyes shuttered. "Unfortunately, I rarely am and

will be plagued for the rest of my life with horrific scenes of abuse, torture, and murder." Kivera stared hard at the young captain, only a handful of years older than her twenty years. "If I am wrong and I invade the mind of an innocent man, I can save his life from the hands of authorities hell-bent on executing his life."

Jexton looked away to the fire, ravaged by an internal debate, before sighing in defeat.

Mavis smiled at Kivera, accepting an explanation when Kivera was ready. Excitement grew in her heart and for the first time in a long time, Kivera found a chance to share about herself with caring ears.

Kivera rose to her aching feet and pat Jexton on the shoulder. "Jexton, I'm truly only here to help." She glanced at Mavis and nodded to the double doors leading to the corridors. "Get some sleep and we'll meet at the guard's meeting quarters after dawn."

Mavis led their way and left Jexton staring at the fire. They reached the door before he spoke. "Arrive with breakfast or I'll throw you out."

CHAPTER NINE

No matter the amount of magic flowing through her veins, Kivera could not stop the hot roll she attacked from dripping onto her navy sweater.

"Dammit," Kivera grumbled but didn't bother changing her nightgown until she engulfed the remaining portion and perhaps another. Food was deposited minutes after waking up as Kivera knew when the maid scurried up the staircase as she unknowingly passed through the shadowy web of alarms Kivera spun. They woke up late since Kivera skipped that morning's run in favor of resting her aching body.

Mavis didn't miss a beat and set off to prepare cups of tea and their plates of food.

"Sit down, Kivera. Sit and eat." was all she would say while giving Kivera a stern look.

Mavis asked nothing of the night before and only helped Kivera out of her clothes and brought her food into the bath. She still didn't press for answers when they went to bed and wished Kivera a good night before falling asleep.

Kivera knew Mavis wanted her to start the conversation about magic but still left Kivera alone to sort through her thoughts. For which Kivera was grateful, down to her bones.

"The beast hurt you, didn't it?" Mavis held up a strawberry cookie but didn't take a bite. Only stared at it. "Something is wrong with your shoulder."

"It doesn't hurt anymore. I'm fine." Kivera smiled at her concern and bit into her third roll.

"Must have been quite the adventure." Mavis bit into the

dessert.

"An eventful day, for sure. Did you enjoy your first day?" Kivera closed her eyes and lashes tickled her high cheekbones.

"I expected nothing quite like that. To be whisked away on a horse by a stranger must happen all the time though," Mavis grinned devilishly, her scar angry and as cruel as the ones who gave it.

Kivera giggled and opened her eyes to snatch a slice of lemon bread.

"Why did you send the message to Jexton and not to me?" Mavis asked after a moment of silence.

Kivera swallowed once, then twice, before answering in a hushed tone. "I know the magic I use is an invasion of privacy, and I didn't want to frighten you."

"You view sending me a message to my mind as an invasion of privacy?"

"I don't want you to look at me like I violated you and take away a hallowed part of you," Kivera focused on the crumbs falling on her gown.

"I appreciate the courtesy, but understand I'm okay with you telling me messages to my mind." Mavis' voice wavered around the word and Kivera fixed her with a steady look.

"Mavis, you deserve a private place for yourself. I do not want to be the person to take that away."

"You're not! I mean, as long as you're not spending all day reading my mind or enslaving me, we're good," Mavis garbled around the food she shoved in her mouth.

"You still trust me? Even after finding out about this?" Kivera sat up abruptly and rested on her elbows.

"Part of me is horrified you can go into my thoughts, but I understand. It helps with your cases. I trust you." Mavis set down the cookie and her eyes glazed with a distant memory. "But if I could read minds, then at least I would know if someone was going to hurt me or not." Tearful whispers choked the last words.

"Mavis." Kivera reached for Mavis' hand across the space

between their beds. "I won't hurt you ever and I will fight anyone who does so."

"I know that Kivera, I do." Mavis smiled and resumed eating. The room quieted as they were both lost in thought. After Kivera finished, she glanced at Mavis chewing her bottom lip.

"What's on your mind, Mavis?"

Mavis smirked and sat back in the armchair. "Funny that you ask. I'm about this pond I visited as a child. When things at home got terrible, I would race to the water and sit there listening to the world."

"What did you hear?"

Mavis frowned, and silver lined her eyes. "A world heavy in sadness. But hope rides on the wind."

The words perked Kivera's ears. "Yes, it does. Did you hear that somewhere?" Kivera picked at her nails.

"I read it in my childhood book." Curious sentence to have in a children's book.

Kivera nodded at her suspicions being confirmed. "Comforting at a young age." Mavis nodded but was unaware of the thoughts racing through Kivera's mind.

Kivera rose from the bed and changed quickly into an evergreen sweater and fleece-lined trousers. With only a wrap covering her chest, Mavis's gaze landed on Kivera's scabbed shoulder.

"You heal quickly."

Kivera shrugged. "Speedy healing is among my magic."

"You're quite the witch." Mavis wiggled her eyebrows.

A flare of rage rippled through Kivera and she shoved the anger down. She wouldn't bite her tongue with anyone else. "I'm not a witch, though that would be a lot easier."

"What do you mean?" Mavis's eyebrows pulled together.

"All that means is I wish I had witch blood instead." Kivera pulled her hair into a high ponytail to catch every scrap of hair. A few lined her face despite all her finagling.

"Question," Mavis said in the candlelight as she reached

for a blueberry loaf slice.

"Yes?"

"Do you- did you see how my life was?"

Kivera stopped messing with her hair and twisted her body on the edge of her bed to scrape for more time to think about the question and how to answer it. Kivera studied Mavis before she said, "I did. I know enough about what you went through." Mavis' memories bubbled into Kivera's mind and she shuddered at the pain inflicted on a scarred, broken girl by those meant to protect her.

Mavis looked away, making herself smaller. "Is that why you offered me a job?"

"I have quite a few reasons I wanted you to work with me. Some for my purposes regarding work, but I'd be lying if I said no. And I do not regret it. You are kind and caring and I selfishly want that in my life. To have a friend." Kivera lowered her head. "I'm so sorry for reading you like that, but I will never violate you in that way ever again. Don't think of this job as a charity but hopefully an answer for calls for help. An answer I think we both needed."

The feeling of another's eyes on Kivera's face made her look up and found blue and white eyes considering her.

After a long moment, Mavis reached out a hand to grasp Kivera's hand. "A small part of me is glad someone else knows about me. I've been forced to live in silent isolation about my horrors, but I'm relieved to know someone else knows."

Kivera smiled in bright relief and gripped Mavis firmly. "I am sorry. If it makes us even, I want to share a secret with you."

"Kivera's, really it's okay. You should share when-"

Kivera interrupted her with a raised hand. "I want to," Kivera took a deep breath before continuing. "My curse is growing at a faster pace now that I'm twenty. I don't know how to be strong enough to control the magic or how long it'll be before I hurt someone."

The confession hung in the candlelit silence and coated

Kivera's tongue in poison.

"There's not only healing and mind reading and making anything appear and disappear, is there?"

The question sounded silly to Kivera, even though Mavis didn't know more than a scratch of the surface. They know each other for only a couple of days, but if she were right about the book, her scent, and what truly lies in Mavis's blood, Kivera's truth must be shared. Mavis doesn't know of the pulsing dark magic consuming Kivera's every cell.

In response to her thoughts, the magic deep in her soul's prison riled at the mockery. The grand display she could display would wring humans' guts with terror.

"Those are only a part of it. A small part." Kivera frowned at the intensity of the magic's desires but reminded herself they are not her own.

"Are you scared?" Mavis nearly hesitated to ask, but Kivera didn't know how to answer. She didn't want Mavis to turn away from her, but Mavis should know regarding her safety.

"It's a scary responsibility to have," Kivera whispered and her shoulders buckled. She nibbled the edge of the loaf but tasted ash.

"Do you know anyone to help?" Mavis pulled on a thick overcoat Kivera brought for her.

"In the mortal lands, I'm all alone," Kivera spoke matter-of-factly, trying to ignore the crack in her heart.

"Not anymore," Mavis leaned to squeeze Kivera's hand once before sliding on a boot and striding to the door, ready to begin the case.

"Not anymore," Kivera mouthed the words and smiled at herself as she followed her friend.

CHAPTER TEN

"We should hunt the creature."

Kivera raised her head from reading the town's newspaper while Mavis gazed at the front doors, lost in thought. Dawn crested over the mountains, and Kivera asked her to have tea before they left for the day. Her body cramped from the draining week. She and the team returned to the crime scene and inspected every bit of the woodlands for any evidence they may have missed. But found nothing. Frustrations rose the previous day between Kivera and Tillirius and Jexton announced they would work in town on the case. Most likely to avoid any altercation. "Mavis, there is no way you will put yourself in danger. Besides, I will take care of it." A plan already formed in between jumps yesterday, and she couldn't afford to worry about Mavis.

Mavis gripped her armchair and leaned forward. "If I am to earn my wages honestly, then I must do something of help."

Kivera snorted into her tea. "You think hunting down bloodthirsty monsters is a part of the job description?"

"I could help if you taught me." Her braids swung as Mavis turned her wide blue and scarred eyes on Kivera.

"I will not put you in danger when you don't even have the capabilities to hunt or protect yourself."

"Teach me."

Kivera's mouth twitched, and she laid down the useless newspaper. "I'll teach you how to run and how to defend yourself. Once you can adequately defend with your hands and then a weapon, I'll take you out on hunts. But I hardly ever hunt monsters, so it's not very often you'll need to. They fill my job with human beasts to capture."

"How often?" Mavis tilted her head, her double braids swaying against her sea-blue sweater. Even sleep deprived, she's aglow with an otherworldly beauty. Another sign confirming Kivera's suspicions of Mavis's heritage.

"Monsters are rare, so maybe a few times a year. Most of the time, it's a bear, wolf pack or mountain lions causing trouble. Monsters don't really exist here."

"But they do? Exist somewhere?" Mavis was quick to latch on to Kivera's slip.

"Monsters exist. Horrors created by forgotten mischievous gods left to hunt and threaten human life," Kivera's amber eyes blazed at the stories of beasts slaughtering children, razing down villages and ripping bodies as a human would tear into a bread loaf.

"Who, or what, do you think created that beast from yesterday?" Mavis picked a crumb off her loose pants.

A clock in the dining hall chimed seven times, and they needed to leave soon before they were late to meet Jexton's team.

"I've been thinking about it. Perhaps someone with access to forbidden texts or a delusional breeder," Kivera attempted to joke, but Mavis winced. Kivera buzzed with the possibility of a magical animal existing in Oakheart. No animal of the human world could compare to the sheer size and brutality the creature possesses. Kivera didn't know if Man could create a monstrosity, but she didn't rule them out yet. If a human was creating monstrous creations, Kivera wondered how and with what supernatural resources?

"Do you think it's someone like you?" Mavis' eyes flicked to Kivera.

Kivera's tea cup halted midair as she mulled over her next words carefully so she didn't share grisly details best left sealed tight in a box. She didn't know if it was for Mavis's benefit or hers. "I haven't encountered another like me in human lands and impossible I ever will. I don't want our time to be wasted on unlikely possibilities." Kivera smoothed her features with a bland smile. The prospect of another with magic like what she caged inside her made her hands tremble.

"Would it be terrible if more of your kind were here?"

Kivera didn't answer for a few moments. Long enough for Mavis to rise to her feet, gesturing for Kivera to hurry, but she didn't move. She couldn't move.

"It would be terrible." Kivera's voice was icy as she stared hard at Mavis.

Mavis nodded as if understanding completely. "We should go. We don't want Jexton to have any reason to be mad at us."

Kivera grinned, a feral slash of white teeth. "We won't be late." Swiveling her head to check if the dining room was empty before summoning shadows. Cool darkness cloaked the length of her body and straightened her curly hair to a smooth glisten. The magic glamoured her pointed ears to rounded ones and changed her dirty sweater to a loose-fitting navy one. Star-flecked clouds kissed her skin before melting away to reveal her once more. One of Kivera's likable powers, she had to admit.

Mavis whistled. "Damn, that's so cool."

Kivera winked. "One of the perks."

They moved to the front door and passed the innkeeper, who didn't bother looking up from her book. Mavis stuck out her tongue towards the old hag and Kivera chimed in with soft snickers.

Kivera sent her magic to find Jexton's mind and found him within walking distance. The guard station was close by, but the moment they pushed through the front door, Kivera rethought walking in the chilly autumn gusts.

Mavis shivered underneath her thick coat and stuck her fists under her arms.

"If I could get us there faster, would you be open to the method?" Kivera glared at the early morning outside. "But there's a slight chance this will hurt your stomach."

"Anything to beat the cold," she nodded furtively.

Kivera held out her hand and Mavis hesitantly gripped it. Once conjoined, dark clouds swirled around them, obscuring their view of the town square before a familiar force yanked them through the darkness. Kivera was barely adjusted to the shadow jumping and Mavis was even less so.

Cobblestones opened beneath their feet and Kivera held onto Mavis in case she stumbled, but she didn't. Only a shade greener, but steady next to Kivera. The corner of Kivera's lips lifted at Mavis, adjusting to the wild force. Magicked stars winked out and the darkness receded into nothingness.

A broad, two-story building and a circular metal sign with crossed onyx swords appeared between the shadows. Beyond the dreary stone wall awaited Jexton's energy bubble, where the rest of his team worked in the guard station. Shops of various avenues and cafes stretched down both sides of the street. Kivera's stomach grumbled wafts of spiced teas and baked goods from a business on the south end. The cloudy sunlight painted pedestrians in a dreary gray haze. A group of men ambled toward the mountains in a near march and carried on their backs lamps and pickaxes.

Kivera started towards the set of large, oak doors under a pointed wooden awning. Vines crawled the stone face and curled around the awning, rattling against the wind. She raced into the building from the chill with an extended hand into the warm air inside.

A fireplace to the right of the entrance yawned flames, basking in a shiny aspen bench at the feet in a soft haze. A front desk worker, manned by a pale man with balding blond hair, squinted as Kivera and Mavis entered. His beady eyes swept over Mavis before dismissing her entirely and glued to Kivera. His small lips curled before gesturing them over.

Kivera rolled her shoulders and raised her chin. Noticing the sudden tension, Mavis frowned at the man.

"We're here to meet with Captain Jexton and his team."

Kivera articulated in a cool voice.

"Your business?" The uniformed front desk attendant crossed his arms with a quirked eyebrow.

"I am Special Investigator Kivera Galveterre here regarding consulting for a case," Kivera answered through gritted teeth. Magic snarled at the man's demeanor and if Kivera were to go inside his mind, it could unleash all hell. Chaos she didn't know she could control.

The desk attendant snorted. "What could a teenager do for a criminal case? Stop wasting my time and-"

"Kivera Galveterre has done more for my team in a single day than you have in the three months we've been here." An icy voice rumbled from the double doors behind the attendant. "Stop wasting *her* time and do something useful with your day for once."

Walking towards Jexton, Kivera grinned over her shoulder and met his rat-like eyes before sauntering away. Soft grumbling reached Kivera's ears and her grin widened.

Mavis followed suit, holding a hand over her snickers.

"You okay?" Mavis whispered behind Kivera, who smiled and nodded back.

"You didn't bring breakfast," Jexton said as a way of greeting and the earlier moment forgotten. He led them past rows of disorganized desks heaped with files brimming with parchments. A circular glass table with wood chairs sat in the center of the room. Jexton's team occupied almost every seat as they milled over reports and maps. The second story of the building exposed, displaying rows of bookcases with a thin railing protecting the few uniformed men milling upstairs from falling below. There were no decorations and dim lighting from the few candles lit.

"You're quick to jump down people's throats early in the morning," Kivera snapped back and her nostrils flared as her temper slipped.

Mavis rolled her eyes at the early morning bickering and surveyed the books above. Her eyes widened with longing.

Kivera agreed and wished for her cottage's small library waiting for her.

They arrived at the glass table. "You promised breakfast, and I said I would kick you out if you didn't bring any." Kivera and Mavis murmured their hellos and the team greeted them, except Tillirius, who glared at their arrival.

Kivera curled her upper lip to bare her white teeth in a feral semblance of a smile. He blinked before returning to his work, dismissing her entirely.

So relations will be like that.

Kivera stepped forward to the table with her hands above and palms facing the empty surface. Summoning food has always been a favorite of Kivera's, and she didn't hesitate to conjure her favorites. Eggs, bacon, and sugary pastry delights from her cottage's kitchen. Steeping tea and fruit juices stacked on the reports and platters of food continued to appear as Kivera turned to Jexton. "I'm not here to disappoint. Sit and eat."

Jexton stared at the food with doubt. "Where does the food come from?"

Kivera chuckled. "From my home. It's not stolen, I promise." Poor Masga would have to order more to be delivered and hoped it didn't trouble the old woman.

Jexton shrugged and piled food onto a plate.

The group mounted their plates with food. Mavis and Kivera pulled steaming cups of tea closer while watching the team. Kivera chose a spot at the head of the table across from Jexton, with Mavis on her right.

Once plates were filled and everyone was comfortable, Kivera straightened her spine, unsure of where to begin. She knew yesterday's incident was heavy on everyone's mind. Her actions did not go unnoticed by the sharp eyes of Tillirius, as if she were a monster to protect his team against. Once everyone settled into their chairs, he didn't give her a chance to open the discussion.

"Are you going to explain why you disrupted our crime

scene?"

Jexton whipped his head to his second with disbelief rippling across his features. The rest of the team halted their eating and cast wary eyes between their Second and Kivera.

"Disruption? You mean when I saved your life?" Kivera's gold eyes flashed. "I've explained to your captain and don't need to with some sniveling prick."

"You forced us to move the body and trample a fresh crime scene. We lost valuable evidence, so we're entitled to a reason."

Jexton moved to interrupt Tillirius, but Kivera beat him to it.

"I don't answer to you, Tillirius. I'm farther up the food chain on this case. But I did what I did to protect the victim and the investigating team." A growl rippled in the room, amplified by thrumming shadows surrounding Kivera. Gods, this man grated on her nerves, but she needed to breathe to rein in the glittering magic before the leash strained too far. She didn't want to spook these humans.

The look in Tillirius's eyes, along with the other squad members, was the reminder that she was not someone to contend with, not an ordinary being to look down on. She wouldn't ever live another day that way again.

Breathing deep through her nose, Kivera calmed her roaring blood. *That short fuse of yours will get you in trouble someday,* a voice whispered from her memories, but she shoved it away.

"I encountered a beast in the forest. A creature I've never seen before." Kivera started the story for the second time without revealing her new transporting ability and focused on Syt. She watched the cogs in her mind whirled rapidly behind her brown-green eyes. Once Kivera finished, her tea long gone and her second steeping before her, the team was silent. Even Tillirius. His snide remarks frozen on his tongue as he chewed on the new information.

Mavis sat through the entire recant, deciphering the

officers' reactions. Whether to defend Kivera or sense their level of distrust, Kivera couldn't be sure. The team didn't glance at her scarred friend anyway and only focused on Kivera with intense gazes.

"Did the animal smell like the victim?" Rex was the first to break the tense silence. Fear of a monster in their lands, something they've never encountered. The unforgettable stench of fear curled around Kivera's nose from the team.

"It was different. I'm not sure if they're connected, but two unfamiliar scents in one day is no coincidence." Kivera couldn't shake the beast's putrid scent, as if wisps of the rotten smell embedded into her nose.

"What did it look like precisely?" Syt asked as she dragged a notepad closer.

Not wanting to tell them again, Kivera showed them. Kivera held out a palm and darkness swirled at the center. Tendrils seeped on the table in a pool of ebony liquid, then shifted to craft into a four-legged figure. A dark head and limbs etched into the shadows to construct a small version of the hybrid monster. After a few moments, the wispy creature bound to the center of the table and waited for Kivera's next commanding thought.

The team watched wide-eyed but leaned in to view the tame miniature figure. Syt jotted down notes, murmuring to herself as her mind churns to unravel the mystery.

"The creature stood well over eight feet tall and with all the sharpest assets in the animal kingdom," Kivera angled her head to Jexton. "We should alert the townspeople to not venture into the woods after dark and to not journey in unless absolute necessary."

Jexton nodded. "We'll need to send out hunting parties to capture it and learn of its conception."

"I'm not sure what these 'hunting parties' would do against the creature. To be safe, I'd rather handle it on my own."

Consideration weighed on Jexton's features, and the rest

of the team appeared content in Kivera hunting it down.

"Do you believe we are weak, witch?" Tillirius sneered across the table.

The cursed magic flared at the insult, but she allowed a smirk. "By all means, I'd love for *you* to hunt it. But for others, I'd rather take their place."

"At least I would have stood up against it like a man rather than run like a coward."

Kivera's eyes narrowed, and the magic simmered dangerously close to the surface, and she clenched her teeth at the effort of not unleashing on this mortal. On the table, the dark wolf-hybrid growled at Tillirius.

Coward rang through her body in rattling peals.

Coward, coward, coward.

Mavis gripped Kivera's clenched fist, her thumb running circles on the back of Kivera's tense muscles. A blue eye glanced at Kivera sideways as she tightened her mouth at Tillirius.

"Get out."

The lethal soft order broke the tense atmosphere, and Kivera snapped towards the source. Jexton's flinty expression faced Tillirius, who sat a couple seats to his right with his face set in a cold rage.

"Jex, she-" Tillirius spluttered, his eyes wide and his hands open.

"You will not represent our team this way to someone I desperately requested to be here. Get out or you're off the case entirely," Jexton's voice rose above Tillirius's.

Kivera appreciated the sentiment, though she didn't need the help in her own battles.

Tillirius's chair screeched as he jumped to his feet and stormed out of the station quarters with filthy curses under his breath. Anyone in his path quickly sidestepped out of his way.

"He's usually like this if it helps you feel better. It's not just you," Maserion joked in a conspirator's whisper, leaning around Mavis. His friendly brown eyes glimmered mischievously under flaming orange hair flopping over his brow.

Kivera grinned back. "I feel bad for your lot dealing with such a grump," Kivera winked and squeezed Mavis's hand once before releasing to reach for the magical creation. The form curled around her hand as if nuzzling her and she could have sworn the shadows vibrated from purring. A ghost of a smile kissed her lips before she swiped the shadow away with a flick of her fingers.

"Where were the other bodies found?" Kivera raised the tea mug to her lips.

"The woods, but a couple were found at locations bordering the forest." Syt reached for a map underneath a pile of papers and pointed to red dots on the map with a vague description of the victim beside the ink showing where the bodies were discovered. Two were near businesses in town, a butcher's shop and tea shop, and four, soon to be five, dots scattered in the forest. Why leave bodies at these locations? What was the meaning? Kivera wondered.

"What did the owners say at the shops?" Mavis asked as she studied the map.

Syt shuffled through her bound notes but spoke from memory.

"Tea shop owner arrived at work in the morning and found the body in her garden. Butcher wasn't there, but his son was and noticed nothing. He found the body in the alley behind the shop when he was taking out the trash in the afternoon."

"How clean was the alley?" Confusion swept the group, but Syt understood the line of questioning.

"Someone from any of the shops would have noticed it. He was just the unlucky number to find her."

"The killer must have dumped the body in daylight. Bold."

"Why not the woods those times?" Maserion twirled his spoon in the air as he spoke through a mouthful of eggs and bacon.

Mavis and Syt wrinkled their noses at the display of chewed food. Noticing their reaction, Maserion grinned, showing bits of the food within, and they rolled their eyes.

Kivera covered her smile behind her hand and glimpsed at Jexton and found his melting brown eyes gazing at her. She didn't have time to decipher the emotion that flashed across his face before he turned away. Kivera lingered on his face for another heartbeat, then turned away.

"To send a message? Sheer convenience?" Jexton exhaled loudly through his nose before biting into eggs.

Mavis nibbled on a banana muffin. "Maybe the locations themselves are important. What if they mean something to the killer?"

"Possible as well. Could mean the killer is a resident of the town." Kivera replied in a hushed voice in case of eavesdroppers. In every case, there are sensitivities when authorities are confronted with the truth that someone in their community can be bloodthirsty murderers.

"A considerable theory to pursue. Cautiously, of course," Syt agreed and to Kivera's surprise, Jexton nodded with her.

"What about the marks? What kind of short blades could do this?" Kivera inclined her head to the weapons master.

Arcian rubbed the back of his neck. "Hard to say. There wasn't just one kind he used. Most likely many sizes, width, design, metals, and so on. Someone familiar with knives made the marks."

"What would the marks show of the blade wielder's state of mind during the torture?"

Arcian blanched. "On each body, miss, I counted the marks in the hundreds and applied to inflict as much pain that I can assume is for his pleasure," A muscle in his jaw spasmed before he continued. "But many marks are shallow and it slowly drained each of blood supply. With no herbs or tonics, the process would have been painful and over a long period."

"Very painful for the poor women." Syt looked down.

"Because he's a bastard conceived of the underworld," Jexton growled, and the rest of the men agreed. Syt remained downcast.

"We will find the answers and bring this person to justice," Kivera told them through thinned lips. Mavis, and to Kivera's surprising, some members of the team, appeared relieved. Barely. "I would like to see the body again. With a more observant eye this time around."

"Rex can go over the body with you. The rest of us are doing fieldwork and some training. Both of you are welcome to join. Though Syt will be researching."

"Training?" Mavis glanced at Jexton with interest, sparking her blue and milky white eyes.

"Unfair to not let a woman train, especially the only woman on the team," Kivera narrowed her eyes at the Captain.

But Jexton burst into snickering laughter and connected his gaze with Syt, who grinned. "Syt is welcome to train anytime. Like I've said, she's vicious with her daggers and puts most of us to shame. She is working on her other duties until she wants to take a break and make us all sweat."

"We're required to maintain a high level of physical strength and to practice with weapons." A goofy grin plastered on Maserion's mouth.

"To be the best?" Mavis' jagged scar crumpled against her freckled skin.

"We think of ourselves as the best, but I outmatch everyone here." Maserion winked.

Mavis huffed a laugh and the rest of the team chuckled under their breath, including Kivera.

"Do you, boy?" Challenge glinted in Arcian's dark eyes.

Before Maserion could fire back, Jexton rose from his seat and met Kivera's eyes before turning to the feast on the table. "It's time to get work done."

With half of a thought, she sent the food and trash away, leaving the files. Everyone stood, purposefully carrying their feet in different directions. Rex waited for Kivera at a hallway entrance to her left with a gentle curve of his lips.

"Kivera?" Mavis's light voice at Kivera's shoulder. "I want to train with them this morning if that's okay with you."

"You want to?"

Mavis shrugged her feather-light shoulders. "Why not? It'll give me a head start on my training with you."

"Good luck, Mavis, and be careful, please. I'm going hunting after I examine the body. I'll find you after. Pay attention to what they tell you. Hopefully, they know a thing or two." A cough from the captain, who pretended not to listen from across the table, tugged on the corners of Kivera's lips. An orb of dark shadows appeared on the table and vanished, leaving behind training clothes for Mavis. She grinned before shooting off to find somewhere to change.

"Don't hurt her spirit. Mavis needs this so if you do, I won't be kind to you anymore," Kivera stepped to the captain, who only raised his eyebrows.

"You've been kind?"

Kivera scowled. "Don't push it. I'll see you later." She sauntered to Rex and lazily waved her hand. A chuckle followed Kivera as she left the spacious room, but heat caressed the back of her neck from the intensity of his molten gaze.

CHAPTER ELEVEN

Kivera could feel the eyes of the dead as she passed through the gray hallway underneath the station. The underground chamber housed the dead bodies of the town and the stone walls reeked of death's rotten scent. The spacious room erected slabs of wood, mostly empty awaiting bodies, save for a few, and torches at the head of each table. Large glass cabinets containing metal instruments, containers of body parts, and brimming with reference books lined the walls. Water basins separated the shelves with empty buckets on the floor beneath prepared for any bodily wastes.

Kivera's boots echoed against the stained floor as she followed Rex. On closer inspection, he was a quiet, small man with a disappearing hairline and a formidable mustache stark against his pale skin. He whistled a cheerful tune through the hallways until they arrived at the mutilated body of the unnamed murder victim.

Kivera peered close at the sliced exterior of the body as Rex chose a safe distance away. He didn't reek of fear like the others, but after one look at Kivera's otherworldly appearance and how far away they were from anyone else, he erred on the side of caution. Kivera didn't blame him.

Arcian was right about the marks. Each wound was different widths, depths, and edging. A dozen different blades at least were used.

Underneath torn flesh and bloodied grime, the girl didn't appear a day older than fifteen years. Choppy dark hair rested on her unmoving chest, and her frail shoulders protruded from snowy skin. Either the victim lived in poverty before her capture or the murderer kept her for a long period and starved her the entire span.

"When will you open her up?" Kivera's voice was quiet, as if afraid she'll wake the surrounding dead.

"This afternoon. Jexton asked me to wait until you inspected the body further." Something twanged in Kivera's chest, but she nodded.

Kivera poured magic into the body to search for toxins or anything strange inside. Dark wisps coursed through the corpse and coated the skin with a faint onyx film to create an imprint of the body. Every slice, broken bone, every inner minuscule detail to be effective for later examination. She nudged the physician's eyes away, helped by magic, so he witnessed nothing it would force her to steal memories about.

"When did she die?"

"Within the last couple of days. Hard to say because of the environment we found her in." Rex didn't lift his head from scribbling notes in a file at the counter near the torchlight.

"They held her captive, like the others?"

"The manacle marks on her ankles and wrists show as much. But for how long? I'm not sure."

Kivera continued to circle around the body and asked pensive questions to receive little information returned. With all his medical knowledge, Rex knew about as little as she did. After a while, she thanked him and they strode away from death's stuffy chambers.

Late afternoon sun beat against Kivera's back and a line of sweat coated her spine. The last of summer's warmth filtered through the vibrant leaves and heated the forest grove. Rodents skirted up towering evergreens and birds cooed sweet melodies. Kivera wished to have time to sprawl under the canopies on a blanket and a book to enjoy the last warm days.

Miles away from the city and to leave the scent of decay far away, Kivera practiced jumping through shadows as she tracked the beast. Releasing some of the coiled magic eased the strenuous tension in her shoulders. She jumped from boulder to boulder through swirling shadows at the rocky base of the mountains. Landing was a challenge. At best, she'd stumble over her feet and fall off boulders at the worst. After a dozen jumps and her body bruised to the bones, she perched herself on the highest boulder and untethered magic to beacon for the unholy creation. She surveyed the area as she refilled her energy with water and packed nuts and apples and kicked her legs with the trilling birds. Nothing ominous disrupted the forest.

Searching for the creature without luck, Kivera trekked back to the city. She sauntered down the main mountain trail leading to the town and slivers of the town peeked through the forestry with the last rays of daylight.

She lifted her hand to gather darkness in the planes of her palm and the whispers of night sky curled against her skin. Blue and green and orange stars glimmered and winked out between swirling tendrils. Though the magic came from her, she never claimed the dark magic as her own, but the power always transfixed Kivera. She dropped her hand to leave the orb of dripping shadows hovering underneath the forest canopy. As she willed, the orb expanded further into the world until a shimmering cloud of night hovered. Without the weight of watching eyes, Kivera pulled her lips back in a wolfish grin before stepping through the cool pressure whipping against her body.

Darkness consumed her vision as it yanked her by her stomach to the torch-lit corridors of the guard station. From habit, Kivera swept her eyes through the abandoned hallways and she was about to walk away in search of the meeting room from earlier when faint grunts and thuds reached her heightened hearing. She followed the noise and there weren't any signs or decorations hanging on the beige walls, making it difficult to mark anything. The thumps and grunting grew louder the farther she walked towards the sounds. Closed doors interrupted the gritty walls before she stopped at a slightly ajar door where the thumps were.

Kivera peeked her head in and found Mavis training. Her sweaty face focused on her movements with a surprising intensity. Sweet, petite Mavis swung her body in driven, focused punches against Arcian's towering figure as he held up pads. Her messy double braids arced through the air as she landed a solid thud against the foam he gripped.

The training room was half the size of the common room, with vaulted ceiling rafters but no windows. Straw dummies, faded targets, and heaps of weapons scattered across the padded floor's grimy surface. Arcian and Mavis occupied the center of the room alone.

"Deciding to sweat for once?" A voice asked from the wall. Kivera didn't notice Jexton stretching by the wall, observing them as Kivera was. He wore a dark shirt cut close to his muscular body, his biceps winking from under the sleeve, and loose shorts that displayed muscular legs.

Kivera's mouth dried but allowed her mouth to curve in one corner as she sauntered to him. "Some of us do real work rather than prance around with sticks and ribbons."

Jexton scowled, but a ghost of a smile lingered on his lips. "Swords and archery are not simply 'sticks and ribbons'. Learning these skills is vital."

She shrugged and cleaned her nails. "Unnecessary and bulky."

"You must use weapons. How else could you defend yourself?"

A serpentine grin etched on Kivera's lips. "I have no use for your weapons, Captain. I have my own."

Jexton flicked up an eyebrow and opened his mouth to ask what she meant when someone cried out.

"Kivera!" Mavis noticed Kivera by the door and stopped practice to skip to her.

Kivera internally groaned. Gods, she has a friend that *skips*.

"How has training been?" Kivera skimmed over Mavis's length of body, noting all the bruises and scrapes peppering her skin, but bright eyes illuminated against her flushed face.

"Arc taught me so much! It's been exhausting, but he's been really patient," Mavis gushed, gesturing to Arcian's crouched form as he leaned into leg stretches. He didn't glance up, but by the red on his ears, Kivera knew he heard her. Kivera wondered if she complimented him to avoid Arcian's arm torn off for how many scrapes Mavis had.

"You look like you've run yourself ragged," Kivera tugged on her sleeve and willed her breath to calm.

"She's learned a lot and did well in her training," Jexton nodded at Mavis and by the redness on her face, Kivera didn't think Mavis had ever been a part of anything like this or even praised.

A hitch pitched whine pierced the air followed by a quick thud. They whirled to Maserion hollering in the rafters, his legs twisted on the beams to allow himself to hang upside down. A perfect shot from the trembling arrow in the center of the target.

"Bloody show off," Arcian grumbled quiet enough only Kivera's heightened hearing caught him.

She glanced at him briefly and snorted. Kivera rounded [over] to the feeling of being watched and found Jexton's eyes scanning the length of her body. She smirked when his eyes found her staring at him and his brown eyes shot away. A blush crept along his cheekbones and Kivera's grin widened.

"Dare you to top that, Arcian," Maserion challenged. In a few maneuvers, he slung the impressive bow behind his back and lifted his upper body up to shuffle along the rafters. He shimmied down the thick rope hanging from the ceiling and bound towards them. A carefree grin plastered on his face the entire time. Maserion slung an arm around Mavis, who rolled her eyes with a smile. "She did excellent, Jexton. Not well."

"We ran, did some muscle exercises, and he taught me the basics for hand-to-hand combat," Mavis gloated and crossed her arms across her chest, proudly displaying her marked skin. Her pride shone brightly despite her exhaustion.

Kivera nodded with approval. "You'll be stronger with each day."

"Did you find any sign of the beast?" Jexton asked Kivera, pulling the conversation away.

Kivera raked her fingers through her hair and exhaled through her nose. "I'm checking a different slope of the mountains tomorrow."

"By yourself?" Jexton straightened. "If I knew you were scaling mountains, I wouldn't have allowed you to search for it."

"Oh, gods. *Allow* me? You wouldn't know how to stop me," Kivera howled with laughter. Mavis grimaced. "I do as I please."

"You should not be wandering mountains alone. You need to be accompanied by myself or Arcian," Jexton ordered.

Maserion cried out he could escort Kivera as well, but no one turned his way.

"I do not 'wander'. I hunt. Your human feet will slow me down." Kivera snorted, but a glitter of annoyance ate away at her patience. Does he not believe in her skills? Or not trust her as much as he's led Kivera to believe?

"Even powerful beings need protection, too." Jexton pleaded for her reasoning. Kivera shrugged but said nothing more. Jexton sighed before talking to the entire group. "Anyone desperate for some food?"

Everyone nodded. Arcian rose from stretching to join them. Jexton named a pub near the inn Kivera and Mavis were staying at to meet once everyone cleaned up.

After the farewells, Mavis and Kivera left without a look back. The latter held out her arm once they were away from the team's eyes, which Mavis begrudgingly accepted, knowing what was next. The shadows pulled them through the station hallway to the coziness of their room.

Mavis set about washing herself off and recanted her day after shaking off the nauseous feeling of shadow jumping.

Kivera listened as she lounged on the bed and ate cookies she stored away on the nightstand.

After a flurry of getting ready, Kivera found it almost comical. Mavis stood in the center of the room with her hands on her hips as she glared at Kivera. She changed into simple-fitting pants and a pale blue shirt that brought out the ferocity of her tumbling auburn hair. Mavis didn't ask where the clothes appeared from, but Kivera knew she had a guess.

"What?" Kivera asked through a mouthful of sweets.

Mavis's nose crinkled. "You have crumbs all over your clothes." Kivera slid to groaning feet before dusting off her bespeckle chest. "How can one person get so dirty from eating?"

"A gift of mine, I suppose." Kivera scowled at Mavis.

"Wearing all black again, I suppose?" Mavis shot back sarcastically.

Kivera waved a hand down the length of her body, and magic shimmered around herself. Her old clothes dissipated away as cuffed obsidian pants and a long-sleeved shirt, exposing her toned midriff, appeared in their place.

Mavis sighed and rolled her eyes. "Purples or oranges or any color would look lovely on you."

"Colors don't help to blend in the shadows," Kivera held out her arm to Mavis, who scoffed, less than enthused to walk through shadows again.

"I'm only doing this *again* because my body can't fathom walking after the beating today."

Kivera huffed a chuckle before Mavis grabbed her arm and the shadows swallowed them whole.

CHAPTER TWELVE

"Why don't we ever choose a quiet place to eat?" Syt groaned for the eighth time as she attempted to review her bounded notes, but her hazel eyes shifted to survey the entire cavernous pub. Kivera couldn't help but agree; the place grated her nerves.

Decapitated heads of different animal breeds overlooked the lounge room and watched everyone. A bar hugged the length of the wall next to the entrance, manned by bored grunts. Corseted barmaids flit from the side of the bar, carrying trays laden with foamy pints of ale. They maneuvered the teeming crowd of folk off work, a rowdy bunch shouting and singing off tune to songs. Piss and rotten food intermingled with the smoke encasing the room's air, nearly choking Kivera's hyper-sensitive nose.

Kivera had nearly walked back out the door, and into her shadows, towing Mavis with her. Before she could even ask Mavis, Arcian's head popped above the crowd to wave them through the people toward their full table.

Jexton chose a table at the back of the pub with the visibility of the pub's occupants. The men of the group appeared indifferent to the rowdy atmosphere and continued with their conversations. Mavis sat at Syt's right hand at the head of the table and leaned over Kivera to greet Arcian next to her.

Tillirius sat to the right of Jexton at the other head of the table and glared when Kivera sat down. She didn't spare a glance toward him. Maserion sat between Arcian and Tillirius, chatting in their usual joyful demeanor.

Jexton smiled at their arrival, appearing handsome in a matching all-black ensemble, and his brown eyes drenched in warmth.

Kivera almost stumbled on her greetings to the team, her mind frozen on him but she tried to shake away all thoughts of the captain a short distance from her and returned her attention to Syt. "Decisions tend to not sway in our favor, I'm afraid."

"If only you could wave your fingers and make them choose what you want." She tugged on her unbound dark hair.

"I don't think it works against Jexton's thick head. I've tried." Kivera's eyes twinkled at the scoff she almost didn't hear across the table. She didn't look up at the eyes burning into her face. "Did you find any of the victim's family members?"

Syt shook her head. "Tilly didn't find any either. I'm wondering if we should expand the search radius to neighboring towns."

"Are there cargo checks on the road leading here?" Kivera remembered on the map from this morning there's a single road leading to the town. No other way in or out without it besides the thin trail Kivera and Mavis traveled through the forest. But the path wasn't big enough for wagons or carts.

"Supposedly. But who knows how well they're doing their job," Syt gave her a pointed look.

"We should focus on the victims. Figure out their last steps before encountering their killer. Do you know of any cases similar to this one?"

"I contacted our chief for similar cases, and he dispatched messengers to neighboring guard stations. So far, no one has had anything like this in their records."

A pretty barmaid stopped at their table and halted all conversations. Everyone ordered drinks and shared a pot of the daily soup. Kivera couldn't fathom how anyone had an appetite with the horrific smell of the place, but she won't refuse the energy refuel. She idly wondered if she should create a shield, both to relieve her nose from the stench amplifying her headache and for the rising pressure of magic if she didn't release some power.

Though nothing compared to the perplexing scent on the body. She wished for a chance to inspect the previous bodies and asked Rex as much, but he said they were buried in unmarked graves behind the guardhouse.

Cemeteries sent skitters on Kivera's skin, but unmarked graves utterly broke her heart. Eventually forgotten about and their mysterious identity never uncovered. Never will the nameless dead have family visiting their graves nor will a family know of the outcome of their lost members. Perhaps she'll visit the graves tomorrow when she has a free hour.

"Kivera?" A voice interrupted her thoughts and blinked away the grim fog at Mavis staring at her, waiting for an answer to a question Kivera didn't hear.

"What did you say? My apologies, my mind was elsewhere," Kivera sheepishly smiled.

Maserion and Arcian peered at her. The former snorted and the latter half-smiled, twisting his ragged scar.

Mavis rolled her eyes. "I was telling them about those fellas from back home you scared half to death."

Kivera shrugged. "You're the one who noticed them getting rough with her. I was checking on you." A malevolent stare tracked her movements, but Kivera's didn't deign a glance towards Tillirius.

The smiling waitress returned with their drinks, along with a platter of bread and cheese. She spun on her heel and hurried through the thick crowd that continued to swell as time ticked by.

Kivera realized the kind, wrinkled eyes were missing from the group. She snuck a glance at Jexton, who listened to what Syt was saying, though his eyes slipped to Kivera's when Syt stared at a bellowing table in the opposite corner..

As if reading the question on Kivera's mind, he mouthed,

He's sleeping.

"You did more than that. C'mon! You should tell them what happened after you arrived at the alley."

Kivera returned to the eager blue and milky gaze and a smile danced on her lips. "You're the hero of that story. You rescued her when you stood up to the bastards." Mavis's eyes didn't waver as she waited for Kivera's to share the ending. Kivera rolled her eyes and leaned towards the trio to continue. Arcian waited with a gleam of interest in his dark eyes. She could have sworn Jexton leaned in a fraction. "Once I saw Mavis up against the men with a blunt knife and a beaten girl behind them, I stepped in. I made sure Mavis and the girl, Janessa, left safely before I had a delightful time with them." In response, tendrils of onyx smoke curled around her fingers. "They were squealing by the time I left the alley."

Arcian flexed his crossed arms. "You left them alive?"

"Death was too easy for their rotten minds but I left them parting gifts," Kivera's voice was bitter and she remembered the glimpse of how truly vile those men were. The stain of their minds lingered on Kivera's own.

A group of men in dark clothing hollered and bellowed incoherently, the sound hammered into Kivera's skull, spearing down the length of her spine. She needed to ease the power before Kivera ripped in half.

Jexton peered at her, his handsome features etched into concern as if noticing her discomfort.

Kivera couldn't twist her neck without lightning striking her spinal cord. Shadow jumping left the magic in a fitful slumber but now reared its ugly head. She would need to unleash some of the pressure when they leave and far enough away from the townspeople.

"Leaving them alive is a gift as well," Arcian argued and his black eyes shuttered with long ago memories.

"It's not mine to decide whether someone lives or dies at my hands but I did not leave them in a better place," She noticed out of the corner of her eye that Tillirius glanced behind them, his eyes flickering towards whatever caught his attention but continued with the conversation with Jexton and Syt.

"What would a shitty mortal's death cost you?" Arcian's sharp question paused Kivera. Every death cost her a piece of her soul. Whether the person deserved death, whatever path they walked, Kivera calculated every factor in ending their life and that choice cost her. Bit by bit.

"Death is not a choice I gladly choose. You know of the cursed gifts I wield. There is always a consequence to each death," the men sat back, content with her answer. Mavis nodded, perhaps relieved her new friend isn't a blood-hungry monster.

Curious to know if Jexton heard her words too, she snuck a glance over and grit her teeth at the disappointment. He was staring over her head at the boisterous men near the bar. Tillirius doing the same. Kivera didn't gather what snagged their attention but didn't ask in front of others, though was half tempted to ask in Jexton's mind.

But the voices of men answered Kivera's question, reaching her ears. She craned her neck, wincing at the stinging pain, and found a circle of ragged men around something indistinguishable. Taunting a moving figure in the middle of the thick-muscled wall. Metal glinted at their sides from brutal weapons, and they each displayed a matching symbol on their forearms.

Mavis followed Kivera's gaze and then back at her, unimpressed. "They're not worth it, Kivera, just being annoying."

"Big shot over here could go rough 'em up for you," Arcian jokes, his large hand thumped Maserion's slim shoulders.

Maserion grinned arrogantly but made no move to rise and eyed his captain warily.

Jexton surveyed them all now, but kept an extra focus on Kivera as if there was a wild animal to watch out for. He shook his head in slight movements. *Not this time.*

With magic close to the surface, her instincts rose in sync. Kivera couldn't stop the slight curl of her lip. Every sense heightened with her predator instincts.

Jexton raised an eyebrow and curled his lips into a crooked grin. Kivera's breathing halted while the rest of the team bubbled with their own conversations without noticing their heated exchange.

Slowly, Kivera breathed through her nose and exhaled a soft gust out of her lips, a huge amount of effort to breathe through the building pressure inside her. Gradually, the pressure ebbed away and her chest expanded unbarred.

When her breathing regulated, she heard the men's voices.

"C'mere, pretty little thing. I can show you a good time."

Slurred words shattered Kivera out of her zen-like bubble. Her head whipped toward the words, unbothered by the pain, and noticed the slim figure to be a barmaid in their midst. Trapped in the middle of the goons, trying to fend them off while waving her arms at the ignorant bartenders.

Kivera braced her hands on the table and honed her ears to the harassed waitress.

"Come back with us."

"We'll put you to work."

"You should stay with us tonight."

On and on they went, winding up Kivera further and further. The caged magic raged to be released to show these wastes of human bodies true, unimaginable power. Voices around her ebbed away as she focused on the breathing of the disgusting men. Jexton and Mavis's burning gazes were on her face, but Kivera couldn't pull her eyes away from the shadows twirling around her hands, ready to shape in whatever Kivera willed them to. Shadows dripped in the corners of the room and flit around torches.

A freckled hand clasped Kivera's wrist. She didn't bother to watch the shadows swarming Mavis's hand.

"We can leave. They're jerks, but she'll be okay." Mavis spoke low, so the others didn't hear her.

"They shouldn't talk like that to her," Kivera said through gritted teeth.

Mavis shook her head and opened her mouth when one of the big men uttered a slur so filthy, Kivera didn't hear the scrape of the chair over the roaring in her ears.

How dare they speak that way to a woman? To anyone in such a way?

Kivera stormed through the bustling crowd in a heartbeat and left the rest of the group scrambling behind her to back her up or drag her away. She didn't know or care.

The crowd peeled apart from shadows to open a path to the woman. Out of the corner of her eye, Maserion and Syt raced towards the bartenders while the rest barrelled after Kivera.

But they were too late.

Kivera was upon them.

"Didn't your mothers teach you how to speak to a lady?" Kivera purred in a voice of death's embrace.

CHAPTER THIRTEEN

The surprise on the circle of men's faces almost sent Kivera into a fit of laughter. They snapped towards her and blood rushed into their faces. Their beady eyes glazed over as they ravaged the curves of her body and she endured the heat flaming her cheeks as long as they kept their attention on her. Behind the front lines of the group, one man grasped the thin arm of the barmaid.

Kivera counted over a dozen of the grimy men and each sported a weapon and the same ugly expression.

"The servant's door is around back," one of them sneered. The leader from the looks his lackeys gave him, desperate for his approval.

"I'll tell you this once. Let go of her." Kivera was stone-faced and her mind eased into lethal calm as her body slipped into a defensive stance.

"She's doing just fine. Could use some of your help." He waggled his eyebrow and grinned a spotty smile. His friends roared with laughter.

"Kivera! Let's go." Jexton grabbed Kivera's shoulder and glared at the snide leader, but she shook off his grip.

"Better listen to your boyfriend. Don't want you to get your hands a little dirty." He stepped closer and his rancid breath slammed into Kivera's face.

"I can use my hands." Kivera pursed her lips and tilted her head, a predator assessing her prey. "Don't make me ask again, boys. I'm quite tired of this." Examined her nails but was loud enough to be heard over the surrounding people but only a few noticed.

"Kivera," Jexton pleaded again in her ear, but she ignored him.

"You shouldn't talk to me like that." The nitwit laughed at his friends and pulled back the dark flaps of his jacket to reveal nasty daggers. His cronies mimicked him to reveal their own hidden weapons.

Not wanting to waste another breath, Kivera struck.

She sprinted the distance between them and as they prepared for her attack; she hurled a shadow in front of her to jump through, only to appear behind the waitress. The man guarding the barmaid didn't know she disappeared until he gripped the star-flecked shadows. Kivera dropped the girl at their table before being swallowed by shadows once more. She swaggered out of parting darkness in front of the red-faced leader.

"Wha-? What the? You shouldn't have done that." He bared his yellow teeth when he realized the waitress had disappeared. "You owe me a ride now, bitch." He jerked his head and a few men stepped from ranks.

Crisp shadows slid against Kivera's hand as a light pressure built in her knuckles. Achingly slow, she allowed herself time to savor the men's reactions as they watched the gold talons slide out of her nails. The men stepped back with their mouths in wide O's and a few even gasped. Kivera inhaled their fear and only the leader stepped forward hesitantly.

His lackeys advanced a beat behind their leader.

"Kivera!" a sweet voice shouted, but Kivera couldn't break her focus and look over her shoulder at Mavis.

Kivera flicked her gold eyes over the middle man's shoulder while he advanced towards her and sneered at the leader before striking again.

She burst forward. Adrenaline shot through her vessels and settled in her muscles.

The man on the right lunged for her first, followed closely by two others. Kivera sliced the wrist holding his plain sword with a quick flick of her wrist. The blade clattered to the floor, and he shouted in pain as he pulled his arm to his chest.

Blood dripped from the curves of her talons. With her other hand, she slit through his jacket and into the flesh of his exposed belly.

The man on the left hurtled towards her in sloppy, lumbering steps. Kivera dodged to the left and ducked low under his raised sword arm. Her claws swiped through his shoulder easily, as if slicing bread. She willed shadows into an obsidian whip and snapped the end around his ankle, yanking hard. The ground rumbled as the giant fellow collapsed on the unforgiving floor.

The third man barrelled towards Kivera at a sprint. She dropped below his defenses to kick his legs out from beneath him. His crash to the ground was louder than a tree toppling in a forest.

More men furiously charged towards her as the coward leader remained behind his wall of muscle and steel. Kivera managed their pathetic assaults and danced around the blood spray in a flurry of flashing gold and onyx tendrils. Violence became a death-song thrumming in her veins and beat with the adrenaline pounding through her body. Blood roared in her ears, blocking out the belligerent cheers from the growing crowd.

Men dropped to the pissed-stained floor like stalks of wheat until they all were groaning in pain.

With fallen men all around her, Kivera locked eyes with the sweaty leader cowering in the corner. His gleaming sword trembled as his beady eyes met hers. She coiled magic into her core to retract all traces of shadows, leaving the talons to glint in the torch-light.

Fear stained the air and curled around Kivera's nose. She inhaled a deep breath through her nose and let out a soft sigh. "I expected a better fight from you."

Anger sparked in his small, dark eyes. He straightened his spine, raised his sword before charging towards Kivera.

In the back of her mind, she heard a scream of terror come from behind her. A scream of terror *for* her.

But she couldn't analyze who cried out for her, not with a sword charging for her head.

Crouched on the balls of her feet, Kivera waited until she could smell his breath before she swiped to his side and stuck out her foot. She turned to watch him sprawl on the ground with his face in something rather unpleasant and his sword clattered to the floor, out of his reach.

Kivera circled around him, and a dark chuckle rasped from her. "I thought you would put up more of a fight."

The gang leader hauled himself to his feet and spat at the ground as he locked eyes with Kivera. "I'm going to kill you, bitch," he snarled before charging again.

Kivera let him within a few feet of her before ducking backwards far enough her hair brushed the floor. Kivera focused on centering her feet to the ground as she raked her talons deep into his side. She spun away from his flailing elbow and, at inhuman speed, she punched the wound as hard as she could. He crumpled to the ground, clutching his side as he rolled around sobbing and he did not rise.

Kivera stood over him. "Let this be a lesson for your abhorrent behavior," she used her coldest voice. She stepped over him and sauntered through the silent crowd that parted for her. Men avoided her eyes, not wanting to attract Kivera's attention. Nervous chuckles surrounded her as Kivera passed through.

The battle frenzy singing in her blood drained away and replaced by shame flooding her cheeks. But she would not bow under their judgment.

Sounds returned to Kivera, and she snapped her head to the crowd surrounding her. Fearful eyes watched her and many cowered away.

Oh, gods, what have I done?

Blood thrummed in her ears but didn't drown out the whispers. She needed to leave quickly, before anything else happened. Pushing through the crowd, though, many stepped back as if she were a plague, and she stumbled into the brisk night. She stalked around the building to a dark alcove and bent over her knees. Kivera inhaled large gulps of fresh air through clenched teeth and scrubbed away the salt-water pricking her eyes.

Disbelief at unleashing completely in front of others and shame stained her cheeks. She couldn't even wonder what Mavis or Jexton thought of her now.

Voices neared Kivera and without thinking, she summoned darkness and allowed the cool caress to rip her away from the pub. Wind snaked around her limbs and thrashed her hair until deposited in her room.

Stone filled her veins at the sight of Mavis's belongings and treacherous thoughts tripped over each other. *What if I scare Mavis away? What if she leaves?*

The room dimmed to an onyx blanket as magic unfurled from Kivera, but she saw nothing. Couldn't muster the energy to chain the power back into her broken heart. Transfixed on a discarded shirt of Mavis's, Kivera's bones settled into unending numbness. Mist coated her flaming skin and enveloped Kivera in the soothing night sky as she drifted to the nearest bed. She curled into the magic and lay there for minutes or hours, staring at the shirt.

Footsteps hounded outside the swirling darkness, but Kivera didn't care. Not if they didn't belong to Mavis. Maybe even Jexton.

Alarms rang in her head as someone neared the door, and she bolted upright. The door opened and a small shape sprinted towards Kivera. A second scent held back at the entrance.

Making a few steps before thudding into the dresser. "It's so dark in here. I can barely see my nose, Kivera," Mavis extended her arms to feel her way in the night but Kivera couldn't move from her shocked sitting position.

Mavis came back.

"Mavis," Kivera's voice broke on her friend's name.

"I'm here, I'm here," Mavis rushed to Kivera's side and wrapped her in a tight embrace. Tears sprang to Kivera's eyes and she let Mavis hold her.

"Did I scare you?" Kivera sniffled and leaned back to look into Mavis's eyes, but she couldn't see through the layers of blackness. Kivera inhaled a deep breath and slowly the folds of darkness furled into her body. Lit candles replaced star-flecked shadows and Mavis could finally see.

Mavis scanned the length of Kivera's body and she realized a beat later that Mavis was searching for signs of injury. Gratitude bloomed in her chest and clenched Mavis's hand. "You didn't scare me. You beat the hell out of those assholes! It was a beautiful sight to see. Are you okay?"

A husk of a relieved laugh escaped Kivera. "Frightened myself about you more than anything. Physically I couldn't be more alive," That much was true, Kivera realized. Down to her bones, fighting injustices is what she was born for and hoped that's why dark magic cursed her. Otherwise, what was the point of this devouring power? She couldn't stomach the alternative.

Mavis smiled. "You're a stunning person with that generous heart of yours." She squeezed Kivera's hand and pulled her from the bed. Confusion must have been clear on Kivera's face because Mavis continued, "Someone is waiting for you outside."

Kivera sniffed at the second scent, and her shoulders loosened when she recognized Jexton. She shuffled through the room and called over her shoulder to Mavis, "Obsessed, isn't he?" She winked and opened the door.

Jexton leaned against the wall and scanned his blazing eyes down the length of Kivera's body. His disheveled hair trickled onto his brow as if he ran fingers through it continuously. Her knees buckled at the intensity, but she raised her chin, even with her core molting into fiery liquid.

His sensuous mouth curved as if he could see the

wetness pooling at her center. "How are you doing, Kivera?"

She shrugged. "It doesn't matter. You don't need to concern yourself with my business."

While she spoke, Jexton shot forward and slammed both hands on either side of her face into the wall. She leaned into the wall but pushed her chest forward. Out of instinct or lust, she couldn't be sure. "I am concerned."

She inhaled his breath, mint and sugar, and her toes curled. But she bared her teeth. "No need. You sat back while I did all the dirty work. That's fine."

A low growl emanated from Jexton's chest. "It wasn't easy watching you fight them while on guard duty," he meant Mavis, Kivera realized with a start. He knew to keep her safe for Kivera's wellbeing. "It was hard."

Kivera smirked. "I'm sure. Standing by seemed easy for you."

Jexton cocked his head, and his lips tightened. "Did it seem so easy to stand by while they could have hurt you?"

Kivera's lips parted. She didn't think Jexton standing by would be hard. He knew what she was capable of, but how? "Why?"

He growled again. "You know why."

Kivera blinked and watched his eyes drift down to her lips and study them as if they were the most interesting sight he's ever seen. His scent changed and Kivera's insides heated.

Oh.

Kivera stared at him beneath lowered lashes, and the corner of her mouth curved. "You're waiting again."

Jexton's eyes snapped up to hers at her seductive purr, and he smirked. "I like a girl who can take the reins." As he said that, invisible tendrils of magic snaked around his wrist and held him against the wall. His eyes widened, and she mirrored his smirk as she ducked below his outstretched arms.

She traced lengthened nails along the muscles in his shoulders and upper back. He trembled under the touch and his burning eyes followed her movements. "Do you now,

Jexton?"

Jexton said nothing, but he didn't have to. His arousal intensified and Kivera noticed the demanding need through his trousers. She could feel his labored breaths under her light touches and nearly drowned in his intoxicating scent.

She rounded to his back and, with appreciation, she stared at his body before pressing her lips to his neck. Tracing where her lips were with her tongue, he groaned.

Kivera smiled. "You know where to find me." She sashayed to her room door, aware of his eyes on her, and prayed her pounding heartbeat didn't give her away. The door between them shut with a soft click and she let go of the restraints on Jexton.

"Cruel, beautiful monster," Kivera heard through the door and she smiled before a thought invaded for the second time that night.

Oh, gods, what have I done?

CHAPTER FOURTEEN

The nightmare clawed through Kivera's mind and ripped apart her soul until her eyes flew open to early morning darkness. Kivera's fingers tightened around a blood-encrusted dagger that was not there. Panting, she sat up, her sweaty body trembling, and she slowly pieced together her thoughts.

Kivera was safe.

Safe at the inn.

The inn room she shared with Mavis. Safe.

Kivera squeezed her eyes tight until her labored breathing subsided.

Soft snores emanated from the armchair in the corner and Kivera looked over to find Mavis curled into an uncomfortable ball with a book splayed on her stomach. With her nocturnal lids in place, Kivera could distinguish the frayed cover of Mavis's childhood book.

The sight almost made Kivera smile. Almost.

Silent as possible, Kivera peeled away the covers and rose from the bed. She padded to the bathroom and cushioned the doors with shadows to absorb any noise. Glittering darkness encompassed the face of the door and she was momentarily stunned at the stars and stardust illuminating the pitch blackness. She propelled the magic in all directions until the entire room bathed in luminescent galaxies and twinkling stars. The magic was a growing marvel to Kivera as she uncovered new faucets to admire rather than used to destroy. A seed of pride planted in her broken soul, bright at what she might create and not the destruction she expects from the dark power. The glimmer of the possibility shone through the cracks and splinters in her heart.

Under the soft glow, Kivera filled the sink basin with cold water and splashed her face. The blissful coolness relieved her heated skin. Kivera would have submerged herself in the tub right then to rid herself of the sticky blood feeling from her nightmare if it weren't for Mavis sleeping in the next room.

An ache for Masga and their sea-cottage in the capital settled in her chest. Kivera hasn't been home in weeks, moving from assignment to assignment with no time off. Soon she'll go back and show Mavis around the busy capital and all the squares, music, and opportunities beckoning, Kivera planned.

Tired of the silent darkness and struck with adrenaline, Kivera itched to be outside. She snapped her fingers to change her drenched night slip into dark pants and sweater. Comfortable boots covered her bare feet, and she was ready to hunt.

Kivera arced her wrist to peel the shadows off the walls and wiped away the galactic canvas. Dark tendrils snaked up her arm and melted into her like a second skin to shield against any threats. Within a few heartbeats, her night sky creation disappeared from the cold bathroom. She slipped through the room to the door before a voice frightened Kivera.

"Where are you going?"

Kivera didn't turn to the armchair. "Go back to sleep, Mavis. I'm going for a walk." The half lie poisoned her throat, but she didn't wish to worry her exhausted friend with Kivera hunting the beast.

Mavis sat up and stretched away hours of uncomfortable sleep. "You're going after the monster."

Kivera winced and turn in place with a hand on her hip. "You don't need to worry about yourself. I'll be back in a few hours for us to go to the post."

"I'm coming with you this time." Mavis bolted from the armchair and began dressing.

"Mavis, this is too dangerous and you've had one day of

training." Kivera started, but the words died in Kivera's throat when Mavis narrowed her eyes.

"I'm joining you so I can learn something. You can protect me and I'll stay out of your way."

Kivera sighed. "When you put it like that, I don't feel like I have a choice."

Mavis winked as she yanked a sweater over her head. With nimble fingers, she plaited her hair back and finished with a smile. "We're doing this together, Kivera, whether or not it's comfortable. But together."

Kivera stepped next to Mavis with a smile and extended an elbow at a crooked angle in invitation. Shadows danced at her fingertips and Mavis sucked in a breath when an obsidian orb appeared in front of them and expanded wide enough for them to walk through. Mavis clasped Kivera's arm and walked through the shadows together.

Darkness and mist and wind tore at them, but they clenched each other through the roaring shadows. Nausea did not grip Kivera like before as they landed and she thanked the gods, but Mavis kneeled forward, clenching her stomach and Kivera held her tighter. She didn't know what would happen if they were cleaved apart between jumps, but won't find out.

Pitch blackness ebbed away into the deep navy of the coming dawn, and the surrounding stars winked out one by one. They wandered under the haunting protection of the tree canopy with the unsettling feeling of eyes on Kivera's back. Tiny bodies scampered up the heavenward trees as they passed.

With nocturnal lids in place, Kivera guided them through the chattering forest by linked elbows. She scanned for any approaching dangers while magic searched the circling area, but found none, to her relief. She locked a shield around them, just in case.

"How are you able to do magic if you're not a witch?" Mavis's question shattered the silence as her gaze slid to Kivera. She kept staring forward, guarding her expression as she carefully worded her response.

Kivera lifted a finger. "One, I do not 'do' magic. I wield magic." She raised her eyebrows and lifted a second finger. "Second, I do not cast spells or anything like that. Only a witch can. I'm a gifted female with magic borne in my bones. But I'm the only of my kind, so my species does not matter here."

Mavis frowned. "Any detail about you matters. How did you learn it?"

"If lucky enough, a mentor can train you, but I learned to control and train myself."

"What do you use your magic for?" Kivera glanced down in surprise at the other female. Mavis kept her gaze down with her eyebrows furrowed, her strawberry braids swaying with each step. Temptation gnawed at her to peek into her thoughts, but she couldn't shatter the fragile friendship between them.

Last night gnawed on Kivera's mind and she thought of her words to be careful of being feared. She couldn't bear it if Mavis would ever be terrified of her.

"I interrogate criminals and investigate the truth. Summon the occasional cake."

Mavis giggled. "If that's all you do, why do you need me?"

"Are you doubting coming with me?" Kivera's question was soft.

Mavis chewed her lip as she mulled over the question for a few moments. "I am not questioning coming with you." A knot eased in Kivera's chest at the words. "But I struggle with not having a place in the world or a home or anything to my name." Unfamiliar savageness coated her words.

"You don't have a home. Yet. You discover your next one. For now, you'll have a place with me and Masga in my home on the ocean." Kivera smiled at Mavis and touched her shoulder.

The forest rustled with a breeze, as if waiting for her response. "Living by the ocean would be a pleasant change," Mavis returned Kivera's smile and Kivera's heart soared. She hid her excitement behind a curtain of hair.

Kivera frowned. "That can't be your only question,

Mavis."

Mavis's braids shook as she chuckled. "I have too many questions. Too many to know what to do with." But after a moment, Mavis opened her mouth. "Why?"

Kivera stilled but forced herself to keep walking. She didn't have to ask what Mavis meant. "I excelled at hunting monsters." Kivera couldn't stop the shadows dancing around her fingers, aching for release. Mavis didn't respond long enough that Kivera assumed the conversation had died. Birds chirped, slow and melodic to the sky as stars winked out one by one.

"Where are you from?" Mavis's eyes darted around as she softly asked the question.

Kivera blinked before sliding her eyes to Mavis. Gods, how she wanted to spill her truth, the entirety of her life, to someone else. Kivera opened her mouth.

A deafening roar split the air.

Feral and wild and ravenous. Only half a mile away, but Kivera couldn't track the direction. Ice swept through Kivera's body, but she would not allow herself to fear. Fear led to mistakes and she could not afford sloppiness. Not with Mavis here.

Mavis stepped closer to Kivera with a face drained of color and she looked around.

Guilt rammed through Kivera. She should have made Mavis stay back instead. She was a fool to let her come and likely will kill her. If anything happened to her, Kivera wouldn't forgive herself until the day she passed into the death god's embrace.

"A home that deserves far more time for its story but that'll have to be another time," Kivera pushed Mavis behind her, and shadows plumed at her feet, bracing for whatever is to come and the invisible shield reinforced around them.

Kivera would be damned if she let anything pass her.

A branch snapped in the trees behind them.

Kivera whirled and dropped into a defensive stance and

angled in front of Mavis.

The worst of nightmares slunk through the bushes. The trees appeared to sway away from the warped creature as the forest froze.

Kivera risked a glance over her shoulder to see Mavis quivering at the sight of the creature and she could taste drenched fear in the air.

She turned back to catch the beast sniffing the air.

Not sniffing the air, realized with no small amount of disgust, but tasting Mavis's fear.

The creature met her glare and pulled back its lips to reveal bone-shredding teeth. An executioner's grin split its face.

Bile roiled in Kivera's stomach at the horrifying sight.

The monster had covered the distance separating them seconds before at impossible speeds, and she was out of time. Most likely thrown into a frenzy after catching Kivera's scent and a second twining with hers.

Talons slid out of Kivera's trembling fingers and shadows danced around her hands and down the length of her body. Darkness tickled her cheek, humming a soft melody into her ears as if to soothe her thundering heartbeat.

A plan was already forming in Kivera's mind, but she needed time. If they were to capture the beast, they couldn't escape from jumping through her shadows. But with Mavis here, she didn't know how likely the possibility would be of capturing rather than killing the creature.

"Kivera." Mavis's voice broke.

"What have you brought me, little pointed one?" The thing spoke with a voice of clashing, guttural snarling and clicking. "Two meals for one, I see."

The beast prowled closer and tilted its dark misshapen head as it circled closer. Kivera's heart constricted as its claws punctured the earth. The thought of them near Mavis roiled her stomach.

But Kivera was not prey.

She was a creature of darkness and nightmares and destruction.

"Quite rude not to introduce yourself," Kivera smirked as she mirrored its movements, leaving Mavis in the circle of impenetrable shadows.

"I do not name myself to my meals." It smashed razor-sharp teeth together and growled deep in its mammoth chest.

The vibrations tickled her toes and she clenched her jaw.

"Quite impolite of you," Kivera mocked him in a crisp voice. "You know what 'impolite' means, right?" Mavis squeezed Kivera's arm in warning.

A snarl slipped from the beast. "How did you escape me, little dark one?" It gnashed its jaws together. "I will surely enjoy sucking the marrow from your broken bones."

"Maybe you're not as smart as you believe." Shadows swelled in her hands behind her back. "I don't die too easily."

"You will scream while I tear your flesh from bone and your cries will be a ballad to my ears. Your friend will watch your blood flow rivers on land before I feast on her, too." It ran a tongue along bared teeth.

Kivera examined her talons. "Your threats are boring. I was expecting more spilling organs and ripping spines apart." The beast snarled and she didn't stop her lip from curling to bare her teeth.

The breeze and forest animals and trees held a collective breath, waiting for the explosion to come.

"I'll enjoy you most." It licked its dripping maw before hurtling forward.

Mavis whimpered.

But Kivera was ready and didn't waste precious seconds bracing herself for the monster charging towards her. She surged deep in magic and shadows writhed in waiting.

Praying this will work, Kivera reached for the darkness and slammed a wall of shadows at the charging beast's mangled face.

For a terrifying second, shadows ensconced the sleek

body. The creature released an earth-shattering roar as it thrashed about.

"Run." Kivera snatched Mavis's arm and tore through the forest at Mavis's much slower speed. To gain extra distance, Kivera spirited them in tiny bursts through shadows and held Mavis close when they landed. Mavis almost lost her footing as exhaustion weighed her down, but Kivera hauled her along.

Vicious bellows echoed behind them.

"Why did you have to make it even angrier?" Mavis hissed. Double braids flew in the wind as her legs pushed her forward, but slower with each pounding footstep.

Kivera will have to find an advantage over the creature.

The creature roared again and the earth vibrated as the fiend barrelled toward them. Gods, the beast was *fast*.

Mavis tightened her death grip in Kivera's hand and did her best to watch her steps with eyes burning in steely fire.

Pride glimmered in Kivera that her friend hasn't complained but pushed herself harder to sprint faster. Hands joined, they sprinted through the forest, black and auburn hair streaming like banners behind them.

But their speed wouldn't be enough.

Trees crashed behind them where they ran past too-short moments before. It was catching on them and, to Kivera's horror, much faster than they could run.

A gurgling stream cut through the forest ahead and Kivera prayed the monster couldn't swim. At the very least, slowed down from the water. An idea flared to study her enemy and search for weaknesses.

A fear gnawed on Kivera's mind. If more beasts were hunting the villages in the outskirts of cities and if, by some miracle she could kill this one, how could she kill others, if any?

Shaking herself to the moment at hand, Kivera saved the thought for her future self.

Something dark blurred past Kivera's left peripheral.

Animal instincts flooded through Kivera anew, and time

slowed as she moved.

In a fraction of a heartbeat, she spirited Mavis away, but Kivera didn't watch her land across the stream. Kivera prayed for her forgiveness.

In the second heartbeat, Kivera launched herself in the air at the same time the beast intercepted her path. She slashed at the creature in wild fury, and a snarl rippled from her throat with her bared teeth.

By the third heartbeat, her gold talons drew coppery red blood while in midair.

A howl tore from the creature's mouth and whipped its large head back to gnash its jaws around her leg. Teeth pierced through muscles and bones before the thing threw her to the ground, but she spun to land on her feet.

A scream ripped from her as pain lanced through her body at the landing. Stars rattled her vision and threatened to overtake her. She stumbled forward through heaving breaths and she launched over the stream.

A strange, warm breeze patted her cheeks as if encouraging her with wispy fingers.

On impact with the unforgiving ground, Kivera crumbled, and familiar darkness swarmed her.

CHAPTER FIFTEEN

Kivera floated through the darkness in skin-splitting agony. She had no sense of self in the sea of pain and could not scream in the suffocation of endless silence.

Is this death? Kivera wondered while she floated in silent screams.

A thud in the black sea jerked Kivera out of the abyss and she blinked at gray skies with branching fingering towards the dawn. A coppery tang wafted to her nose and the last moments before unconsciousness slammed into her.

The beast, a stream, and Mavis.

Kivera bolted up, but the world tilted, and she focused on her breath. Oh, gods, where was Mavis? She wasn't resting on the stream bank and Kivera flared out magic when a snarl crackled behind her.

A mutilated, triangular face stared at Kivera a few yards away in the tree cover, then it slowly rose to its feet. The creature bared its teeth, but the pain in its black eyes was unmistakable. Kivera sneered at the deep gashes in its side, dripping blood. At least she landed one decent hit.

Kivera scrambled to her feet and grit her teeth at the waves of pain threatening to drag her back into oblivion. She raised her hands, dark wisps curling around gold talons, and she bared her teeth.

Familiar energy brushed against the searching magic and she almost wept at Mavis a safe distance away. Using a flick of magic, she nudged Mavis to run.

Kivera would buy her time.

The magic chained in her core thrashed to be released to dull the razer-edge of the straining magic. But this time she would not tighten the chains if she wished for any chance of survival.

A bit, Kivera crooned to the dark creature prowling beneath her skin. She loosened some restraints and ebony flames consumed her taloned hands. Despite the pain and terror coursing through her, Kivera smiled at the monster.

The creature lowered onto its back legs before exploding into a spring.

Fast as an asp, Kivera threw shadows at the creature and, as she hoped, it zig-zagged to avoid their hit. She allowed the creature close enough she could see bits of flesh between its knife-length teeth. Revulsion careened through her, but she threw a shadow-orb and the beast danced from it, victory lighting its eyes but did not see the onyx whip she aimed at its legs. The magical whip snaked around its legs and she yanked as hard as her strength would give.

The beast collapsed not three inches from her boots.

Shadows gathered in her hands as the beast attempted to stand on all fours, but the magic tightened around its limbs and it collapsed in a thunderous shriek. With her other hand, Kivera curled her whip around its legs.

"Untangled me, filth." It pummeled against the restraints.

"As if," Kivera laughed and sprinted away, ignoring the growls behind her. She bound through the trees, following the magic trail until she found Mavis bent over retching with bright eyes.

"Are you okay, Mavis?" Kivera hurried over to her and held Mavis's braids as she scanned the surrounding woods. "We have to go, but this will be over soon," Kivera rubbed her friend's back as she waited for the monster to jump out.

The beast still struggled in the magical ropes for now. Until the magic wears thin from a distance and the shadows will dissipate into mist. By then, Kivera hoped to have a plan to ensnare the beast.

"That thing was so ugly and, of course, you had to make it angry. Do you piss off bears for fun, too?" Mavis snapped in between retches as Kivera continued with the reassuring circles. A cooling obsidian mist emanated from her now talonless fingers until the surface of Mavis's skin shimmered.

"Only when I can't find any mountain cats to antagonize," Kivera smirked at Mavis's back.

"You are insane, Kiv," Mavis coughed and straightened, not noticing the slip of a nickname.

Kiv.

Kivera sounded the shorter name in her head before mouthing the pronunciation when Mavis wasn't looking. She's never had a nickname before.

Despite everything happening, a small smile budded on Kivera's lips.

Kiv.

"I know. You'll love that about me. But we need to hurry." Kivera extended her hand.

"You and Arcian will train me into shape," Mavis grumbled as she accepted Kivera's cold hand. Together, they dashed away but didn't run far before a roar ripped through the air, and the magic holding the beast wore to nothing. Kivera's bones shuddered at the malevolent cry and pushed her legs further, pulling Mavis behind her.

If only Mavis gained a bit more training, this would be easier but Kivera was the one who caused the delays so the mistake was hers, she seethed at herself.

Tomorrow they'll start running in the mornings together.

"A little further," Kivera barely huffed.

A familiar rumbling of the earth wobbled Kivera's feet.

The monster was closing in on them.

"I need to get you out of here, Mavis," Shadows whirled around their joined hands.

"I don't think my stomach can't handle spiriting again,

Kivera." Indeed, green tinted her skin. Another jump wouldn't do well to Mavis's delicate body, but to make up for her body's queasiness, Mavis pumped her limbs harder than before.

Snarls and nail-shredding of the earth sounded closer to them. Kivera poured all her strength into her legs and urged Mavis faster.

A gurgling sound bubbled ahead, and Kivera almost shouted in relief. An idea shaped in her head. "I have a plan. I can hear a creek ahead, so we only need to cross it."

Mavis nodded, too focused on keeping their brutal pace. Yet, she didn't give up.

Foliage shattered behind them, too close for Kivera's comfort. She threw orbs of coiled darkness over her shoulder to blind the beast and stalled its progress for a few short heartbeats before the beast shot off again, even more enraged than before.

The creek was too far ahead and without knowing how high the waters were from recent rain storms; the plan became dangerous but there were no other options. She had a risky idea to get the horror off their back until they crossed the creek, but she would have to leave Mavis.

One more glance at the monster behind them confirmed Kivera must be swift.

"Keep running," Kivera said under her breath to Mavis before dissolving in the shadows. Before darkness swallowed Kivera whole, she saw Mavis maintaining the pace as she shot through the forest like a deer being chased.

Kivera could only guess where to reappear. In her short time spiriting, guessing was the best she could do. Darkness spread its wings from Kivera's vision and when she appeared in the creature's blind spot on its right side, she slashed deep into the night black fur with her talons. With the creature's momentum, she had to hold on to the warm body as her talons shredded through its side.

Before shrieks erupted from the creature, Kivera had already disappeared through shadows and continued running beside her friend.

Snarls began anew, but at a comforting distance away.

Mavis had slowed down and regret flashed across her features.

"You feel sorry for the creature?" Kivera asked, not unkindly as she grabbed Mavis's hand to yank her along. If only she could carry Mavis, but she had a feeling Mavis needed to *feel* this hunt.

"Maybe it didn't ask for this when it was made," Mavis panted, her red face straight ahead.

Kivera squeezed Mavis's hand. "It's safe to say it's asking to eat us right now, Mav. I'd rather you breathe than that thing."

Lapping sounds were ahead and close enough for Mavis to hear the joyous noise. The trees broke and a pregnant stream appeared beneath a rocky ledge. They needed to run down the incline to cross the water. The stream was fuller than Kivera expected, but she didn't have time to check the water depths with the creature gaining on them at inhuman speeds.

Kivera turned to Mavis who wore an odd expression of fear, uncertainty, and relief as she stared at the swollen water.

"Can you swim?" Kivera asked and Mavis's mixed expression wiped away to leave dread in its place as she shook her head. Kivera scratched one option out mentally.

Smooth terrain leveled out from the slippery decline and the creek side beyond.

The beast crashed through the trees at the top of the small hill and a fierce roar split the air but Kivera didn't dare glance back.

Spiriting to the other side was out of the question with Mavis's condition so there was one option left.

Kivera gathered the strength to her legs, bracing them with a reinforcement net of black tendrils, and clutched Mavis's smaller body to her before launching across the width of the creek.

"Hold tight."

Mavis's shocked gasp pierced Kivera's ears, but she paid no mind. She was too busy cherishing the air caressing her neck and face. Gods, she missed the feeling of flying like a missing lung she ached to have once more.

Within two heartbeats they arced over the creek and landed in the shallow depths of the creek. Kivera stumbled before catching her footing and released Mavis from her grasp.

"Kivera!" Mavis screamed.

Kivera turned in time to see the beast skidding down the hill and lean back on its haunches. In horror, Kivera stared at the beast bound over the creek, stealing Kivera's idea. She had enough time to raise her hand to conjure a feeble shield against the sharp claws and bared fangs.

But someone else acted quicker.

Mavis hurled herself in front of Kivera and threw out her arms towards the mid-air creature. Water slammed into the beast in a magnificent wave and swallowed its thrashing body downstream.

The creature stumbled in the current as it struggled to right itself, but the females bolted, not commenting on the water magic, and followed the winding stream south to the cliffs above.

Splashes echoed through the trees and the earth vibrated once again as the beast won against Mavis's waning magic as their distance lengthened. The earth trembled as the animal chased them.

Under her breath, Kivera spits a stream of curses and pushed her quaking limbs harder. She had a few ideas, and each was crazier than the last. None Mavis would enjoy, either.

"Kiv, what do we do now?" Mavis exclaimed as she tripped over a loose rock.

Kivera reached out a steadying arm. "We're going to find out exactly how foolish and hungry this monster is," Kivera answered, as vague as the idea forming in her mind.

The treeline faded into a rather impressive view of the city nestled in the mountain's bosom. Evergreens blanketed below with staggering peaks at their backs, spearing to the sky and guarding the small valley. Puffs of white painted the vast blue sky, cruising on the biting autumn wind tearing at Kivera's clothes.

Mavis and Kivera had ventured higher than Kivera originally thought. They carefully toed the edge of the cliffside and peered over the ledge to the plummet below.

Mavis landed terror-filled eyes on Kivera and hugged her elbows. "What do we do now?"

Branches snapped, and the beast slunk forward, oozing malevolence. Blood dripped to the ground from its side in tattered ribbons. Kivera angled Mavis behind her after whispering instructions in her ear.

"I will enjoy your filthy blood. She won't mind me tasting you," the abomination clicked and growled, edging painstakingly closer as if devouring their fear.

Mavis shook and whispered prayers to gods who didn't care for her.

Kivera would know. They answered none of her prayers. But her mind mulled over the creature's slip. *She.*

"You have yet to draw a single drop of mine, beast. Your empty threats are very unbecoming of you," Kivera taunted and flicked out her talons.

Its answering snarl rode the breeze across the world and sunk deep into Kivera's bones.

"You have nowhere to run and no more tricks. You are nothing but a warm meal for me to eat on a frosty morning, worm."

Kivera raised her arms and positioned her body for a fight, but pasted on a smirk. "I'll turn you into a new rug to place in front of my fire, or perhaps a fresh coat for the coming winter. Or I could send your pieces to your master. She would probably be delighted."

The creature bared its dagger-like teeth and tore at the ground with its massive paw. "I wear no leash, pointy one."

"You're a lackey. You do all her dirty bidding," Kivera

coaxed, digging to gain more about this mysterious woman. She prodded its mind and submerged into an oily spider web filled with unspeakable horrors. No matter how hard she tried, Kivera can't enter inside the animal's mind but this creature was something *other*. Intelligent enough to have consciousness, but not one she's ever encountered. Sifting through this mind took longer to scrounge through its mind and time wasn't on her side. Not with a cliff behind her and a bloodthirsty beast before her.

"I will enjoy draining the life from my food. You will end slowly."

"Like I said, I don't die easily." Kivera drew a long, onyx whip from her shadows and aimed a strike at the beast.

Or where the beast *had* been.

With lightning reflexes, the creature dodged Kivera's assault and crossed half the distance in a few bounds.

"Kivera, when she-?" Mavis's strained voice cracked Kivera's heart.

Kivera grit her teeth and swung the whip harder to antagonize it further, but interrupted Mavis's question as the beast barrelled towards them at top speed. A vicious chorus of unbridled fury clanging through the open air and Kivera snarled back.

The beast was nearly upon them and Kivera slammed her whip once more into its side. When it glanced at the distraction, Kivera raised her other arm and sent a blast of raw darkness.

"Now!" Kivera looked over her shoulder in time to watch her friend inhale a deep gulp of air and sprint to the edge of the cliff.

And *jumped.*

Kivera didn't indulge the fears of failure but tiptoed to the edge as well and counted her breaths. Three breaths and the beast cleared its vision and tore through the last few yards.

The beast's hot, vile breath wafted up Kivera's nose as she coiled her whip around its paw before launching herself off the cliff.

The creature didn't notice until too late and attempted to claw at the rock and snag anything to hold its weight. It roared one last time, frantic this time, before free-falling through the sky.

Not wasting time or air distance, Kivera spirited to Mavis's twisting body, almost a third of the way down to the ground. Screams ripped from her throat by the plunge and tears streaked from her squeezed eyes. As gentle as she could, Kivera enveloped Mavis and dissolved in a slip of darkness.

The landing was rough. Kivera slammed hard on her feet and the force jolted her to her knees. She never wanted to do that again, no matter how much her blood sang at the rushing air in her face. Mavis collapsed to her hands and knees after Kivera let go of her and coughed on the ground.

Kivera's stomach roiled, but she couldn't vomit yet. She was waiting for something. Something to hit-

A faint crash of trees and a loud thump echoed somewhere nearby.

"Rest here, Mav. I'll be right back." Mavis nodded in between heaves and Kivera didn't waste another second and spirited away.

Kivera didn't have to travel far. She had to jump a few hundred yards away in the impact's direction and she tracked the rotten stench the rest of the way.

Broken branches littered the ground around the creature's broken body. Dark limbs splayed in every direction and leaves coated its fur. Dead eyes stared at nothing with a jaw lying crooked.

The sun warmed the back of Kivera's neck as she crouched to inspect closer. Blood coated the gashes on its side and she used the tip of her talons to pull the skin flaps apart and sniff the decaying smell delicately.

Who did this beast know in human lands? How will Kivera find this woman the beast spoke of? Could the woman the beast spoke of have any relation to the murderer Jexton was hunting down?

Done minutes later, Kivera spirited away in a swirl of shadows and landed where she left Mavis, who was rubbing the back of her hand across her mouth. Her unreadable blue eye was bright on her ashen skin.

"It's dead?" Mavis asked.

Kivera nodded and stepped closer to grip her upper arm. "That was a lot to take in. Are you alright?" Kivera couldn't let her concern subside any longer. Her guilt wouldn't let her. She chided herself for being stupid enough to let Mavis join her on a dangerous hunt.

Mavis smiled. "After a steaming bath and strong cup of tea, I'll be better. Can we-we spirit back to the inn? I need to clean myself up."

Kivera knit her eyebrows together. "If you wish."

At least there Kivera can ask about the water magic after Mavis cleans up. She wouldn't mind walking back to town if it meant Mavis felt better, but Mavis only crooked her elbow and Kivera linked her through before shadows devoured them.

"How do you feel?" Kivera set down her book and popped a berry into her mouth.

"As I jumped off a cliff," Mavis dried her hair while she padded from the bathing room in her nightclothes.

"The monster is dead and we're alive. Pretty lucky with all things considered," Kivera scooted to make room on the bed.

Mavis folded herself on the bed to sit cross-legged and she played with her soaking hair. She chewed her lower lip. "You knew, didn't you? About the water magic?" Mavis asked slowly, without meeting Kivera's eyes.

Kivera sat up and set aside her book. "I did. When we first met, I saw the forefront of your mind and your gift... presented itself. Magic-wielders also have a unique scent from their magic."

"Is that why I'm here? Do you feel bad for me or something?" Soft-spoken Mavis didn't raise her voice but was close at the end of the sentence. Tears shone unafraid in her eyes.

Kivera couldn't deceive her friend if she wanted an honest, liberating friendship her heart ached for. She lowered her eyes to stare unblinking at her clenched hands. Kivera swallowed. "I saw my eyes in yours. Alone and sad in a way, yes. Your magic, on the other hand, was a danger to you and your kin." She couldn't help the growl coating the last word. The thought of them enraged Kivera. "But in the alley, you were courageous and kind with only a knife in hand. I thought, maybe if neither of us was alone anymore, maybe this could be a chance to be completely ourselves with another soul."

Kivera looked up and Mavis didn't meet her gaze but stared straight ahead and chewed her lower lip. The silence ate at Kivera.

"Are you mad?" Kivera held her breath.

Mavis remained transfixed on nothing. "Well, I am confused. I never thought of doing anything with the ma-magic. It always scared me."

"Having magic makes you different, of course, but do not shy from who you are." If only Kivera followed her own words, but the *creature* inside her was wholly different. "Your magic is a part of you, but your choice on how to wield it. Learn enough to control it so you aren't torn apart and you can live a mundane life. That's fine, too, Mavis."

"Would you still want me employed with you if I didn't choose magic?" Mavis reached for the apple slices on the platter between them.

Kivera raised an eyebrow. "Shouldn't you care more about working with someone with sharp talons and dark magic?"

Mavis laughed. "I guess I should, but I don't."

Kivera joined in a beat later. "Of course I want you around. It would be nice to be around someone who didn't feel inclined to crucify me for witchcraft." She shrugged. "You would, at least, understand what I am."

"Am I like you?" Her voice was soft and tentative, searching for an answer she didn't know if she wanted.

Leaning over, Kivera sniffed Mavis closer and her eyes widened fractionally. She sat back and cocked her head.

Kivera rubbed the side of her temple. "Similar yet not. Interesting."

"What does that mean?"

"You're like me, but different. In a way that cousins are similar, I suppose."

"You're saying I'm a freak!" Mavis exclaimed, throwing her body into the pillows.

"Not at all. We are grotesquely different from those around us now. But we are not freaks of nature, Mavis." A memory from a locked box in her head pushed to escape, but Kivera swiped the thought away. "We are born from faeries. Or Fae, as we call ourselves. You can distinguish the race with full-blooded Fae and some half-blooded Fae with these." Kivera lifted the glamor from her ears and their point emerged from the obsidian mist. "In faerie lands, they're separated by their elemental abilities into reigning territories. But how you are here and able to wield water magic somehow is a mystery I don't have a clue about."

Silence clenched the air and Kivera held her breath as she waited for Mavis to respond.

"You wouldn't turn away from me if I didn't choose to be a faerie?" Weary blue and white eyes met Kivera's.

Kivera's shoulder shook with silent laughter, but she cascaded in relief. Letting someone else see one of her scars was her first breath of air. "Of course not, Mavis. That's a silly reason not to be friends. You're part human, but who you choose to be is forever your choice."

"Would you hate me if I didn't want the same as you?"

The giggles died in Kivera's throat as she looked into her friend's eyes. Pain and worry wrinkled around Mavis's eyes, feathering around her savage scar.

"Now, I'm confused. I just told you we're a part of a supernatural race stuck in human lands from another world."

"Well, if we're being completely honest with each other, there are things about me you may not like," Mavis rambled and stared at the ceiling to avoid Kivera's eyes. "I'm sure you saw my truth in my mind anyway when we met, which I'm okay with, I just-"

"Mavis, I don't know what you're talking about. If you're comfortable sharing, I'm here, but don't feel pressured to do so."

Mavis swallowed once, then twice, but tears shone in her eyes before dropping like stones. "When I was younger, there used to be a family that lived next to Mother's. My brother and I could play with their children, but that never happened for very long. There was a girl my age, Daizi, whom I was lucky to get along with. She was sweet and listened to me."

"My brother caught us one day... being close. She was my first kiss." Mavis swallowed again. "But when he caught us, he pushed me in the mud while she watched and screamed at him to stop. He dragged me home by my hair after scaring Daizi away and told my mother the 'abominations' he witnessed and she was not pleased." Mavis' throat bobbed, but her face remained stony. Shadows passed over her eyes from unspoken horrors. "I never saw her again after she ran away."

Kivera's tongue struggled to unlatch itself from the roof of her mouth and couldn't form any words to say. "Are you worried I'll hate you for being attracted to women?"

A single tear slid down Mavis's cheek. "Yes."

Kivera burst into laughter. "Mavis, faeries don't care about gender limitations. I knew plenty of people attracted to the same sex or did not care at all who they were with, myself included," Kivera smiled and Mavis peered at Kivera. "My world had no qualms with who you love. An opposite notion compared to the human world. I only want you to be happy."

Kivera could appreciate Mavis's beauty, her brutal scar

was striking even. But at that moment, when she beamed at Kivera, she was simply stunning, as if the sun radiated beneath her delicate skin.

"You don't care if I'm attracted to women?" Mavis bent her elbow to rest her chin on her fist.

"I could not care less who you snog," Kivera winked. "As long as you're happy and that person is good to you. Besides, I've seen how you and Syt are staring at each other."

Mavis reached for Kivera's hand and squeezed tight, sealing their friendship.

"Thank you, Kivera." Mavis's blue eye twinkled.

Kivera grinned back and squeezed her hand back. "Since you shared your secrets, I'll share a truth of my own." Kivera slid off the bed onto her feet and stood in the center of the small room. She double-checked the magical web she spun and strengthened the shield around their room before pulling off her black shirt. The cold air of the room kissed Kivera's exposed skin with only a slip of fabric on to cover her chest, and she couldn't resist a deep shiver.

In a slow circle, Kivera exposed her back to Mavis and inhaled deeply through her nose, and exhaled. Every day for years, Kivera painted a glamor over her inhuman body, but for Mavis she allowed the magic to drip off her skin like paint drizzling down a canvas.

Mavis gasped and scrambled from the bed closer to Kivera.

Darkness rejoiced and flickered throughout the room as Kivera's unfiltered delight surfaced. Streams of metallic gold lined her olive skin in a strange pattern. Rather, outlines of some design and Mavis leaned forward for a clearer visual. The whorls of designs were rooted at the center of her spine, divided into shapes and veins spreading to the planes of her shoulders to the definitions of her biceps.

Mavis inclined closer before going rigid as stone as realization struck.

Those were feather outlines.

Kivera flashed her a wicked grin over her shoulder. "Want to see them?"

Mavis dipped her chin. She couldn't fashion a sentence.

A small smile remained on Kivera's lips as she unfurled her wings.

Shadows whispered against Kivera's skin before seeping into her skin. As one, the gold lines and obsidian lifted from her skin. The lines on her forearms peeled back and stretched to the ceiling.

Tendrils of shadows floated to the floor as the darkness and gilded lines formed into wings borne of night. They encompassed almost the entire length of the room and trembled with the effort to not stretch further.

The wings were magnificent and beautiful and terrifying.

In a graceful arc, the wings fold on Kivera's back as she faces Mavis. The exhilaration of her wings freely released a tension in her chest she could never escape.

"Holy gods, Kiv. They're beautiful." Mavis breathed, awe radiating on her face. She pushed to her feet to stand in front of Kivera. A smirk played on her mouth. "Of course you can fly. Why wouldn't you be insanely powerful and beautiful and not be able to fly?"

Joy dimmed from Kivera's heart. "I have wings but I cannot fly."

"Why's that?"

Tears welled in Kivera's eyes and she coiled the magic back within herself. The glamor settled into place and the wings dissipated into her skin once more. "I've been alone for a long time. I don't have anyone to help me learn."

CHAPTER SIXTEEN

"Someone is in our room."

Mavis and Kivera halted to a stop outside the dining room with their arms laden with boxes of sweet treats from the sweet shop across the street from the inn. The former straightened to scan the inn while the latter peeked in the dining room, checking to see if it was empty before shoving Mavis in and depositing their boxes unceremoniously on the floor. She checked the web around their room before gathering magic.

"I'll be back," Kivera spirited away with a wicked grin.

"Wait!" and a reaching hand followed Kivera as the darkness swept her away.

The dark room was lit by a half-standing candle on the dresser Kivera left for their return. She appeared in the bathing room, swallowed by folds of darkness, while she observed a figure walking around their beds toward the dresser. For how large the person was, they moved on silent feet as they rummaged around for something.

Talons slid out of Kivera's fingers achingly sweet and stepped out of the bathing room cloaked in darkness.

This fool wouldn't leave alive.

She moved on noiseless feet until she was behind the hulking figure inspecting papers on the dresser. A man by his scent and familiar to her but couldn't place where from.

"Find something you like?" Kivera's croon was razor thin. A death whisper.

The human spun in surprise and reached for his side,

presumably for a weapon, but her talons glinted in the candlelight as Kivera moved, a wraith of night, as she slammed the intruder's wrist on the dresser. A clatter clanged on the floor.

"Argh, you bitch!" The brood exclaimed.

A dark tendril grasped his other arm and yanked him to his knees. He roared as his knees slammed into the unforgiving ground. Kivera gripped the other wrist in an unbreakable hold and cut shallow slices into his skin with her talons.

"Invading my privacy is quite rude. Don't you have any manners?" She leaned down and sniffed. Tillirius. She let out a deep exhale through her nose and threw his hand out of her grip.

"How dare you?" Tillirius thundered. His dark eyes met hers, full of raging hatred. The tendril locked around his wrist forced him further to the ground. Kivera snaked another around the wrist she discarded and yanked harder.

"You're in my room, idiot. Why were you snooping?" Kivera's voice was guttural.

Another signal through her dark web thrummed through her, but a familiar person this time.

Mavis burst through the door and torchlight from the hallway streamed in. Her eyes gazed at Tillirius kneeling before Kivera, spitting with rage.

"What the?" Her eyebrows knit together before ushering herself in, shutting the door behind her. She breezed through the room to light more candles.

Kivera forgot about her different eyesight. If Mavis was like her, what physically heightened gifts was she given?

"Stones for brains here was going through our rooms," Kivera glared down at him with a faint smirk dusting her lips. Tillirius didn't seem like a man to kneel for anyone, not even for a lover. Her smile spread further.

"I was delivering a message from Jex, you stupid bi-" His eyes widened imperceptibly as Kivera snarled in his face and flashed her gold nails. Fear secreted from his faintly trembling body.

"Be nice or I'll rip out your tongue," she promised in a soft voice.

"What did you say, Kivera?" Mavis asked near the bathroom, still lighting candles.

"I encouraged him to use manners, Mavis," Kivera lied and eyed Tillirius's shaking form, daring him to object.

Mavis only grunted as if not quite believing her, but asked no more questions.

"I'm here to deliver a message. It's in my pocket," Tillirius eyed an outer jacket pocket and Kivera reached in, careful not to touch anything else.

"Was the message also underneath all our paperwork, too?"

He looked away.

The paper was small and folded into a neat square. Kivera unfolded the parchment to a neat scrawl.

The victim's sister claimed the body.
Need you at the station. Sorry.
-J

"What does it say?" Mavis asked at Kivera's shoulder and she handed the message over. "We should go then."

The dark restraints vanished from Tillirius. He jumped to his feet and stepped toward Kivera.

She shifted Mavis behind her before pointing a single talon at his throat. "Give me a reason." A growl emphasized each word of the promise.

Tillirius's jaw clenched and his fists worked themselves before he stormed out of their room. Kivera heard his thunderous footsteps down the hallway and out the front corridor.

Kivera faced Mavis, who rolled her eyes at Tillirius's dramatic exit.

"Syt was right. He is dramatic. Can't seem to handle a loss to a woman, either." Mavis stepped closer to Kivera.

Kivera snorted and held out her hand. "Technically,

we're females. That's how faeries reference each other. Humans are men and women. But you choose how to call yourself."

Mavis hummed but placed her icy hand in Kivera's and watched shadows swirl around them before spiriting away.

Kivera didn't care any longer about who saw magic. After she lost her temper in the pub last night, she knew word would spread swiftly about her power. Let them see a glimmer of what lies underneath her skin and maybe draw out the killer.

The round table was the first to appear from the darkness in the torch-lit room. Uniforms milled the massive room and hollered in surprise at the dark power filling the room. Most reached for their weapons as forms shaped into Kivera and Mavis.

Thankfully, Jexton noticed the shadows and called for swords to be dropped. Regardless, Kivera kept a firm shield around them both. She didn't trust the number of guards following Kivera.

Jexton smirked once the officers moved on. "Quite the entrance, Kivera Galveterre."

Kivera grinned and raised two fingers to her brow. "I like to have some style, Captain."

Jexton met her and Mavis with a calm smile. "Hello, Mavis. I'm sorry to interrupt your day, but this couldn't wait." An underlying question laced his words. Kivera assumed about why they requested the day off after a few days of being on assignment. But that was Kivera's business.

Jexton escorted them down a hallway that led deeper into the building.

"What made your day interesting?" Jexton asked casually as the trio walked past countless doors. The few people they encountered eyed Kivera with suspicion.

Kivera shrugged. "Mavis and I ran into our good pal out in the mountains."

Jexton snapped his head to Kivera. "You found the

creature? What happened?" His eyes were wide with something like fear.

Kivera recanted the story, and by the end, the tension between them was palpable. He stopped them outside a plain door.

Kivera looked up from their destination to find Jexton glaring down at her. "You're angry?"

"You brought Mavis to hunt a bloodthirsty monster?" Jexton clenched his fists and crossed his arms.

Kivera's temper rose to the surface. Who does he think he was for being upset with her? After sending Tillirius, of all people, to deliver a message to her?

"Mavis performed outstanding and would outdo you against a supernatural creature, given the opportunity." Kivera slid a gaze to Mavis, whose face was set in a grim smile. They turned to Jexton with matching glares. "Mavis asked to come, and that's her choice to put her life in danger. Not your call to make, Captain."

"You could have stopped her. Not taken her in the first place," Jexton raised his voice.

"My place isn't to rip choices from people," Kivera countered in cold fury. He has no position over Mavis or to berate Kivera like this. "You called us here with your bull-headed lackey, so what do you want?"

"My what?" His eyes narrowed, but a feather twitch in his jaw caught Kivera's attention. He didn't know what she was talking about.

Kivera planted a hand on her hip. "You didn't think to send someone with less of an inkling to stab me in the back of our room?"

Jexton's face reddened, and he opened his mouth to spit something back when Mavis interrupted.

"Jex, to be fair, couldn't you have sent Syt or Mase to deliver the note? We all know Tillirius isn't very fond of Kivera." Mavis stepped up to put a hand on Kivera's shoulder.

Kivera's temper ebbed away at the calming touch, and

she stuffed her hands in her pockets.

"I didn't know Till delivered the note until now, but I hope he wasn't a complete bother." Jexton's bewildered eyes bore into Kivera's and she rolled her own after a moment.

Kivera rolled her shoulders. "Whatever, it's fine now. Someone is here to claim a body?" Like that, Jexton snapped back into his normal self.

"The sister of the latest victim. The sister's name is Sonia, and she's through this door with Syt. I'll be taking her to the morgue after you're done talking to her. She's a wreck, so be nice," Jexton raised a brow and Kivera made a face before opening the door.

Mavis's soft chuckles followed behind her.

The secluded meeting room was bare save for a mediocre painting of a doe in the woods and a long table occupying the room's center. Two people, Syt and an unfamiliar woman, occupied the table sitting next to each other.

The woman, Sonia, looked up at Kivera with a mixture of fear and unending grief. Hair of rich chestnut framed eyes of tilled soil. Her round cheeks glistened with tears, but her vacant eyes didn't falter from Kivera's.

Syt flashed the newcomers a grim smile before returning to her notes.

"Hello," Kivera used a hushed tone as she sat down across from the two women, and Mavis sat to Syt's left. Jexton remained by the closed door and Kivera forced herself to not glance at him. "My name is Kivera and I'm here on behalf of the Alcerian Royal Council to investigate the recent deaths in town. This is my colleague, Mavis. Would you be comfortable discussing your sister with us?"

"If it will help," Sonia rasped. "Her name is-well was- Eileena, and she is-was- a maid in some lord's household. She is quiet and works hard for our family back home."

"When was the last time you had contact with her?" Kivera tilted her head and kept her expression neutral.

Sonia readjusted in her seat and lowered her head. Red

crept up the sides of her neck and ears.

"For a couple of months. We argued over a stupid boy and stopped talking. But Mama hadn't heard from her either, so I rode here to check on her."

"Have you already visited this lord's household?"

"I checked, but the staff chief didn't recognize her name or description," Sonia sniffed, and a tear rolled down her cheek.

"Dark hair, light skin, average height, with green eyes. A notable scar on her shoulder," Syt murmured to Kivera without being asked. The latest victim had a white scar on her shoulder under brutalization and grime.

Ice filled Kivera's veins.

A cough sounded from the door, but Kivera didn't spare a glance.

"Is she here? Is my sister here?" Sonia looked at Kivera. Tears pooled and threatened to overfill her pretty brown eyes. Her lower lip quivered.

"Captain Jexton would like to escort you to the morgue to look at a victim who matches her description. But, Sonia, I can offer you another option," Sonia lifted her head and everyone's attention in the room focused on her. A feeling of Jexton's eyes on her back burned her skin, but ignored him. "I'm gifted with powers to provide a way for you to view the body without seeing her that way. A way of being kinder to her memory, Sonia."

Confusion flashed across Sonia's face, but she nodded once.

Wasting no time, Kivera held out a hand above the table, and darkness blossomed from her palm.

Sonia gasped and jumped out of her seat to the opposite wall, but watched with wide eyes.

Syt leaned forward to study the dark mass, unaffected by now with magic from Kivera, and Kivera peeked a look over at Mavis's encouraging smile. Jexton's brooding presence rested heavily on Kivera's back, but she kept her eyes forward.

Darkness floated the length of the table, halted midway, and melted together to allow a form to shape. Two tendrils split into legs from a torso and two more wisps split to create vague arms. Shadows rounded into a sphere at the top to create a head. Darkness swirled for a moment or two before a layer of shadows melted off to reveal a charcoal replica of the dead woman beneath Kivera's feet.

Every detail was as precise to Kivera's memory in a shimmering gray sheen without the gruesome wounds that marred the actual corpse's skin.

Sonia screeched in surprise, but took a cautious step forward to inspect the magic closer. Tears streamed down her cheeks and her lips wobbled as her eyes inhaled every detail of the projected image. Once her fearful eyes reached the shoulder with a scar dull in the faint glimmer, an emotional dam broke inside her. Sonia's fists hit the table, and she heaved a terrible sob.

"That's her. That's my sister," Sonia's voice broke, and she slumped into the chair. Mavis sucked in her breath and tore her gaze away. "How did this-? Who could do such a-?"

Kivera blinked back tears and swallowed her rising emotion.

"We're still working out those details, ma'am. We are all so sorry for your loss," Jexton spoke for the first time.

Sonia didn't lift her eyes from the shadow body.

Kivera peeked over at him to see the pity contorting his handsome features and he met her eyes without looking away.

"I need to go home to tell Mama and Father." Sonia rose to her unsteady feet and slid on her coat. Syt rose to her feet to escort Sonia. "Tell us when you find this monster."

Kivera stood on rickety legs and nodded. "Thank you for your time and I wish you healing at this time of loss."

She hated this part of displaying magic to random humans, but she couldn't shake the ingrained precaution. Magic entered Sonia's mind, simple as most human minds were constructed, and Kivera slid in undetected.

Sonia's eyes didn't even flicker.

Bleak memories canvassed Sonia's mental walls and a familiar face dominated most of the space.

Her dead sister.

Dread pooled in Kivera's gut and she studied the pretty face for a fraction of a heartbeat longer than necessary before she pilfered through for the memory of Kivera. With expert precision, Kivera carved out her image like shearing animal fat off muscle and warped the memory into one with Kivera absent.

To protect me, Kivera reassured herself.

The invading magic slid out unnoticed and the moment Sonia walked out with Syt, she never remembered Kivera in the room. She wouldn't remember the dark figure of her dead sister instead of the murky essence of a memory viewing her sister's body. Nothing concrete for her human mind to grasp as the brain will naturally push out the image to not be devastated. Kivera only encouraged the human mind's defense system.

When Syt escorted Sonia out into the hallway, Jexton rounded on Kivera with burning eyes. "Why did you do that? She needed to make a proper identification downstairs."

But Kivera didn't care for the handsome man fuming at her, despite their hallway encounter, and she raised a perfect eyebrow. "Have you ever seen the dead body of your brother or sister? A body of someone you care deeply for?" Jexton shook his head at her flat-voiced question and opened his mouth to start, but she merely held up a hand. "As someone that has walked that dark path, I couldn't do that to someone as well. Especially if I can help."

Mavis touched Kivera's arm, her eyes full of concern. Kivera gave her a small smile in return. Anything else required more energy.

"The policy is to have the body identified through correct processes," Jexton tried again.

"I don't give a damn about cruel mortal policies. It's

taken care of and we have a lead to follow. Don't be unsympathetic." Kivera rolled her eyes and examined her nails. Dark tendrils snaked around her long fingers and wiggled her fingers for them to dance. When Jexton didn't respond to her insult, Kivera lifted her eyes to find Jexton transfixed on Kivera's fingers. When he caught her gaze, Jexton's eyes snapped away and pink crept on the tops of his ears.

Kivera couldn't name the reason her stomach clenched at the secret look. Flustered and a bit annoyed, Kivera rose and Mavis followed. Kivera skimmed Jexton's broad chest with feather-light fingers and she forced her eyes past the impressive muscles to meet his unreadable eyes.

"This is a team. You can't go off doing things on a whim. Sonia could have given us useful information," Jexton played his hands outwards.

"She didn't," Kivera said softly with all the conviction she could muster.

Jexton's eyes flared, but he didn't respond. Rather, shrugged and led them out.

"What about this lord? When will someone talk to him?" Mavis asked next to Kivera.

"Till already interviewed him, if I'm not mistaken. His name is Lord Huron." Jexton shrugged as they strode through the musky hallways. "He checked out."

Kivera snorted. "He will be re-interviewed if the victim allegedly knew him. Even if Tillirius interviewed him."

"Did Lord Huron mention any member of his staff missing?" Mavis intervened as Jexton's head whipped around to Kivera with a growl on his lips.

"Till did not mention it in his report."

"That is an important detail to leave out. Wouldn't you want to find out what happened to someone who spent time in your home?" A wicked smile twisted Kivera's mouth. They entered the lobby and headed straightaway for the round table in the center occupied by Syt, Rex, and Maserion.

"You want to go talk to him, then?" Jexton smirked over his shoulder.

"Incompetency needs second eyes, so yes," Kivera fluttered her dark lashes.

A few yards away from the oak round table, Jexton spun to glare at Kivera. "What did you-"

"Oh, don't get your knickers in a bundle. It's easy to tease." Kivera poked the taut muscles of his shoulder with an unsheathed talon before she breezed past him. She didn't see Mavis's apologetic smile to the captain.

"I swear, she only likes you," Jexton huffed to Mavis, not knowing or caring that Kivera could hear him.

Mavis chuckled and followed Kivera with her hands in her pockets.

Syt glanced up from the notebook she carried around when the trio arrived at the table. Her mouth parted when her gaze landed on Mavis.

Mase and Rex were reviewing slips of parchment, and the latter held a candle close to the paper.

"That was quite eventful," Syt observed of the meeting without a greeting. Mase and his grandfather looked up and waved at the newcomers. "Sonia said nothing about witnessing magic afterward. It was odd."

Kivera looked away. "I couldn't let her leave with knowledge of magic. Such knowledge in the wrong hands would be problematic, in the least." She perched herself on the edge of a chair Mavis sat down in. "Besides, her mind will be okay. She won't contain a memory of her sister's body."

"Invasive others might argue," Jexton muttered at Syt's side, peering over her shoulder to examine the book she held. A detail of interest caught his attention and Kivera watched his lips twist in a flash of a smile before it was gone in a heartbeat.

"Compassionate, declare the wiser." Kivera shot back.

"Arrogant, say the experienced."

Torch lights flickered and Mavis gripped Kivera's arm and squeezed it gently, but with firmness to remind her to breathe. The calm reassurance Kivera's raging blood needed.

Mavis's serene water to Kivera's raging fire.

Mavis slid her eyes at her, but Kivera knocked on the wall of Mavis's warm mind. A request to be let in. Nodding her head, Mavis allowed Kivera to whisper in her mind.

I don't know who I want to shove in front of the beast more, Tillirius or Jexton. What is it with mortal men?

Mavis snorted, but she covered it with a cough. The team was immersed in their conversations and no one noticed.

Pretty boys are irritating, Mavis's soft voice spoke back.

Spending too much time in front of the mirror, I'm afraid. Not enough substance to fill those pretty heads.

Leaving all the work for us females.

Interesting how Mavis already uses the Old Language, Kivera noted. Female rather than woman or girl.

Lazy asses.

At that, Mavis chortled and received odd looks from the others. All of which the two females ignored.

"Those two are strange," Rex whispered mischievously in Maserion's ear, loud enough for Kivera to hear.

She grinned in the pair's direction and they grinned back. She liked them, Kivera decided.

Jexton, not missing the friendly interaction, said nothing but stared hard at Kivera's face. His gaze had a heating force on her cheeks, but she couldn't meet his intensity.

"We should meet this Lord Huron," Kivera rose to her long legs. "What do you say, Mavis?"

"I don't think I'm given much of a choice," Mavis grumbled, but her eyes alight.

"You always get a choice with me. You practically run this show," Kivera mockingly scoffed and linked her elbow with Mavis's.

"Report back to the team when you're done." Jexton continued his intense gaze on Kivera, challenging her to object. She stuck out her tongue before shadows immersed her and Mavis.

CHAPTER SEVENTEEN

"How did it go?" Syt's melodic voice encompassed the training room where the shadow magic deposited her and Mavis at. Syt wasn't training alone. Across from her waited Maserion, equally sweaty, wielding twin daggers. Syt brandished a beautiful staff Kivera ached to touch.

On the other side of the room, in a shaft of sunlight, Jexton and Tillirius dueled shirtless. Arcian presided over to bark various instructions. The circling men discarded their shirts on the floor where Rex sat reading a chunky book. Sweat shone on their sun-kissed skin and Kivera's mouth dried at Jexton's body. Her steps even faltered toward Syt.

"Kivera!" Mavis hissed at her when Kivera stepped on her toes.

"Sorry, sorry." Kivera broke her stare and faced where Syt was waiting with Maserion's arm wrapped around her shoulder.

"Lord Huron was a strange fellow and not a big talker," Kivera smirked when she and Mavis were near the pair.

Syt chuckled. "He didn't confess right away?"

"Nothing at all. When I checked his mind," Kivera peered over her shoulder at Tillirius, Jexton, and Arcian striding their way and she didn't want to rehash the argument of reading minds. Rex remained on the floor, content with his paperback. "His mind was blocked."

Syt's brows furrowed. "Blocked? You couldn't read it?"

"I couldn't access anything tangible about Eileena and any other victims," Kivera shrugged. "There could be several reasons, but it's still strange, especially with a human. I would say he's a person of interest."

"Who should be a person of interest?" Jexton asked at Kivera's shoulder, his breath close enough to kiss her hair. He and Arcian nodded their greetings, Tillirius glaring at the new arrivals, Kivera in particular.

"Lord Huron didn't divulge too much," Mavis answered when Kivera couldn't. "Something was off about him."

Kivera cleared her throat. "We couldn't pry too much from Huron, but he's sending his head of staff here later today. I'd like to interview him if no one else wants to." The snively butler crawled under her skin, but she'd stomach the feeling of trying glancing in his mind. Huron frustrated her even further by not being able to enter his oily mind.

Syt met Kivera's gaze. "If you don't mind, I would like to join."

Kivera nodded. "That would be perfect."

Out of the corner of her eye, Jexton nodded.

"We should all get back to training until then. After that, we'll survey farther out neighborhoods to find other families of the victims," Jexton announced to the group. "Mavis, you're welcome to go with us or Kivera. We need to train and you're both welcome to spar."

"Mavis wants to train with me," Syt hooked Mavis's arm through her out and led her to the mat she and Maserion had occupied. Mavis glanced back to Kivera with wide eyes and a creeping blush on her cheeks.

Maserion trailed behind and hopped around them in a flurry of words.

Tillirius peeled away without a word and Arcian followed after a quick smile to Kivera.

"They're quick friends, aren't they?" Jexton commented and leaned closer to Kivera when they were alone.

"Interesting, isn't it?" Kivera agreed with a knowing

smile, then laughed at Jexton's perplexed face when he twisted to her.

"Are you going to train with us mere mortals or are you leaving?" Jexton smirked down at Kivera. Her blood heated at his molten brown eyes and she forced herself to look at Mavis. Kivera's heart overflowed with joy at Mavis's smile while she practically fawned over Syt's instructions.

"What do you have in mind?"

"How about two against one?" Jexton raised a tawny brow and held his hands behind his back.

"Unfair odds for your lot, but if you wish to," Kivera gave him a wicked grin before sauntering towards Arcian and Tillirius and pulling her arm into a stretch across her chest.

"You against *us*?" Jexton trotted at her side. "That wouldn't be possible."

Kivera waggled her eyebrows. "Scared of defeat, Captain?"

"On the contrary, I don't want you to break a nail or mess up your hair," he smirked back. Kivera scoffed and peeled off her jacket, laying it on a nearby chair. "You think you can beat us both?"

"Wiping that smirk off both of your faces will be easy," Kivera waved her hand as if swatting a fly.

"We'll wipe that grin off yours, girl." Tillirius curled his upper lip and glared at Kivera.

Kivera hummed a light tune as she began light stretches while the men watched her like a trio of cackling hyenas, as if confident of their win already. As if they underestimated her. As if they forgot that bloody night in the pub. Their own foolish mistake then, Kivera thought as she ignored the disappointment burning in her chest.

"Need any weapons?" Tillirius joked across the mat. He and Jexton grabbed their broadswords and grinned at each other like schoolboys.

"I have my own, or have you forgotten?" Kivera lifted her hands in front of her face and waved her fingers. Before their eyes, golden talons slid from her fingers with wisps of smoke kissing the brutal sheen. "Rules, Master-of-Arms?"

A soft growl rumbled deep in Tillirius's chest. This was a fight for the two of them; defeating Jexton would be the cherry on top.

"Yielding means defeat. Shallow cuts only." The Master of Arms glared at them all and lingered on Tillirius the longest, but finished with his dark gaze on Kivera. "No magic, either. We are still a team."

Kivera dipped her chin and shook out her arms at her sides. Her opponents shook off the last of their pre-ritual jitters, their faces focused with lethal precision.

If only they knew of the beast roaming under Kivera's skin.

"Three," Arcian took precautionary steps back from the brewing storm.

"Two."

Jexton met Kivera's eyes as gold talons slid out of her knuckles. She didn't miss Tillirius's swallow.

"One."

Tillirius shot forward on surprisingly nimble feet. His feet touched within a few yards of Kivera within a few heartbeats and his sword flashed in the sunshine streaming through the high windows as he raised the blade over his shoulder. He was close enough that her heightened hearing detected his thundering heartbeat before she burst forward.

Every heartbeat, every breath, and every step carefully measured. Muscles rippled as she sprinted forward and eyed Jexton holding the rear on the defensive.

Fast as a leopard, Kivera slid low on her knees and dropped below Tillirius's guard. His eyes didn't register her speedy movements until he saw with wide eyes Kivera swing her right arm to tear into his inner arm's soft flesh. Jumping on light feet, Kivera spun to drag her talons along the wrist holding his sword. Before his body turned towards the near-invisible movements, Kivera stuck out her foot in front of his moving legs.

A thud shuddered the ground, but she bounced past Tillirius's reaching arms towards Jexton with a delighted smile tugging her lips.

Jexton held steady like a cliff against a stormy sea.

"Don't go easy on me now, Capt."

Jexton cocked her head. "Do you think I'm soft-hearted, Kivera?"

Her toes curled from the way he purred her name. Kivera mentally shook herself and raised a hand to beckon him forward with her forefinger.

In an incredible burst of speed, Jexton lunged forward with his sword clutched in both hands close to his ribs. Kivera couldn't help admiring the graceful speed his body moved.

Kivera parried the blade with both her talons and danced around his back.

Tillirius swayed to his feet but bared his teeth.

"That was good, Kivera," Arcian commended.

Kivera swept a leg back and sketched a deep bow.

Slight rumblings up her shoes alerted Kivera to Tillirius sprinting towards her. She straightened into a loose fighting stance in time for Tillirius to raise a sword in front of her.

Kivera windmilled Tillirius's confident strikes with curved fingers and the clash of different metals rang through the air. Her blood sizzled with the weapons clanging.

"You are a vile creature," Tillirius hissed venomously near Kivera's face when her talons held his blade at bay. He poured his strength into the blade and pushed it against Kivera's hands. "Mavis is too good for you. She should have stayed on her own."

"You enjoy hearing your voice, don't you?" Kivera rolled her eyes and his eyes flared. She dropped low to kick out Tillirius's knee as Jexton circled to her side.

Kivera would admire the languid movements of Jexton's body if he weren't running towards her as he struck Kivera's side. The sword slit through Kivera's black shirt and drew blood from the shallow cut. Any deeper would have pierced internal organs had she not flit away.

A hiss seeped from Kivera's lips at the burning cut. She glared at Jexton's cocky grin through slits and she bared her teeth. Kivera angled her body towards the huffing men and cracked her neck. She wiggled the gold talons and breathed deeply to calm the rising beast that dragged its claws beneath her skin, craving release.

"Tired, girl?" Tillirius sneered.

"Says the *boy* with his ass in the air most of the match," Kivera matched with her sneer and flicked off flecks of his blood near his scuffed boots.

"You little bi-" Tillirius spit at her and sprinted forward.

Kivera shot forward like an arrow released from a drawstring and the clash between the two weapons exploded through the room. Jexton followed suit, but Kivera could have sworn he rolled his eyes before joining the scuffle.

The trio whirled into a violent dance. Kivera blocked a quick jab from Tillirius and spun to launch her own attack on Jexton. Blades and talons and bodies were a flurry of movement.

A slip in concentration at Jexton's focused expression cost Kivera a deep gash in her bicep from a wide-toothed Tillirius. She snarled viciously before unleashing herself into a whirlwind of flashing gold. Kivera wore their stamina down as she danced around them until their chests heaved and perspiration stained their shirts. Before long, the men slowed from her antics and their blades lost momentum. Jexton landed a few shallow cuts while her mountain-cat like lacerations riddled their bodies and their shirts shredded in ribbons.

Kivera had to bend backward to avoid Tillirius's brute swing and returned a savage assault on his exposed forearm. He stumbled back a couple of steps and his free hand gripped the trickling wound.

In the same heartbeat, Kivera whirled on Jexton before

he could twist his wrist for the next jab. She dropped to a lunge and kicked out Jexton's feet from beneath him. She relished the vibrating earth when Jexton crashed to the floor. He rolled on his stomach, groaning.

She circled back to Tillirius and tilted her head at the fire burning the forges behind his dark eyes. Tillirius's sword arced in front of him to keep Kivera at bay, but she batted the sharp weapon away as if it were only an irritating gnat. Moving like a dark blur, Kivera slit her talons along his massive thigh and pounced as he crumpled to one knee.

She whirled her body to slam him onto his back. Without Kivera's magic, she strategically pinned him down mid-thigh so his legs were useless as they flailed about. She laid her hands on his sternum and poured inhuman strength down her arms and forced him to stop moving. She moved her hand to his neck and curved her fingers into claws, and caressed his skin with the tip of her talons.

"*Yield,*" Kivera growled a few inches away from Tillirius's face and dug in her talons encircling his massive neck like a lavish necklace. Blood bloomed on the tips of her claws like beads of rubies adorning jewelry.

Tillirius groaned and squirmed his body to buck Kivera's weight off, but to no avail.

Kivera only grinned at his struggle.

"Jexton, you useless twit. You can't ever back me up." Tillirius seethed at Jexton, groaning a few feet away but didn't concede.

"Yield, Tillirius."

He whipped his head back and forth, spewing a slew of curses.

"Now." Her talons pierced deeper in emphasis.

"I yield," Tillirius rasped through gritted teeth and the depths of the underworld burned in his eyes.

Kivera leaped off his body, painfully aware of the warmth from his body underneath her own before he could lay a hand on her.

Kivera returned to Jexton, still gasping on the mat floor.

The heat of the fight ebbed out of her blood, the fire now a mere simmer. Despite the victory, all she felt was cold burrowing under her skin. Not even men twice, even thrice, her size can defeat her. It left her heart empty.

"Do you yield as well, Jexton?" A flat question even to Kivera's ears.

"I do." Jexton moaned into the sweaty mat. His sword lay discarded a few feet from his writhing body.

Feeling the weight of the victory heavy on her shoulders, Kivera turned to Arcian, who studied her carefully.

"Well? Do you feel worse than they do?" Arcian's eyes were unreadable.

"Yes," Kivera whispered.

Mavis and Syt halted their exercises some time ago to stare at the quick fight and smirked at the fallen boys. Mavis seemed to hear the quiet words and strode over with comforting touches and warm eyes.

"Are you hurt, Kivera?" Mavis asked soft enough so the others wouldn't overhear.

"I hurt them. Mavis, I beat them." Kivera met her friend's eyes, but even to her ears, her voice was haunted.

"Kivera, it's okay. They're okay." A warm hand wrapped around Kivera's wrist and squeezed tight. "You knocked them to the ground. You were incredible at fighting."

"Incredible? She's extraordinary. Nothing I've ever seen before," Arcian interjected, his face etched in surprise and respect. Syt and Maserion joined Arcian by nodding as the pair raised matching thumbs up. A small piece of Kivera lightened at the sight. "Kivera handed those fools their asses."

"I've never seen Tilly so chafed with anyone. Much less a woman," Maserion snorted and crossed his arms. His smooth brown eyes crinkled at Kivera without a flicker of fear in them. "Teach me how to fight like that. I need to use a few new moves on Arcian and Tilly."

A ghost of a smile tugged at Kivera's lips.

"You're only shoving salt in their wounds," Arcian grumbled under his breath.

"I'd go outside their training, too," Kivera nodded her head back at the two men rising on unsteady feet. "After this mess, I would want outside training, too." She winked. "I'll show you a few moves sometime. Nothing extensive."

"What are you talking about?" Jexton groaned, leaning heavily on a slouched Tillirius with a hand clutching his stomach. "It was a good fight. But I've never felt so old in my life."

"Mase is pissing on his entire training from us." Arcian glanced over at Rex, expecting a defense for his young relative but he was lightly snoring on the floor's cushions with a book splayed on his chest and Arcian shook his head slightly.

The phantom smile widened even further at the old man, oblivious to his surroundings.

"He's being ungrateful. That's what he's talking about." Syt rolled her eyes and met Kivera's eyes. "Though I am grateful for all my training, it would be unwise to not learn from you. Especially if Maserion is. I couldn't let him beat me."

A laugh erupted in the sudden air. Kivera raised her brow as she peered at the pink-cheeked Mavis.

There was an unmistakable twinkle in the scholar's eyes that Kivera had to look away from. The pang in her chest squeezed tighter.

"Best learn your competition. Otherwise, you'll end up on your arse from a tiny woman with gold nails." Tillirius groaned but attempted to straighten but winced.

The group chuckled hesitantly and eyed Tillirius and Kivera. She didn't pay him any heed, but the smile remained pasted on her lips.

Finally realizing Kivera's talons were unsheathed, she retracted them and relished the aches in her knuckles.

The tension in the air lessened and afternoon heat bore into the room like a cozy fire and melted the frost threatening to encase Kivera's vessels, her heart, her soul.

"When can we start?" Maserion asked in the quiet, settled air.

Something in Kivera loosened and breathing came easier.

A rumble of outcries from the men made the question sweeter.

"Now, if you'd like." Nothing delighted Kivera more than the round of nods that spread through the group. Especially from the hesitant ones from the master of arms and the men she just defeated.

Well into the bosom of night, Kivera slid into the blankets of her bed and moaned at the comfort and warmth. She sent a lick of power to warm the sheets and snuggled herself deeper, tugged into exhaustion by her eyelids and a sigh loosened her lips.

In the bathroom, Mavis was splashing cold water on her face. "I don't think that bath could clean all the dirt under my nails. Today was disgusting. I'm exhausted," Mavis groaned.

Kivera knew Mavis felt worse than she sounded. Despite living a life free of training and workouts, Mavis did well with the intense day.

Kivera led the team through grueling exercises, snapping instructions and correcting their forms when necessary. Only a few whining complaints from the group and minimal dagger glares from Tillirius, but plenty of encouraging smiles from Mavis.

The investigation team improved over the hours as sunshine drifted across the floor. By the end of the evening, the humans left Kivera's training session limping but satisfied grins plastered on their faces.

Tillirius growled at any instruction and lunged to bite Kivera's finger off anytime she critiqued him in the slightest. Not that she didn't revel in his discomfort. She searched for any minor correction about his form and couldn't contain her smug smile at each comment.

Out of everyone, no one impressed Kivera more than Mavis. Her friend soaked up the lessons like she was breathing air and sweat to execute them to her satisfaction as her blue and milky eyes focused wholly on Kivera's demonstrations. At the beginning of the lessons, her body was awkward and clumsy, but evolved into smooth movements.

Alongside Mavis, Syt was a razor-sharp fighter. Her assaults were lethal on Maserion when the group was instructed to pair off. Any of her hits not blocked by the quick auburn-haired youth were landed with fatal efficiency. The woman could *move.* A storm of her own nature. Syt received a few blows and danced around him like mist on a breeze. How Maserion could remain upright after such an opponent was beyond Kivera.

Jexton and Arcian didn't worry about Kivera. Like well-trained soldiers, they remained quiet and diligent in their exercises. Neither one uttered a single complaint when Kivera gave instructions and corrections. The former gave Kivera secret smiles and nods of encouragement.

At those, Kivera would look away to avoid him noticing her flaming skin.

Now deep under covers, Kivera grinned at Jexton's smooth smiles and the way his *godsdamned* body moved with graceful speed. A small, wild part of Kivera relished the way his brown eyes had followed her around the training room. Occasionally, she held his heated gaze before his eyes snapped away. Part of her fluttered every time.

"Why are you smiling, Kiv?" Mavis shattered Kivera's daydream as she retreated into her haven of covers.

"I don't want to move for a week," Kivera ignored the question and turned on her side to look over at Mavis.

A strawberry brow was already raised as she peered at Kivera. "You were smiling about something. Or someone?" A cheshire smile widened on her pink lips.

Kivera rolled her eyes but said nothing. A whisk of dark

wind blew out the candles, masking the room under a blanket of darkness.

"Kiv?"

"Yes?"

"Are you okay after the training today?" Kivera knew what Mavis meant but couldn't bring herself to talk around the lump of emotion clutching her vocal cords.

"I'm not sure." The whispered confession, saved for the serene safety of darkness, tore at Kivera's soul but she didn't dare speak dark truths even to a kind-hearted friend. She couldn't lose her new companion so soon.

"Whatever you're feeling, I'm here to listen. Now or later. Whenever you're ready and comfortable. But don't let your chaos consume you. Your warm heart does not deserve that heavy burden." Mavis voiced in a feather-soft voice. Kivera heard her heart stumble along with the words. "You'll always have me to bring you back to the scary witch we all love."

"I swear I will gut the next person to call me a witch." But in the folds of darkness, Kivera smiled, grateful for that fateful pub night she met Mavis.

CHAPTER EIGHTEEN

Autumn bleached into early winter as a couple of weeks passed in a chaotic blur, beginning and ending before Kivera could finish a cup of tea. She enjoyed her mornings with Jexton and Mavis as they ran for miles around the mountain slope. No one spoke unless necessary, but Kivera didn't mind the quiet companionship. She felt less alone in her thoughts.

They spent days in grueling training sessions, led by Arcian's barks or occasionally by Kivera's demonstrations if she was in a good mood. Mavis took part in each session and followed along with incredible accuracy.

Syt and Maserion were by Mavis's side at each session as supportive pillars with unending encouraging smiles and words of advice. Elation thrummed through Kivera at the sight and squeezed her chest.

After training against Jexton and Tillirius, Kivera didn't return to the mat unless she was asked to lead the demonstrations. After defeating the two men, the sight of the mat rolled her stomach and bile rose to the back of her throat. To support Mavis, Kivera constructed a small working space for herself by the windows with a little table she dragged in. She spent days poring over piles of books about runes, rituals, and anything else relating to the symbol carved into the bodies, but found nothing.

Kivera constantly discovered Syt's greedy eyes on the books and joined her as much as her schedule would allow.

By the time Kivera grew tired of the team each day working on the case and training, the sun was deep beneath the mountains. A few nights, Kivera had to drag Mavis out of the training room, but once out in the clear air, she moaned about hunting down dinner.

Unable to stand the inn's food any longer, the pair discovered new stews, roasts, and even more desserts in hidden restaurants and drunk on cheerful conversations under dazzling stars. They spent dinner alone and conversed about every topic ranging from Mavis's childhood, cases Kivera investigated, and her latest findings in the case. The last topic didn't last long, much to Kivera's frustration. Light conversations carried them out of restaurants into the biting air until Kivera wrapped them in a cocoon of warmth as they strolled into the woods for nightly walks. Kivera mentioned in passing one week how she adored the forest in the moonlight and Mavis insisted they should venture through each night.

With a smile, Kivera agreed.

After the meal, Kivera and Mavis stalked through the forest under the moonlight, heated in a bubble of Kivera's magic. They didn't stray too far from town, so they attracted nothing with teeth and claws, but on an occasional night, they found a smaller path branching off. Mavis led the way with Kivera holding the rear with talons flicked out.

Three weeks after their arrival, under the belly of the full moon, Mavis and Kivera roamed a favored path with staggering views of the mountains above them. "When did your magic present itself?" Mavis asked with her face tilted upwards in the moonlight.

Kivera looked over at Mavis and studied her friend's thoughtful expression. "Since I was young, there was always a glimmer in my veins. When I was a tot, magic exploded out of me when I threw tantrums, laughed too hard, or when I needed to pee." But she didn't mention the beautiful magic she once had before her world went to shit and she fell into the mortal world with new twisted magic flowing in her veins.

"You must have been a babe straight out of the Underworld," Mavis teased.

Kivera chuckled and rolled her eyes at the shadows in between branches. "I was. The other children hated to play with me in fear of one of my outbursts."

"Poor cowards."

"When did yours present itself?" Kivera cautiously dared to ask and peeked out the corner of her eye at Mavis. They hadn't discussed Mavis's magic for a few weeks, not even after the stream's wave Mavis conjured. Mavis blew off anytime Kivera tried to introduce her magic, but Kivera didn't miss the curious gleam in Mavis's blue eye anytime Kivera used magic.

Mavis paused in the swollen darkness. "I was almost a teenager and my brother was still rough with me still." Her eyes fogged over, and she cleared her throat after a moment. "He took me to this pond near our home and felt grumpy that day. He pushed me to the ground and slapped my face. I don't need to tell you the rest. But after a while, I was getting really mad. He was my brother, and he was doing this to his little sister?" She swallowed and her hands clenched into fists at her sides.

The same thoughts hounded Kivera. How could anyone relentlessly hurt someone of their own blood? Every day, she wished to travel back to that shack and return the cruel favor.

"After the third or fourth slap, I felt something stir inside me. Like part of my soul woke up. It sounds silly, but it's the only way to describe how I felt. The pond *listened* to me and a wave of water splashed him in the face. I could run away and hide."

Unending rage and darkness fluttered the branches around them as Kivera heard her voice crack. Crack from the years of pain at the hands of loved ones. Crack from the years of loneliness in a house with a wretched brother and mother.

Kivera nearly spirited away to the squat cottage to rip apart Mavis's only living family. Mavis was the only tether to ground herself and to keep walking.

"When I returned home, my brother had already told Mother about the entire incident. She was spitting mad."

Mavis's shoulders curled in. "Mother made her objections about the magic, so I never tried again."

"What did she do, Mavis?" Silence answered Kivera's question, and she had to breathe in deep to wrangle control of her waning restraint. Only Mavis and the gods would ever know what happened. "I understand. We don't have to talk about it any longer. But I want to show you something," Kivera stopped their walking, peering at Mavis. The moonlight shone on her face and illuminated the scar ravaging her milky-white eye down to her cheekbone. Mavis nodded, curiosity limning her eyes.

Kivera smiled and closed her eyes. Nothing happened for a moment save for violet and obsidian lights tracing the edge of her skin. Her whole body rippled with darkness and her skin hummed with the night sky's dark energy. She inhaled a deep breath and exhaled out of her lips.

But the air didn't come out.

Stardust and night sky and galaxies poured out of her lips. Magic surrounded the females, lifting their hair with its wind, and filled the forest with glittering darkness full of purples, blues, and colors not of the earth.

"Wow," Mavis spun slowly on her heels, amazement bright on her face. She lifted a hand to a star that burst into a flurry of red, purple, and gold. The beautiful darkness expanded and bubbled around them as they walked through galactic whorls.

Kivera smiled at this other realm with glitters of stars in the velvet darkness. With a swift joyful shout, Kivera's gold-flecked wings tore through her jet-black sweater and stretched to their full width. Stars burst everywhere they touched and the explosion of color on her obsidian feathers captivated Kivera's attention.

At this moment, Kivera Galveterre felt otherworldly free.

"When could you do *this*?" Mavis' incredulous voice twined through the stars, her eyes whizzed around to drink in every detail.

"Not long. I've practiced when I can't sleep." In moments of being awake, she kept the nightmares at bay by unfurling the magic inside her to soothe her mind in short bursts of roiling galaxies that were like the one encasing the females now.

"I wonder what the others would say if they saw this."

Kivera snorted. "They might like me more but ole Tilly-bear will still want to kill me, screaming that I'm a bloodthirsty witch." But even to her ears, her voice sounded flat.

"Kivera, they are coming around. All of them have by now but if they saw this side of you, not just the slasher talons and brilliant eyes, this process might be easier for you. Not so much heartache involved, either." Mavis linked her arm through Kivera's and pranced through the forest.

"I know and I agree." Kivera clenched her jaw. "It's better since we started training as a group, but that doesn't stop me from wishing this case was over. Then I could finally show you the capital," Kivera had been raving about Tymern, the mortal capital of Alceria, since the two met.

"I'm thrilled to see it, too." Mavis's eyes lightened. "But while we're here, you can charm them over with who you are. Anyone would adore you if you let them."

Kivera twisted her lips to stop an oncoming snort. "Like they would ever feel comfortable next to a female with shredding talons and dark magic."

"They hardly care now. Arcian has probably been strategizing how to weaponise you. We'll assume him free of ill thoughts towards you." Mavis shrugged her slim shoulders. "Jex and Tilly will completely get over it, eventually. Perhaps after the twin bruises on their asses fade away."

The females howled with laughter at the memory of Jexton and Tillirius's defeated faces.

"That may be too soon for their egos," Kivera chuckled again but stared at a passing star cluster after the sound died on her lips. "I don't need them and frankly don't care for a man's opinion, but it would make one's existence easier if the surrounding people were pleasant. Besides, I'm craving the most chocolate cake of all time and to eat many sinfully in bed. Are you with me?"

Mavis chuckled, and Kivera grinned widely.

"What do you think-" Kivera began, but a shift in the wind cut her off.

A wind of burnt sugar and decay.

Magic was near that didn't belong to Kivera or Mavis.

Instincts flooded Kivera's system and the magic surrounding them darkened into black smoke before flooding in to form a hardened shield around Mavis. Her wings disappeared in a flash, leaving behind a wisp of dark smoke. Her secret once again embedded itself into her skin.

"Kivera? What is it?" Mavis asked in alarm and Kivera thanked the unhearing gods that Mavis spoke in a whisper.

Kivera's gold talons slid out of her knuckles and she lifted them in a ready stance. Her eyes adjusted to the darkness as second lids slid into place within a split of a heartbeat and she combed through every pocket of blackness. The magic coiled within her sprang free, eager to search the world for the unknown magic source.

With no luck.

"Something is here. With magic." Kivera whispered back in a death-soft voice.

"Is that what the smell is?"

Kivera nodded. "We must be careful." She didn't want to take risks, especially with Mavis present. The magic shuddered through her as it snagged on the magic source less than a mile away.

Too close for Mavis's safety.

Kivera would have to track it down alone.

With a serious expression, Kivera turned to her friend.

"Tell Jexton to be ready and I will send for him if I have need."

"Wait, Kivera!" Mavis's voice rang out before Kivera

spirited her away. She whispered an apology in Mavis's mind as she traveled between the folds of the world.

CHAPTER NINETEEN

Kivera barrelled through trees as she tracked the strange wind's trail and landed in a clearing. Moonlight sprinkled the forest floor through the thick canopies. Snow dusted the ground but didn't reveal any tracks.

In a pocket of shadows near a thick tree base, another unknown scent mixed with the forest. Kivera crept closer, scanning the nearby trees as she followed her nose, but her eyes immediately snapped to the darkness. The world slowed to a halt as she recognized the stench. Bile rose as she inspected the freshly upturned earth hidden in shadows and recoiled at the fresh smell of death.

A whip of silver flashed in the woods and dragged Kivera out of her reverie and she forced herself forward away from the body. She muttered prayers for forgiveness, for herself, and for failing who was buried.

For miles, Kivera felt like she was chasing a will-of-the-wisp. No matter how much she pushed her legs faster or pumped her arms harder, her only reward was glimpses of rippling pale hair between the trees.

Once her breathing turned sharp, Kivera rounded back to the body with a string of curses on her tongue. She knew she was close when the reek of death worsened with each step. The smell slammed into her nose when she stood over the tilled ground. For a few minutes, she stared at the ground in silence.

With a sigh, Kivera knelt and dug her fingers through the frigid ground. Dirt clumped together easily but froze Kivera's fingers so she paused every so often to blow into her fists. Three inches of dirt covered the body, and the first feature to appear was the face. Kivera stifled a grimace as she brushed away the last bits of dirt off the high cheekbones and thin eyebrows.

She couldn't stomach any more and lurched to her feet and shoved an arm over her nose and mouth.

The magic inside Kivera nudged her. *I can help...*

Kivera hesitated, but eventually resigned to the magic. Touching the body would send her over the edge and vomit all over the clearing. She waved a hand over the mound and a dark wind swept away the last layer of dirt. A wool blanket covered the small woman's body. Her limbs were tucked in at awkward angles and her mousy brown hair tangled in clumps. But the most startling detail of all, besides the splattering of bruises on her harrowed face, was the silver collar clamped around her neck.

Oh, gods... she was chained and leashed like an animal. They all must have collared.

Without realizing what she was doing, Kivera rubbed her wrists as unwelcome memories rose to the surface of her mind. Panic seized her heart. In her younger years, Kivera would have resorted to profusely praying. But if any gods were listening, they ignored the slain woman's pleas as they turned away from her pleas.

In response, the monster inside Kivera grazed her skin with obsidian claws. Then again but more insistent. Stars appeared in the corners of her vision and she begged her lungs to expand. They moved in tight, restrained movements, but one by one, the stars blinked away. She despised how a long time passed before her heartbeat settled.

A breeze washed over Kivera's face and kissed the tears that had unknowingly escaped. She scrubbed the wetness off her cheeks with fists and inhaled one final deep breath.

The past would have to remain as dead as her sister. She only wished to escape its chains.

Kivera knelt to inspect the collar closer and dragged a

finger along its cold, scratched surface. Using her knuckle, Kivera turned the corpse's head to the side for a clearer view. A simple key lock interrupted the worn surface beneath the earlobe.

Attached to the victim's wrist was a manacle halfway unlocked, a key still inside the hole. A mistake of the killer from Kivera's interruption. The metal of the handcuff was stripped and dinged from what Kivera assumed was from the victim's failed attempts to break them off.

Jexton and the rest of the team should be here.

Kivera delved into her well of power and cast it out into the world on a dark wind to search for Jexton. Within a few moments, she found his wary mind.

Out of respect, Kivera brushed the chambers of his mind, seeking permission to speak to him. Kivera could feel a deep sigh before he reluctantly allowed her in.

I know it's late, but there's been another body and I interrupted the killer dumping her. You need to bring the team. I can guide you through the forest.

What are we dealing with?

Kivera sent him a mental image of the dead woman. Rage simmered on the other side of the mental bond.

Gods. We'll leave now. Do what you have to do to get us there.

Kivera closed the mental bond to a sliver to keep the communication line open in these treacherous woods to lead him through. Holding her stiff hands out in front of her, she gathered darkness in her palms. A violet orb illuminated the night in a soft glow.

A satisfied smirk touched her lips.

In the next breath, shame flooded Kivera's cheeks as a nagging voice rose in the back of her mind, chastising her blatant arrogance.

Only fools are caught in the pride's web, it said.

Kivera shook off the warning and shoved the orb into the air. Her eyes followed the magic until it was lost in the sea of shadowed leaves, searching for Jexton.

While she waited, she stationed more orbs throughout the trees for muted light to allow the others to see but not to attract the predators of the forest. A knot nestling deep in her chest loosened after each ball of the night sky was created as if unraveling the knot string by string.

Nocturnal eyes watched over Kivera's movements and didn't make any move to disappear, despite her efforts to throw sticks and rocks near their saucer eyes. On multiple occasions, Kivera snarled at predators that sniffed out the victim's death scent prowling through the brush and attempting to break through the ring of trees. She spread her magic around the area to ward off any intrusions.

Kivera couldn't escape the deathly rot woven into the air or spare another heart-wrenching glance from the broken body. At the sight of the collar, Kivera's stomach twisted at the degradation of the human woman. Less than the life once was bright in the world and now snuffed by a cruel hand.

You have a cowardly pit in the center of your chest. You cannot even look at her, a nasty voice sneered in Kivera's mind.

There is no weakness in empathy, Kivera shot back.

A change in the silent woods pricked Kivera's ears. Hoofbeats pounded the earth, and she checked her mental connection to Jexton and relief flooded through her as his mind was near her location.

A flash of purple light burst through the trees, followed swiftly by waves of hoofbeats.

Cloaked riders atop horses broke through the trees in the eastern corner of the clearing in swift pursuit of Kivera's messenger sphere. The animals broke through some of the magical spheres mounted on the perimeter, but the glowing shadows swarmed together to knit back into shape. The riders gathered closer to Kivera on their horses before dismounting.

A familiar shape leaped off her horse and bounced across the grass and enveloped Kivera in a hug. Sea salt and wild grass wrapped around Kivera's nose and she hugged Mavis tighter.

"Are you hurt?" Mavis pulled Kivera at arm's length and scanned the length of Kivera's body. On the way up, she met Kivera's eyes with a relieved expression, followed quickly by annoyance. "You won't like it, but we are talking about how you *spirited* me away."

Kivera winced. "I'm sorry, but you needed to be safe. It was too dangerous for you."

"You could have asked! I could have helped you," But Mavis's voice died off at the end when Kivera shook her head.

"I couldn't even catch her. She was *fast*."

"What happened, Kivera?" Jexton walked up to them, his face partially obscured by his dark hood. His cloak didn't hide the metal at his side gleaming in the moonlight. The team filed in a loose circle around Kivera as she relayed the story, save for Rex, who wandered over to the corpse for a closer inspection.

Once she finished, Tillirius and Syt joined Rex at the body, speaking in soft tones.

Kivera watched Tillirius inspect the corpse's body with surprising gentleness.

"Where did she disappear?" Jexton pulled Kivera's attention back.

A rush of embarrassment flooded through Kivera and straightened her spine.

"The person ran through those bushes." Kivera turned and pointed at the trees on the northwestern edge. "I tailed the scent for a few miles before it went cold. We didn't pass through water, so they most likely used magic."

"By spiriting away, do you mean? What did you do to Mavis?" Jexton peered down at Kivera with a suspicious gleam in his eye. As if he knew Kivera had a secret she kept from him. Which, Kivera supposed, wasn't untrue.

"The same."

"How do we know you didn't do this?" A voice sneered behind Kivera.

Jexton's face reddened at his Second's outright disrespect. On most days, Tillirius ignored Kivera with frigid silence, with only a few snipes towards her. Although, he followed her lessons under the back row's invisibility. This was his first distrustful question in a couple of weeks, and the effect rippled through the group.

Kivera and Jexton opened their mouths when a quiet and cold voice sliced through the air.

"Say one more word against Kivera and I'll make you apologize on your knees." Mavis raised her chin. The whistling breeze halted, the very moisture held still in the air, frozen in fright at the power that boomed through the woods.

Never had she heard that voice from her friend and shock seeped into Kivera's bones. Mavis with a sweet smile and a kind word to offer.

Kivera felt the ripple of Mavis's power against her skin and rallied against the magic caged in her soul. It was near impossible to ignore the seductive purrs that rumbled through her and beckoned to her heart.

Kivera stared at Tillirius, and his whole body slackened with shock at the young female threatening him. His mouth opened in an askew O and he watched Mavis as she returned a withering glare. Something like fear gleamed in his eyes.

Mavis would not stand for any more shit.

"It's okay, really, Mavis," Kivera gripped her friend's arm and pulled her closer but couldn't stop the rising giggle.

"I-I'm sorry. I didn't think it was her." Tillirius held out his hands as if encountering a wild animal snarling at him, but his eyes didn't look any less suspicious when his eyes flickered over to Kivera.

"I was with her the entire night and if you still have a problem, take the issue up with us now, or don't bring it up again." Mavis nearly growled and stared at him down her nose.

Kivera smirked at Tillirius before nudging Mavis. She would need to control her power before alerting anything more treacherous to their location. Mavis's power grew by the day and was forming into a massive well of magic. As an extra precaution, Kivera threw a shield around the area to contain

Mavis's groaning power.

Breathe. Keep your emotions in check. They're human, but not stupid. Kivera knocked on the antechambers of Mavis's mind and a minor flood of relief coursed through her when she allowed Kivera in.

I have an inkling that's not the case for our dear Tillirius. Mavis sniped back in Kivera's mind and Kivera stifled a chuckle.

He is a cranky bastard, but not worth the energy. Reign in your magic and sharpen your focus.

"Kivera, could you trace where the killer went through the magic?" Jexton asked to dissipate the awkward moment.

"If I knew, wouldn't I be there instead?" Jexton rolled his eyes at Kivera's smirk.

"This may be an obvious question, but now there's actual magic in Alceria? Besides from our lovely Kivera," Maserion spoke for the first time and his eyes twinkled with friendliness when his brown eyes landed on Kivera. He pulled back his hood and crossed his lean arms over his chest. A magnificent bow peeked over his shoulder, with knives strapped to his thighs.

"It appears I'm not alone." Though Kivera knew differently, she remained silent. Kivera couldn't share the secrets engraved into the groves of her bones.

"Kivera, how could someone be here with magic and no one knows? Especially you?" Jexton watched Kivera with his sharp eyes as she led the group to the body.

Kivera's stomach roiled at the glint of the collar and manacles, but she pushed one foot in front of the other. She would not faint, or worse, vomit, in front of her colleagues.

"They hid well and will change everything." No one could be in Alceria with magic. Even Kivera stumbling into Alceria was an anomaly. They were hunting for a cold-blooded supernatural murderer to contend against that has been in Alceria for gods-know how long.

Kivera's meal threatened to rise at the thought.

"Why would someone with magic draw attention to

themselves?" Syt murmured as she peered closer to a mark on the body's collarbone. Perhaps the murderer's signature mark.

"Maybe you should ask the Queen Witch," Tillirius grumbled, once again bent over the body for closer inspection. Everyone ignored him.

"Maybe out of desperation?" Arcian offered.

"What are we looking at? Sacrifice? Ritual? Spell?" Jexton knelt beside Tillirius.

"They all have this mark and the collar, so could be ritualistic." Syt pulled down the blanket to reveal the unique mark slashed into pale-blue skin beneath the protruding collarbone.

But Kivera wasn't looking at the mark. Instead, her gaze froze on the collar. Memories demanded her attention, but Kivera batted them away and her knees trembled with the strained effort. Kivera prayed no one was watching her inner turmoil that threatened to burst from her skin. The team continued sharing their questions and observations. Kivera didn't know whether to be relieved or hurt.

"Did any of the others have these same afflictions?" Not even the deep tenor of the captain could yank Kivera out of her reverie.

"It was suggested, but the town's coroner couldn't confirm on the bodies I didn't see myself," Rex nodded.

"Tell him to do another inspection of his notes. How long do you suspect they held her?"

Kivera flicked her eyes up to Jexton's stony face, but the weight of another's eyes burned on her face. She scanned until she met depthless black eyes. Tillirius regarded her coolly and Kivera lifted her chin, defiance flaring in her stomach. But wondered if he watched her skin leach of color or hear her rapid heartbeat on the whistle of the dark wind Kivera created by accident.

After a long moment, Tillirius wrenched his eyes away with a glower and a primal part of Kivera elated at his submission.

"She was a prisoner for weeks," Kivera murmured in a soft voice as she cut off Syt's answer. Silence fell like a heavy blanket on the group. "If not months."

"How do you know?" Arcian spoke as soft as Kivera had spoken with his dark eyes fixed on her.

"You wouldn't put a collar on someone for short-term needs. The continued degradation feeds the sadist's pleasure," Kivera kept her voice steady but didn't raise her voice in fear of emotion breaking through. Mavis grabbed Kivera's icy hand and squeezed. Kivera nearly collapsed on her friend's shoulder.

"What did they do to her?" Maserion's youthful voice cut through the tense silence. No one answered him, but they shared the same conclusion about what this broken and dead female endured.

"Horrible things that we will repay the poor bastard who did this when we find him," Kivera growled with lethal finality.

An unfamiliar sound shattered the air, and the team straightened on alert. Horses were flying across the earth and vibrated the ground beneath Kivera's boots. She threw an uneasy glance at Mavis, who mirrored her concern. Kivera threw a shield around the group and threw her magic towards the oncoming horses. With a lazy slash of Kivera's wrist, a dark wind blew out all the glowing orbs. The group of riders was close, and Kivera chastised herself for the millionth time that night for not remaining focused.

"Assassins or thieves wouldn't announce themselves like this," Jexton grumbled, but still rested a hand on his sword's hilt. The rest of the team created a barrier around the body with hands on their weapons.

"There are half a dozen riders and closing in fast," Kivera announced in a rasp. Shadows crawled up her skin, simultaneously comforting and eager for a fight. Her knuckles ached from her talons, desperate to escape, but she wouldn't release them unless necessary.

"Captain Jexton! Are you out here?" A voice bellowed over the trees and Jexton released a breath while simultaneously groaning.

"Over here, Turnen!" Jexton cupped his hands over his mouth.

"Who is it?" Kivera turned to Jexton and hoped Mavis didn't notice her small step to put her behind Kivera's shoulder.

"The city's Chief of Watchmen. Grumpy bloke but hospitable enough," Jexton answered before he nodded at Maserion. "Light the torches from the saddlebags and search for tracks."

"I'll go with you," Mavis volunteered and gave Kivera a knowing look. Kivera wrapped her magic around Mavis in a warm hug and watched the pair chat animatedly as they walked away.

"You're protective of someone you've only met recently. Or is that what you do normally?" Jexton observed the trees for the guardsmen, but Kivera didn't miss the curious spark in his eyes.

"And?" Kivera shrugged, but the thought nagged her. Never on a whim would she employ anyone to save them from their home troubles.

That's not it and you know it, Lady of Darkness. The voice in Kivera's head sneered, but she knew it was right. The bound magic in her soul recognized Mavis's bulb of magic and she didn't want to be alone in a bare, mortal world.

"I've been wondering if you would be here if it weren't for her," Jexton guessed, and she would not tell him he was wrong. The thought of leaving Mavis with her vile family tore Kivera to shreds.

A deeper part of Kivera wondered if she was led here from a divine entity to the symbol on the corpses with a water-gifted female in tow. Coincidences weren't a possibility any longer.

"I would be here, Jexton." Kivera stared straight ahead, but a corner of her mouth quivered. "You are quite a convincing man."

The trees Kivera was watching burst apart as the small

horde of riders broke through and skidded to a halt. Kivera's counts were correct and who she assumed was the leader of the six riders was a broad pale man with snow-capped hair and whiskers to match, grinned widely.

"What a ruckus you've created, Jexton."

Chief Turnan ambled off his graying horse and his large gut barely crested over the saddle as he landed with a heavy thud.

"I didn't realize we woke you, Turnan." Jexton's lips dipped in a frown that disappeared once the Chief stepped in front of them and they clasped hands.

"You didn't, which is the problem. Next time alert me," Chief Turnan's eyes flashed, and he finally noticed Kivera's presence. His tongue flicked out like a desert lizard to lick his thin lips. Two of the guards remained with the Chief and the rest bypassed to go to the body. Tillirius peeled away to join them.

"Chief Turnan, this is a special investigator of the Alcerian Council, Kivera Galveterre." Jexton introduced the two and the Chief greedily reached for Kivera's hand to his wet lips. She stifled her gags at the touch and was grateful Mavis was away from this man. But she pasted on a fake smile.

"I heard a special investigator was here, but I didn't know she was so beautiful. The pleasure is all mine." The Chief said in what Kivera thought was his purr and he bowed slightly at the waist.

"Thank you, Chief Turnan. I wish we weren't meeting under these circumstances." Kivera couldn't think of a time she would ever want to meet this man. "But we'd love the manpower and men familiar with the terrain."

"Whatever you need, little Kivera." His ale breath slammed into Kivera's nose and her restraint to not vomit on this man's grimy shoes threatened to snap. But she nodded anyway.

A lanky guard to the Chief's left leaned into his ear and distracted the Chief for a moment.

Kivera tracked Mavis and Maserion, chatting quietly on the rim of the trail as they continued to light the torches. A knot loosened in her chest at the sight.

Out of the corner of Kivera's eye, Jexton tapped the side of his temple. Any onlooker would believe him to be rubbing his head, but Kivera knew otherwise.

He's all roses and rainbows, huh? Jexton's smooth voice joked down the bond as Kivera wove between them.

I've smelt horse stalls better than this guy. Kivera was careful not to inch any deeper into Jexton's mind. The other guard didn't pay them any attention rather on his tiptoes, craning his neck for a peek of the body that Kivera blocked with her body.

Dare you to tell him so and I'll buy you a cake at Frantin's. At least that creepy look will be off his face. Jexton and Kivera walked by Frantin's Sweets every morning and she drooled over the display cakes.

I might just leave you with him so I can take Mavis home. Kivera threatened mischievously and her toes curled in her boots as he leaned down. His hot, minty breath washed over her.

You wouldn't dare. But his mouth curved into a crooked smile and Kivera's insides melted into molten lava.

"What's the girl's story?"

Kivera and Jexton whipped their heads to the Chief and found him already watching them. Too immersed in their mental conversation, they didn't notice his attention land on them. Chief Turnan narrowed his eyes and his face was unreadable.

Eager to draw the attention away from their moment, Jexton launched into a summary of the night's events. He twisted the truth about Mavis and Kivera to keep their magic secret.

Kivera inhaled fresh air as he spoke to clear her wild thoughts and scolded herself for the lack of focus. Now she just was embarrassing herself.

He can't keep his eyes off you. Jexton noted through the magic a live wire between them.

Kivera flicked her eyes over to where Mavis and Maserion were nearly finished, lighting the torches and continuing to chat with ease. Kivera strengthened the dark power around Mavis and hid Mavis further in the shadows, despite the torches they were lighting.

I should pull out his eyes with a teaspoon. Jexton stilled at Kivera's words.

That would be a political nightmare on your hands, but I'd hold him down for you. Jexton's words lifted the corners of Kivera's mouth and she bit her lip to prevent a full-blown grin.

"Do you have any leads?" Chief Turnan asked Jexton, but his small eyes slid over to Kivera every so often.

Bugs crawled all over her skin at the visual touch.

"Not yet, sir. But with more evidence we've gathered, we're closer to solving the case." Jexton opened his mouth again, but stopped at the sight of Chief Turnan's face.

His lips thinned. "But no suspect? Not even a lead?" Chief Tunan scoffed, his ears a deep red, and turned his eyes on Kivera. A shade of his earlier affection remained in his eyes. "Even with the help of this so-called 'Special Investigator' that looks about my youngest niece's age, you have yet to solve it and the killer dumped another body on our hands."

The insults were not the first Kivera has received on the job and she didn't bother to react.

"Ms. Galveterre is young, yes, but incredibly gifted. She may be the only person in this city able to stand between the murderer and your niece." All of Jexton's earlier friendliness disappeared, and a man carved out of ice replaced him.

The older man's face blanched and redness crept along his face.

"Yet, we have a dead girl behind you who says differently," Chief Turnan raised a pudgy finger at them. "Ms. Galveterre has been here for how long?"

"She's been here a couple of weeks and I'd suggest

lowering your finger, Chief Turnan" Whether it was the cold fury on Jexton's face or the violence promised in his voice, Chief Turnan lowered his finger, swished his eyes between Kivera and Jexton's before he stormed off with guards in tow.

"You shouldn't have done that," Kivera turned on her heel to look up at Jexton and rested a hand on her hip. "I'm used to old men like him. His treatment isn't new."

"You shouldn't be *used* to behavior like this. No woman should be used to that." Jexton burned her with his steely gaze.

Kivera snorted. "You need to get out more often, Jex. This isn't a new notion to a woman even allowed to work." His tough exterior cracked with a small smile.

"I know, but it's difficult to watch." He laughed at Kivera's pointed look. "Let's go before Turnan becomes too grumpy."

For the next few minutes, Kivera and the team answered questions Chief Turnan and his lanky lieutenant had. Their onslaught of questions pulled at Kivera's eyelids and grated down her bones. Dawn passed hours or days ago, Kivera couldn't remember. After the heavy magic usage and chasing after the killer, Kivera's head and body were done for.

The team prepared to go when a grim coroner and his hefty wagon reached a nearby clearing near to the main path to retrieve the body. Chief Turnan and his guards were to stay and document any other evidence and ensure the body safely traveled to the morgue.

Kivera was grateful for the opportunity to leave and finally be able to close her eyes and be off her feet. She searched for Mavis and Maserion but didn't find them among the trees or by the horses. Panic crackled in Kivera's veins and she released a burst of magic to find Mavis's own magic. There was no sign of Mavis or Maserion anywhere in proximity.

Her legs propelled her forward before Kivera's mind registered their movements. She was in front of Jexton before she could blink. His shadowed face flashed with surprised concern, opening up his mouth, but Kivera didn't give him the chance.

"Mavis is gone." Both magic and Kivera's eyes searched through the woods in case her first round of searching missed her.

"She's with Mase. They're taking care of the torches." Jexton frowned.

"But they're not around here. I've checked." Kivera curled her lip as fear roared in her chest. How stupid did he think she was?

"They shouldn't be far." Jexton glanced around with his own eyes.

"They're not here," Kivera repeated and the chained magic opened an eye. Kivera needed her control in front of the mortals.

"What's going on, Jex?" Attuned to his Captain, Tillirius walked up to them and ignored Kivera entirely.

"Mase and Mavis are gone. Kivera can't track them."

"I sent Mase to escort Mavis back to the city." Tillirius shrugged and glanced over at Kivera, a satisfied glint in his eye, before focusing on Jexton again.

If she wasn't thoroughly panicked, Kivera would have gutted him right there.

"I'll see you in the morning," Kivera looked Jexton in the eye before turning on her heel without bothering a farewell to Chief Turnan, who was speaking to the couple of guards by the body. The rest had ventured into the woods to help the coroner.

Kivera needed to be a safe distance away before she could spirit away and find Mavis. She was past the torch-lit envelope when Kivera realized how quiet the dark forest was. Kivera inhaled the solitude with a deep breath.

Branches snapped in the nearby distance and alarms raised throughout the magic twined in the woods. Talons immediately snapped from her knuckles and she leaned into a defensive stance to face whatever was hunting her.

CHAPTER TWENTY

A low rumble of whispers trickled through the forest, and Kivera slammed a shield around herself. She would not be caught unaware again today. Out of the corner of her eye, three figures strode straight toward her, attempting to be quiet.

Adrenaline seared through Kivera's system as her instincts rose to the surface

Leaves crackled, and one of them swore.

"Oy! That hurt!"

"Shut up or the witch will hear you, idiot."

A growl erupted in Kivera's chest, but she stifled the sound swiftly and retracted her talons.

Witch.

"Where are you, sweet girl?" One of them called and chuckles followed.

"Come out, little dark witch, come out," another lilted in a hushed voice. Another raspy round of chuckles followed.

Kivera risked a look over and saw a guard uniform in the dim night.

Chief Turnan's men? They were supposed to be in the opposite direction from the coroner.

A dark part of Kivera wondered if they waited for an opportunity to catch her alone. She fought the urge to release her talons again but told herself if the opportunity will come with patience.

"Hello?" Kivera transformed her voice into an innocent terrified sound and placed herself in their direct path with a faux stumble.

Kivera decided she had a little time to spare to have some fun.

"Oh, sweetheart, you lost?" The middle one asked within a dozen yards away.

"I'm afraid I can't find the path to the city. I'm lost," Kivera relieved a shade of the glamor covering her eyes and allowed them to illuminate in the darkness. The effect was obvious on their transfixed faces.

"We can take you there, doll." The stubby man on the right grinned a gap-toothed smile and Kivera pasted on a relieved smile. They circled her like hyenas and led her deeper into the forest and she noted in the wrong direction of the path.

"You shouldn't be walking out in the forest alone, sugar." Up close, strong ale reeked on his body and a deep flush was apparent in the moonlight on the guard's cheeks.

"I was so tired and I didn't want to bother anyone while they were working *so* hard, so I started walking back," Kivera laid the dramatics thick with her sigh as if she were an utter idiot.

Let the hyenas be fooled by the leopard in antelope's skin.

"What a shame. We're glad to be of assistance." The middle guard wore a lupine smile.

Too soon the guards pressed too tight, and the casual touches were too often and their eyes glazed over. Kivera's patience wore thin, and the magic coiled tight around her heart ached with a war cry to be released.

"But there is a small fee for us getting you to the city," Stubby grinned.

"Oh, I don't have any coins on my hip. I'm sorry. I wish there was something I-" Kivera wore a mask of worry and fear as she pretended to search her pockets.

"Don't worry, little Kivera, there is," Tall Oaf matched Stubby's grin.

Kivera didn't know who grabbed her coat first, and

she yanked the coattails out of their hands. "Stop that right now." Kivera faked a shrill voice and attempted to run. Hands grabbed her before she could escape and they threw her against a tree. The back of her head slammed into the tree trunk and stars filled her vision.

Kivera swore to the gods she would spill the guts of these men as she scrambled to her feet, using the tree's support. The tips of her talons grated against the bark and she retracted them before her harassers caught sight of them.

The men descended upon Kivera once more, sneering at her.

Tall Oaf licked his lips. "I wonder how a witch tongue will feel on my-"

"Fellas, what's the problem here?" A voice in the darkness snapped them to attention.

Familiar to Kivera, yet unnervingly misplaced.

A liquid shadow walked forward and crossed arms over their massive chest.

Tillirius glared down at each of the guards, cold fury clear on his features.

"We were taking Ms. Kivera safely to the city, sir." Tall Oaf couldn't say the words fast enough.

"Were you?" The guards nodded in Tillirius's face and he chuckled. A sound that skittered across Kivera's skin. "It looked like to me she was about to flay you alive and pick her teeth with the shards of your foolish bones."

"Sir, nothing happened!" Each of the guards cried out similarly and whipped their heads back and forth.

But they didn't look at Kivera until her exhaustion wore thin and she pulled her lips back in a wolfish grin and slid the talons free.

The guards' faces made the entire ordeal worthwhile when they realized fully the predator before them. She lunged forward to swipe a talon across Stubby's forearm. Kivera admired the dark copper on the talon and flicked her tongue out to taste the blood, locking eyes with him the whole time.

A deep growl of animal satisfaction reverberated from Kivera's chest, and their faces paled even further.

Kivera waved Tillirius away. "This is a bad time, Tilly. Come back in an hour." Kivera played into Tillirius's game and wove shadows around her tighter and let the men see the nightmares under her glamoured mask.

Kivera savored every second that pulsed with their fear. She flicked her eyes over the guards' shoulders to catch Tillirius's reaction, and he seemed as pleased as her. His dark eyes met her own and for a moment held her gaze with an appreciative flash before shuttering.

Rage exploded from Kivera's heart and a snarl gnashed her teeth. She narrowed her eyes at Tillirius and didn't bother to watch Chief Tunan's guards flee. Kivera marked their faces and would repay this night.

"Don't look at me like that again or I'll pluck out your eyes."

"What happened here?" Tillirius scrubbed his face.

Kivera snorted. "Like you care." She was adjusting her coat when Tillirius perched himself against a tree to wait for her answer. She sighed and walked to the tree next to him to lean against the uncomfortable bark. "You know what they were going to do and what was going to happen. You're not dumb."

"I figured as much." A shadow passed over his eyes but was gone in a heartbeat. "You looked like you were about to have those bastards for a meal."

"It feeds my evil witchcraft powers." Kivera bared her teeth at Tillirius's nauseated expression. She needed to get to the town and make sure Mavis was safe. Then stuff a chocolate scone the size of her face into her mouth.

"You're kidding."

"You'll only have to find out." But Kivera rolled her eyes. Silly, gullible mortals. She would rather be anywhere but here with Tillirius. The man who caused this shitty night. "I'm going now. Run back to Jexton like a good little pup."

"You sure you don't need a *little pup* to go back with you to the city?" Tillirius cocked his head and frowned at her.

"I don't need a man to watch over me from some moral obligation or to *rescue* me like a damsel." Kivera clenched her hands and shadows crawled closer to her and wove themselves into her body. She knew how to care for herself. Years alone in a foreign world hardens one.

"I could hardly rescue you. I was saving those idiots from their deaths," He huffed and furrowed his brows.

Kivera blinked, her only sign of surprise.

"Why?" Kivera regretted the question before the words spilled out of her lips from the way Tillirius's eyes darkened.

"Anyone could guess what would have happened if you were any other girl." He clenched his jaw. "I should have let you tear them apart and keep on walking by and whistling the entire time. But my feet pulled me here instead."

Tillirius's honesty silenced Kivera.

"This would have been a mess for Jexton." He said to himself, but he sounded unconvinced.

"Next time, I'll maim other guards to avoid any trouble. But right now, I need to find out where Mavis is." Kivera pushed off from the tree and walked away without a farewell. Shadows cascaded around her body to prepare for use.

"Check your room first. She was ragged," Tillirius called out, and she didn't look behind her before spiriting to her room.

Where Mavis snored softly under the covers.

CHAPTER TWENTY-ONE

The moonlight rippled across the lake like pearls and onyx diamonds. Mountains slumbered in deep sleep behind the trees beyond the shoreline. A soft breeze whisked along the water before biting the fisherman's ears. The cold was worth not being home listening to his wife's constant yammering. He preferred the solitude of a full moon and a fishing line over most conversations. His wife's especially. He could cast out at a new fishing hole all the men shopping with their wives from the market whispered excitedly about this week. There were great talks in between the salt vendor and butcher's shop about recent bountiful catches worth a pretty coin.

Maybe he could catch enough fish to leave town and the wretch at home. The thought propelled him to cast the line with the best bait he bought from the market.

The lake bubbled the moment bait touched the water. The bubbles started small, then grew into palm-sized bubbles before they disappeared entirely.

The fisherman breathed a sigh of relief, peering at the jug of ale he brought and attached it back on his horse.

"Bad batch," he grumbled.

Splashes from the lake drew the fisherman's attention back to the water.

What he witnessed shook his knees.

Three heads bobbed in the water and floated to the beach until massive bodies walked out of the water. They were the largest men the fisherman had ever seen, with wicked weapons glinting at their hips. He fled to nearby bushes, but his horse barreled through the forest and left him behind.

He watched them through the shrubbery walk past his fishing spot on the shore without a glance to it and murmured in soft, musical voices. They neared his hideout after following his exact footsteps and he ducked beneath the leaves, trying to hold his breath.

A deep voice spoke to his companions in a foreign language. One he's never heard at any of the various ports he's traveled to around the continent.

Another grunted his answer in the same strange language.

The third answered in a voice of the coldest night that sent the fisherman into a fit of shivers and the leaves that nestled around him trembled.

Out of foolishness or dire curiosity, the fisherman quaking in his loafers, risked a peek over the bushes to glance at the men walking near his hideout. Their enormous bodies bore strange clothes and moved with unnatural fluidity. Two were identical in huge brutish stature and all golden looks and the other of silver, but all had the striking similarity of pointed ears and harsh features.

The gruff voice grumbled once more and their steps disappeared through the trees.

The fisherman's mind went wild with the sight. He would have thought anyone that spoke of men with pointed ears walking out of the middle of the lake would be mad had he not witnessed it himself.

He waited until the branches rustled with creatures went silent again and he crept out of the woods on silent feet before breaking into a sprint in the opposite direction to his home so he could tell his wife.

Tensions rose between Kivera and the rest of the city's

guards after that night with Chief Turnan's guards. Kivera struggled to tell Jexton what happened, and he didn't ask why the Chief went to no end to make the investigation harder and over the next couple of days, Chief Turnan insisted on attending all of their meetings and didn't allow Kivera a moment to speak. She left meetings fuming, vowing to slit out his tongue, but Mavis always cooled her down until the next round of Chief Turnan's interference.

Multiple times, Kivera had to snarl off some guards that picked a fight with her or with a member of the team. The confrontations irritated her to no end, but Mavis made her laugh within minutes and loosened the tension in the back of Kivera's neck. Multiple times throughout the day, Kivera found a guard following them. She would pull Mavis down an abandoned alley and spirit away when out of sight to a safe place. Kivera told Jexton about the incidents, but he patted her on the arm and assured her he would talk to him. Whether he did, Chief Turnan's efforts didn't lighten up.

Once or twice, she caught Tall Oaf or Stubby following her or passed by at the station. Kivera would flash them a wicked grin and they would scurry away.

On top of the annoyance with the city's guards, the case was no closer to being solved. She pored through books regarding the engraved symbol with nothing to come of the endless research. Despite the hunt for the mark engraved in her memory, Kivera found nothing.

Once they saw the collar, it threw the entire team into an angry frenzy, going over every detail with a fine-tooth comb. Physical proof of the treatment and imprisonment ripped everyone apart.

Training sessions were further apart but lengthier with more aggressive techniques. The team fought with the image of the broken, collared girl branded their minds. Tillirius and Kivera never spent a moment alone again a couple of weeks after the incident and he barely glanced at her when they were in the same room.

But Kivera couldn't forget his expression when she terrified the guards, nor forget the appreciative gleam in their dark depths.

She couldn't forget the way her stomach pinched at the look, either.

Kivera loathed Tillirius even more.

The entire team and Mavis were in the training room following Arcian's instructions. Kivera lounged sideways in a plush armchair in the room's corner and held a book about beasts from legends in her lap. The lore of forgotten and vicious creatures always intrigued her imagination.

A sharp cry from the mat pulled Kivera's attention from a beautiful depiction of a winged lion. Syt's slim arms pinned Mavis to the mat and she let out a loud groan.

"I won't beat anyone. I'm too weak," Mavis grumbled.

Syt hopped to her feet and extended a hand and smiled at Mavis. "You will. With practice, you will knock down anyone."

"That's her nice way of saying you'll get the snot kicked out of you lots before you're any good." Maserion hopped up to them and placed an arm around Syt's shoulders, a playful smirk on his lips.

Syt's elbow flashed out to jab his ribs, but she smiled up at Maserion anyway.

Kivera stifled her smile.

"Syt's right and learned to get the snot kicked out of her just as you did, boy." Arcian stepped up behind them and crossed his arms. His voice was stern but a ghost of a smile danced on his lips as he looked down at the trio.

Maserion laughed, his cheeks reddened to apples.

"Wait for the fight that leaves you coughing blood and broken teeth. Near dead alone in the mud and rain." Kivera mused in a non-flippant manner as she dragged a finger down the majestic mane of the winged lion and traced its gold etches. "Those build character."

"Who was this mentor of yours again?" Arcian scratched

his jaw.

"One who builds character, obviously," Maserion sniped under his breath. Quiet enough Kivera barely heard the retort with her heightened hearing. Syt jabbed him again in the ribs.

"You don't get to sit over here," Kivera swiveled her finger to show her reading space, "by no effort. Syt's right, though, you'll love seeing your own snot," Kivera met Mavis's eyes and nodded.

"Oh, shut up, grumps." Kivera shot her head up to the source of the too-sweet voice and Mavis flashed her a feline smile.

Kivera was about to shoot back a retort when the doors burst open. Jexton strode through the doorway and his face flushed with anger, with Tillirius hot on his heels.

"Jex, what's-" Kivera sat up.

"There's been another body found, close to the eighth." Jexton seethed as he strode for the weapons closet in the back of the room. He methodically strapped various daggers and twin swords to his back. "Turnan's men just told me when I walked through the doors."

Kivera growled and wasn't the only one to cry out. There was a grumble or a scoff from the others.

"No one notified us." Arcian followed his captain's movements and strapped weapons to his body. The rest of the team did the same.

"We need to get there first before we make any other mistakes," Jexton rose tall and looked them all in the eye. "This is the last one. The last victim."

His steely eyes rested on Kivera's as he spoke the last words, softening slightly. Kivera's cheeks heated, and he looked away before she could say anything.

The team nodded at their leader's words, Mavis included with a grim expression on her face.

"Let's hurry." Jexton nodded at them once more before he strode out the doors, a walking storm that left them all scrambling to follow.

After returning a few hours after sundown from the crime scene, Kivera and Mavis skipped the late-night meal with the team in favor of desserts and sweets in bed. The day drained every dreg of energy either of them had.

Not to mention sucking out all the emotional heartaches.

They splayed the ninth victim out as the others, but without the collar or manacles. Bruising around the victim's wrists and the sides of her neck suggested she had been in both before death, but Kivera was grateful not to see the metal restraints.

As with the others, there was no evidence, no scent, no suspect.

The case needed to be solved soon, Kivera thought as she and Mavis strode through the front doors into the stuffy inn after another late night. Almost a month and a half since they've been here, and they were no closer to figuring out who the killer was. Kivera wrangled with her rising frustration daily at still being in Oakheart.

Not bothering with the immersed innkeeper in her book, the two continued on.

"Oy!" the innkeeper called out and gestured with an arthritic wrist. They shared a look before stopping at her desk. "For you."

The innkeeper's withered hand handed over an envelope and her sunken eyes scanned Kivera up and down before returning to her book with a harrumph.

Kivera viewed the envelope, and shock fluttered through her system at the blue seal on the front.

The Arcerian Royal Seal.

"I'm not a mail service," the innkeeper smarted into her book.

Kivera grunted at the old woman as she stared unblinking at the seal.

Mavis stared around Kivera's shoulder. "What is it?" She jumped on the pads of her feet as they left the innkeeper to her book without another word.

"If I had the power to look through the paper, I'd tell you," In a near savage motion, she ripped the seal off the envelope. Tearing the turquoise wax in half.

On a gray paper, her name was beautifully scripted and the words below it summoned her presence for a meeting with the Royal Council. Short and with no room for rejection. But it was the other paper behind it on silver and cream paper that worried her the most. An invitation to the Winter Solstice Ball a few days from then.

"A ball?!" Mavis squealed, jumping as she clapped her hands, but Kivera groaned.

They were going to the ball.

CHAPTER TWENTY-TWO

The back road drove Kivera and their caravan southwest to the capital. The mountains watched their backs with ominous eyes. Kivera glared at the waning sunshine as purple clouds enclosed the skies. A brisk wind stirred her hair, so she sent a magic shield around Mavis and herself to block out the cold. Within minutes, a storm descended on their traveling party. An onslaught of torrential rain slammed into their party as they pounded through rolling hills, the coverage of the forest long behind them.

But Kivera was ready.

"Stay close!" She shouted over the slap of the wind and delved deep into the magic and threw a shield of darkness over their heads. The rain didn't dagger Kivera's face, and she threw a quick look over her shoulder. They formed a diamond, with Mavis in the center and Tillirius covering the rear. Much to Jexton's chagrin, the rest of the team stayed behind to continue the investigation and keep the trip to the capital as swift as possible when he received his own invitation for the council meeting.

Kivera led at a brutal pace and stopped only for quick bathroom breaks. The clouds darkened into angrier, purple-black shades. The rain froze into sheets of snow and an enraged wind tore through Kivera's heavy coat. She widened the dark shield to cover their flanks, but her magic couldn't save them from the biting cold. But she didn't allow the pace to slow.

Hours passed in that miserable state until the snow passed, but thick clouds remained. Kivera's stomach grumbled as the last flurries grazed her cheeks. Her breathing was haggard from the excessive magic use and it flayed her energy thin.

She spotted an oak with overflowing branches and a dry patch of ground beneath it. Kivera slowed her horse to a trot and nudged her to the tree. She didn't look back to see if the others followed and only focused on staying astride the panting horse's back. Under the safety of the tree's cover, Kivera slid off and stumbled to the ground. Her knees slammed into the frozen ground and her body slumped over.

"Kivera!" a voice called out. Seconds later, a hand touched Kivera's shoulder, her face, and Kivera opened her eyes to Mavis's concerned eyes.

"Sorry, sorry," Kivera rasped through chapped lips. Gods, her body hurt all over. "A little tired, is all. I just need a moment to rest."

"You don't say." Mavis frowned down at her. "Did you use too much magic?"

Kivera only mumbled an unintelligible reply.

"Will she be okay?" Jexton's voice asked with equal concern nearby.

"She needs to rest and eat," Mavis answered.

Kivera wanted to snap at them to not speak of her as if she weren't present but couldn't manage more than her lips scratching against each other.

"We'll rest here for an hour so we can arrive at Tymern before dark," Jexton told them, and Kivera heard him rummage through his pack. A few moments later, a heavy blanket was laid on her body. She didn't realize she had been shivering until the blanket trembled.

"It's too cold for a fire, so we'll have to sit close to each other and the horses." Tillirius sounded far away.

Kivera must have dozed off because her eyes snapped

open to Jexton, Tillirius, and Mavis huddled close together eating bread and apples. The horses lay in a circle around them and Kivera was grateful for their body heat against the chill tightening her bones. She pushed up to her elbows with a deep, unladylike groan. Her entire body ached in protest and tilted the world on its axis.

"Steady there," Mavis gripped under Kivera's arm and eased her against her horse's body. Mavis passed her a loaf half and a water flask. Kivera devoured the bread in a few bites and guzzled the water. Mavis refilled each and Kivera smiled gratefully.

"Are you feeling better?" Jexton asked to Kivera's left, and she slid her eyes over. He didn't appear any better than how she felt with windswept hair and frosted skin. Next to him, Tillirius appeared even worse from his position in the back as he savaged apart his loaf.

"I didn't protect myself properly, but I'll be okay soon," Kivera rasped around a mouthful. For the first time in a long time, the magic was panting on the hard ground of its cage. If she wasn't exhausted, Kivera would smile.

Jexton smiled. "Well, good. For a moment there, you had us worried."

Tillirius rolled his eyes and bit into his bread.

"Falling off one's horse is a terrible entrance." Somehow, Kivera's mouth pulled into a smirk.

"Not too graceful." Jexton's mouth twitched. "We think we're about a half a day's ride to Tymern. Even less with pleasant weather."

"Gods, do I wish this was done with," Tillirius muttered under his breath.

"No one more than I," Kivera narrowed her eyes at him and Mavis covered up a laugh with a cough behind her hand. Exhaustion shuttered Kivera's eyelids, and she welcomed the darkness once more.

A hard shove to Kivera's shoulder woke her out of a restful sleep. Her eyes sprang open to Tillirius's scowl. Jexton and Mavis were gone, their horses absent as well.

"I was going to wake her up, Tilly," Mavis hissed from somewhere behind Kivera.

Kivera bared her teeth at Tillirius and rose to unsteady feet with the blanket clutched to her chest. Kivera's mare unbuckled its lean legs and stood to full height. She waited until the mare shook out its coat before she approached.

"Thank you for your strength and speed." Kivera raised a gloved hand to rub the horse's cheeks. While the others readied their horses for the last half of the journey, Kivera evaluated her own body. Magic reserves were low, muscles sore from clenching too long against the frosty weather, and her lower body screamed at her for not choosing to use a saddle.

"How do you feel?" Mavis walked around Kivera's horse to stand next to her.

"Tired and aching," Kivera inspected her friend. Mavis's braids were nearly pulled out across frosty cheeks, but her blue eye was bright. Rain soaked both of their outfits and Mavis retrieved thick, dry sweaters and coats from her pack. They hurriedly changed while Jexton and Tillirius were occupied. Kivera stifled a moan at the dry clothes and Mavis appeared to feel the same.

"Thank you, Kivera. The men will be jealous. They look like drowned rats," Mavis snickered.

A grin tugged Kivera's mouth and she winked. "And smell like one. We did all the work! They did nothing but stay astride a horse, so it's not our fault if they don't pack extra riding clothes."

"We are certainly inferior to you and deserve nothing more." Jexton's voice came behind Kivera and she turned to his sardonic grin. A drowned rat indeed. Jexton's mouth hung open crookedly for a brief second as he stared at her. At her mouth, Kivera realized as she traced his eyesight and heat crept up her neck.

"It's good you accepted it sooner rather than live in denial," the corner of Kivera's mouth curled up.

The frozen air heated into a heart-hammering tension as Kivera and Jexton stared at each other.

Mavis coughed. "Let's try to leave soon," Mavis turned away to her horse and waved a hand behind her.

"How are you feeling?" Jexton leaned over to pat the mare's face and neck. Each step brought him closer to Kivera. Scent of snow and rich soil clung to his overcoat and Kivera breathed in deep. Gods, his scent was intoxicating.

"The ride hurt my ass but will be worth the trouble when I'm back in my bed tonight," Kivera lifted a shoulder.

"Well-deserved reward," Jexton chuckled, and Kivera's stomach did a few flips. "Thank you for taking care of all of us. You didn't look too good when we stopped." His eyes darkened and concern crinkled the edges of his eyes.

Kivera laid a hand on his upper arm and smiled up at him. "I feel bruised and slightly embarrassed, but otherwise I feel fine," She shook her head and some hair stuck to the side of her cheek. But she wasn't lying to him. After using nearly all the magic in her core, she felt loads lighter.

"Want to know a secret?" He peered around before he whispered loudly. "Tillirius has been beside himself because he has to stay in your home."

She laughed. "Poor Tillirius." Jexton smiled and Kivera looked up at him under her lashes. Jexton's laugh died off. "How do you feel staying at my cottage?"

Lightning crackled in the air between them. Jexton searched her eyes before he leaned in and cinnamon washed over Kivera. His sensual lips tugged into a crooked grin and Kivera nearly spirited them away so she could explore those lips herself.

"I am beside myself, Kivera."

"Jexton! You ready?" Tillirius shouted from a distance and Kivera was grateful for her horse's body shielding her flaming cheeks from the lieutenant.

"Yes, give me a minute!" Jexton called back, his eyes never leaving her face. "Don't exhaust yourself the rest of the way. We men *can* handle escorting you." He walked back to his horse and a smile replaced the melting grin from moments before.

With a final wink, he disappeared behind his horse before Kivera registered his words. A moment later, silent laughter racked her body.

CHAPTER TWENTY-THREE

The moon arced high over Kivera's head when they galloped over the crest of the final hill above the capital. Stars sprawled the ebony depths of the sky and their familiar designs welcomed Kivera like an old friend. Moonlight glimmered along the deep emerald rolling hills along the coastline. Huge, wooden farmhouses spotted the expanse of land, animals slept in dark heaps in the fenced grass.

But it wasn't the glow of the city or the lively music that wafted to her heightened ears that caused her heartbeat to skip.

It was the endless sea covering the horizon. Viciously black with tendrils of pearlescent moonlight snaking along the ocean's surface.

"I've never seen so much water." Mavis slowed to a trot next to Kivera, her face awestruck.

Kivera peered over her shoulder to find Jexton and Tillirius surveying the woods but their gazes snagged on the view ahead of them every few seconds.

"This is the Meriake Sea. Legend goes, sea monsters and sirens sunk hundreds of ships to the bottom of the bay," Kivera waggled her brows at Mavis. With the edge of her boot, Kivera nudged her horse into an easy trot and Mavis kept beside her.

Another pair of horses followed in their wake and Kivera couldn't distinguish Jexton and Tillirius's conversation.

Mavis slid into place next to Kivera. "Do you think the

legends are true?"

Kivera's mouth twitched. "There are an awful number of ship wreckage at the sea floor. The capital was built in record time reportedly from the creatures but whoever really knows."

Silence enveloped the females. Kivera veered them off the path to the outskirts of the city walls and straight for the echoes of crashing waves. The hills steepened into a rocky cliff and Kivera slowed their pace.

A sliver of a trail zigzagged down the rocks enough space for a single file line.

The city wall was not any better, curved around Tymern from one end of the rounded harbor to the other horn. Bleached to the color of stale bread from the harsh sun and a massive gate was built at the center of the wall armed with City Watch with the royal emblem above the opening, an eagle dripping in blood clutching swords in its talons. A stone bridge covered the length of the gap between the cliffs and the iron gate.

An ugly design, in Kivera's humble opinion, but the waste didn't come out of her coppers.

Mavis stared silently at the ocean but even in the dark, color bloomed on her pale cheeks.

Kivera cleared her throat. "What do you think?"

"It's beautiful and daunting," Mavis murmured so low, Kivera almost missed her answer.

"We can go tomorrow after the meeting. What do you say?"

"That would be fun." Mavis beamed as bright as the moon above. "Afterwards, we can go dress shopping!"

Kivera laughed despite the wretched plan. She despised shopping but would go along for Mavis.

"Isn't the gate the other way?" Jexton called behind them.

"I'm taking a shortcut to my flat. Going through the capital would take too long." Kivera said over her shoulder. Once they made it to level ground, Kivera nudged her horse into a gallop and the others fell behind. They were half a mile from the looming city wall, running parallel to its massive height and approaching the eastern gate. Grass thinned to thick sand and a saltwater breeze curled around Kivera's nose. A black shape interrupted the smooth wall surface and a sliver of exposed beach winked at the end of the wall.

They neared the black archway and halted in front of the iron grate. Between the metal squares, forms moved in the shadows. Two guards, not much older than Jexton, poked their heads through the grate.

"What do you want at this hour?" The voice was familiar to Kivera, but he didn't recognize Kivera in her dark cloak in the darkness with his human eyes.

She prodded forward and removed her hood to show her face under the full moon. "Hello, Huron. This is Kivera Galveterre. I apologize for the late hour."

Huron's face pushed further through the grate to inspect closer. His grin flashed in the light. "It's good to see you again, Kivera. You've been gone awhile this time. Who's with you?"

"Friends and an oaf from my current case. We're headed to my place. You?"

"A fresh face from the academy. Better than the cranky bastard from before." Huron joked before their forms stepped back and seconds later, the gate lifted with an ear-splitting screech.

Kivera started forward and waved at Huron and the other guard leaning against the wall. The thick walls were damp with humidity and seawater and she didn't know how anyone could stand the stench more than passing through.

"Have a good night," Huron called after Kivera when the four horses walked through. Kivera waved her hand but didn't turn around.

"Almost there," Kivera nudged her mare into a swift pace and kicked up sand as she flew across the beach. Waves crested to her left, and the cliffs staggered above her on the right. The bone-white cliff faces dipped into smooth terrain as homes sprouted down the land. Illumination from the capital bloomed ahead, but Kivera slowed at a modest home settled in the hill's curve facing the ocean.

Kivera's home.

"Your house is right on the beach?" Mavis asked, her eyebrows having disappeared in her hairline. She clustered close to the men.

Kivera stuck out her tongue. "I told you."

Mavis shook her head.

"It's not that bad," Jexton commented.

Kivera frowned. "Not that bad?" Out of everyone, she was must nervous about what he would think.

"Not what I was expecting, is all. Your home is pretty."

"I was expecting a cemetery and gargoyles out front," Tillirius grumbled.

Kivera snickered under the safety of her hood and swung her leg around the horse's body, landing with a soft thud. "Sorry to disappoint. I'll ask Masga to set some out in the morning."

The others dismounted and Kivera had to shake off the sand from her boots after Jexton's hard landing.

"Masga?" Tillirius asked from Kivera's left as she unstrapped packs from her horse.

Kivera stepped over to help Mavis. "You'll meet her in the morning. She lives here to watch over the house while I'm on assignment."

"You've shared so much about her. I can't wait," Mavis smiled and shouldered her pack.

The group walked the horses to the side of Kivera's house, where they were tied to posts on the side of the house.

"They'll be fine here for the night. Masga will enjoy meeting them in the morning." Kivera waved them to the side door that led inside. She dug through her pockets to pull out a brass key and unlocked the door.

The heat of the fireplace and the scent of cloves welcomed Kivera home.

"Masga?" Kivera whispered into the dark and held open the door for the others to walk through. A couple of candles burned on the table to the door's right, allowing some visibility. An open kitchen with cheery yellow cabinets and tiled countertops to the left. Soft snores halted at the whispers.

"Kivera?" a weak, familiar voice garbled close by. Masga.

"Yes, it's me and some visitors. Sleep, old woman." Kivera answered Masga and turned to the others cloistered around the table. "Bathroom and bedrooms are straight ahead. Formal tour in the morning."

Jexton and Tillirius ambled down the hallway with their bags thrown over their shoulders without another word.

"Do you want your room or stay in mine?" Kivera murmured softly to Mavis as they followed the men through the dining area and past the moonlit living room on the right.

A body, Masga, lounged on the long couch that faced wide windows. Soft snoring resumed under the mass of blankets.

Kivera tapped Jexton's shoulder and pointed to doors on the left and the men entered without a word.

"Yours if okay with you," Mavis whispered back to Kivera, and they continued toward a door at the end of the hallway.

Kivera opened the door to a pitch black room and ushered Mavis through the door. She fumbled around for a candle until she found one on top of a table. A stone and flint lay next to it and Kivera rubbed them together until sparks lit the candle. Kivera circled the room, and the attached bathroom to light candles.

Mavis dropped her pack on the floor. "Your room."

Kivera's room was nothing much, in her opinion. A simple vanity table and mirror on the far wall with a chest of drawers beside it. A bronze gilded mirror leaned up against the wall next to the bathroom door. Her massive four-poster bed occupied most of the room but didn't compare to the overwhelming mass of haphazardly stacked papers on nearly every surface of the room.

Kivera shrugged. "I use it as a closet and extra room for my work."

"Do you sleep upside down in the attic, then?" Mavis snorted.

Kivera scowled. "No, dork. Usually on the couch."

Mavis's feet were planted on the spot as she gaped at Kivera's room. Kivera realized with a start that her room easily tripled the size of Mavis's room back at her mother's hovel.

Kivera gave her friend a warm smile. "You'll like the rest of the place."

Mavis walked to the side of the bed and dropped her bag next to the nightstand. She pulled out night clothes from her bag, once Kivera's that were too small for her now, and meandered to the dim bathroom.

"Holy gods," Mavis exclaimed and Kivera winced. She couldn't remember if it was a mess or not.

Kivera threw her bag on the bed and strode into the bathroom. "Sorry if it's messy. I should have-" She found Mavis staring at the massive tub occupying most of the room, easily able to fit three people without their shoulders touching.

"You have a pool next to your toilet," Mavis said from a distant place in her mind.

Kivera frowned but summoned magic. The faucet twisted and scalding water poured from the spout from the water basin heated by coals from her magic underneath the tub.

Kivera opened cabinets beneath the sink for a basket she used for bath items. Her long fingers plucked out oils, salts, and scrubs to set on the mantle at the tub's lip. Methodically, Kivera dispensed fragrant oils and salts and set aside a cloth next to the scrubs.

Mavis remained quiet the entire time. The silence grated Kivera's nerves.

"If you're mad about the house, I'm sorry but I can't help what I do. I'd just rather not live in the castle," The words rushed out of Kivera's mouth in a bursting geyser. "I can't bear your silence, Mavis."

Finally, Mavis tore her eyes away from the tub. Her blind eye seemed duller in the candlelight while her blue eye was bright.

A whisper of a smile brushed against Mavis's lips. "I couldn't be upset about the life you've earned for yourself, Kivera." She lowered her eyes. "I don't want to put my dirt on the pretty surface."

Kivera reached over to grab Mavis's hand. "Dirt is more appreciated than the stuff between Masga's toes." The corner of Kivera's mouth quivered when Mavis huffed a chuckle, achieving the desired reaction.

"Okay, fine, you're right," Mavis rolled her shoulders. "It's just a tub."

"I'll leave you to it," Kivera left the doorway, pulling the door shut as she said "Shout if you need anything," and the door clicked shut.

Breathing in the familiar clutter and enormous bed Kivera surveyed the comforts of her room. Gods, she missed her room.

Kivera changed into a soft nightgown that hugged her skin. In the morning, she would bathe after a run. Sleep called to her now in deep reverberations through her bones.

With light steps, Kivera was out the door and heading for the kitchen, food for bed on her mind.

A warm body slammed into hers before she made it out of the hallway. Hands grabbed Kivera's waist to prevent her from falling.

"Ow!" Kivera called out in hushed tones.

Jexton grinned down at her, his eyes dancing with amusement. "You should probably be more careful."

Kivera was aware of his hands at her hips and she cleared her throat before taking a step back. Fire licked up her spine and goosebumps spread across her skin. She hoped the darkness covered the blush on her cheeks.

"I hope the two of you are comfortable." Kivera tried amicably but sounded out of breath.

His smile widened. "We are more than accommodated, thank you."

Before she knew to stop, Kivera wore a matching idiotic grin. She maneuvered around his body and strode to the kitchen. She plucked cookies out of the cabinets Kivera hid from Masga's bloodhound nose.

Jexton studied her with predatory focus and she focused on not sparing him a look. Her willpower would disintegrate from the fire barely contained in his eyes.

Kivera stepped on her tiptoes to reach the cabinet next to the sink for two glasses and her nightgown traveled up to the tops of her thighs. When she set them down and swiveled slowly on the pads of her feet to face Jexton. His eyes were transfixed on the length of her legs with a clenched jaw.

Heat filled the room, tingling Kivera's skin. She forced her eyes on the glasses and what she was doing.

"Jexton?"

"Hmm?"

"Why do you think the Alcerian Council summoned us?" The question was eating away at Kivera. The council never summoned her like this before.

Jexton turned away. "Perhaps they're receiving pressure from the king?"

Kivera shook her head. "The king cares more for his wine and young servant girls than the wellbeing of the kingdom."

"There's nothing to worry about, Kivera. They are a bunch of fussy, old men." He walked over to lean against the countertop within the breathing space of her.

Kivera blew out air. "You're probably right."

"I usually am. You've just never noticed before," Jexton leaned down, close enough for Kivera to smell horse and raindrops on his skin. Flutters tickled along Kivera's ribcage and spine.

"Never noticed you?" Kivera fluttered her lashes and bit

her lip. His eyes followed her with razor focus and he lifted a hand to brush a strand of hair from her cheek. "Impossible."

A riotous snore struck them like lightning and the two jumped apart, both panting.

A nervous laugh bubbled up from Kivera's chest and she scrambled to the cool safety of the sink. She pulled glasses closer to fill them, grateful for the precious seconds to cool off her flushed skin. Every few seconds she peeked through her hair over her shoulder to find Jexton watching her with a hungry gleam. But thankfully he remained on the other side of the kitchen. Kivera would burst into flame if he touched her. "I should get to bed. Dawn is in a few hours."

"A good idea." Kivera summoned a dark wind to carry snacks and water glasses as she walked down the hallway.

"Running in the morning?" Jexton matched her strides.

"Perhaps a light stroll on the beach. My legs won't forgive me if I go any harder." She winced and stopped by his door.

"This is me." He didn't move toward the door, instead leaned down close to Kivera's face. "Have sweet dreams, Kivera."

His scent washed over Kivera, and she almost combusted into a puddle.

"Good night, Jexton." Feeling brazen, or deliriously exhausted, Kivera reached up on tiptoes to run fingers through his hair. Kivera kissed the top of his cheekbone near his temple. She pulled back enough to look into Jexton's eyes, a question of her own.

Jexton's breath halted and his hazel eyes turned molten. His eyelids drooped low and his lips parted.

"Jexton?" Tillirius called from the other side of the door and it swung wide open.

Jexton shied away from Kivera and she stumbled backward but not before catching an expression of horror on Tillirius's face. It smoothed over in the next blink.

"I see." Tilly sneered.

"Enough," Jexton didn't spare a glance to Kivera before

he disappeared into the room, his face red as beets.

Alone in the dark hallway with Tillirius, Kivera adjusted the straps to her nightgown and realized how much skin was exposed and she crossed her arms.

"I was getting snacks," Kivera defended and backed away in small steps.

"Will you say goodnight to me like that?" The sneer deepened.

A growl rumbled in Kivera's chest and she threw a ball of darkness at his face. Tillirius grunted as it slammed into his face. She stalked to the bedroom door and slid it closed with a soft click.

Chuckles resonated through the door.

Kivera groaned and threw her body on the bed. "Are you good there?" Kivera called out, grateful that her voice was steady.

A noncommittal grunt answered her and Kivera laid back into her pillows.

She couldn't wait to be done with the case so she could be back in her bed permanently. Perhaps she would take a vacation to sit among her friends of written words and eat to her heart's desire with Mavis. Perhaps spend time in the capital and enjoy the glamor of the city for once.

Kivera dozed off on thoughts of book kingdoms and pear tarts and woke up to Mavis sliding under the sheets. In the back of her sleep-deprived mind, Kivera crawled under the sheets. "You're back," Kivera snaked a hand out of the warm satin sheets and conjured a weak wind to snuff out the candles.

"That was a magnificent bath. Might have to be a daily occurrence," Mavis sprinkled the sheets with rose oil, vanilla, and a faint citrus Kivera couldn't pinpoint.

Kivera's eyes began to drop. "This is almost better than chocolate."

Mavis giggled. "Goodnight, Kivera. Sleep well." Mavis's voice sounded far away and Kivera fell asleep before she could respond.

CHAPTER TWENTY-FOUR

Kivera woke to gray light filtering through the curtains. She sat up with a start, realizing where she was, and vaulted out of bed. She peeked between the curtains to the familiar ocean, stark charcoal in the coming dawn light.

Mavis slept soundly under the covers, so Kivera spirited out of her room and into the living room in search of Masga. She always woke up at this hour.

The couch was empty, and Kivera breathed in the room. She found the old woman's scent and followed it outside.

Masga had her back turned to Kivera and was surrounded by the horses as they nipped her hands for apples.

"Good morning, Masga," Kivera announced herself to not frighten the blind woman.

"Hello, Kivera." Masga turned to the sound of Kivera's voice.

Kivera walked closer and laid a hand on Masga's shoulder before she pulled the woman into a hug. Cedarwood and a sweet-smelling smoke wafted into Kivera's nose and she inhaled the comforting scent.

"I've missed you, Mas," Kivera let go and ignored the pricking in her eyes. She missed the old woman, their nights of Kivera, reading books to her or sitting by the beach in content silence.

"I've missed you, too, sweet one," Masga pat Kivera's cheek before she resumed feeding apple chunks to the impatient horses.

Kivera turned to the ocean and pink clouds dotted the sky and danced on the water's surface.

"Something has changed." Kivera's confession hung in the air and she forced herself not to check Masga's weathered face for her reaction.

"What will happen to you?"

"As much as I don't wish to, I have to go with this direction of change and adapt to the coming chaos," but the words tasted like ash on her tongue.

Kivera checked they were truly alone, and she released the glamor on her body. She needed a moment to let herself be for a moment. The marks on her back warmed and her wings drifted off her skin. Magic melted off her ears, and she reached up to the blissful feeling of their elongated ridges.

"Change may be what you need after all these years alone with me. Only showing your true self to someone with blindness must be lonely," Masga crooned.

Kivera raised her arms to the sky and stretched the obsidian feathers to the sky. "I made a friend. Her name is Mavis and she's incredible."

Masga hobbled a few feet over and felt the air around Kivera before she rested a hand on Kivera's shoulder, then floated to the rustling feathers at her spine.

"Is she here now?"

"Kivera? Where are you?" Mavis's voice answered Masga's question from inside the house.

"By the horses!" Kivera shouted back.

The side door opened and Mavis strode out barefoot. She was bundled underneath a thick knee-length sweater and hurried to where Masga and Kivera stood. She stopped in front of Kivera with a warm smile on her face.

"I like you best like this," Mavis lifted a hand to touch the tip of her round ear. "You look like yourself."

Kivera looked down. "The glamor is exhausting sometimes, but a required sacrifice to hide our secret."

"It won't be like that with me around. You'll have to learn how to take me wherever I want." Mavis winked before she moved her attention to Masga, who listened to their exchange with amusement. "Hello, my name is-"

"I know who you are, Mavis. My Kivera is excited for me to meet you." Masga hobbled to Mavis and feathered the air until she placed her wrinkled hands on Mavis's face. Masga's thumb brushed the planes of her face until she grazed Mavis's ravaged eye and down the raised skin of the scar. "Oh, dear child. Who did this to you?"

A shadow flashed across Mavis's eyes. "It was a long time ago, but he can't hurt me anymore."

"Your pain is deep yet your soul is still bright and kind," Masga sucked her tooth. "You'll smooth out our ragged edges soon enough."

"Kivera?" A deep voice rang from the kitchen, but would venture outside to check for her soon.

In the split of a heartbeat, shadows swarmed Kivera to cover her secrets. A warmth caressed her skin, and the darkness disappeared quickly. In their wake, round ears and an unmarked back were left.

Masga returned to petting the horses.

"Want to meet the boys, Mas?" Kivera asked her.

"Later, my dear. I have not had enough tea to deal with men this early."

Kivera and Mavis doubled over in silent laughter as they walked back into the house. But Kivera couldn't shake the feeling of the phantom limbs weighing down her back.

"I have a question for you," Jexton announced at Kivera's side.

"Shoot it." Kivera stared at the market they strolled through. Two-story stone buildings rose on either side of their group and they weaved through the cobblestone street. Banners drooped from the second landings across the market in colorful displays. Early morning workers rushed around the cobblestones streets. Bakeries seduced Kivera's senses with sugary breakfast goodies and tea shops wafted mixed spices that made her toes curl.

The morning had passed in a blur with a quick breakfast after a quiet run on the beach with Jexton, a change of clothes, and out the door, all under an hour after dawn. They walked on the beach toward the castle and trudged up stone stairs installed on the cliff-side that led to the city. Kivera lived near the castle and with the right shortcuts through the city, the walk there is swift. Stairs merged into teeming streets waking up in the bright morning light. The same light blinded Kivera as she squinted up at Jexton waiting for his question.

"I never asked, but I was wondering about the journey here. Does the Council know *what* you are?" Jexton cocked his head.

"No, I told them the information was too dangerous for them to know and when I threw a bit of magic around, they didn't ask questions after," Kivera narrowed her eyes into a passing glass storefront of a jewelry shop and noted vibrant pieces to inspect another time with Mavis. Why would he care anyway?

His brows crumbled into skepticism. "That doesn't bother them?"

A devilish grin flashed in the glass's reflection. "Oh, they're bothered endlessly but I haven't budged for years."

"Do they trust you enough to not protect themselves with guards and their own devices?"

"I'm assuming by 'devices' you mean protective charms or relics?" Jexton nodded and Kivera continued, "They tried with silver, blessed water, and ashwood charms."

"Do any work?"

Kivera thought for a moment as she studied his face, wondering why he would want to know her vulnerabilities. A nasty voice in her mind pricked at his question, doubting the trust they built over the past couple of months they'd worked together.

"No, they don't."

"Kivera, how much longer?" Mavis asked behind Kivera, interrupting their conversation. Mavis struggled underneath a pale pink gown she had picked out from Kivera's closet and Kivera pitied her. Which is why she wore loose gray pants and a charcoal sweater.

"Soon."

A few minutes later, the arched iron castle gates edged into view at the end of the market. A line of people awaited at the entrance to pass through the wall. Mostly servants were in search of work or food, but guards stationed at the post turned away all.

Kivera strode to the guards with a raised chin and the others filed behind her in a tight-knit circle. She glanced over her shoulder to find Jexton and Tillirius huddled close around Mavis and pushed against anyone who stepped too close. Gratitude sang in Kivera's heart.

The guards watched Kivera approach with weariness, but quickly straightened at the sight of the Royal Seal pinned to her chest.

"Good morning, ma'am," A gold uniformed guard with fiery red hair walked over to inspect Kivera's papers and waved to the others to open the gate once he found them sufficient.

"Good morning. Pleasant day so far?" Small talk bored Kivera but anything to keep them moving as the gates slowly lifted.

He gestured at them to pass. "Yes, ma'am, thank you. You're all clear.".

They entered a courtyard shaded by skinny trees with wide leaves framing the cobblestone walkway. Underneath some of the trees on the shaded grass were cushioned benches. Two-story walkways that led to other parts of the castle enclosed the greenery. Elegant arches beneath the second-story railings marked different passageways but Kivera continued to the end of the long courtyard without sparing a single glance at the servants flurrying around in preparation for the day.

With each step, a dispassionate and cold mask slid into place over Kivera's face and suffocated her soul.

At the end of the courtyard were double doors at least twenty feet tall with intricate engravings of crashing waves.

Jexton and Tillirius rushed ahead to open the doors before guiding them back to a soft close. They stepped into a foyer that split into two hallways and a staircase that led to the floors above. The walls of the foyer were adorned with ancient paintings of long-dead royal families and an abundant amount of royal pets. A sea breeze drifted on Kivera's skin and she inhaled the sea spray lingering on the gust.

Familiar with the way, Kivera chose the staircase to the left and led a grueling pace. The stairs passed floor after corridor until she stopped at a landing with the Royal Seal engraved on the stone floor. A single door marked the hallway at the end.

Willing a breath into her constricted lungs, Kivera turned around. "You all know me as this sweet, kind, and loving person." Jexton and Tillirius scoffed but feigned coughs when Kivera frowned at their outbursts. Mavis crossed her arms and rolled her eyes. "But there, I'll be different. I'll become who they want to see me. I don't want you to take my behavior personally." Kivera looked at the door and the guards that awaited.

Tillirius grinned. "You're five feet tall and not that intimidating, sweetheart."

"Don't tempt me into shoving you over that railing," Kivera grumbled, but a knot in her neck released. She viewed Mavis and a shade of green tinted her cheeks. "You can wait out here or I can take you back."

But Mavis didn't scare easily. Not after the scars that forged her fearlessness. "I'm ready. Let's get this over with."

With a smirk, Kivera led the way, and the wicked glamoured mask compressed more into place. They approached the great double doors, guarded by gold cloaks, and Kivera sent a rush of dark magic to open the doors before the soldiers could. After yesterday's draining ride, the magic bonded to Kivera shuddered at the use. She needed to survive this meeting, then she could rest.

The others scrambled to follow Kivera's long strides. The council room echoed her boots slapping against the polished marble. She used this moment to gather her surroundings and mark all the exits. The room appeared to be carved out of a massive slab of marble. A reminder of the riches the kingdom once had that are now measly coppers filling the coffers. Veined pillars rose from the floor to the wood arches in the high ceilings. The room might have felt like one giant cavern if it weren't for the three floor-to-ceiling windows facing the expanse of the coast.

More staggering than the magnificent view were the number of gold-uniformed guards that manned every inch of the room. Shoulder-to-shoulder, guards gazed impassively ahead with hands ready on their weapons.

In the middle of the room was a beautiful table the size of a tree and sitting around the gleaming surface were seven of the highest officials in the kingdom. Another layer of guards waited in the shadows behind the Councillors seated around a table. The High Court of Alceria was second in power behind the King but grew in power as his care for his kingdom lessened. The seven men watched Kivera and the others approach with unblinking eyes, but the unmistakable scent of fear wafted to Kivera's nose. Every man sitting knew she was not to be trifled with. The thick layers of guards displayed showed she wasn't to be underestimated.

A table was set up a good distance away from the powerful men, with only two chairs to occupy one side. Kivera's thunderous footsteps halted a few feet away from the table and the entire room held its breath.

Kivera didn't speak, and neither did the Councilors as they waited for her to start. She cocked her head as she stared at the table as if contemplating how to destroy the bland features, then raised her narrowed eyes to the Council.

"I assumed you received my earlier message about my guests." Her sharp, cold voice clipped through the room. A few guards and a couple of councilors jumped from their skin.

"We did. The servants couldn't scrounge up anything more." A man with a black beard spoke, his beard rippled with each word uttered, and Kivera recognized Councilman Andello.

"Out of the entire palace?" Kivera raised an eyebrow and peeled back a layer of the glamor camouflaging her face and let the men see a flicker of the monster underneath. It was necessary, or they would treat her as a youthful welcoming mat.

"Our apologies. We'll do better next time, Miss Galveterre," Andello bowed his head.

Kivera only blinked. This was all a silly game for them to test her.

"No worries. I usually have spares," Kivera snapped her fingers and the two chairs at the table disappeared and four larger obsidian chairs replaced them. Sweat beaded in her palms as the magic trembled after too much use, but she ignored the sign. Kivera strode forward and pulled the middle left chair with a cord of dark wind and sat on the plush seat. Mavis sat to her left; Jexton on her right and Tillirius on his right.

"Tell me, gentlemen, why did you interrupt an ongoing investigation for this meeting and attach an invitation to a silly, terrible party?" Kivera questioned in a voice hard as granite. Everyone in the room shifted to Kivera's harsh words. The punishment for speaking against the Council was imprisonment or worse, public execution. But Kivera couldn't let them know she was afraid of those consequences.

"Oh, Gods, Kivera," Jexton choked and cleared his throat. "Councilors, what she means to say is-"

"I meant nothing different from what I asked. Questions

they should wisely answer soon." Kivera cut him a warning look before she turned slitted eyes at the men before her.

"Watch your snake tongue with us, girl." The eldest of the councilors, Councilman Martess, seethed as he leaned forward, his wrinkled face flushed.

"Should I now?" The words flowed out of Kivera's mouth in a lethal purr.

"Who are these people you've brought?" Councilman Andello asked, attempting to diffuse the tension.

"I brought my Second, Mavis, and Jexton brought his hound, Tillirius." Tillirius scoffed at his introduction but did not make any move to correct her. Not in front of the Council when she was like this. Later in the ring, he would exact his vengeance on Kivera. His glare confirmed as much.

"You did not clear this decision with us to hire a Second, much less bring her on your illegal investigation," Councilman Martess tsked. His tone raised Kivera's hackles. The councilman loved any excuse to jab at her, but his last two words caught Kivera. *Illegal investigation?*

"Not everything I do concerns you, *mortal*." The growl slipped out of Kivera's mouth and the mask squeezed her heart. She hated her friends seeing her in this persona.

"You are under our employment and everything you do concerns us." The elder bared his yellowed teeth. His words rang through Kivera.

"What illegal investigation?" Mavis murmured next to Kivera but even her soft voice carried to everyone in the room.

"Did she not tell you, young lady?" Councilman Andello steepled his fingers on the desk.

"My name is Mavis, not 'young lady'." Mavis jutted out her chin. "No one told her about any illegal investigation, either." Kivera nodded at her words and a flare of pride burst in her chest at her friend's ferocity.

Councilman Andello rolled his eyes. "Someone better start explaining, otherwise we have half a mind to throw you all on the gallows."

Kivera blinked with surprise and Jexton's breath hitched next to her.

"This is my fault, High Council," Jexton pushed from his lavish chair to rise to his full height. "I went personally to Kivera Galveterre to request her assistance under false pretenses."

"Did you, now?" A silver-bearded councilman, Vernis, asked as he stroked his facial hair.

Jexton bowed his head. "I did, sir. I'm fully prepared for the consequences."

"How did you know I was in Tymern?" Kivera asked the council softly. Even in the expansive room, Kivera's restrained fury carried throughout the walls.

The councilors shifted in their seats as they struggled to speak, opening their mouths like fish. Even Councilman Martess's thin mouth gaped as he mulled over his next words.

After a minute, no one answered and Kivera clucked her tongue. "Gentlemen, you've been spying on me?" She expected the betrayal to hurt, for her to explode in anger, but she wasn't entirely surprised. Kivera would be disappointed if they weren't following her and was angry at herself for not finding out sooner.

"We meant no harm in it." A younger councilor spluttered, one she didn't recognize.

"What did you expect from us mere 'mortals'? To let the most powerful weapon in the country roam free?" Martess sneered down at Kivera.

Weapon.

The word stilled Kivera.

Weapon.

"That is not Kivera's fault. Without your permission, I requested her to join us-"

Jexton rose from his chair, but Councilman Martess held a hand up. "Kingdoms don't run on excuses, Captain," Councilman Martess's voice snapped. "Your treasonous acts are grounds for execution, Kivera, and we must be convinced otherwise."

Kivera's table erupted in raised voices at the outlandish words. The air in the room tightened around her throat, but she didn't allow herself to succumb to panic. She locked unblinking eyes with Councilman Martess and allowed herself time to settle her thoughts.

"If you tried to kill me now, you'll never discover how magic returned to Alceria." Gasps rolled through the council.

"Explain this." The man to Councilman Martess's right leaned forward with a twitching mustache, Councilman Leno.

Kivera summarized the last month with the briefest of details, leaving out Mavis, and one by one, each councilman's face ashen at the news. One magic wielder is enough, but two or three, if Kivera was accurate, would be their doom.

"You can vouch this is the truth, Captain Jexton?" Councilman Andello broke the silence when Kivera finished. He watched Kivera during the entire meeting with a hawk's stare and she didn't know, nor cared to know if it were to unnerve her or study her.

"Yes, sir." Captain Jexton nodded like the polite, good soldier. "What Kivera has said is the truth."

"Your superior will discipline you for not following the chain of command and leaving your post." A rich, tenor voice commented and melted against Kivera's skin. The voice belonged to the beautiful man with skin the color of night and glittering onyx eyes on the far right side of the panel. Councilman Lenxo. Kivera only heard whispers of his brutality during his time as the army's general.

"I understand, sir." Jexton nodded.

"Why have you allowed this investigation to go on for this long?" Councilman Mastress snarled. The question and rage flickered in Kivera's heart.

Shadows in the room jumped.

"Allowed this?" Kivera's mood plummeted to a dark place within herself as the images of the dead women's faces burned the back of her eyelids. She would not be blamed for a magic wielder murdering scores of women. But she was already growing tired of this game. Each side between her and the Council vie for power, dominance, and blood. A headache pounded against Kivera's skull.

"I did not-I didn't mean-" The councilman backtracked, realizing his mistake, but it was too late.

"I am not responsible for these deaths. Nor is Jexton." Kivera stared hard into each council member's eyes. "Should any of you feel differently, I will bring you along to share your insights with the murderer's beast." She didn't inform them she already slayed the monster.

"We did not mean any disrespect. We meant-" Andello scrambled to de-escalate the situation.

Kivera's eyes narrowed. "I know what you meant. Your harsh accusations are feeble from your thrones above the city."

"What are you saying, Kivera Galveterre?" Councilman Martess peered at her. A cruel glint in his wrinkled eyes roiled Kivera's stomach.

"Far away from the bloody mess, you all are concerned more with having my head on a pike than the evidence that Alceria may be in more trouble than any of us realize." Kivera took a shallow breath to quiet her wild heartbeat.

"How is it possible for magic to be in Alceria?"

"As of right now, we are investigating this as an isolated incident from a single individual until evidence proves otherwise," Jexton answered in a clear, confident voice. Kivera wondered if that's what he felt in his gut as the council stared down at him. "Kivera has been diligent in her search for other magic beings since we made this discovery."

"How did this one escape your attention, Kivera?"

"I didn't know to look for anyone else. There has been no indication of gifted folk in Alceria since I've lived here." Kivera shrugged. "There's not exactly a club to join."

Tillirius snickered under his breath.

"We'd like this investigation closed by the end of next week. Or the next summons will not be as pleasant."

Councilman Leno said with a measure of finality and pushed to his feet. The other councilors followed suit, albeit begrudgingly at the dismissal.

Kivera's friends rose to their feet, their chairs scraping back with a screech, but she only leaned further into her seat. Blood pumped loudly in her ears and she clenched her shaking hands into fists on the table.

"I'll leave you all with a reminder." Her voice was hewn from glass. The air itself quivered from the small amount of power Kivera released. "Threaten me or my friends again on fruitless accusations and I'll rip through your feeble minds and Alceria will be rid of this council."

"Excuse me?"

"A vile girl!"

"How dare you say that to us?"

The councilmen exploded into spitting outcries, the loudest from Councilman Morvolino. His black beard trembled with anger. A scar that trailed his jaw pulsed with each gesture.

"I'm growing tired of this game we play. Do not trifle with me again," A shark's grin pulled back Kivera's lips. "Or you will learn how truly mortal you are and how sharp this weapon can be."

Then did Kivera rise from her seat like a dark queen leaving her court.

She sauntered back through the doors and clasped her shaking hands behind her back. Kivera prayed to the gods her racing heartbeat didn't echo against the marble walls. Her friends filled tightly behind her.

None of the guards made any move to intervene against Kivera or her friends, but she didn't breathe until they crossed the threshold and the heavy door slammed shut.

Kivera kept her arms folded behind her back through the corridors and she turned a sharp right to an empty hallway.

"What are we doing down here?" Mavis asked and before Kivera could answer, Kivera yanked open a utility closet and upended her breakfast in a bucket on the ground.

"Oh, Kivera," Mavis closed the door behind them, leaving a crack of light in. She reached over to hold Kivera's hair as more vomit burst from her mouth.

"That was the worst." The sorrow in Kivera's voice chilled the darkness.

"You were... different," Mavis struggled with words but rubbed Kivera's back in soothing circles.

"I have to be. When I first arrived here, they were hard pressed on killing me." Kivera coughed more bile into the bucket. "I had to scare them witless so they could find me useful as a *weapon* and not a young corpse."

"You did what you had to do to survive," the circles continued.

A single tear slipped out of Kivera's eye. She pushed up against the wall and pulled crisp darkness around her body.

"I'm tired of wearing a mask. I wish to be myself," Kivera's voice broke on the last word. Another tear slipped out of the corner of her eye, but the weight off her chest lifted as the confession held in the air.

"You should show the world who you are. It's a disservice not to," Mavis fumbled in the dark for Kivera's hand and gripped hard.

"No one befriends a monster of darkness," The bitterness in Kivera's voice shocked them both and she felt Mavis's wide eyes on her neck.

"Monsters make the most interesting of friends. Monsters can play with demons," Mavis countered and laid down a thick blanket of understanding over them both. She squeezed Kivera's hand, and she returned the pressure.

"Everything okay in there?" Worry lay thick in Jexton's voice through the door.

"All good. Be out in a second," Kivera called back. She pushed to her feet and found Mavis's hand in the faint darkness and lifted her. "Thank you, Mav."

They embraced briefly before Kivera pulled away to fix her hair and scrub a hand across her face. When Kivera opened the door, Jexton and Tillirius stood on guard with blank expressions on their faces.

Kivera could have sworn she heard footsteps further down the hallway before they scuttled away.

Concern replaced the stoic expression on the captain's face. He scanned Kivera's body for any sign of harm and met her eyes at last.

"Let's get you something to eat and a little sea salt to cheer you up." Jexton wrapped a warm arm around Kivera's shoulders and she leaned into the touch.

"Sounds perfect." A soft smile hidden away in the darkness from years of solitude tugged Kivera's lips.

Quiet bickers from Tillirius and Mavis behind Kivera about gods know what, and her smile deepened. She found the company she may keep after all.

CHAPTER TWENTY-FIVE

Kivera emerged from the bathroom, and Mavis let out a low whistle.

"Whoa."

A red velvet dress clung to Kivera's curves and extended down the length of her spine to her wrists. The fabric rippled against her body and she lined her eyes using kohl with a sweeping stroke and dappled rouge on her cheekbones and lips. She used wisps of darkness to smooth her hair in an onyx sheen. Her hair now fell to her shoulder blades after a couple of months without being tended to.

For the first time in a while, excitement bubbled in her stomach and Kivera didn't dare name the reason. Jexton had already left for the castle, complaining about how long women need to get ready for a "ridiculous ball" in his words.

Mavis stood by the door in a radiant evergreen dress. Soft material cuffed her pale neck that drifted down her body to the floor and exposed skin from her shoulder to fingertips. Her makeup was simple, with a smear of pink on the top of her cheekbones and her lips. Her ragged scar shone in stark contrast to her beautiful ensemble, but rather than hinder her beauty, the scar fashioned Mavis to be devastating.

Kivera's brows raised. "You're stunning, Mav."

"I'm sure I'll make a mess of myself eventually. Nerves rattled my stomach," Redness crept on Mavis's cheekbones. She clutched a cream wrap Kivera lent to her around her slender shoulders and opened the bedroom door. Mavis ushered her friend to walk quicker.

A smile tugged at the corners of Kivera's blood-red lips.

Drawing her shoulders back, Kivera followed at a leisurely pace and followed her friend through her house to the awaiting carriage she had called on earlier to their night of festivities.

Kivera and Mavis followed the partygoers that trickled through the hallways, the crowd knowing where to go. Lovely melodies floated to Kivera's ears and her blood thrummed with the music. Silver pine trees spotted the wide hallways and gleamed against the opalescent walls. Snow-dusted garlands looped the top corners of the walls with silver bedecking the pine needle tips.

The flood of courtiers wound through castle corridors before the swift music was near deafening and they walked through a tall archway into a golden ballroom.

The castle's ballroom was spectacularly bedecked into a winter's night dream in streams of holly and frosted pine cone garlands. Striking pillars lined the massive room, lit with twinkling lights twining around their impressive heights. Ornaments and bright garlands ordained thick evergreen trees with ornaments and colorful garlands throughout the floor in strategic positions. Golden-wrapped presents littered the ground beneath, strategically placed by careful servant hands. Tiny droplets of light dripped down from the snow-frosted ceiling and set silver glistening icicles aglow dangling beside them.

Courtiers filled the room in a flurry of dances and animated conversations, donning ridiculous outfits of furs and feathers on their billowing clothes. Lustrous jewelry and adornments bespeckled all the courtiers.

But Mavis absorbed the ball with wide eyes, her eyes darting to each detail. With each passing step, the glow on her face intensified. Kivera internally sighed and vowed to let nothing spoil Mavis's night, no matter the cost of her boredom. Mavis deserved a fun, extravagant night.

"Let's find food. I'm starving," Mavis whispered at Kivera's side.

From her survey of the exits, Kivera knew where to go and she looked down at the awe-filled female. "At the far wall near the windows is food. Hold my arm," Kivera extended a ruby velvet-clad arm and brokered a path through the bustling crowd. She summoned shadows to clasp ankles ahead of her to pull the courtiers unwittingly forward a few steps.

They arrived at a decadent feast table that caused Kivera's mouth to water. Cakes and macaroons and pies were on tantalizing display.

Kivera and Mavis turned to each other and grinned.

Kivera marked the servants in red and black meandering through the crowd with trays of bubbly flutes in their hands.

"This is a splendid party," Mavis commented as she pounced on the table. Kivera followed suit.

Warm peppermint cookies melted on Kivera's tongue, followed by buttered, salted caramel tarts. Her fingers itched for the other goodies, but she refrained.

"We have to try it all," Mavis garbled around a mint chocolate cake slice. She let out a soft moan and closed her eyes.

"You'll be up all night on a sugar frenzy if you overindulge." A voice came from behind them and Kivera turned to Jexton's glittering brown eyes. In a navy and cream uniform tight on his massive body, Jexton was dashing. She watched his eyes rake down her dress and her cheeks flamed as his eyes dragged on her curves, before his eyes met Kivera's again. He swallowed once before stuffing his hands in his pockets.

Kivera's mouth dried.

"You both look great," He nodded at Mavis, but his heated gaze flicked to Kivera. She couldn't form words around her twisted tongue.

"You look handsome yourself," Mavis beamed and pinched Kivera's side and she jolted to attention.

"I'm excited to return tomorrow. I hate to leave Arcian in charge for *too* long. He becomes antsy and even more cranky than usual," Jexton sighed. Grateful for the safe topic, Kivera tore her eyes away and inhaled a shallow breath. "The others will hopefully have something new by the time we arrive."

Kivera nodded as she reached for a passing tray of a rose-gold liquid and grabbed two. She passed one to Mavis, who accepted with delight. The females tapped their glasses and Kivera watched the smile on Mavis's spread with each mouthful. Each one was more greedy than the last. "I'm eager to get back, too."

Kivera lifted the flute glass to her lips and sipped the sweet sunshine.

"Are you enjoying the party?" Mavis's eyes were bright.

He rubbed a hand on his neck and shrugged. "Enjoying the party is an overstatement, but I don't mind the company." Jexton grinned with an award-winning dazzle and turned his gaze onto Kivera. Onto her lips, to be exact.

And gods-forsake her, Kivera was dazzled.

"I couldn't agree more." Kivera's voice, gods strike her down right then, sounded out of breath. What was wrong with her?

"Would you like to dance?" Jexton held out a hand to Kivera and his eyes met hers with a challenge glittering in his eyes. Her stomach tightened in response.

"She would love to!" Mavis pushed Kivera forward, and she stumbled towards him and caught herself by clutching his arms. She tilted her eyes towards his and they stared into each other's eyes for a long heartbeat.

They severed contact, remembering Mavis behind her, and Kivera looped her arm through Jexton's and smiled at Mavis. "What will you do?"

She laughed with a carefree, tinkling sound. Her first in a

while. "Dance, eat, chat. Who cares?" Mavis stepped a few paces back before melting into the crowd.

"Come on," Jexton escorted Kivera through the crowd until they were in the center of the room. The music slowed to a waltz and Jexton didn't give Kivera a chance to prepare before he whisked her around with a steady hand on her waist and clutching her hand with tender firmness. Light on his feet, Jexton maneuvered them with an expert touch.

"You're not too bad at dancing, Captain," Kivera twirled under his arm and he dipped her low into his arms. He pressed his body close to Kivera's and his gaze traced the bare skin of her chest, up the length of her throat, and landed on her molten eyes. A fire lit behind Jexton's eyes and Kivera couldn't tear her eyes away.

He lowered himself by her ear. The stubble on his chin scratched her cheek, and his voice rumbled in her ear. "Surprised?"

"Men and their egos," Kivera rolled her eyes but grinned. Flexing her core, she arced up painstakingly slowly to give his eyes a full view of the front of her dress. Jexton's eyes blazed as they roamed and his lips parted. A carnal smile slid on Kivera's face.

"Women and their satisfied egos," Jexton smirked down at her, but his eyes didn't lose their intensity. "I like the dress." His breath tickled Kivera's neck and goosebumps rose on her skin at the purr in his voice.

A breathless laugh burst from her chest after another spin. Jexton yanked Kivera close to his chest and a hand drifted to her lower back. Flames licked up her spine where his hand gripped her and a growl almost slipped out of her chest. Flames trailed her spine, following where his wandering fingers touched her gently.

The orchestra ended with a final drawn-out note and the crowd burst into applause. But Kivera and Jexton didn't join in and were content to stare at each other.

"My turn for a dance." Mavis appeared at Kivera's elbow

as if made of shadows and Kivera stumbled out of Jexton's arms. She smoothed the front of her dress to allow her cheeks enough time to cool off and snuck a gaze at Jexton's face. Hurt and sadness flashed across his face before vanishing.

"Of course, my lady," Jexton winked at Mavis and bowed at the waist. He disappeared into the crowd before Kivera could lift a finger or say a word to him.

The orchestra moved to an uptempo tune and Mavis pulled Kivera to the center of the room, almost tearing her arm from the socket.

A furrow in Mavis's brow appeared. "How do you dance with a girl? I've never even danced before."

Kivera winked. "It's better than with a boy, trust me. My sister taught me how." She waited for the usual gut-tightening sensation and choked airways when she talked about her sister on the rare occasion, but none happened. Kivera didn't know whether to be surprised or upset. She guided Mavis's hands up to her shoulders and placed her own on Mavis's slim waist. They twirled to the beat in uneven circles but giggled the entire time.

"Everyone's staring at us," Mavis swiveled her eyes and Kivera did the same. Indeed, everyone stared at the only women dancing together.

"How sad is their life to judge and stare," Kivera lifted a shoulder in a shrug and grinned wider, and slid Mavis into a low dip. Mavis mirrored Kivera's grin as her hair cascaded behind her.

Shadows trailed their movements as if followed by the joy from their master. They wove through the hem of Kivera's dress and in the curls of Mavis's strawberry hair. Kivera peeked at the surrounding crowd to search for any sign of the humans noticing the magic, but there was no reaction that she could see.

Out of the corner of Kivera's eye, a stout man with a bushy mustache strolled onto the front stage next to the orchestra and the music trailed off to a soft lull.

Sweat gleamed off his balding head while he clapped as the song softened. "Thank you all for coming to the winter ball hosted by the lovely Crown! The royal family is thrilled about the attendance of their great friends and welcomes all to the festivities. But unfortunately, they fell ill and urgently retreated to their chambers and expressed their regrets." The crowd clapped toward empty thrones in a booth on the upper floors, including Mavis. "However, we have a magical night ahead of us with a glamorous act, certain to wow you. So, please, raise a glass to an exhilarating night ahead of us." He raised his own as the crowd lifted their flutes. The crowd burst into cheers after the sip.

The orchestra began an upbeat tempo, and the crowd dissolved into dancing or moved to the edges of the room to chatter. Ladies held the arm of their dancing partners as they twirled their corseted bodies, dipped, and swayed throughout the room.

Mavis and Kivera danced with renewed vigor, a giddy gleam in both of their eyes. They danced for a few songs and Kivera enjoyed the event. She suspected the elation was because of her company. She caught flashes of Jexton in the crowd before the writhing crowd swallowed his illuminated hazel eyes.

"I need something to drink," Mavis breathlessly said.

Kivera held out her arm for Mavis and she led them back to the dessert table and noticed a passing servant. She pulled two flutes off his tray and extended one to Mavis.

"This is a lot of fun, Kivera," Mavis beamed as she sipped her champagne.

Kivera smiled. "I'm glad you're enjoying yourself. This has been better than I thought it would be. I wonder what the entertainment will be."

"Ladies and gentlemen," a voice boomed around the ballroom and Kivera craned her neck to find the source. A man in an all-black tuxedo and top hat strolled onto the stage as he opened his arms wide. The torchlight dimmed to near darkness, save for the torches at the front stage, casting malevolent shadows on his narrow face. He scanned his kohl-lined eyes over the crowd. "Thank you all for attending this lovely ball. My name is Theodore Raske, and I'll be your host for tonight's entertainment."

A round of applause erupted, and his mouth twitched. Kivera cocked her head at the mysterious man. Alarms rang in the back of her head.

"Tonight, your blood will heat with danger of what I'll show you this evening," A gasp rang throughout the room and Kivera rolled her eyes.

"What kind of danger do you suspect he means?" A husky voice murmured in Kivera's ear, and she swiveled to Jexton's handsome features, smirking at her.

"Perhaps a rogue band of pirates will take a courtier hostage and demand a hefty ransom," Kivera mused, to give herself time to cool off from his heated gaze. Gods, when did the room heat?

"Or a magic show!" Mavis clapped her hands together and her smile widened when she noticed Jexton.

A faint drum hummed through the room and vibrated Kivera's bones. Masked men in dark vests and trousers marched through the room and carried sheeted objects resembling overgrown bird cages throughout the room. Kivera counted almost a dozen sheeted cages as they halted at different spots in the room amidst the crowd.

"What do you think those are?" Mavis whispered as she tried to peek over the crowd on her tiptoes.

Kivera shrugged. "Someone tied up?"

"Gentlemen, unveil your dangerous secrets," Mr. Raske's voice boomed through the room. Anticipation mounted as everyone's eyes frantically scoured the room to watch the masked men rip off the sheets in unison.

Gasps of awe bounced throughout the room as spectators toed closer to exotic animals pacing in their cages. Dangerous wild cats prowled their confinements and hissed at humans inching too close. Leopards, cheetahs, and lionesses occupied most of the cages. Tigers and a pair of wolves placed too close together with their knife-like teeth bared and snarling at the observing crowd. The humans closest jumped away with a shriek.

Most horrifying of all was the glass enclosure writhing with dozens of venomous snakes, wriggling over each other's bodies. Their hisses reached Kivera's ears and goosebumps raised the length of her spine.

"Hold your ladies, sirs, or even the slightest misstep close to the leopards or the tigress will cause the loss of a fine woman's arm." The host grinned with yellowed teeth smile. "Don't drink too much, men or your buddies will throw you to the wolves. In literal terms."

A dark chuckle rode through the crowd waves, Jexton included. Kivera only knit her eyebrows together.

"Good thing Arcian and Mase aren't here. They'd be trying to play chicken with the creatures," He said with the sigh of an exasperated father.

Kivera snorted. "I can only imagine the bloodshed." But she focused her attention back on the ringleader when his voice clanged through the room again.

"But these vicious creatures aren't the most dangerous predators roaming within these castle walls," Raske paused for a dramatic effect and a smug expression flashed across his features as hushed whispers quieted the crowd. "No, dear friends, my hunters found a creature so terrifying and bloodthirsty, my men didn't return home the same as they left. The ones that returned at all."

Torchlight dimmed, and the drumming continued. The sound jolted through Kivera's blood.

"For the first time, the world will see the black demon terrorizing the northern forests. Razing down villages to slaughter parents and rip out their children's throats." Raske enthralled the crowd and Kivera watched them fall entirely under his thumb, but dread filled her stomach.

The drumming heightened as the ballroom doors flung open to reveal a black sheeted cage that trembled from the beast inside. Hooded figures walked beside the rolling cage and carried lanterns.

"I present you, the Black Demon of Alceria."

They ripped the sheet off metal bars and drifted slowly to a pool on the floor.

The creature roaming the small confinement jolted through Kivera.

A behemoth-sized panther prowled the edges of the cage with a sleek body of powerful muscles rippling. Its coat was the deepest color of night and its triangular head easily towered over Kivera's head. Scars reflected along its body in a ravaged masterpiece.

But it was the creature's eyes that Kivera couldn't tear her eyes from.

Eyes of blue fire flared while the panther roared against imprisonment and snarled at the observing humans.

Realization struck Kivera's gut and knocked the wind out of her lungs. To be sure, she inhaled the scents in the air and pierced each part before she found the panther. Shock reverberated through Kivera's bones and she reached out for Mavis's arm but struggled to form the words.

"Kivera? What is it?" Mavis's eyes flit between the panther and Kivera, her brows furrowed.

Kivera leaned closer so no one could overhear her clenched words. "That's not a normal panther."

"What do you mean?"

"She's a Fae panther," Kivera studied the animal and maneuvered through the crowd in a trance-like state. Mavis scrambled behind her, but Kivera didn't notice. The world blurred from her senses and she couldn't hear the host babble on about the legendary creature over the roaring in her ears.

Those who knew where to look witnessed shadows quivering and jumping up the walls. Kivera's only sign of emotion. She wanted to roar with the poor creature at this treachery.

She hurried to the front row with Mavis on her heels when she made eye contact with the creature.

Can you understand me? Kivera slid into the creature's mind. Select Fae animals can understand mental connections from their two-footed Fae cousins with telepathic abilities.

Mavis blinked at Kivera for the briefest of a second, knowing what was transpiring between Kivera and the panther. The wild cat blinked at Kivera as if acknowledging her words, but the cat returned her focus to the pressing crowd. With humans threatening around her, the panther couldn't risk losing her focus on those within perilous proximity.

You will have your freedom again, my wild friend. I will rip out the throats of every single captor.

The panther huffed what Kivera thought to be a doubtful sigh and continued to pace.

"What's she saying?"

They will make legends of your release.

The panther exploded into sharp snarls and Kivera yearned to join in with her feral roar. Instead, she slinked through the bustling crowd with Mavis by her hand.

"She deserves her freedom and gods be damned, I'll fight to release the poor girl." They looped their arms together and slipped through the waves of bodies. They found Jexton in the same spot they left him, albeit with a fresh drink in his hand and concern crinkling his face.

Jexton's hand twitched towards Kivera, but appeared to think twice and shoved a fist in his pocket. "What's wrong?"

Mavis was going to explain but cut short by a glance from Kivera. "It's better if you don't know."

"Why?" His face strained. "So I don't get in trouble or I won't stop you?"

"Both," the females replied in unison.

Jexton looked up at the ceiling. "Gods help us."

Agreed, Kivera thought to herself. Gods help the poor fools imprisoning the panther.

"I need to go," Kivera told them both, and Mavis's expression plummeted. "You're welcome to stay here, Mav, should a certain brute monitor you."

As part of their improvised plan, Mavis's eyes brightened and clasped her hands together, turning the full power of her enormous eyes on Jexton. "Stay with me, pretty please?"

"Fine." Jexton groaned, but a faint smile played on his lips. "We'll be back no later than midnight." He gave Kivera a knowing look.

Kivera nodded and reached out for his arm, ignoring the knife in her gut, twisting further. "Thank you." She flicked a look back at the caged, beautiful animal that prowled her cage and a lone tear slipped out of her eye.

"Will you be okay?" Mavis peered closer at Kivera.

"I will be. Have fun, you guys." She turned away, letting go of Jexton's arm, and strode for the double doors out of the room. Shadows separated the crowd to keep her thunderous footsteps moving.

One last scan of the caged creatures and Kivera was gone.

Stragglers and couples in feverish embraces spotted the hallways. Kivera hurried past them.

"Kivera?" She whipped around to see Tilly sharing a dark bottle in a hidden alcove with guards. From the sigil pinned to their bosom, most likely personal guards to one of the courtier families. Tilly frowned at her, but she continued past him and his footsteps hounded after her.

"Wait, Kivera!"

But she didn't. Not with the onslaught of images of the imprisoned panther and those terrifying eyes. Kivera knew the feeling of being chained and humiliated. How do humans have the arrogance of imprisoning such beautiful animals none other than a Fae cat?

That was what the Alcerian council wished to do to her once they figured out how to overpower her. Stuff her in a cage, rot in there unless an enemy speaks against their law and they unleashed her as their weapon.

A vision flashed across her mind and Kivera saw herself rather than the panther pacing in her cage. Wide, golden eyes terrified as she hissed.

A hand wrapped around Kivera's arm and yanked her out of her thoughts. She whirled and bared her teeth at whoever grabbed her.

Tillirius's growl met her face but died off once he glimpsed her face.

"What is it?" He let go of her arm but gestured to an abandoned hallway and she followed him. He leaned against the wall to wait for her answer.

"Nothing." She said through gritted teeth and crossed her arms.

"Nothing doesn't wet your cheeks like this." She didn't notice the tears and scrubbed her face. Heat flamed her skin from Tillirius's observant gaze and rage roiled her stomach. He was the last person she wanted to see her like this.

"They captured wild beasts and placed them on *display.* As if their suffering and treatment are worth applause and money." Raw bitterness and rage clipped Kivera's words.

Tillirius's mouth gaped open and shut it close again like the words caught in his throat.

A pained roar bounced through the marble walls, and rounds of applause followed. Kivera winced, and another tear slipped out.

"Will you do something about it?" Tillirius cocked his head.

A feral, wicked smile spread across Kivera's lips and she stepped backward into the gathering darkness and disappeared.

CHAPTER TWENTY-SIX

Kivera slammed into the hardwood floor of her dining room, and her knees groaned in protest. A crash exploded around her and Kivera scanned the low-lit room. Shattered remnants of a teacup surrounded Masga, where she stood in the kitchen as she clutched her chest.

"Gods, girl, don't scare an old woman like that."

"I apologize, Masga. Next time, I'll wear a bell around my neck," Kivera hurried to her room and undid the laces on the back of the dress in awkward motions.

Masga shuffled into the room behind her and walked the familiar steps to Kivera's bed and sat down. "Why are you tense, Kivera?"

The dress pooled at Kivera's feet and she kicked it into a corner of the room. Her satin slippers landed next to the red fabric.

"The foolish mortals captured an extraordinary creature and I intend on freeing her," Kivera moved to the bathroom and splashed cold water over her face. She scrubbed off the meticulously placed makeup from her skin.

"Explains all your thundering about," Masga held out her palm and Kivera sighed, knowing what the old woman was asking for.

A platter of sweets from the ball flashed onto Masga's wrinkled palm. Masga smacked her lips together and popped a berry tart into her mouth.

"They imprisoned a female panther from my homeland." Kivera stepped into her closet and picked out an all-black ensemble.

"A panther? How were they able to capture her?" Masga asked around the dessert in her mouth and Kivera placed an image of the big cat in the woman's mind and watched her jaw slacken.

"I don't know, but I'm going to find out. This is the third creature born of my world here in Alceria, and that cannot be a coincidence, especially since starting this case." Kivera waited for Masga to disagree, but the older woman nodded as she popped another sweet into her mouth. A part of her wanted to be wrong.

"Even the smallest cracks in a door can allow any creature to pass through." Masga's hushed words froze Kivera's arms in midair as she pulled a dark sweater over her head.

Never in her years knowing Masga did she mention a lick of knowledge about the gates between Alceria and Kivera's native world. Faeries were forbidden decades ago to reveal the world's nature to humans and leave such dangerous knowledge in human hands. They burned any evidence of faeries from human minds, along with the existence of all the magical creatures that once inhabited their world. Or worse, they slaughtered those who resisted.

Faeries sealed off the portal to each side to protect each race after migrating their race to faerie lands, so neither race could harm the other. Histories between the two were bloody.

A secret Kivera's sister died for and nearly claimed her own life.

"I don't know what you're talking about," Kivera said softly and slid the sweater down her body.

But Masga rasped a dark chuckle. "I may be blind, but I am *old,* girl. My parents lived long lives and their parents even longer. My family spoke of the wicked legends from ancient times in whisperings around the campfire. Do you think I didn't know what you were the moment we met? Feel the power in my bones of someone *other* in my presence? You're not like the rest either, are you?"

"I've always been open about what I am-" Kivera began, but Masga waved her gnarled hand.

"Yes, yes, you have been. But you have not been open about what your magic unlocks. Even a blind human knows you are different, even among your kind."

"You knew." The words rushed out of Kivera's mouth in a breathless whisper. She left the closet and kneeled next to Masga. The old woman wrapped a frail arm around Kivera and pulled her tight. Wild grass and sea salt enveloped Kivera's nose, and she breathed in the peaceful scents deep into her chest.

"I always have. You are not as bloodthirsty as the legends proclaimed your kind to be," Masga snorted and rubbed Kivera's shoulder. "Whatever is your past you ran from those years ago has finally caught up to you now, Kivera. You must face it and the consequences."

Kivera closed her eyes and the phantom knife in her heart twisted. "I don't want to."

Laughter wracked through Masga's body. "The gods don't give us that luxury. You are meant for greater than a pawn in men's silly power games."

"I wish to stay here with you and let Mavis explore life as she should," Kivera sniffed, and buried her head into Masga's bony shoulder.

"Neither of you were made for that life, my sweet Kivera. You both are gifted with tremendous power. Mavis is welcome here but she may be set on fighting at your hip." Masga ran her fingers through Kivera's hair and kissed her forehead. A tear trailed down Kivera's cheek.

"I don't have to leave. I can figure this mess out and seal the gates forever from this side." But doubt crept into her voice and didn't fool either of them.

"Fate may keep you here or push you towards a path you are completely unready for. But you must not resist what's meant to be."

Kivera rose gently to her feet for the sake of the more frail woman and found boots at the edge of the bed. The words, truthful or not, sliced at her heart and tears flowed from her eyes.

"Damn the gods. I'll live with the consequences. They've taken enough from me. I can live with their displeasure." Kivera nearly gagged on the bitterness coating her tongue and glared at her shaking fingers lacing the boots.

"What scars lay on your heart, child?" Anguish wove into Masga's voice.

Kivera instantly regretted allowing her wounds to bleed.

She walked back to Masga and leaned down. "Time has been good for me. There is no reason to trudge up the past. I'll see you later." A kiss on her wrinkled cheeks and plucking a treat for the journey, Kivera strode out the door and strolled through whorls of darkness.

Kivera thanked the stars for a moonless night as she crept on silent feet around the enormous alabaster circus tent. Nocturnal lids slid down to navigate the night, and can see when the Fae cat returned to the circus's domain. She had been waiting for hours, listening to the sounds of the balmy night. The roaming employees below would only have to look up to her outline, stalking their movements, but all focused on moving the animals to their cages. She held tight to the pole, spearing to the heavens and scanned the bodies in each cage. Big cats, wolves, and more predators than what they presented at the night show hissed Kivera's way. Her heart wrenched at the sight.

A bellowing roar to her left snapped Kivera's head to face the sound. The panther wrestled within the cage's confinements as the workers wheeled her inside the tent. Kivera could have sworn she scented the panther's fear from there and was grateful Mavis wasn't there to witness.

She crept down the sloping tent to the tent's eastern entrance and nearly stumbled on the slick surface, but righted herself by gripping one of the smaller poles at the edge. Kivera peered down the circular edge for any passerby before she vaulted off. She loosened her knees for impact and landed with a slight jar, but slid into a swift sprint.

The last cage behind the panther passed under the tent and Kivera cast out her magic to mark any of Raske's cronies patrolling near her. A couple of men stumbled along the right side of the tent but didn't notice Kivera slinking in the shadows through their boisterous laughs.

Cloaked in shadows, Kivera sprinted forward on cat-like feet and held her breath as she searched the side of the tent wall to find a way inside. She found a flap along the tent and she crept inside. Giant wooden crates lined the sides of a makeshift walkway that branched off into haphazard paths. The crates towered over Kivera's head and she lost count of how many lined the perimeter and wondered what lived within.

Kivera wends between crates and casts out magic to create a mental map of the warm bodies moving around. Torchlight stands were placed among the rows in sporadic disarray from a lazy touch, so it was easy for Kivera to sneak around. Shadows fogged the edges of the tent and pressed down in a gauzy fall to the ground, allowing Kivera an image of the tent's inner workings.

A bead of sweat slid down her torso at the high usage of magic. She would have to deplete her resources at a steady pace to avoid burnout.

One by one, cage after cage, empty, hungry eyes in the container depths watched her pass. Large locks at the front of the cage doors gleamed in the hushed light. In the folds of darkness, Kivera unsheathed her talons and stepped to the nearest cage. With a quick swipe, the lock thumped to the ground. She would not leave a single soul in imprisonment till her last breath.

But Kivera prayed their sharp teeth didn't near her as she raced past the rows of cages, slashing as she went.

Snarls exploded throughout the stretches of the tent from the center. Kivera raced towards the sound, continuing to slice locks as she passed. It surprised her at the lack of workers patrolling their stock. Part of her, the hungriest part, desired to repay their kindness with streams of their blood in the grass.

Kivera turned a corner to find shadows waving in the grass to alert her of the humans blocking the path. Their jeers reached her ears half a second later, and she scrambled up a crate to avoid the men and laid on her stomach as she angled her body to face the panther.

A crowd of men surrounded the panther's cage as she paced the small quarters. She was spitting out snarls and swiping at the close bystanders. They howled with laughter when a bottle exploded against her side. She growled viciously and Kivera echoed the sentiment.

Minutes have passed, and it was only a matter of time before-

"Animals have escaped! The beasts are gone!" A voice shouted from the southern edge of the tent.

The men shoved each other and dispersed through the pathways. Guttural growls followed soon after and the horrible sound of flesh shredding and screams filled the tent. The coppery tang of death and fear filled Kivera's nostrils, and a hidden part of her relished the scent from the horrible humans. But the area around the panther's cage was empty within moments.

She spirited through the shadows before Kivera landed in front of the panther's cage. The lock dropped a split second after from her talons. Kivera watched the cat's startling blue eyes as the door creaked open. The panther lifted her lips to reveal her fangs, but did not move.

Kivera waited, but the cat stilled. "Come on."

The cat sat on her haunches, not breaking eye contact with Kivera. Her tail flicked next to her paws and her teeth stayed exposed.

"Someone will come soon. You need to leave. Now." Kivera waved her arms and pinched the bridge of her nose after long seconds of attempting to break free from the cat. "You're an insufferable soon-to-be coat."

The panther only blinked.

Kivera pointed a talon at the beast. "It's your ass I'm saving here."

"Stop right there!" a voice bellowed to the left.

Forms ran in her peripheral, raising swords above their heads, and Kivera hissed for not staying focused on her surroundings.

Kivera spirited behind the three incomers and was a blur of burnished talons and shadows. In two heartbeats, Kivera tore into all the men's arms and had them moaning on the ground.

She turned to the panther in the cage. She watched the entire encounter without moving toward the open cage door.

Kivera rolled her eyes. "Fine. You had your chance, but you'd rather be a mongrel's *pet* than live in freedom." She turned around and faced a sword pointed at Kivera's heart.

"You released my inventory, bitch." Raske's beady eyes pierced down at her and he bared yellow teeth under the full mustache that canopied his lip.

Blood thundered in Kivera's ears, but she gasped in mock surprise and lifted a taloned hand to her chest. "Little ole me unleashing bloodthirsty monsters?"

"Young ladies are supposed to stay out of a man's business," Raske thrust his sword arm and Kivera didn't have enough time to raise her arms against his stab.

A breath of wind stroked Kivera's face and hair sliced into her eyes.

The strike didn't come and Kivera opened her eyes, one at a time.

Raske was gone. Save for a shoe sideways on the ground.

A breath whooshed from her chest. "What the?"

A shadow with brilliant blue eyes lifted from behind a crate. Paws touched down in the light and the panther sauntered out, licking her bloodied lips.

Kivera bowed her chin and shared a wicked grin. "Well met, friend."

She could have sworn the panther dipped her chin, but Kivera couldn't be sure with her onyx fur.

Time was running out, and they needed to leave before authorities captured Kivera. Shouts burst nearby, Kivera spun on her heel and broke into a sprint. She freed three-quarters of the cages already and with Raske's crew busy with the chaos of released hunters, Kivera raced for the remaining cages. She prayed they wouldn't find his body until she was long gone.

Footfalls thudded next to Kivera, and the panther dashed to her right, barely ahead of her. Kivera ran through each row of cages until she broke each lock and left on the ground before fleeing. The freed animals surged around her in a feverish stampede and she focused on keeping away from the sharp claws and dagger teeth crowding her. The big cats and wolves dispatched anyone that tried to stop them.

The last cages were in the northwestern corner of the tent, and Kivera slid to a stop. Animals parted around her and didn't stop the momentum of their herd, save for the female panther snarling at the other predators to back away from her and Kivera.

Kivera focused on the cages and groaned out loud as temptation gnawed at her to leave them behind. Three clear paned top-less containers were filled with hundreds of snakes wriggling over each other. Kivera's skin crawled, and she ached to scratch her skin, but she shrugged the itch off.

Time was running out.

Kivera summoned a concentrated amount of darkness to push the cages over with the gentlest touch. She cushioned the edges of the cages, so the landing didn't disorient the snakes within. They swarmed the grass and Kiera corralled them with hardened shadows to follow the mammals far ahead.

The act took precious seconds away, but the look from the observing panther at a nearby crate made Kivera think releasing them was the right decision.

The pair were careful to stay out of the snakes' path and raced ahead. The slit in the tent from the animals ripped into a small gateway and Kivera jumped through and the panther hopped out after.

A mental check of the map Kivera created of the tent confirmed she freed all the animals, but they were running straight to the edges of Raske's company. They set makeshift tents and wagons up for temporary housing. Fires dotted near the tents and where the fire burned, men occupied the surrounding seats.

When the wave of animals was upon them, screams started before something savagely cut them off. Bloodcurdling snarls echoed, and Kivera sprinted harder without interfering to allow the animals their revenge. She didn't want to stop them even if she could.

Slain bodies of wolves with knives embedded in their hides littered the ground, and Kivera murmured a soft prayer for their gentle departure. Howls filled the star-kissed night from their mourning brothers and sisters. But where the wolves fell, a big cat stalked in wait before pouncing on the humans.

Out of the corner of Kivera's eye, fallen men in between tents spasm and convulse from the writhing serpents on the ground. She glanced closer to watch the dozens of snakes cover the men, toppling over each other for the flesh to sink their venomous fangs into. The weight of their wriggling bodies muffled their screams.

The escaping animals were reaching the far edges of the castle grounds off the coast. Freshly cut grass turned to dirt, then fine-grained sand and Kivera's steps sank deep into the thick sand.

Freedom sang in the wind, and Kivera howled to the

stars. She kept up easily with the carnivores, but needed to leave as soon as they were clear. The suffocating feeling of the world is easier to bear under the soft night sky and ocean spray in the veins. A mile outside of the capital, down the vacant coast, Kivera slowed her steps to a jog before stopping entirely.

The panther continued and a piece of Kivera's heart panged at the sight, but the onyx cat glanced back before stopping in her tracks. Her elegant tail swished in annoyance like the thrill of a run under the stars called to her very blood. Kivera knew the ache like an old friend.

Kivera squinted at the retreating figures of the pack of lionesses, wolves, and their fellow refugees. "Take care of them. You're free now."

The panther watched the pack run without her until they disappeared around the bend of the cliff.

Outrage exploded in Kivera's chest despite the fissure in her heart at the thought of her being gone. "What are you doing? Go with them! Have your freedom!" All that work and the stupid beast won't leave.

Instead, the panther turned to Kivera, and she stretched low, her belly brushing the wet sand.

Kivera crossed her arms. "You're not running with them."

In response, the cat lifted a paw to her face to clean the dirt and blood, caking her black fur on her claws.

Kivera toed the ground, coyly peeking through the raven black curtain of hair. "Do you want to stay?"

It was the right question.

The Fae creature rose to her full height and radiated unbreakable strength. Her limbs rippled with each step towards Kivera and each time her paws struck the ground, something *else* thrummed through Kivera's soul.

An ocean breeze swirled around them as old magic dusted the atmosphere.

A feeling unknown to her before settled in Kivera's bones as the powerful animal inclined her head and dipped in a bow.

Old recollections of Kivera's studies of bonded fae named this moment a 'yielding'. The animal will bow down their life for their chosen Fae distant cousin to yield their life entirely and soul to their companion. The two-legged Fae would do the same and yield their entire soul to the animal counterpart.

These types of bonds were rare and Kivera only remembered flashes of old faces from her past life, with a Fae monkey and robin at their side. But never a creature as powerful as the one before Kivera. A part in the back of her mind balked at what this pairing meant.

An exasperated huff from the panther pulled Kivera out of her thoughts. The panther waited on the ground but didn't appreciate the delay. Kivera stepped closer to her and slowly knelt in case the cat changed her mind.

Kivera held her fingers up. "Let me touch your face. I promise I won't hurt you." She waited for a sign of approval and after a long moment, the panther blinked and lowered her head a fraction of an inch. With tentative fingers, Kivera raked them under the panther's chin, the ebony fur soft. A purr emanated deep in the panther's throat, and she closed her sapphire eyes.

A knot in Kivera's chest eased. She inspected the length of the obsidian cougar and found dozens of scars and tufts of fur missing. Fury flared in her heart at the mistreatment this animal has endured for gods know how long. Kivera wondered when, or ever, gentle hands touched this animal.

Another noise broke from the panther and she opened her eyes once more. She flicked her head back, gesturing behind her, and Kivera understood.

The wind howled from the ocean, the sea salt breathing around them, and Kivera unfolded from her crouch and waited for permission from the cat. Her colossal head bobbed once as she stared straight ahead.

A warm breeze washed around them and the Old Magic

sang to the magic restrained in Kivera's soul.

Kivera swallowed down her emotions and swung her leg over the panther's massive body and settled onto the warm body between her legs. Her hands explored the soft area between the cat's shoulder blades and marveled at this graceful body rising to her feet. Kivera's weight didn't burden her movements, but her liquid muscles shifted easily upwards.

"Do you have a name?" Kivera tilted her face upwards and inhaled the world at this height. She felt the panther's neck shake under her legs. "We need to change that."

A ponderous moment under the cover of stars brought a name to Kivera's lips. A name from ancient stories of Fae warriors and their legendary animal counterparts. One of Kivera's favorite warrioress, Nyrabella, tore through kingdoms and ripped apart her enemies with a golden lioness, Zyra. Her favorite legend was the fair saving an orphanage full of unwanted females from a drunken horde of males.

"Zyra."

The name carried through the air, tasting the world. A pleased ear-splitting roar belted from the magnificent beast that allowed Kivera to ride her, despite the horrors she endured.

The roar resonated to the heavens and Zyra dug her claws into the sand and hurtled them down the beach. They formed a living shadow streaking along the coast. Zyra unleashed her full strength but panted after a few minutes from lack of exercise in imprisonment.

Issuing her own howls, Kivera joined Zyra as they rounded the dark cliffs and the capital glimmered ahead. Kivera shrouded them in darkness in case a night guardsman noticed the stolen animal. An interruption in their swift journey was a hindrance Kivera wished to avoid.

Long minutes passed in a comfortable blur and Kivera looked in time to catch the end of the capitol walls and the beginnings of the lush fields on the cliff-side landscape. Their freedom beckoned.

Gods, Zyra's speed amazed Kivera. Despite her exhaustion, Zyra sprinted down the beach in remarkable time and arrive at Kivera's house with an impressive time.

Candlelight illuminated through the wide windows. Zyra slowed to a trot and stopped near the side door. The horses Kivera and her company brought scampered to the far reaches of the field when Zyra pranced through.

The side door opened, and a figure rushed out of the house and Kivera recognized Jexton in his rush. She watched as he practically fell back when he caught sight of the enormous predator Kivera was atop.

Soft snarls rippled from Zyra when Jexton came into view, and Kivera patted her shoulders.

He's a friend. Kivera assured Zyra's mind, and the rumbles stopped.

"Is that the panther from the ball?" Shock and scraps of fear laced Jexton's voice, and he remained near the safety of the door.

Kivera slid to the ground and approached Jexton. "Yes, she's Bonded to me."

Whether he understood the meaning or didn't want to ask, Jexton didn't push further. "She's much larger up close in person." He leveled a gaze at Zyra, but didn't move closer. "Does she have a name?"

Kivera nodded. "Her name is Zyra." She inspected Jexton further and noticed the panic in his eyes. "What's wrong, Jexton?"

A moment passed before Jexton finally looked away from Zyra and met Kivera's stare.

"Syt's missing."

CHAPTER TWENTY-SEVEN

"What do you mean, Syt is gone?" Kivera choked out.

A muscle twitches in Jexton's jaw. "When we returned from the castle, a message was waiting for me from Arcian." He swallowed once, then twice. "She didn't report back to Arcian and has been missing for a day."

The world tilted beneath Kivera's feet. "Oh, gods, Jex. We'll leave straight away and find her. Where is Mavis? Does she know?"

Jexton nodded. "She's gutted and inside with Masga and Tilly."

Kivera let her worry subside for one more brief minute. "Does Arcian know anything else?"

"Nothing that he wrote in the message. He'll brief us when we return to the guard station," Jexton raked a hand through his hair.

"We're going to find this person and make them regret ever taking Syt," Kivera stepped around Jexton into the house. Zyra trailed in her shadow as Kivera opened the door.

A tearful Mavis sat at the dining table with Masga hovering nearby. Tillirius, with his back to Kivera, sat across the table from Mavis.

Mavis's head snapped up when Kivera entered the room, but they slid quickly to Zyra behind her.

"You saved her," Mavis breathed, awe bright on her tear-stained cheeks. Tillirius swiveled in his seat and the blood from his face drained.

He pressed his body as close to the table. "You said to *rescue* the panther, not make her your pet."

Masga sniffed the air and surveyed the room. "You kept the poor creature?"

Kivera sighed and moved around the table to sit next to Mavis. "I cannot simply keep a creature like Zyra. She chose me and chose to stay."

Zyra slunk under the wide table and her tail flicked against Kivera's shins.

But Tilly leaned forward. "The castle will punish you for stealing a smuggler's prized stock. They already want your head."

Kivera bared her teeth. She was tired of this never-ending day. "Raske and his men are dead and my scent will be in the wind. We're leaving in a few minutes and by then, the smugglers won't find me or any of their 'stock'. Besides, would they risk confronting me with a pissed-off female Fae panther at my side?"

From the look of horror on Jexton and Tillirius's faces, Kivera knew what they were thinking. "No, I didn't kill anyone. That was not my revenge, to be exact." Her voice was clipped.

No one would search for an abnormal panther that could have slaughtered Raske. The news would break from many wild creatures' escape and suspicion wouldn't touch Kivera. Not with Mavis parading around the ball with a magicked shadow replica of Kivera. The drunk partygoers would only see glimpses of the infamous Royal Investigator, but not a genuine look on her face as the replica passed through the hallways or just slipped out for the bathing chambers.

Shaking his head, Tillirius shoved from the table to stand next to Jexton, grumbling under his breath.

"When do we leave?" Mavis's lower lip wobbled and Kivera's heart ached. Syt imprinted on Mavis's tender heart.

For her friend, Kivera would tear herself apart rather than witness her tears.

Kivera set her chin. "We leave in ten minutes. I'll spirit us back and we'll find her."

Mavis's eyes widened to saucers, her scar stretched tight over her face. "Kivera, you can't transport that many people and Zyra."

At the same time, Jexton and Tillirius voiced their outrage.

"I am not being sucked into the darkness with perfectly nice horses outside."

"You'll end up leaving me in some pocket of space, never to be found again." Tillirius fussed.

But Kivera held up a hand to silence their uproar. "The choice is yours, but that could mean wasting a precious day to find Syt alive."

Silence enveloped the room.

A faint smile tugged at Masga's lips as she tasted the room. "Kivera would not offer this sacrifice if life wasn't in peril. I suggest you take it to find your friend, boys."

The *boys* shared a look, discussing in soft tones, and Kivera stole the moment to reach under the table to scratch at the soft wrinkles between Zyra's brow.

"Can you spirit us all back to Tymern?" A voice tickled Kivera's ear, and she found Mavis staring at her. Tears wobbled in her eyes and the edges of her lips tugged down. The words weren't meant as an insult to Kivera or her abilities, but as caution at the influx of power. Especially after the night's events.

Kivera pat Mavis's arm. "I hope so." She left Mavis and Zyra at the table to pack a couple of things. Each step forward, Kivera delved into the steep descent into the well of power. She would have to take care not to waver too close to the solid bottom or burn out will break her.

Right at ten minutes, the group gathered outside for Kivera to have enough room to summon magic and not send the inside of her house through a tornado. Jexton and Tillirius stood awkwardly off to the side of the building, near the abandoned horse post. The horses didn't like Zyra's presence and fled to the far reaches of the field.

Masga followed Kivera and Mavis outside into the night, her movements slow with exhaustion, but her spine remained straight. Masga's hand lifted to search for Kivera's arm, so Mavis ambled closer, placing Masga's hand on her arm.

"This case differs from the others, am I correct?" Masga's weathered voice cut through the chilly air. Kivera's shoulders sagged, but she nodded at Mavis to continue to Jexton and Tillirius. Zyra watched as Mavis slouched away. Masga's gift to cut through any issue was Kivera's worst yet most valuable asset.

"You're right."

Masga nodded and sucked a tooth. "What will come of this?" The question cleaved Kivera's heart as the fear of losing this case, or worse, not solving it.

Her shoulders curled inward further. "I don't know," Kivera whispered. The honest uncertainty clouded Kivera and choked her airway. The number of Fae players presented since the case began was not a coincidence to be ignored. Kivera didn't know what could happen once they finally unmasked their murderer.

Kivera's troubles didn't fall on Masga. "Wherever the wind blows you, Kivera, sweet dear, you will conquer your way. You have gained precious, ferocious friends with even fiercer hearts. Allow them to fight with you."

Kivera blanched at the thought of Mavis wielding a sword against the murderous magic wielder. "I couldn't ask-"

"True friends won't wait for an offering, child." A knowing smile tugged at the old woman's pursed lips. Her arthritic knuckles reached up to brush against Kivera's cheek and Kivera leaned into the touch, wondering if she would see this woman again. Gods, she wanted to. So why did Kivera feel like this was the last time she'll see Masga?

In an unusual display of affection, Kivera pulled Masga's frail body to hers and inhaled the wild grass and sunshine that clung to the older woman's hair. A small *oophf* whooshed out of Masga, but she enveloped Kivera with the same measure of warmth and a surprising amount of strength.

The embrace lasted a few short moments before Kivera extracted herself gently out of Masga's reluctant arms and brushed away the moisture coating her cheeks. "The house is yours. I'll arrange for someone to care for the structure and bring food. I will do my best to come back."

Masga bobbed her head. "You do yourself well and take care of Mavis and Zyra." Without another word, Kivera's oldest friend in the human world stepped back and let her go.

A deep, vital part of Kivera cracked at the sight of the small yet vast void of space between them. A single tear that Masga would never see dropped from Kivera's eyes.

She spun and strode a few yards to Mavis and the others.

Zyra immediately perked to attention and sauntered over, her eye-level gaze concerned.

Kivera cleared her throat and tangled a hand in Zyra's thick fur. "Everyone ready?"

Tilly frowned. "Do we have a choice?"

"Not this time." Kivera beamed back. She plunged deep into the well of power and summoned wave after wave of ebony power. The power stimulated Kivera's blood and sparked into her vessels, easy to become intoxicated by the dark power.

The wind around Kivera howled in response and the ocean waves thrashed relentlessly. Tillirius and Jexton looked around anxiously, but said nothing.

They formed a close-knit line so Kivera's magic didn't reach too far and Zyra's tail wrapped around Kivera's ankle. Mavis gripped Kivera's hand and squeezed.

Hold tight. You won't like this feeling too much, Kivera murmured into Zyra's mind. The panther constrained Kivera's ankle tighter and planted her hind legs down.

Kivera hooked her elbows through Jexton's as the brisk rush of dark magic exploded from within her. Soft whimpers from Zyra joined the magic's roar and she couldn't see the others' reaction through the curls of shadows.

A breath in the air caused Kivera to pause. The writhing darkness cracked open to reveal one last view of her cottage by the sea and her friend listening to Kivera's departure. That quiet second allowed Kivera to look at the fragile, insignificant life she built for herself on this beachside.

This shred of life didn't truly belong to Kivera and was on limited time.

The thought unsettled Kivera more than Masga's hesitant wave. An idea struck Kivera as a last-minute gift to Masga.

This is me. And the others. Kivera popped an image into Masga's mind of their group, exhausted and terrified, but a gleam of fight in each of their eyes.

A grin broke on Masga's face that only Kivera could see. Kivera's last image of her borrowed life before shadows swarmed her vision was Masga's lips mouthing a *thank you.*

Darkness swelled and overcame Kivera.

CHAPTER TWENTY-EIGHT

Soft whimpering tugged Kivera from the darkness, and a warm body comforted her cold awakening. Kivera tore open her eyes to a scratched floor and her cheek plastered to the sticky surface. She scrambled to her feet and a wave of dizziness rocked her back on her heels. Stars flickered in the corners of her vision and a hollow ringing echoed in her head. Every inch of her body ached down to the bone marrow.

A hand steadied Kivera. "Easy there, Kivera," Mavis's lilting voice wrapped around her. "We're back at the guardhouse. You got us all here."

The blinding dizziness ebbed away and slow seconds passed before the guardhouse training room appeared between the dots in Kivera's eyes. It was nearly empty, save for Maserion watching from Kivera's research corner, devastation stark on his face. Circles puffed below his bloodshot eyes and Kivera wondered when the last time he slept.

Zyra monitored Kivera in a sitting position next to her. Her brilliant eyes never wavered from Kivera's position. Relief shone in her gaze and her enormous face crinkled when Kivera faced her. Mavis crouched at the panther's side.

Kivera scrubbed her face, and kohl stained her fingertips. "What time is it?"

"A few hours before dawn. You were out for a few minutes," Mavis answered the next question in Kivera's eyes. With an absent hand, Mavis rubbed the side of Zyra's neck. The panther hesitated for a moment but allowed the touch without biting Mavis's finger and drifted her gaze on Kivera.

"Where is everyone?" Kivera assessed the spring of magic within herself and found the normally overflowing well nearly drained. Never has she emptied the magic to dregs.

"Jexton and Tilly are gathering information and planning with Arcian at the round table. Jexton said to let you rest," Mavis answered and led the way through the training room.

Kivera nodded and followed her. Zyra rose to her feet and padded next to her, their heads level with each other. Kivera ran a hand down the panther's body and sent a thank you down their Bond.

Soft footsteps trailed behind them, and Kivera knew Maserion trailed after the Fae trio.

Voices floated to Kivera's ears before they were out of the training room. Kivera and Zyra shared a glance. The latter's hackle rose and her entire body straightened to the sound.

"Why did you permit Syt alone to go to his house in the first place? I instructed you to follow up with witnesses and not interview the *only* person of interest!" Jexton's voice hollered, and when Kivera rounded the corner, a tense scene appeared.

The large room of desks was empty save for Jexton, Arcian, and Tilly; their faces had different shades of red. Officers watched the ordeal from the balconies and the edges of the room. Most likely waiting for an all-out brawl between the Captain and his Third.

Jexton's eyes found Kivera the moment she walked in and allowed him to slide his eyes down the length of her body, searching for any sign of injury. Her cheeks flamed at his gaze. She gave him a weak smile in return, unable to conjure anything more. Exhaustion leaden through her bones.

"Enough, Jex. Fighting won't help us now. Everyone else returns to work," Kivera's voice cut through whatever Tillirius was about to gripe about and she maintained enough energy to add a growl to the ends of her words directed at the observing guards. They scattered under her scowl. She neared the table and leaned against the solid frame, grateful for the support of her shaking knees. "What do we know?"

Arcian turned towards them and had a double take at Zyra, next to Kivera. His mouth flopped open, but he recovered quickly before Kivera reached the table and he cleared his throat. "Syt visited Lord Huron's household to interview him once more. She wanted to scope out his staff to see if anyone would talk about their master in secret. She didn't report back last night."

Kivera nodded and sat in the nearest chair for the sake of her buckling knees. Zyra and Mavis flanked the high-back chair. "Poor fellow will have us to answer to. We'll chat with him first." Not a single person in the room missed the creature that roiled behind her gold eyes. But they didn't see the exhaustion flagging her movements or crinkling the edges of her eyes.

Lord Huron will regret meeting the monster underneath Kivera Galveterre's skin.

Preparations were scrambled chaos. Jexton's team rushed to gather their uniforms and weapons as Kivera and her sisters-in-arms watched. Kivera spent the time coaxing the last of her magic supply to the surface with her eyes closed.

"Rex will stay here and watch over Mavis," Jexton's voice carried from the training room as he assembled his weapons.

Mavis's eyes slid to Kivera from the seat next to her. "Do I have to stay?"

Kivera shrugged. "Your choice. It'd be safer for you here, but I couldn't make that decision for you."

Mavis nodded and bent to pet Zyra, now laying on the floor monitoring the hectic scene. "I'll stay near Zyra if we find danger."

Blue eyes flicked to Kivera, and she met Zyra's gaze, an

unflinching promise to protect Mavis from harm. *I will protect your friend should danger arrive as you saved my life.* The silent oath eased tension from Kivera's shoulders.

"If you won't use your magic, then stay armed and remain by Zyra's side." Kivera's own armory slid through her knuckles and Kivera tapped them on the table.

Without another word, Mavis burst from her chair with renewed energy and sprinted towards the training room. A single braid bouncing against her back.

Once Mavis disappeared from sight, Kivera slumped against the chair and closed her eyes again. A few moments of quiet passed before the peace shattered.

"No preparations needed for a great warrioress?" Rex's raspy voice asked from the other side of the table.

Kivera kept her eyes closed. "Is meditating not considered prepping anymore?"

"Indeed, forgive me. Others grind their swords to a vicious point and some need a nap." Rex smirked when Kivera cracked an eye open.

"Conserving energy is as important as weaponry care."

He chuckled, but the sound died quickly. "I want to ask something of you, from a wizened bag of bones to a young warrioress." Something in his voice made Kivera open her eyes. The normally cheery man was absent and in his place stood a twitching, exhausted grandfather. His eyes, bloodshot and fearful of what he knew to come, met Kivera's.

She cocked her head. "What is it?"

Rex played with the leather bracelet on his wrist. "My grandson is skilled in archery and combat. But he's young enough not to have experienced the trauma of watching a friend die or ending the life of a criminal." He cleared his throat as if the next words strangled him and a muscle in his jaw clenched. "I would like to hug my grandson again, Kivera. If he can't walk away from a training match with you, I pray to the gods he will walk away from whatever you all will face."

Kivera rose slowly to her feet, and she stood before the man.

Zyra grumbled from underneath the table at the interruption.

"I swear to you, Rex, that your grandson will come back to you," she crossed a fist over her heart. "I will protect him with my life."

Rex's shoulders sagged, and he surprised her by grasping her hands into his own warm ones. "Thank you, Kivera. Thank you so much."

Emotion clogged Kivera's throat and tears sprang in her eyes. Rex tugged on her heartstrings.

With a smile, Kivera nodded and opened her mouth, but a voice interrupted their moment. "Kivera! The horses are ready!" Arcian called to her from the building's side door.

Kivera pulled out of Rex's hand and smiled again before striding for the door. Zyra padded next to her side within seconds and together they left the building, but a new heaviness weighed on Kivera's shoulders.

Zyra slunk low to the cobblestone road, Kivera atop her, as the entourage neared Lord Huron's manor and Kivera leaned deep into her warmth and exhaled. She saw her breath and shivered. There wasn't enough magic in her body to fight off the winter night.

Hoofbeats clobbered on the neighborhood's street as Jexton's team approached the estate. Under the guiding light of the clouded moon, the group crept closer to the front gates through the shadows.

From Kivera's position behind Huron's foliage, there was not a single candle lit from within the household. The front facing wall yawned like a skull waiting in shadows.

Lone trots reverberated behind Kivera, and she turned to find Jexton staring at the grim manor. He frowned. "Is she in there?"

Kivera shook her head. "I don't think she's in there." What magic she had left swept through the manor, but she couldn't find Syt's familiar presence within.

A flash of disappointment swiped across his features but disappeared as quick as it appeared. "Stay here until I say." He kicked his horse forward before Kivera could huff a word.

She snarled and poked out her tongue at his back. "Whatever you say, *Captain*."

Immediately, Tillirius ambled forward to ride next to Jexton with a hand resting on his pommel and a smirk in Kivera's direction. She curled her lips at him in return and exposed her teeth.

Kivera nudged Zyra to saunter backwards to Mavis and the others. Arcian's eyes followed his superiors over the hedge line until they disappeared behind the growth.

"I don't like it," Arcian frowned. Mavis nodded in agreement and Kivera couldn't disagree. Nothing about this felt right.

Heavy knocks beat the front door. After a beat of silence, trios of knocks trailed after another until the door whooshed open.

"What do you want?!" Kivera's ears perked at the furious man and would recognize the pompous tone from anywhere. Lord Huron.

"Lord Huron, you are being summoned for questioning regarding the recent disappearance of missing women, including a member of the Alcerian Royal Authority." Jexton's stony voice answered the lord's question.

"At this time of night? Do you realize the time?"

"Yes, sir. We apologize for the inconvenience…" Kivera tuned out Jexton's peaceful approach and settled with twirling tufts of Zyra's fur into tight locks. She grew bored with Lord Huron's denials to Jexton's questions and occasionally listened to their mutterings.

"What are they saying?" Mavis leaned down from her horse to whisper to Kivera. They were near eye-level from

Zyra's massive height.

Arcian's eyes flicked over in warning but returned his focus to his captain.

"Bunch of garbage questions and the mustached toad denies knowing anything about the disappearances," Kivera said absentmindedly as she twirled her finger around another tuft.

Mavis's mouth twitched as she leaned back into her saddle.

Jexton's words floated to Kivera's ears again. "If you choose to not cooperate, we have other methods allowed by the Council to extract the truth."

"You cannot torture a Lord for your little interrogation. You don't have that much power, Captain." Lord Huron sneered and grated Kivera's nerves further.

"You're right, Lord Huron. Torture is against procedure, but we have other unpleasant means," Kivera heard a smug smile in his voice. "I believe you've already met Special Counsel Kivera Galveterre."

That was Kivera's cue to dismount Zyra, and she rounded the hedged gates. In the darkness with her hood up, Kivera appeared as shadows given form. A demon shrouded in the Underworld's dark cape. A mask to extract the truth.

Lord Huron, from his perch on the front steps, studied Kivera's every step., but his fear wafted to Kivera's nose and coaxed her inner predator to the surface.

She walked to where the front steps extended from the entrance and she stopped in between Jexton and Tilly. Kivera pulled off her hood and issued Lord Huron a granite expression.

Lord Huron's eyes narrowed. "It's you again."

The corner of Kivera's mouth jerked upwards. "Hello again, Huron."

His eyes flashed. "It's Lord Huron to you."

Both men on either side of Kivera bristled, but she shrugged off the venom.

"Makes no difference to me who you are. You all smell the same to me," Kivera made a show of delicately sniffing at Lord Huron and scrounging her nose up. He stepped farther into the safety of his home.

"You're all imposing on my sleep schedule and I suggest you vacate my property before I summon the entire regional council." Huron bared his yellowed teeth and moved to shut the door.

"Oh, quit your haughty chastising. We don't care or have the time. You stole something from us and we're here to retrieve it." Kivera inspected her nails and could have sworn the older man choked.

Lord Huron stayed silent for a moment. "I didn't take any women, and I think it's time for you to leave."

At that, Kivera grinned viciously. "Got you." With everything she could muster, Kivera conjured the wisps of magic burrowed deep and hurled them straight for Lord Huron's mind. Her magic cut easily through his defenses and in the split of a heartbeat, Kivera clasped his mind in a steely grip.

Lord Huron cried out, the scream loud enough to alert the neighbors, and Kivera hurriedly clenched his vocal cords. His yowling cut off and his body crumpled like a discarded puppet as magic swarmed his brain.

She controlled her movements within his mind carefully, not to let exhaustion cause a mishap. One wrong touch, one misstep and the human's mind would deteriorate to a mushy bowl of potatoes. Worst-case scenario, their soul forever departing their body.

Shock rippled through the bodies pillared on either side of Kivera, and they hurried to hold up the mogul.

Magic from another source clouded his mind in a thick mist that Kivera labored through. Tastes of winter and chaos and solitude stained the man's mind and Kivera urged her waning energy to fight through. Kivera clenched her teeth at the incoming burnout.

Rest will come. Rest will come. Rest will come.

Rapid-fire mental images sprung to the forefront of Kivera's conscious as she breezed through Lord Huron's mind. A dusty barn; pale-headed figure; Syt's brown eyes, wide open and filled with terror.

"Oh, gods, Kivera, his eyes rolled to the back of his head!" A voice exclaimed from faraway.

Weakness shuddered through Kivera, and her knees wobbled before buckling completely. Gloved hands caught her momentum before she collapsed. Kivera looked up to blue and milky-white eyes, filled wide with unease. Kivera slid out of Lord Huron's mind and she gulped fresh air.

Mavis frowned. "You faint too much."

"Too much practice, I'm afraid," Kivera sniffed and forced herself to stand on shaky legs.

But Mavis wouldn't shake off so easily. "Will you be well enough for the rest of the night? It wouldn't be shameful to rest on the raid."

Kivera's eyebrows disappeared in her hair. "And leave the investigation in these fools' hands? No, thank you. Not with our murderer borne with magic," she juts her chin towards Tillirius and Jexton, standing over Lord Huron's unconscious body. A softer smile touched her lips. "I'll be fine with you and Zyra watching over me."

Zyra rubbed against Kivera's hip in confirmation she wasn't leaving Kivera's side.

Mavis nodded but didn't appear convinced and chewed her lip. "What did you see in his mind?"

Kivera relayed the mental images to her and the eavesdropping ears around them. By the time she finished, faces around her etched into concern.

Arcian towered over her, scratching his head. "I may know of a barn from looking at the maps, maybe a few miles from us. That could be where Huron took Syt."

Kivera nodded. "In his memories, the barn felt close for comfort, yet far enough away to not be associated with the

Huron name."

Jexton nodded once and looked over at Kivera from the top of the stairs with one eye trained on Huron. "Could you find out who has Syt in the farmhouse?"

But Kivera shook her head. "Not with his head befuddled heavily with magic. Huron could have lost his mind and soul to the wielder." For the first time in her life, Kivera felt remorseful at the lack of magic filling her veins. Every other day she breathed, power plagued and splintered Kivera apart.

"We'll make do and check out the farm you know about, Arcian. We're going to find her. Right now," Jexton didn't spare another glance at anyone before he left Lord Huron snoozing uninterruptedly in a heap on his own doorstep. Kivera already swiped every memory of her and the team from his mind to avoid unnecessary retribution.

Tillirius blinked at his commander, then stared at the unconscious man for a second longer before following in Jexton's footsteps.

"Shit, I thought I was dramatic." Kivera rolled her eyes at Mavis. The other girl husked a laugh but died on her pink lips. The sight tugged Kivera's heart and in a brash moment, she pulled Mavis into a hug. "We are going to find her or spend our last breaths torching the world until we do."

Mavis sniffed and nodded into Kivera's shoulder. She let go quicker than Kivera anticipated, following Jexton's lead, and she stumbled after Mavis.

"Hoorah," Maserion spoke for the first time since arriving at Lord Huron's estate.

"Hoorah," Arcian mimicked but Kivera didn't glance back at them as she strode to the huddle of animals.

One by one, the group mounted their horses and Zyra respectively, leaving behind Lord Huron on the steps of his ivy lined manor.

CHAPTER TWENTY-NINE

After half an hour of hard riding through the maze-like forest and a gut-wrenchingly wide river their caravan nearly drowned in, the investigative team arrived at the barn Kivera viewed in Lord Huron's mind as the sky lessened from black with glistening stars to indigo. The beginnings of a winter storm pricked Kivera's nose.

A faded white barn peeked through the trees and Zyra crept low to find a closer peeking vantage. Zyra stalked on deathly quiet paws as her instincts took over and made their scouting undetectable. She stopped on a cliff overlooking a small valley where the barn lived and provided a well-positioned viewing point.

Jexton and the others dismounted some hundred yards back to avoid detection from supernatural ears. Their near silent footsteps followed Kivera and soon, five sets of eyes peered at the barn next to Kivera's perch.

The old barn was built in a break in the woods with waves of grass surrounding the ramshackle building. A corner of a tiny cottage protruded from behind the barn and curls of smoke escaped the chimney.

But that wasn't what stopped Kivera in her tracks and her beating heart nearly collapsed. Not the eerie quiet gripping the forest the closer they neared the farm. It was the smell of burnt sugar piercing her nostrils.

The smell of dark, abhorrent magic.

For the second time that night, Kivera mentally kicked herself for the barren fountain of magic within the belly of her soul. With full power, she could scan inside both of the buildings and slice through the slayer's mind with half a thought. Ending the entire case. She cursed herself for not being able to defend herself and others properly.

Instead, Kivera crept closer with her talons out and held her breath.

"We'll stick to the shadows all the way to the barn and locate Syt before we begin our hunt for this bastard," Jexton's whispers puffed in the frigid air.

Kivera nodded once and flicked her eyes to the barn every few seconds.

"What if we find the killer first?" Maserion asked from behind Kivera. Her promise to monitor the young man floated back to her mind. Heaviness tugged at her.

"We'll rain down justice, but finding Syt is our key priority. Without Kivera's magic, we'll be blind, so watch each other. We don't know what the hell we're walking into," Jexton answered, and met Kivera's eyes briefly. Their warm depths were now cold since Syt was taken, softened fractionally when their eyes met before Jexton strode away to begin the creeping pace down the cliff. The rest of the team followed his quick, purposeful strides, with Zyra and Kivera covering the rear.

The group crouched through the shadows and wended through the trees until the barn loomed above them and blocked out the moon. Owls hooted as if warning them to leave this horrid place. Jexton signaled for the group to split; each half of the group circled the building and converged at the entrance. Kivera swallowed her concern at splitting, but they had little choice and she led the way for Maserion, Mavis, and Arcian.

Through their Bond, Kivera nudged Zyra to watch over the captain and the big cat trailed after the men, after giving her Fae counterpart a side-eye. Kivera nearly cackled at the sight, had it not been for their purpose for being at the farmhouse.

A low whistle thrummed behind her and Kivera turned her head to find Maserion staring at the talon's unnatural gold gleam even under the cover of darkness.

"Would hate to be the unfortunate fellow on the other side of these doors." Kivera raised a brow at Maserion's words and a nasty grin arose to her lips.

"They will regret the day they stole one of our own," Kivera hoped she sounded brave despite the overwhelming sense to snatch Mavis and Zyra and leave this place. Kivera leaned back on her haunches and held a ready stance.

Silently, they crept around the barn without incident or any sign of whoever lived there. Any scent on the wood was stale. They rounded the corner to find Jexton and Tillirius's confused expressions, mirroring her own.

Kivera could read their minds without magic. *No one standing guard?*

A detail strange to Kivera, but without the luxury to dwell on the unsettling feeling seeping in. The two halves of the group crept closer to each other until joined at the front doors, careful not to stand by the tall gap between the door and the ground. The doors were double Kivera's height and four times as wide, but scratches marred the surface in uneven stretches.

"Your scent," Kivera hissed as quietly as she could afford. Comprehension bloomed on Jexton's face, and he stepped back from the wooden doors. She cocked her head and mouthed to him, "Zyra?"

Jexton thumbed behind him, indicating the cottage cloistered on the side of the farm.

She nodded once and placed her rounded ears to the door slab and listened to the stillness inside.

Nothing rustled on the other side and Kivera nodded at the all-clear.

Jexton reached over to open the door to let Kivera slip inside. The room was dipped in pitch blackness and Kivera allowed her eyes the split second they needed for the nocturnal lids to slide down.

Musty hay, blood, and cow shit slammed up Kivera's nose, and she forced herself not to cover her nose, or gag, from the eye-watering stench. Loss of the senses is an advantage for the opponent.

Tall wooden stables lined each wall at the top of the vaulted ceiling. The stables were all closed and deadbolt shut. Soft rustling reverberated behind some doors, but nothing, or no one, peeked out.

By the gods above and below, what a damned hellhole.

Nothing of immediate danger alarmed Kivera and she nudged into Jexton's mind the coast was clear. Her team flowed through the entrance like inky water in their all black ensemble. They split off to inspect the perimeter and Mavis jogged to Kivera's place, ragged uncertainty blazing in her eyes.

"Where could she be?" Mavis whispered at Kivera's shoulder. She was about to answer when something tugged at her.

A scent caught Kivera's attention and she delicately sniffed and her legs followed the path. It led her to the stable farthest away from the door, tucked away in the darkest corner of the barn.

Decay and gore slammed into Kivera, and she toed a step back.

"Mav, go wait outside," Kivera murmured behind her. The hitch in her voice was unmistakable and footsteps swarmed towards her. But Mavis stubbornly remained by her side.

"What is it?" Jexton was at her side and worry coated his voice.

"Did you find her?" Tillirius's voice asked behind Kivera.

But Kivera ignored them. She crept forward without breathing and swiped at the locks with her talons. The metal clamored to the floor, and she held her breath, listening and waiting for anyone coming to investigate the noise.

Kivera stepped forward and opened the creaking door and nearly wretched at the sight inside. She was grateful the others couldn't see the horrors filling her beloved darkness.

In the center of the bare stable was a post scaling to the ceiling, past the upper railing. Chained to the wood beam, Syt hunched over herself and partially undressed. There were featherlight movements in her chest and Kivera breathed a sigh of relief. Behind Syt's unconscious body was a form doubled over from the same chain that wrapped around Syt's torso to the other prisoner.

A couple steps further in, and Kivera realized the source of the reek. Kivera gagged as ice washed down her spine and she threw an arm over her nose to escape the smell.

They chained Syt to a post with a dead body.

"Oh, gods." Memories threatened to overcome her and it took every scrap of energy Kivera had not to be distracted by the demons of her past.

Kivera stumbled forward and, without looking at the mutilated body, she slashed down to cut through the chain as if cutting bread. She scooped up Syt's small body and rushed out of the stall.

Kivera gently transferred Syt into Arcian's arms before she vomited at the base of the stall door.

"Oh, Kivera!" Soothing circles began on Kivera's back and a wave of gratitude rolled through her. Though a peek over her shoulder would tell Kivera that Mavis kept one eye focused on the other woman.

"What else is in there?" Jexton made a move to enter the stable slot, but Kivera held up a hand to push the door closed.

"Don't go in."

"The female is right. Snooping through someone's residence is a bad idea." A cold, terrifying voice slid through the barn. A female, no less.

Kivera's body straightened at the voice, and she shoved Mavis behind her. She bared her teeth, and she flashed her talons. Her instincts scream at her to *run* and her earlier sickness forgotten.

The only sound in the room was the unsheathing of blades by the humans around Kivera, but those would be like twigs to the fangs on the female's creatures flanking her.

A small frame silhouetted the barn door, but remained in the darkness. Pointed ears, much longer than Kivera's own, broke through the other female's silver curtain of hair. A row of beasts, identical to the supernatural wolf that Kivera slayed, snarled behind the female, awaiting their master's orders.

"An obedient Fae in the clutches of Alceria? A sight to behold." The wintry voice mocked.

"How are you here?" Kivera's lip curled, but she couldn't mask the building curiosity since discovering magic at the first crime scene she visited.

"Unfortunate luck and a tragic story," the female sighed and drifted farther into the barn. "Why are you here, little one?"

"To hunt the monsters of our home and protect the humans that live here," Kivera replied equally coldly.

To this, the female laughed at the sound of the loveliest melody Kivera ever heard. "Hunt your own kind? For these *dogs*?"

"You are hereby under arrest for the death of multiple women, as well as the creation of those ungodly creatures. You will be brought in for questioning to the Royal Council." Kivera ignored the snipe and straightened her back to glare at the female.

The female's hand waved through the air in dismissal of the arrest charge. "Don't you wish to know *how* I'm here?"

"I'd rather cut your tongue out to shut you up rather than hear another word spew from your wretched mouth," Jexton grinned without a touch of the warmth Kivera had grown accustomed to. The captain raised his broadsword higher.

The female ignored him and gave Kivera a pointed stare. "I bet you're curious about how I traveled here and remained caged in this cesspool nation."

Kivera couldn't argue. She'd been mulling over who this killer might be and why they were in Oakheart, of all places, slaughtering people. But she wouldn't confirm that. "I care only for the victims you ruthlessly slaughtered for a pointless cause."

"Pointless?" The female scoffed. "Returning to the home of my kin is not *pointless*, stupid girl."

Understanding surged through Kivera, but she didn't hint at the realization.

Kivera theorized the markings were symbolic to a spell, but she didn't know enough of that subject of magic work to tell the difference. But coaxing the information from the female was far easier than mulling over useless literature.

"We can never go back. That was the purpose of the gates." Kivera pointed out.

"Gates?" Tillirius whispered to Jexton's ear, but Kivera ignored him.

The female cocked her head. "Did you not tell your humans about the gates imprisoning their kind?"

"Protecting them," Kivera snarled at the same time Jexton spoke.

"Not the matter at hand. You'll come with us in full cooperation or make the situation harder than it needs to be."

He was successful in capturing her attention. "You wish to chain me for a few girls, human? What do they matter to you? No worries now... you'll be dead soon enough, anyway."

A light clap rang through the barn and light burst into the open space. Pale, emerald flames burst from the female's figure and Kivera flinched at the pure wrongness of the fire. Burnt sugar flooded Kivera's nose and down her throat, nearly choking her.

The female standing in the doorway to their freedom was worse than Kivera imagined. Slight in frame, appearing no older than teenage years, with moonlight skin and hair to match.

But her eyes were wholly black.

Her creatures of nightmares growled and pawed at the ground. The animals would have been beautiful had someone properly cared for them.

The team sucked in a collective breath.

"I won't let a traitorous bitch and foolish humans prevent my return to home. My name is Lady Reanna, and I will not wait any longer." The pale-haired female moved to raise her hand, but a flash of fluid shadow behind the pack of beasts caught Kivera's attention.

A warm hum through Kivera's soul confirmed her hope.

"I know how to open the gates."

Shock rippled across the other female's features. A moment of contemplation seized her mind, and a sneer pulled at her lips.

"How would you know this? And do not think to lie to me. I'll spill your humans' blood quicker than you'll finish your lies."

Kivera cocked her head, stealing precious time. "I'm acquainted with the creator behind the gates." Not a lie, but not the entire truth.

Disbelief contorted Lady Reanna's face. "That's impossible." Snow-white eyebrows scrunched together and the misshapen wolves behind her growled. "The only person who knows is...."

Something clicked behind the female's depthless eyes. "You're his daughter." Her gaze inspected Kivera closer, down the length of her body, and sniffed the air. "But smell like her... she never told me..."

A shiver skittered along Kivera's skin and she was about to ask what she meant when a shadow appeared out of thin air as a flash of dagger claws and rippling snarls. Zyra tore into Reanna's shoulder and ripped flesh from the bone.

A screech belted from Reanna's bloodred lips, and she grasped Zyra by the scruff of her neck and yanked her bulky body off her own.

The movement of pure strength stole Kivera's breath.

Kivera spun around and maneuvered Mavis into the corner at their backs. Her hands found Maserion's uniform next. Instincts took over Kivera's system and placed him in front of Mavis, who was scrambling to her feet. Confusion scrunched both of their faces, but the look on Kivera's face cut off their protests.

"Strike down anything that comes close. Protect her at all costs." Kivera gave him a flinty look and something wild must have sparked in their golden depths, and Maserion unsheathed his bow swiftly.

Arcian deposited Syt's lifeless form gently on the wall behind Mavis. With one last look toward his friend, Arcian returned to the half-circle they created.

A quick nod to Mavis before Kivera whipped back around and sprinted toward the nearest set of vicious teeth with talons extended.

Battle cries rang behind Kivera, and she didn't need to look behind her to find the remaining men of the team engaging the beasts.

Kivera dodged a wolf's massive paw aiming for her and she struck at the soft flesh of its shoulder socket, then danced a few steps back before jumping forward to shred the lean tendons below the wolf's knee. The wolf slammed forward into the ground and Kivera went in for the kill, jamming both sets of talons into the vulnerable area between the shoulder blades.

Blood spurted up Kivera's fingers and coated her wrists. She squeezed whatever organ her sharpened claws were near. The wolf struggled underneath her grip and Kivera jumped backwards to avoid flailing limbs from the dying animal.

Kivera heard snarling to her left, and she spun in time to watch a wolf open its jaws at her face. She raised her arms up to protect herself.

A dark blur slammed into the wolf's flank and sank into the beast's neck and the pair went rolling. Kivera lost sight of her bonded animal under fangs and claws. She clung to the psychic bond that they have not killed Zyra, her only reassurance. Her eyes turned to her next target.

Reanna lounged on the banister railing above, watching the entire scene with a small smile on her full lips.

Around the airy room, the men each batted their own wolf and sporting a wound. In the dark corner Maserion and Mavis occupied, the former fought off a wolf with brilliant skill while the latter pressed herself to the wall of the closest stable, clutching a blade in a white-knuckled grip.

Kivera raced forward but was intercepted by a pair of wolves and she slammed on her heels. She hissed at their snapping jaws and drew her arms into a ready stance.

The wolf on the right lunged forward and Kivera swiped to the left but caught a paw to the shoulder. Pain lanced through her arm and she staggered back a few steps back.

The wolf on the left used the opportunity to circle around towards Kivera. It leaped forward and Kivera grit her teeth at the pain lancing through her body to meet the beast head on.

She raced forward before dropping to her knees and slid by the wolf. It whipped its head back to snap at Kivera's passing body and she shoved her claws into the wolf's flank.

Howls echoed through the barn and Kivera looked up to find the rafters empty. Red flickered in her vision, but she didn't have long to look in other areas before the wolf on the right was upon her and extended claws for her throat.

Kivera rolled on her side and jumped to her feet, pushing forward with her hands. Pain speared up her arm and whimpered, but kept moving. Exhaustion slowed her movements to human speeds, so she'd have to find Reanna before anyone else gets hurt. She turned to the wolf and snarled before sprinting forward.

She knocked away the wolf's paw with talons and ducked beneath the next swipe. Kivera clipped at its snout and earned a chilling, earsplitting roar.

The animal leaped onto Kivera's chest and talons sunk into her flesh. She cried out and raised her arms above her face to avoid the dagger-like teeth snapping an uncomfortably close distance to her head. She held the creature by its jaws inches but was losing the battle quickly.

Kivera kicked the back leg until the wolf lost momentary focus, but a moment was all she needed. She let go of the snapping jaws with her right hand. Hot breath wafted an inch from her face and slammed her talons into the wolf's eyes as hard as she could.

The wolf stumbled and howled in agony before flopping down, slowly panting to its death.

Kivera surged to her feet and roared in victory, her eyes wild for the Fae female. Her eyes found the horrific sight of Reanna dodging Jexton's blows with her strange green fire. Kivera's stomach filled with queasiness at the sight.

Tillirius and Arcian fought off two of the wolves together, having dispatched one on the floor near the door. The men were bloodied and their swords singing, but their movements did not tire. But they couldn't have seen Jexton off fighting Reanna.

Zyra crept through the shadows and stationed herself near Mavis and Maserion as he fought off a smaller wolf. He sported a nasty cut down on his freckled neck, but otherwise appeared unharmed. Zyra's paw swatted at the beast, accompanied by a ferocious growl, as if it ventured close to Mavis.

Kivera turned back to the fight between Jexton and Reanna and ran towards them, but a green flame struck her throbbing shoulder. She didn't have enough time to raise a shield and fell hard to the stained floor, her breath whooshing out of her chest. Stars twinkled in the corner of her vision and for a moment, Kivera rolled on her spine as pain lanced through her body.

Gods help us. Please.

But the gods don't answer the prayers to a

nonconsequential, pointed ear female. She would become a force to be reckoned with if they continue to ignore pleas.

Kivera turned on her side to ease back up. Her eyes followed Jexton's fluid movements and couldn't help but marvel at his sword skill. The fight became a lethal dance that Reanna laughed delightedly in.

But Jexton faltered a step, and Reanna struck. Her fire struck Jexton's palm, causing him to drop his sword. She moved past his defenses like a shadowed blur and pulled him close to her body to hold a lick of flame near his throat, holding him into a lover's embrace.

The flame colored his tan skin a sickly hue and Kivera heard his breath hitch at the effortless dismantling.

"What can humans actually do if they fight terribly?" Reanna mused through the battle in the room, but Kivera knew the words were meant for her. "Breeding and servants' work."

"Let him go." Kivera groaned and tried to push to her feet, only to be betrayed by her wobbly limbs.

A cruel laugh tinkled among the bloodshed. "You can't even stop me, girl. What makes you believe you could stop me from drinking the blood from your precious human?" Reanna inhaled Jexton's neck.

Panic screamed in Kivera's head.

"You do not wish to make me your enemy, Reanna. You will die if you harm a single hair on his head," injecting as much fear and power into her voice, but even to Kivera's ears she sounded weak.

"What could you do from the ground, child?" Reanna laughed and inched closer to Jexton's ear. "Could she stop me, human man?"

"She is a dreadful thorn to her foes," Jexton replied through gritted teeth, but Reanna only smiled.

"Nuisances are boring. But maybe she'll be a little more fun after this...." Reanna locked eyes with Kivera before the darkling's finger dragged along Jexton's neck. A faint green line followed the trail and brightened once before Reanna lifted her finger.

Ruby beads pooled from the dimming green necklace and Jexton's mouth gaped into an O. Blood gushed from his neck and the world stopped turning as Kivera watched from the ground.

She screamed and screamed and screamed as Jexton's body tumbled to the ground. The world froze as the red ribbon around his neck poured out his lifeblood and he stared at her with unblinking eyes.

CHAPTER THIRTY

Kivera stumbled to his twitching form and collapsed next to his body. Her clumsy fingers fumbled at the wound around his neck to staunch some blood remaining in his body.

The remaining beasts retreated to their master in the momentary lapse of confusion, and Kivera's friends ran over to form a loose, protective circle around Jexton and Kivera.

She looked around for anything to help but found nothing and held the two edges of the frayed skin together. Only found the lost and agonized eyes of Jexton's team.

Kivera locked eyes with Tillirius and she saw the soul behind his eyes shatter as he watched his captain and best friend bleed out on a dirty barn floor.

Faint laughing echoed around the room and Kivera looked over to find Reanna smirking near one of the semi-upright wolves. "Who is he to you? A lover, perhaps? Won't matter soon when my creatures shred your bodies apart and you'll be dead next to him." She continued to laugh.

Unending rage flooded through Kivera and settled into a deep descent into her well of power, scrounging for anything to silence Reanna. A shrill ringing started in Kivera's ears.

"You'll regret this," Tilly shouted and broke into a sprint, his sword pointing straight at Reanna's chest.

He didn't make it a few yards before Reanna lazily waved her arm and Tillirius flew across the room, towards the stable Syt was imprisoned in.

His attack only delighted Reanna more and she brought her hands together.

Wave after wave of rage consumed Kivera, and she scratched at the bottom of the power woven into her soul, digging for any scraps, pleading for *anything*.

A fission cracked the rough, strewn surface and Kivera, in her rage, punched and kicked and slammed every ounce of her soul into the crack. Screaming to give her something. It splintered into thousands of hairline cracks and Kivera gave it one more tremendous hit with the last of her depleted energy.

The bottom exploded, and Kivera's soul free fell into the abyss beneath the well of power. Shadows cocooned her bleeding soul and seeped into every crack of her shattered heart and filled her empty carcass with raging power. Kivera swam in this new cold power, momentarily marveling at its unending expanse, and hauled it toward the surface at hurtling speeds.

Kivera had enough time to say to her friends, "Get back." before brilliant darkness exploded from her body. Shadow winds howled and whipped throughout the room. Tendrils tickled Kivera's skin as they wiggled to be let loose.

Kivera lifted her hands and unleashed the nightmare underneath her skin. Talons lengthened to their full size and the glamor concealing her Fae body melted off. Obsidian shadows speared for the few injured wolves and pierced their coats to sink into their flesh. Reanna deflected the ones assaulting her with some difficulty in a conjured shield of fire.

Wounded howls echoed through the room and to the mountains beyond, but Kivera didn't waste time.

Fueled with this new power, Kivera sprinted forward at supernatural speeds. With her right hand, Kivera threw a shield around the team.

Reanna lifted her hand to fling her power at Kivera, but she was too weak against Kivera's cold fury.

She was feet away from the foes when she halted to a stop and snarled as she lifted her hands.

A thunderclap deafened the room, and darkness smothered the torches. Reanna's beautiful mouth was ajar and was the last image Kivera noticed before everything went black.

But with her nocturnal lids in place, Kivera could see through the blanket of blistering night to notice ashes on the ground. The only remnants left of Reanna and her wolves after the ebony magic incinerated them.

The world, suffocated by shadows, was eerily quiet.

"Kivera?!" a strained female voice called out and all the newfound energy rushed out of her body. She breathed deeply to allow the shadow magic to ebb away and tighten the chains on the power once again.

Slowly, light returned from the gray predawn skies as the shadows dissipated.

Kivera limped to where the team crowded around Jexton and she dropped to her knees, pulling his head into her lap.

"I'm so sorry. So sorry." Tears spilled onto his cheek and he stared up at her with wide eyes. She waved her hand over his head and overeager shadows encased the length of his body like liquid night. The shadows eased his pain and Jexton's body loosened.

"Can you do anything?" Tillirius's gruff voice cracked and Kivera shook her head, ashamed of the curse of great, terrible power without the ability to save the people closest to her.

Kivera's fingers raked through Jexton's brown hair that flopped over his brow. "Peace be with you, Jexton, as you pass into the next world." More tears rained onto his face, most of Kivera's and a few of his own. "You fought braver than any warrior I've met. It's an honor, Jexton, to know you. You are the kindest man I've ever met and wish we had more time together."

Someone sobbed behind Kivera.

Kivera watched as Jexton's blood spilled from his neck and life drained from his eyes. He gurgled from blood choking his air pipe and red trickled out the corner of his mouth. But his eyes warmed as he stared at Kivera and his friends behind her.

Jexton shuddered one last time before his chest stopped moving. His eyes were wide and staring up at Kivera.

A sob ripped through Kivera and she bent over his body, unleashing the silent tears building inside her. She didn't move for some time and heard the others disperse to chew on their grief with tasks.

They needed to finish this case and get the hell out of there.

But Kivera couldn't move. Darkness tugged on her soul and slowly she sank.

And sank.

And sank.

When Kivera lifted her foggy head, the world swam in saltwater and she kissed his lips one final time before she pulled away from Jexton's body.

Somehow, she rose to her feet. Everything screamed at Kivera to sleep for weeks with each forced step. Everything was a haze, and she blinked again somehow outside and she didn't know how.

By the gods, do I need a deep sleep. Perhaps forever.

Kivera's eyes wandered out the open barn doors to the sky that painted the day with a rosy blush. What a cruel sight after a bloodbath night, she thought to herself.

"What would he want?" Kivera's voice rasped, her vocal chords constricted. She didn't know who the question was for, but an answer came anyway.

"He would want his ashes to float down the river to the sea where his own family perished," Tillirius replied in a raw voice as he stepped by her side.

"We'll take him to the river halfway to Oakheart," Kivera decided. Another decision came to mind. "What of the others?" She couldn't form the words of the grotesque remains that awaited in the stalls.

Yet, birds chirped, and the wind carried a dance through the branches and the sun rose above the mountain. How could they when something tragic happened in their presence?

"They should be burned. The entire barn should be torched to the cursed ground," Arcian chimed in from far away.

Kivera arched her neck to find where he stalked off to. A stark expression of disgust and horror was clear on his face as he surveyed the stables.

"What is it?" Kivera's quiet voice carried through the crypt-like barn.

"She... changed the bodies, warped them. The victims, I mean." He could barely choke the words out.

Before reason stopped her, Kivera's legs carried her through the barn to where Arcian stood on the threshold of a stall. Rotting death and excretion slammed into her nose. She clenched her stomach to not vomit and squinted against her watering eyes.

A single look inside the stall and she bit down on a scream with her fist. The image of that *thing* was plastered to the forefront of her mind.

Kivera wished she had been slower with Reanna's death.

The lifeless body inside was once a human woman, until she broke all the bones in her limbs to unspeakable angles. Fingers disfigured into upside down clawlike curves. Ugly slashes slit from her mouth across her beaten cheeks to the holes where her ears used to be. Patches of hair remained in long, matted ribbons atop her head and across her naked body.

The girl must have died before Reanna completed her wicked transformation.

Kivera's stomach roiled at the thought of the beast she killed weeks back. The savage creature was once a woman ordered to her death.

"We'll burn it down. They don't deserve the disgrace of being gawked at in the worst state of their lives." Kivera walked towards Mavis and hooked her arm through hers. They strode into the winking dawn after one last look at Jexton's body. Tillirius stood over him with his head bent over shaking shoulders. Sunlight streamed onto his back as he wept, casting a shadow over Jexton's body. Tillirius draped his cloak over his best friend's body before bending down to lift him into his arms.

No one voiced their opposition nor peered inside the stables. No one whispered a single word until everyone was gathered outside. Their friend's body wrapped in Tillirius's cloak on the ground in the middle of them all.

Maserion carried Syt out of the stables and volunteered to return Syt to Oakheart after their goodbyes to Jexton. Rex would need to inspect the nasty cuts and bruises covering her body. Mavis attached herself to her side and watched her every breath.

Arcian scraped a flint and rock over hay and with a few maneuvers, sparks flew to the hay and flames licked the surface before spreading across every bit of the wooden structure. Everyone stepped back from the raging heat and stared at the engulfing flames rising toward the new morning sun.

Arcian murmured prayers as he watched the fire lick up the exterior walls.

Kivera wished she knew the victims' names and loathed that she would never find out. Instead, she inhaled the stench of rot and decay and prayed for their souls to pass to the next world in peace.

"Why did Lady Reanna do this? Kill all those women?" Mavis asked as she observed the fire.

"A lonely, angry person with nothing to lose, desperate to return home, is the most dangerous combination," Kivera replied and her response quieted the team until they watched the barn topple to a pile of ashes. Some drifted in the wind and swirled to the woods and beyond. They left it smoldering on the ground and began a slow march for the river within Kivera's earshot. Maserion led the horse, carrying Syt's swaying body with Mavis by her side.

The sun had not cleared the eastern curve of mountains when Kivera and the team arrived at the serene river overlooked by willows. Zyra slunk next to Kivera and occasionally, she lifted a hand to rub underneath her fuzzy chin.

The walk had been grueling to Kivera's body on top of the magic burnout and sleepless night, but with each glimpse towards Jexton's body, exhaustion faded entirely from her mind.

They approached the gurgling river, and the procession stopped.

Kivera glanced over to Syt and the struggling woman blinked open her bleary eyes. She opened her mouth, but her eyes fell to the covered body on the river banks. Kivera watched her survey the group and count the number of faces in their group before the light clicked behind her eyes. Suddenly wide awake, deep sorrow haunted her chestnut eyes and tears swarmed her gaze.

A moment passed, as if everyone was waiting for someone else to start the ceremony. Mavis hooked her arm through Kivera's and placed a hand on Syt's leg. Zyra scaled up the nearest tree to monitor the forest beyond and their tiny ceremony below.

With a sigh, Arcian stepped forward and lifted Jexton's body from Tillirius's massive arms that trembled. Arcian eased the limp form on the ground and peeled back the cloak to reveal Jexton's bloodless face and his slashed throat.

Maserion choked on a sob.

Arcian cleared his throat and clasped his hands together in the front of his body. "Jexton was a remarkable leader and an even better friend. I couldn't imagine being where I am today without his help. Thank you, my old friend. I look forward to our rambunctious times with the gods of the underworld." Tears strangled his voice and Arcian stepped back, wiping his face. Kivera did the same with the wetness coating her cheeks.

Maserion inched forward and rubbed his hands on his thighs, but kept his eyes trained on Jexton's body. "Jexton was a good man and an encouraging trainer I'm grateful to have met.

I will miss him until the end of my days." He wiped his nose before retreating to a tree trunk to lean on. Many eyes tracked his movements with pity.

"He was kind and stern, funny and serious, open and resilient. A wonderful human to be my longest friend and my brother for life." Tillirius didn't move and spoke in a hushed voice. He stared with bright eyes at Jexton and his throat bobbed before being able to speak again. "Life will be a challenge without you, brother, and one I wasn't prepared to do. But now you can look out for me from above and be with your family again."

Mavis choked on a sob and buried her head into Kivera's shoulder. Kivera wrapped an arm around Mavis's shaking shoulders and blinked through her own prickling tears.

Silence enveloped the group, and Kivera waited a moment before peering over at Tillirius. Tears stained his cheeks and a small timid part in Kivera's heart ached at the sight.

Knowing the last words were shared, Kivera disentangled from Mavis's grip and knelt down to his body. The scent of decay slammed into Kivera, but this was Jexton and she forced herself not to recoil away.

"Take care, Jexton. I'll miss you terribly. I wish I could have told you everything," Kivera's voice cracked and tears fell onto his face. She brushed her lips against his cool skin. The lack of warmth on his forehead cracked her heart. Never again would she watch Jexton's kind and warm eyes twinkle after a joke or his brows furrow at Kivera.

Kivera cupped her hands into a makeshift bowl above Jexton's unmoving chest. Darkness pooled in the center and overflowed into his body. Within a few seconds, enough shadows spilt onto his body and encased the entirety of him. Only his face remained bare. Kivera rocked back onto her heels and pushed to her feet, returning to her spot in the group.

"Are you ready?" Kivera asked no one in particular though knowing no one was ready. She clenched her hand into a fist. The shadows on Jexton's body expanded to his face and hardened into an ebony casing.

A breeze lifted the threads of Kivera's hair from her call of magic. Piece by piece, Jexton's body disintegrated into onyx ash and floated on the wind. The pieces carried on the wind before settling into the water and drifting down the current.

"Well, that's one way to say goodbye," Maserion commented, and Kivera could have sworn the air vibrated with a heavenward laugh.

CHAPTER THIRTY-ONE

Kivera opened her eyes to complete darkness. After a dreamless sleep, her bones finally didn't ache as much.

Holy gods, I'm ready to go home.

She stretched a seeking arm for fur to pinch but found cold, empty sheets. In a panic, Kivera sat straight up, scanning the room.

"Easy, there. I'm right here," Mavis perched herself in the armchair and basked in the full moon's light flowing through. She lowered the book she was reading by the candlelight to her lap. "How do you feel?"

Zyra lay at Mavis's feet dozing and she peeled her eyes open before closing them again and snores continued. She scrunched her enormous body to fit on the floor between the chair and the bed.

Kivera stretched her taut muscles, and an ugly groan escaped her mouth. "Like I was resurrected from a dragon burning me to a crisp."

Mavis snorted. "That good, huh?"

Kivera waved her arm, and the rest of the candles in the room flickered to life. "What time is it?"

"The sun went down a few hours ago. The city has been in a fit of celebrations since then." Kivera must have worn a puzzled expression, and Mavis continued. "The streets are safe now and the town's guards want to commemorate a fallen hero."

In an instance, a heavy cloud settled on Kivera. The previous night rushed back, and she slumped back into the bed. After the teary goodbye to Jexton the day before, Kivera announced to no one in particular that she was leaving to go to sleep before spiriting Zyra and herself. Mavis stayed by Syt's side until the afternoon and Kivera heard her slip into bed.

"I thought it was all a dream. A terrible, tragic dream," Kivera whispered.

Mavis sat forward slowly, as if chewing on the words she was about to speak. "He would want us to keep moving and cherish the time you had together." She placed a warm hand on Kivera's foot.

Zyra opened an eye at the emotional disturbance that fluttered through their bond. She raised herself up to jump on the bed and plopped her head on Kivera's lap.

Kivera raked her fingers absentmindedly through Zyra's soft fur. "I can't stop seeing his eyes. If I blink, I see them. If I sleep, I see them. I see them everywhere and I can't escape."

"He was your friend and someone possibly becoming more. Take the time to grieve, my friend. Zyra and I are here for every step."

Kivera could have sobbed right there on Mavis's chest, but her stomach interrupted with a growl. Mavis cracked a smile.

"I think it's best if we found some food and relaxed the rest of the night." Mavis folded the page she was reading on and ambled to her feet. She stretched her arms to the ceiling and groaned. "I heard some folks celebrating downstairs, but I've heard them quiet down in the past hour. Perhaps it's safe."

Kivera slid out of bed and slid on clothes over the nightshirt she wore. She glanced down at Zyra's unmoving form. Her blue eyes blinked tiredly up at Kivera. *Go hunt or something, you lazy kitty.*

A grumble down their connection line almost cracked a smile on Kivera's face, but darkness shrouded her heart and the smile did not come.

Zyra huffed and stretched languidly to her feet, slow as possible to get moving.

"Must you be so swift?" Kivera lamented and stepped around the slow-moving beast. The trio left the room, despite Zyra's reluctance, and went down the staircase to the main floor.

Gasps and quiet murmurs followed in their footsteps from humans meandering through the lobby and the dining tables. Kivera nearly snarled at the onlookers for staring too long, but after a second look, she realized they were ogling at the Fae panther padding next to her.

A slip of satisfaction raced through Kivera's blood.

Mavis slipped off to find seats while Kivera opened the door to allow Zyra outside.

Can you stay nearby? The woods are safer, but not entirely friendly. Kivera said down their mental line, and Zyra dipped her chin before disappearing through the door.

A ball of anxiety knotted itself in her stomach, but she swallowed around her fear and turned around to find Mavis.

Every table was occupied with celebrators vocal on the death of their town's murderer. Ale tins overflowed with foam and a haggard wench zipped around the room in a constant blur of activity.

Kivera found Mavis's twin blonde braids with ease, but she wasn't alone. The whole investigative team sat in silence, sipping on ale mugs, including a pissed-looking Syt. No one saw Kivera enter except for a pair of dark eyes that snapped up.

Tillirius's eyes met Kivera's across the room and Kivera waited for a fraction of a second. Waiting for what she didn't know. But he nodded once and returned to glowering at his drink.

She let out a breath and wended through the tables and the vacant seat next to Mavis. The entire table looked up, except for Tillirius. Rex beamed with unsaid gratitude at Kivera, but a shadow of grief flashed across his weathered eyes.

"You look as rough as we feel," Arcian commented, a

brief twinkle in his eyes before it guttered, but she noticed his attempt to raise the team's spirits and Kivera played along.

Kivera gave him a sardonic look. "Don't talk too fast, Arc. You're not looking like a rested beauty yourself."

A rumble of chuckles, ghosts of the laughs they shared when *he* was alive, rode through their group. A small victory, at least.

"Did you rest well?" Rex asked as he lifted the mug to his lips.

"Not until I leave this godsforsaken city, will I have a true deep sleep," Kivera grumbled and signaled the flitting wench for two ales. She grunted before shooting off towards the bar. "How long do you all plan on sticking around Oakheart?"

Everyone shifted uncomfortably in their seats before Maserion answered Kivera. "We think in the next couple of days and we debriefed our commander the outcome of the case," Maserion gulped as he brushed over Jexton's death, but continued on. "There will be another unit's captain to assign us a new case in the next few days. We have to settle things here and we'll be gone soon."

"We don't want to stay here longer than we need to, it's just…" Arcian's tenor voice trailed off, but Kivera followed his mental crumbs. The team needed time to say their goodbyes to their captain before traveling away from his body floating on the river.

"He's with the wind now and able to guide you wherever you go, no matter how far you travel," Mavis intervened with quiet reverence. Syt reached over to grip Mavis's hand and stroked her thumb on the back of Mavis's hand.

Kivera couldn't fathom a world where Jexton's soul didn't exist, much less coast on the wind. A flash of image scorched Kivera's vision; Jexton gasping for breath, staring up at Kivera with pleading eyes. She sighed gratefully when the ales were delivered to their table and interrupted her thoughts. She reached for her mug and held it up.

"To a brave soul and an even kinder friend," The others

lifted their drinks as well with a chorus of "Jexton". Kivera drank deeply and wiped foam from the top of her lip with the back of her hand.

"I remember this time when I was first training with Jexton, he was showing me different angles to fire off arrows. He decided a fun exercise would be for me to learn how to dodge an arrow.. from above," Maserion sniffed and took another swig.

A rumble of chuckles roved through their group.

"What happened?" Mavis leaned forward.

All eyes turned to Maserion and a tired grin split across his face. "He shot the arrow straight in the air and I made damn sure not to be pierced in the back."

Syt's nose turned up. "He did not. Jexton would never."

Maserion's smile widened further. "He did. I'll prove it."

Quicker than Kivera could process, Maserion whipped off his coat and pulled down his shirt collar before anyone could protest the stripping. A four point scar marred the muscle beneath his shoulder blade. He looked over his shoulder with a fox grin spread wide on his lips. "I told you."

Syt sniffed, but a trace of a smile taunted her lips.

"That's nothing," Arcian gulped the last of his ale before slamming it on the table, wiping the foam from his lips with a forearm. "Jexton tricked me into a duel with a bear. I barely escaped with my ass intact."

An eruption of laughs rumbled the table.

Kivera spluttered on the ale she drank. A devilish bud of a smile appeared on her lips. "Do tell us more, Arcian."

An animated Arcian replayed the entire story, happy tears in the corners of his eyes before unashamedly coursing down his face. Once he finished, Maserion delved into another story of Jexton. Everyone around the table piped in with their own story, even quiet Mavis and Syt.

Kivera watched the energy vibrate among their little group, laughing over tales of their fallen friend. Emotions rolled through her and held the looming darkness at bay. Time passed in a bittersweet blur and Kivera felt content enough to sit there for hours.

A tremor in the world demanded Kivera's attention. She forced herself not to react outworldly and instead cast a magical net as far and wide as possible until she found the source.

Or to be precise *them*.

Three of them.

Under the table, Kivera reached over to squeeze Mavis's hand. She tapped on the chambers of Mavis's mind to ask for permission to speak inside. Her friend opened the mental door immediately. *What's wrong?*

There is Fae here. I'll talk to you when I can.

Mavis nodded imperceptibly out of the corner of Kivera's eye. She excused herself to the bathroom in the middle of the clamor, and the group waved her away, barely registering her words.

Kivera hurried out of the dining room and rather than turn left to the stairs to her room, she turned towards the front doors out of the team's sight. She stepped outside into the crisp night and before the door shut, Kivera disappeared in whorls of darkness to spirit to the location of the faeries. She sent a message of the strangers to Zyra wherever she may be hunting. If these were more of Reanna's friends, Kivera would provide them with similar treatment that she gave Reanna at the barn. She had enough magic flowing in her veins to confront them, though a cramp pierced her lower back, signaling a burnout would be near if she weren't efficient with the usage. She sent a message down her Bond with Zyra and she could have sworn a growl reverberated in the night air.

Darkness parted in a wispy curtain and she landed in the woods on the northeastern edge of the city. Right behind three hulking figures. They were watching the city as they quietly conversed with themselves.

Zyra's eagerness for a fight rippled through their bond and Kivera felt her hunting for her location.

Kivera's knuckles tingled and magic simmered close to the surface, encasing the whole of her body in the blackness, saving her face. Nocturnal lids slid down to provide perfect vision of the strangers. Cramps burned her lower back, but she was numb to feeling anything.

"Are you lost?" Kivera used her most sultry voice, and a thrill went through her as the hooded figures jumped and spun around with inhuman speed. She shoved her hands in her pockets.

Deep growls echoed to where Kivera stood, some twenty feet from the males

"State your name." One of them snarled.

Kivera cocked her head. "Not how this works, fellas. Tell me who you are before I destroy your minds and slit your throats from ear to ear."

More snarls and protests from the males erupted, but the middle one watched Kivera with a frozen stillness.

"You do not belong here." The frigid one sliced through the other males' outcries.

Kivera grinned. "Neither do you."

"My name is Raagir and I've been ordered to return you to the King for your interrogation."

Kivera narrowed her eyes. What king could he speak of? Last she remembered of the faerie lands, there were High Lords and Ladies but no kings. Those were mortal terms that the Fae looked down their nose at.

"It's time for you to go." Kivera bared her teeth.

The one on the left cackled. "Not a chance, I'm afraid, princess."

A figure hurtled through the woods and skidded next to Kivera and let out a roar. Zyra glared at the incomers and dug her body low in preparation to attack.

The three males stumbled back and raised their weapons.

Tensions raised Kivera's blood temperature and, unsure of how this fight would turn out, she sent the conversation to Mavis and let her watch the encounter through Kivera's eyes. At least someone will know what has happened to Kivera should she be taken or killed.

"We've been charged with bringing you to the King once I have found you. It's a crime to open the gates," One of the hooded males protested still behind Raagir.

Kivera gave him a long look, and Zyra sensed her annoyance and snarled at the male. "You're not in any place to disagree, I'm afraid."

Kivera. Mavis called, but Kivera couldn't focus on answering. Her magic was expelling too fast.

"We don't want any trouble, but the order is strict. We have to bring you back or he'll take our heads and send worse males to hunt you. Something is wrong with them and threatens the safety of every territory, human and faerie," Raagir reasoned and tried a step.

Kivera. Mavis tried again.

"You'll have me to contend with if you try to take me unwillingly," Kivera snarled, and magic throbbed in the air.

The two shadowed guards on Raagir's sides unsheathed sets of axes and flexed their muscles.

Kivera. This time, her name was a command rather than a summons.

Now is not the time, Kivera grumbled down the line, readying herself for the fight.

Zyra pawed at the ground and hissed at the males.

You should listen to them first. If your people need you....

You have met none yet, but fae males tend to be dramatic. It's most likely a ploy to put me in chains.

An interesting ploy if they've traveled this far just to bring you back and ask to.

Mavis's words struck a cord within Kivera. She was right, of course, to Kivera's chagrin. The journey from the Fae lands to the human continent was impossible. Kivera tripped into the portal by accident and woke up in Alceria, coughing up lake water but unable to go back.

Kivera shrugged. "Sorry, but I've made my peace to live out the rest of my immortal life in the human lands. I do not belong in Faerie nor want to. Your *king* can eat shit."

Raagir blanched, and the males behind him stilled with inhuman ability. Lightning sparked in the atmosphere, and Kivera readied herself for whatever could happen.

Perhaps she could finally release the ball of grief knotted in Kivera's stomach with a drawn out fight.

A low growl rippled from Zyra in warning.

"Please help us and come back with us," Raagir tried again and splayed out his hands.

Kivera bared her teeth. "I asked for help and prayed endlessly to the gods for help. No one listened to me then and I will not listen to you now."

Raagir and his males began slow steps towards Kivera.

She flashed her magic once more and the ends of her fingers ached in anticipation. Kivera took one step towards the males and Zyra's tail twitched against the back of her legs.

Kivera, stop.

Her footsteps stopped, and she cocked her head. *What?*

Raagir and his comrades wore confused expressions, but Kivera didn't pay them heed. They halted, but kept their weapons ready.

Maybe... maybe you should listen to them. Hear out what they have to say.

What are you saying? Kivera guffawed.

Would it be so terrible if we went there to figure out more about Lady Reanna's words and come back after it's all done?

Terrible? It's fucking dangerous and compact full of psychopaths. They wish only for their bloodthirsty games and games of power.

And if you contained the power to change that world, would you?

Kivera pondered for a brief heartbeat.

I wouldn't even know where to begin. Besides, we have a home here. Do you truly wish to leave it?

A pause in their connection from Mavis contemplating Kivera's words.

If it means I can learn to use my magic and to help others, I believe the journey is worth it. I couldn't save Jexton and I don't know who I am.

I can help you with the magic part. It's different, yes, but-

How could you train me when you're afraid of your own power? You're terrified of what is beneath your skin.

Mavis had a point, Kivera begrudgingly admitted. What Reanna said of her parents niggled her mind.

You can't spend the rest of your life that way, Kivera. You are more than that.

Kivera didn't answer her and stared at the three males for a long minute. Until she decided and dark tendrils of her magic swirled in the air and through Kivera's hair, tickling her ears. Kivera brushed a hand on Zyra's side and asked for a favor in their Bond.

"Zyra will guide you to the Gate. Go with her and I will find you both and follow you to this king," Kivera ordered before darkness swallowed her whole as the males shouted at her to wait.

CHAPTER THIRTY-TWO

Moonlight cascaded through the cocoon of darkness Kivera conjured before revealing the inn in its dingy glory. She rushed through the oak double doors and strode for the dining room.

The team sat at the same table Kivera left them at, but a couple of drinks further in. Mavis was the exception. She sat calmly in her seat, but followed the rim of her mug with a finger.

Stepping through the drunken crowd, Kivera maneuvered her way through and touched Mavis's shoulder.

"That took forever. Sorry, everyone," Kivera announced breezily and flipped her hair behind her shoulder. But she couldn't force the lighthearted tone this time. She pierced them with a golden stare. "Mavis and I are leaving tonight. It's sudden but urgent, I'm afraid."

A mix of shock and despair shined on their faces. Then Maserion burst to his feet in outrage.

"It's the middle of the night! You can't leave! You can't leave us!"

"We can take care of ourselves, Maserion," Kivera countered, but an ache sat heavy in her chest. She glanced at Tillirius and found his dark eyes staring unblinkingly at her.

Kivera couldn't look away fast enough. Not fast enough for the ache to spread further.

Syt gaped at Mavis, waiting for her to deny it. But Mavis

gave her a sad smile and shook her head before standing. "It's true."

"Will you be back?" Arcian questioned with a heavy-lidded, sad look and crossed his arms across his chest.

"We're hopeful, but only if we survive the mess," Kivera shook her head and put her arm through Mavis's own.

"So this is it? This is your goodbye?" Tillirius quietly challenged and Kivera raised her eyebrows.

"I wish it weren't like this, but *she*," Kivera cocked her head towards Mavis. "Wanted us to leave."

"She is right. I am pushing for us to leave sooner. I wish we could-" Mavis stared at Syt's hurt face with pleading eyes but was drowned out by Arcian and Maserion's protests and Tillirius's constant groaning about leaving so soon after drinking ale.

Rex stood on unsteady feet but raised his chin to meet Kivera's eyes. "Ignore these boys, ladies. Our time together is over, but the impact will last the rest of our lives." He hobbled to Kivera and wrapped her in a swift but tight embrace. He stepped back to the table with a twinkle in his bloodshot eyes.

The team followed suit and moved around the table to take turns embracing forearms. Lots of "be safe and take care of yourselves", "thank you for everything" and Kivera's favorite from Maserion "watch out for batshit murderesses and mutts". She couldn't help the belly laugh from exploding.

"Take care of yourself too, Mase," Kivera smiled at him. The tops of his ears reddened, and he dipped behind Tillirius's mountainous frame.

"This is it. Our goodbye, I suppose." Tillirius cocked an eyebrow and glared down at Kivera. Mavis chuckled under her breath as she said goodbye to Arcian.

"I know, I'm sorry," Kivera reached for his arm and squeezed once before dropping her arm. "But, I have to. This is where our paths part, but I'll miss your grouchy face."

Tillirius cracked a smile and put a hand on her shoulder. "Jexton cared about you a lot and was very persistent for me to cooperate with you. I hated him at the time, but now I'm glad. It's been a pleasure having you on the team for a while. No matter how many times you dropped me on my ass."

Kivera laughed and put a hand on his wrist. "I'm glad to leave you in more capable hands."

A dark chuckle came from Tillirius, and a wicked grin spread across his face. "Anytime, little girl."

Kivera matched his grin. "I'll keep you to that, no matter what time in your lifetime I return."

She strode for Syt, and the latter simultaneously opened her arms to Kivera. The enveloping hug warmed Kivera's soul, and the ache spread deeper in her bones.

"I'll miss you terribly, Syt," Kivera buried her nose into Syt's shoulder.

"I'll miss you, too, Kivera. Whatever you two are up to, be careful and watch each other's backs." Syt squeezed before releasing Kivera, wiping away the tears on her cheeks.

Kivera turned her back and strode towards the lobby. The innkeeper read her book and was slurping something questionable from a vast bowl, and Kivera waited near the front doors.

Still hovering near Syt and the others, Mavis chattered away with goodbyes, sorrow plain on her face.

"Mav, we need to leave sooner rather than later," Kivera called and went to pay the innkeeper by placing a heavy sack of gold coins on the counter.

"Will there be a panther droppings fee included?" The innkeeper clucked around the thick accent.

Kivera frowned. "Of course, madam. Everything's in order for the utter destruction of your pit stain room."

The old woman's face appeared unfazed and continued her reading. "Goodbye then. Come again. If you want."

Kivera made a face but stood in the lobby, waiting for Mavis. She was in the middle of hugging Syt and Kivera made sure to not listen in to their conversation.

Mavis broke away with blotchy and tear-stained cheeks.

She faced Kivera with hunched shoulders and rushed to her side.

Kivera wrapped an arm around her shoulders. "It's okay. It's terrible now, but we'll come back after it's all over."

Mavis smiled but said nothing.

"Are you sure about this?" Kivera searched Mavis's eyes.

Mavis nodded her head, and the corner of her mouth quivered. "We need to go and you agreed with me. It's time to face whatever those males were talking about."

"Wait!" a woman exclaimed at them and the females whipped their heads to Syt, now running to them with her eyes trained on Mavis. "I'll follow you wherever you go to any world. Let me come and I'll help in any way I can." Syt reached for Mavis's hand and kissed Mavis's cheek.

Kivera stepped away with tears springing in her eyes.

"This is dangerous and I don't want you to get hurt," Mavis sniffled and stared at Syt with silver-lined eyes.

"I'll come to monitor her," Tillirius stepped forward and smirked at Kivera.

"Oh, gods," Kivera rolled her eyes, but a smile lined her lips. "This is not a safe place for mortals. We'll all be hunted the moment we step through the gate, and there are monsters worse than me in those lands. None of us may come back."

Tillirius gave her a long look. "I want to find out about the monster who murdered my brother."

All joking was wiped off Kivera's face. "We'll find out who she was fighting for and bring them down, too."

Tillirius nodded, then turned to his brothers-in-arms and clapped them each on the back. Syt disentangled herself from Mavis and hugged her team. Their goodbyes were short but soft-spoken.

A smile tugged on Kivera's lips at the sight and felt Jexton's warmth cascading around the team. *You'd be proud of their bravery, Jexton. I'll bring them back.*

Syt and Tillirius detached themselves and strode to where Kivera and Mavis waited. "Ready?" Tillirius asked, and

Syt wrapped an arm around Mavis's waist. The latter leaned into the touch and she smiled.

"Whatever you say," Kivera groaned and looked back at the remaining team standing around the table. "It's been real wonderful slaying monsters and murderers and all that but take care." She waved as darkness spooled from her palm and dripped on the floor. The drunk bystanders didn't notice the obsidian shadows creeping on the floor and the corners of the room, pulsing to ready for Kivera's departure. Rex, Maserion, and Arcian waved their goodbyes and Kivera did the same. Warmth bubbled in Kivera's chest at the sight of her new friends and she prayed to the gods she would see them again.

"We need to pack our stuff and we're ready," Syt murmured to Kivera, and she nodded.

"Don't we need to pack our stuff?" Mavis asked Kivera, and she gave her friend a look. A look of understanding dawned on Mavis's face. "Oh, right, I forgot. I don't think I'll ever be used to magic, *ever*."

Kivera chuckled through the tendrils of darkness. "It's okay. I live to surprise you. The look on your face is always worth it."

And darkness whisked them away.

Following the tug on Kivera's bond with Zyra, she found the panther and the three males pacing trenches on the shoreline of Lake Drear. Zyra glanced up from where Kivera and the rest appeared from shadows on the higher ground amongst shrubbery and dry, wild grass. Kivera detoured to the guard station, where Kivera explained about the males and the King they were being escorted to while Syt and Tillirius packed their belongings. They hurried, and they spirited through the darkness ten minutes later.

Low on energy and magic after the splurges of her resources, Kivera stumbled when she landed in the wild grass. Mavis and Syt held her upright until Zyra bound the hundred yards to them. Tillirius unsheathed his broadsword and held it at the ready, eyeing the males below. Mavis settled Kivera's arm across the panther's back and the group began a slow descent towards the males on the lake shore.

Moonlight danced across the rocky, dark surface and Kivera shivered at what creatures wade through its waters.

The males held weapons and straightened at the sight of Kivera and the rest. A hiss slithered from one of Raagir's guards.

"Are you hurt, Kivera?" A wrinkle appeared in Raagir's perfect brown skin between his brows.

"No, but we need to hurry." Kivera quickened her speed and eyed the water wearily.

Zyra supported Kivera while she watched every movement on the flatlands surrounding the great lake. *I hope your home looks better than this dump.*

Kivera snorted.

"You know what you're doing? We got through by sheer luck from the king and he assured us you would bring us back," Raagir asked ahead of Kivera and she gave him a dirty look.

"I'm sure this will be like last time," Kivera growled, but she toed into the freezing depths and shuddered as the frigid water seeped into her toes through her boots. Last time, she was cut all over her body and the water bubbled wherever her blood dropped. The last time Kivera fell through the gateway, she was bloodied and fell into the aquamarine pool in Faerie. Without a single incantation or riddle, Kivera transported through the Gates fabric. A mystery befuddling Kivera to this day.

She allowed a talon to slide out of her index finger and slashed a line across her wrist. Holding her arm over the water, blood dripped into the lake as swirls of ink.

Nothing happened and Kivera waded deeper into the water with her wrist over the waters.

When Kivera was nearly resigned to fate, a faint glow flared through the murky waters. A distant light that brightened as it grew in size. Bubbles floated to the surface, releasing scents of lilac and summer breeze. The water illuminated to an almost too-bright blue light that blinded her.

Murmurs of awe sounded from behind her, but Kivera could only frown at the waters and what awaited her on the other side.

"Ready?"

A chorus of footsteps inched through the luminous waters and followed behind Kivera. A low whine hummed from Zyra and she sent a wave of reassurance down their Bond and the panther's massive head floated next to her.

With her other hand, Kivera bared her palm parallel to the waters and summoned roiling waves of darkness. They cascaded onto the surface before sinking below.

The light flashed to a blinding white below, dimming to a vibrant rose, and the bubbles stopped.

The Gate to Faerie was open.

Frantically, Kivera reached for Mavis and Zyra as they continued to walk deeper through the waters. Mavis clasped hands with Syt and Tillirius gripped Syt's shoulder. Raagir and the two males stood behind Kivera and waited for her lead. The water burned as Kivera stepped into the light and the magic rose her legs then torso and constricted her chest. She savored her last view of the human world with a blanket of stars above her before the water swallowed her whole.

ABOUT THE AUTHOR

Hannah Hanvey

Hannah was raised in Colorado but moved to Scotland in 2021 to be with her partner and two dogs. She visits castles and museums and writes in coffee shops older than her birth country on a too-often basis. She's an avid nature explorer and vegan baker.

You can follow her Twitter and Instagram pages @hannahlhanvey to stay up to date on her writing.

Printed in Great Britain
by Amazon